Praise for *The Cutting*

'A gripping, chillingly believable book that holds a mirror to the dark side of high society. *The Cutting Place* is Jane Casey's best book yet – and that's really saying something'
Erin Kelly, author of *He Said/She Said*

'*The Cutting Place* is SO good. I love Maeve so much and this is a really gripping, timely plot'
Elly Griffiths, author of the Dr Ruth Galloway Mysteries

'Jane Casey is among our very best crime novelists and this is her best book. So far . . .'
Liz Nugent, author of *Lying in Wait*

'Her best yet. Heartpounding and SO MOVING! If you haven't read the Maeve Kerrigan series, start RIGHT NOW'
No. 1 bestselling author Marian Keyes

'The sexual tension between Maeve and her boss DI Josh Derwent is one of the highlights of this complex and gripping police procedural'
The Times

'Jane writes one of my very favourite police series, and this is her best yet'
Sarah Hilary, author of the DI Marnie Rome series

'Topical and deeply disturbing . . . a superb crime novel'
Sharon Bolton, author of *The Craftsman*

'The Maeve Kerrigan series is truly the gold standard for police procedurals'
Catherine Ryan Howard, author of *Rewind*

'Jane Casey is a masterful storyteller'
Charlotte Philby, author of *Part of the Family*

'Full of intrigue . . . a captivating read'
Olivia Kiernan, author of *Too Close to Breathe*

'Tense, dramatic and sharply written'
Sinéad Crowley, author of the DS Claire Boyle series

'Engaging, smart and addictive . . . superb'
Will Dean, author of *Dark Pines*

'A terrific book . . . Jane Casey's books are a must read'
Patricia Gibney, author of the Detective Lottie Parker series

'The best police procedurals I've read'
Claire Allan, author of *Her Name Was Rose*

'*The Cutting Place* is pitch perfect. I ripped through it, unable to stop myself'
Sam Baker, author of *The Woman Who Ran*

'A chilling and inventive read'   *Woman's Weekly*

'I couldn't love Maeve Kerrigan or Josh Derwent more'
Cressida McLaughlin, author of the Cornish Cream Tea series

'Simply stunning'   *Heat*

'Her best yet, and ain't THAT saying something'
Lucy Mangan, author of *Bookworm*

'Pacy plotting is underpinned by authentic relationships between the female cops'   *Sunday Times* Crime Club

'A classy, astute, timely, whip-smart read'
Lucy Atkins, author of *The Missing One*

THE
CUTTING
PLACE

Jane Casey has written ten crime novels for adults and three for teenagers. A former editor, she is married to a criminal barrister who ensures her writing is realistic and as accurate as possible.

This authenticity has made her novels international bestsellers and critical successes. The Maeve Kerrigan series has been nominated for many awards: in 2015 Jane won the Mary Higgins Clark Award for *The Stranger You Know* and Irish Crime Novel of the Year for *After the Fire*. In 2019, *Cruel Acts* was chosen as Irish Crime Novel of the Year at the Irish Book Awards. It was a *Sunday Times* bestseller.

Born in Dublin, Jane now lives in southwest London with her husband and two children.

🐦 @JaneCaseyAuthor

Also by Jane Casey

THE
CUTTING
PLACE

JANE CASEY

HarperCollins*Publishers*

HarperCollins*Publishers* Ltd
1 London Bridge Street,
London SE1 9GF

www.harpercollins.co.uk

This paperback edition 2020
4

First published by HarperCollins*Publishers* 2020

A catalogue record for this book is available from the British Library

ISBN: 978-0-00-814911-6 (PB b-format)
ISBN: 978-0-00-837850-9 (CA-only TPB)

This novel is entirely a work of fiction.
The names, characters and incidents portrayed in it are
the work of the author's imagination. Any resemblance to
actual persons, living or dead, events or localities is
entirely coincidental.

Typeset in Sabon LT Std by Palimpsest Book Production Ltd,
Falkirk, Stirlingshire

Printed and bound in Great Britain by CPI Group (UK) Ltd, Croydon CR0 4YY

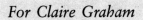

For Claire Graham

'Ask yourself "Am I satisfied that I have done all I can?"'

from the Domestic Abuse, Stalking and
Harassment and Honour Based Violence (DASH 2009)
Risk Identification and Assessment
Checklist for Police Staff
Laura Richards, BSc, Msc, FRSA

1

For a few moments, it was the quietest place in London. The area under the footbridge was as hushed as a chapel while the black mortuary van was pulling away. A little group of us had gathered there to show our respects, photograph-still: uniformed officers, forensic investigators, a team from the Marine Police unit in their wetsuits, a pair of detectives and a small grey-haired woman in waterproofs and rubber boots standing to one side, her arms folded. Then the van disappeared from view and the picture dissolved into movement. Back to work. Life goes on.

The woman in waterproofs turned to me.

'Is that it, then? Can I go?'

'Not yet, if you don't mind. I need to hear your account of what happened.'

Kim Weldon gave a deep, testy sigh. 'I've been here for hours. I've told you everything I know already.'

She hadn't told me, because I'd only been there for a few minutes, but I decided not to point that out. I was used to arriving at a crime scene last of all, the detective sergeant coming in with a notebook and a pen and an endless list of questions when everyone just wanted to go home. 'I know it's frustrating, Mrs Weldon, but we'll try not to keep you for much longer. Do you need to let someone know you're running late?'

She shook her head. 'I live alone since my husband died. No one's waiting for me. But I got here at five this morning and I'm tired.'

'Early start.' The comment came from over my shoulder, where DI Josh Derwent had apparently decided to take an interest in the conversation. 'That's keen.'

'Of course. It's the best time to be here. Before all of . . . *this*.' She gestured at the footbridge over our heads, where the tide of commuters heading to work in the City formed a second river, flowing as ceaselessly as the Thames towards the great dome of St Paul's. 'It's so busy now. I can't even *think*.'

It seemed quiet enough to me, but Derwent nodded. 'Let's find somewhere more peaceful where we can talk. A café, or—'

'The best place to talk around here is down there.' She gestured over the wall to the foreshore, a strip of shingle a few metres wide that extended to the left and right along the river bank. 'I can show you where I was. Easier than having to describe it all.'

'How do we get down there?' I asked.

'There are steps.' She set off towards them, moving briskly, and we followed her obediently. 'But you'll have to come down one at a time and mind how you go. It's steep and it gets slippery.'

The steps were concrete and more like a ladder than stairs. The treads were so narrow I had to step sideways, juggling my bag and clipboard awkwardly, off balance. My long coat threatened to trip me up at every step. Kim Weldon was short and had a low centre of gravity, unlike me, so that explained why she had found it easy. On the other hand, Derwent was taller than me – just – and he had rattled down in no time, as light on his feet as a boxer despite his broad-shouldered build. He stood at the foot of the thirty or so steps and watched my progress, which didn't help.

'You could come down backwards.'

'This is fine.'

'Do you need a hand?'

'I can manage.'

'Only we all have other places to be.'

'I know,' I said through gritted teeth, concentrating on placing my feet carefully. The shingle below shimmered in the morning light, out of focus and dizzy-making.

'Like a cat coming down a tree. I can call the fire brigade out to rescue you if you like. It's not as if Trumpton have anything better to do.'

'I'm fine,' I snapped, and ignored the hand he reached up to help me down the last few steps. He stuck it back in his coat pocket with a grin that I also ignored as I made it to the shingle at last. Kim Weldon was watching us with interest. Considering I spent so much time assessing witnesses it shouldn't have surprised me to remember it was a two-way process. I tried to see us as she might: officialdom in dark trouser-suits and polished shoes, Derwent's hair cropped close to his head in a way that hinted at a military background, broodingly handsome. I was younger than him as well as junior in rank and aimed to be as neat, though my hair was already beginning to spiral free from the bun I'd trapped it in. We stepped around each other with the practised ease of longstanding dance partners. As a rule, Derwent was rude enough to me that even people who knew us well suspected we were sleeping together, or hated each other, or both. The truth was that we'd never slept together, and I only hated him from time to time. We were closer than most colleagues, it was fair to say – friends, after all we'd been through together. There was also the fact that he was my landlord. I currently lived in a one-bedroom flat he owned, though I fully intended to look for somewhere else to live. I just hadn't got around to it yet. We bickered like children and trusted each other's instincts without even thinking about it.

No wonder Mrs Weldon looked puzzled.

'Where do we need to go?' I asked her.

'Along here.' She gestured to the left of the bridge. 'That's the way I went this morning. I came down the steps around five, as I said. Sunrise is about half past five at this time of year but it was starting to get light. I could see well enough without a head torch.'

'Do you do this often?' Derwent asked.

'Most days.' She smiled, looking out across the river and breathing deeply. The air was fresh down by the water, and the hum of the city seemed to recede. Seagulls hovered overhead, peevish and mocking as they floated on the cool spring breeze. 'This is my place. I'm a licensed mudlarker. I take what the river chooses to give me, whether it's treasure or trash.'

'Treasure?' Derwent scuffed the shingle with the toe of his shoe. 'What kind of treasure?'

'Nothing valuable, exactly. But items of historical interest. And sometimes the trash is interesting too.' She bent and picked up a small white tube. 'What do you think this is?'

I peered at it. 'A bit of china?'

'It's the stem of a clay pipe. I can't date this without having the bowl, and the bowls are harder to find, but it could be from the 1600s. The pipes were in common use up to Victorian times. When they broke, they couldn't be repaired and people would chuck them into the river.'

'An antique fag end.'

She looked at Derwent sharply, her eyes bright. 'You don't see the appeal, Inspector. But that's a little piece of London's history. The man or woman who smoked it is long gone and forgotten, but we know they were here. I might be the first person to touch it since they flung it in the water.'

'What sort of things do you find?' I asked.

'I've found Roman glass once or twice, and coins, and bits of pottery. Last year I found a medieval die made out of bone. How did it end up here? Maybe someone flicked it into the river because they'd had a run of bad luck, or maybe they stumbled as they boarded a skiff to cross to the other bank and it fell out of their pocket. There are a hundred possibilities, a hundred stories in one small scrap of history. My favourite was a bone hairpin that was a thousand years old. That's in the Museum of London, now, with my name recorded as the person who found it. That pin will still be there long after I'm gone too.'

'And people will know you were here,' I said.

The fan of wrinkles around her eyes deepened as she grinned. 'Everybody wants to leave a trace of themselves behind, after all – some evidence they walked the earth. One day someone might be grateful I was in the right place at the right time to find something special. That keeps me coming back.'

'So what was different about this morning?' I asked.

'Nothing. Everything was the same as usual. At least it was until I found it. Then everything went sideways.' A low chuckle. Kim Weldon struck me as the kind of person who didn't allow herself to be unsettled by anything; if what she had found upset her, she had got over it by now.

But I noticed she said 'it', rather than what she had found.

'Where were you when you saw it?'

She pointed. 'See the white stripe on the wall? I was halfway between here and there. I always give myself a marker to reach because it's too easy to get distracted and forget to keep an eye on the tide. You can get caught out – never happens to me but I've seen other people get soaked. So I always give myself a limited search area and then I go once I've covered it.'

A Thames Clipper barrelled past, ferrying commuters up the river, and the wake sent a wave that splashed over one of Derwent's shoes. He stepped back quickly, swearing under his breath, shaking his foot.

'It's all right, the water is quite clean these days. They've even found seahorses down the river, near Greenwich, so it's fresh. But you really need boots like mine, and you need to be more respectful of the river.' She looked wistful. 'I've seen grown men tipped over by a wave like that.'

'I'll bear it in mind.' From his tone of voice, I strongly suspected that he wouldn't be returning to the foreshore any time soon if he could help it, boots or no boots.

'This way.' The slight, upright figure crunched away from us to where a wooden post stuck out of the shingle, frayed with age and the action of the water. 'They used to tie up barges here.' She pointed at the sandy edge of the river. 'This is where it was.'

It.

'And it was just lying there?' I checked.

She looked baffled. 'What else would it be doing?'

'No, I meant – it wasn't buried, or wrapped in anything?'

'No, no. It was lying there on the shingle. I thought it was a tree root at first – you do get them washed down the river from upstream where the banks are overgrown. I was going to take a picture of it to put on my Facebook page, because it looked like a hand. But then, when I got a bit closer, I thought it looked a bit too much like a hand. And then, of course . . .' She shrugged. 'It *was* a hand.'

'Did you touch it?' Derwent asked.

'Before I knew what it was. I turned it over. It was palm down, with the fingers curled under it, you see.' She held up her own hand to demonstrate, a loose fist with knuckles to the sky. 'Then when I felt it, I knew it couldn't be a root. Too soft. Too much give in it. But it wasn't until I saw the fingernails that I was sure. It was such a strange thing to find that I couldn't quite admit to myself what it was. I took some pictures of it and where I found it and then I picked it up. I was afraid it would be washed away before anyone came to recover it.'

'You must have had a shock,' I said.

'Well, you expect to find bones here – this was London's rubbish dump for thousands of years, and this area in particular was full of markets. But the bones tend to belong to sheep or pigs or cows. Sometimes you find a bit of a fox. I've never found a hand before.' She faced into the breeze and smiled. 'But then you never do know what the river will give you.'

At the top of the stairs, the Marine Unit were packing up to head back to their base at Wapping.

'Finished for the day, lads?' Derwent demanded as they went past us.

The sergeant stopped. He was mid-fifties and serious. 'Tide's coming in. We're not going to find anything else here today.'

They had found three other pieces of tattered bone and flesh that had all been carefully preserved in coolers for transportation to the mortuary along with the hand. Thinking of what Kim Weldon had said about animal remains, I asked, 'Are you sure that what you found is human?'

'No idea.' He heaved a bag onto his back. 'But the pathologist will tell you if it's not.'

'Where's the rest of the body?' Derwent asked. 'In the sea?'

'Could be. Could be we'll find some more bits in the next few days. We'll be looking. Where we find things has a lot to do with the tide and the shape of the river. The way the water moves through it depends on whether the banks are concave or convex. You get lots of stuff washing up around Greenwich, for instance, and at Wapping, and at Tower Bridge. You won't find as much on the opposite banks. So we have a few places to look.'

'I never really thought about the tide coming up the river,' I said. 'I thought it flowed out to the sea and that was it.'

He shook his head, not even trying to hide his scorn. 'Why do you think the flood barrier exists? There's a clue in the name, love.'

'I'm not saying I couldn't have worked it out,' I protested. 'I've never thought about it before.'

He grunted. Clearly I was worth even less of his time now, which was a shame because I needed his expert knowledge.

I tucked a stray curl of hair behind my ear, widening my eyes to play up the helpless look. 'As you can tell, I don't know much about this. The river flows in both directions, so does that mean we can't tell where the body parts might have gone in? Could they have been moved up here by the action of the tide?'

He wrinkled his forehead, considering it. 'The tide moves things up but then it moves them back again on the way out, if you see what I mean. That makes it hard to pinpoint where items enter the water. They sometimes wash around the same area for a while.'

'Could they have been dumped off a boat?' Derwent asked.

'Yeah. But why draw attention to yourself by hopping in a boat to dump body parts when you could slip them into the river from the shore? No one would have noticed if it was small parts, which is what we've found. People don't realise but the river is a busy place. You wouldn't want to be out there midstream and not know what you're doing.'

He was right. I'd never realised how busy the Thames was with constant boat traffic: commuter boats, tours, barges loaded with building materials, small speedboats and larger vessels crewed by competent-looking people in high-vis overalls.

'If the body parts turned up in this area, does this mean they were all thrown in the river here?'

'I wouldn't want to try to guess, love. But we only found four pieces. Better hope there's more to come.' He nodded briskly and strode away.

'Thanks for the help,' I called after him.

'I don't know much about this,' Derwent cooed in my ear. 'Please explain it to me, Mr Police Diver.'

'And did he explain it to me?'

'Sort of.'

'So it worked.' I put my notebook away. 'But don't get used to it.'

8

2

'Hello, you two.' The pathologist Dr Early barely looked up as we walked in; at the best of times she was a fast-moving blur in scrubs, humming with nervous energy, and she didn't waste precious seconds on elaborate greetings. 'I was wondering who was going to be lucky enough to get this one.'

'Nothing like a nice easy case to start the week,' I said.

'And this is nothing like an easy case.' Dr Early gathered an armful of files and headed for the door.

'I was going to say that.' Derwent was actually sulking as we followed the pathologist through the security doors that led to the morgue.

One of her assistants was photographing a collection of objects that lay on a metal table under the glare of a bright light. He was heavily built but he moved with precision and focus as he skirted the table.

'Here we are.' Dr Early slipped a pair of gloves on and pulled her mask up over her mouth and nose. 'You need protective kit too. Then it's jigsaw puzzle time.'

'I'm not a doctor, but it looks as if you're missing a few pieces,' Derwent said before he tied his mask on.

'And I'm not a detective but it looks as if it's your job to find them.' Dr Early raised her eyebrows at him meaningfully and I smirked to myself under the cover of my own mask: victory to the pathologist.

None of us had forgotten where we were or what lay on the table beside us, but banter was one of the only ways to feel normal when your job involved looking closely at fragments of a human being. Not that I would have known what I was looking at, if I hadn't been told. No piece was bigger than a shoebox. The skin was yellowed, bleached by the river, and the flesh underneath it was pale and ragged, bloodless. White bone gleamed under the bright lights that shone on the table.

'So. What we've got are four pieces of what seems to be an adult female. She was probably IC1, probably light-haired and probably younger rather than older, but I'm not putting most of that in my initial report because it's an educated guess at the moment – it's purely for your benefit.'

'Why do you say it was a woman?' I asked.

'I'm going on the size of the hand and the joints that we've recovered – they would be average for an adult female. The muscle development and fat ratio suggests a reasonably fit, relatively young woman. The body hair was removed from the legs at the root – waxed, epilated, something like that. She had very fine light brown body hair on her hand and shoulder. And the fingernails were painted at some stage because I can see tiny traces of dark polish around the cuticles. It is still possible that it was a man, but I think it more likely we're looking at a woman. No tattoos, no scars, no distinguishing marks so far.'

'Any idea when she died?' Derwent asked.

'I'd guess she's been in the water for a couple of days. Do you want me to talk you through her piece by piece?'

'No, but you probably should.' Even with the mask obscuring most of his face, I could tell Derwent wasn't enjoying himself.

Dr Early pointed. 'This is an easy one. It's a right hand.'

'That's what our mudlarker found.' I leaned in to see it,

trying to imagine how it might have looked on the shingle. 'She didn't know what it was at first.'

'It's out of context, isn't it? We don't expect to see something like that without the rest of the body to go with it.'

'What other bits have we got?' Derwent was peering at the three other pieces of flesh on the table. The way they were laid out reminded me of a butcher's window.

'We have one part of a thigh, one part of a lower leg and a left shoulder joint. We won't get all of her but it would be very helpful if your lot could track down a few more pieces. Currently this doesn't tell me very much at all. The rest of the torso would be a great help. And the head would be the best thing of all to find, if we're going to identify her. Unless her DNA is in the database, of course. Then it'll be straightforward. I've submitted a sample already so cross your fingers.'

'Is there anything to suggest how she died?' I asked.

'Not so far. All I can tell you is that she was already dead when she was cut up.'

'That's something,' I said, and the pathologist nodded.

'They did a very thorough job on her, I have to say.'

'Was she cut up deliberately? Could it have been an accident? A propeller, something like that?' Derwent asked.

'Definitely not a propeller.' Dr Early turned one of the leg pieces so we could see the end of the bone. 'When you cut into a bone like this, the marks you leave are called kerfs and they can tell us a huge amount of information about the instrument that made the cut. See this notch here, about a centimetre from the end? It's a false-start kerf, where whoever dismembered her started cutting into the bone, stopped, and moved down to begin a new kerf. Second time, he managed to cut through the fibia. The first cut is precisely parallel to the second. He didn't move between the two attempts and her body wasn't moving as it would have been if the cuts had been made in water by something like a boat's propeller. This was deliberate dismemberment, not an accident.'

'Can you tell us anything about what they used to cut her up?'

Dr Early frowned, her forehead puckering. 'I knew you'd ask that. I'm not an expert in this but I've been reading up on it. I'm going to get one of my colleagues to take a much closer look once we've cleaned the bones up, so again, this is preliminary information. I can't give you a detailed description of a cutting tool that you can use to eliminate suspects. But if you look up close at this cut, you can see lines running horizontally across it. They're called striae and they're made by the teeth of a saw cutting back and forth. It tells me this wasn't done with a knife or an axe. They use a chopping motion, not a sawing one.'

'Could it have been a handsaw?' I asked.

'That's what I think it was, but that would be a long, slow process, especially given the size of the pieces.' She leaned forward again, beckoning us in for an even closer look. 'Then this part here – the small step at the bottom? That's called a breakaway spur, where the bone finally fractured and gave way. The saw didn't cut cleanly through the entire bone because it didn't need to – the weight of the bone itself snapped it. If you find the other side of the bone, there'll be a matching notch in it where this bone came away. Think of breaking a green stick. You don't get a clean edge – you take a bit of the other side of the break away with you. The size of the spur varies but, in general, the more powerful the saw, the larger the spur. These are small.'

'Messy,' I commented.

'And slow. Cutting someone up isn't the kind of job where you want to take your time. Bodies are cumbersome and it's a horrible working environment. On the other hand, if you want to avoid attracting attention, a handsaw has the virtue of being quiet.' She straightened up. 'The kerfs will help us narrow down the kind of saw you're looking for – the number of teeth per inch, the direction of cut, the set of the blade and so forth. We'll be able to find out a lot more once this lot is under a microscope.'

'Looking forward to it.' I ran through my notes. 'You said she'd been in the water for a couple of days. Any idea when she actually died?'

Dr Early shook her head. 'Too many variables. We don't know where the body was kept before or after it was dismembered. If it was refrigerated, for instance, that would have delayed decomp. I don't have enough of her to tell you anything so useful.'

'And we don't have any trace evidence to speak of because of the water.' Derwent's shoulders slumped. 'It's almost as if they didn't want us to work out who killed her.'

'It's not playing fair, is it? She's going to be a bit of a mystery until we can find some more of her. Or unless you work out who she is, obviously. That would help.'

'Wouldn't it, though?' I closed my notebook with a snap that made the pathologist's assistant jump. 'It shouldn't take us long to look through the missing person reports for a woman—'

'—or a man,' Derwent chipped in helpfully.

'Who disappeared at some time or other that wasn't in the last two days, probably, and *might* be twenty-something and *might* have light brown hair—'

'—but otherwise has no distinguishing marks—'

'—on about ten per cent of his or her body,' I finished.

'At least you were paying attention. It sounds as if you've got quite a lot of work to do.' Dr Early nodded at the door. 'Better get on with it, hadn't you?'

We were almost at the car when Derwent's phone rang.

'Boss.'

I waited, watching his face, trying to read what he was thinking as the boss – DCI Una Burt – talked on, and on, and on. Derwent wasn't her biggest fan, and the feeling was entirely mutual. He started out looking irritated but that faded, replaced with grim resolve.

'Yeah. OK. I understand. No, it's fine.'

Silence as she spoke again. He rubbed his face with the hand that wasn't holding the phone and turned in a tight circle, impatient now. I could practically hear what he was thinking. *Get on with it.*

'Yes. As soon as I can. Yes. *Yes.* OK.' He ended the call and stood for a moment, staring down at the phone absently. His face was bleak.

'Everything all right?'

'I have to go to Poplar.'

'Why?'

'Another case.' He put his phone away and started searching his pockets, distracted. 'A cot death. Suspicious circumstances.'

'Oh.'

'The boss doesn't want to send Liv. She thought it might hit too close to home.'

'Oh,' I said again, this time with more understanding. Liv was six months pregnant, at the stage where you couldn't miss it. Sending her to a cot death would be hard on her, and hard on the parents whether they were guilty or not. 'So she's sending you?'

'She asked me if I minded.'

'And you said you didn't?' I raised an eyebrow at him.

'Look, it's not my favourite kind of job but I'll do it. She's getting Liv to help you on this one instead.'

I didn't know if I was relieved or disappointed. By swapping a detective inspector and a detective constable, Burt was effectively putting me in charge of finding out who murdered the woman in the river. It was a vote of confidence.

I could have wished it had come on an easier case though.

'And who are you working with?'

'Georgia.'

Of course. I did my best to look blandly interested. Detective

14

Constable Georgia Shaw was more or less the last person I'd want to work with, but Derwent didn't mind her. She was pretty and ambitious and overwhelmingly irritating to me. If Derwent had been describing her, he would have stopped at pretty, and that seemed to be good enough for him.

He was still patting his pockets, swearing under his breath.

'I have the car keys,' I said. 'If that's what you're looking for.'

'Why didn't you say?' He held out his hand for them and I shook my head.

'I'll drive.' I wanted him to have time to prepare himself for what lay ahead, to get his game face ready. He wasn't as tough as he pretended to be, I knew, and when cases involved children he struggled to maintain his objectivity. Taking on this case would cost him something he'd never admit, even to himself. But I couldn't say any of that out loud. 'I need to get back to the office and I don't trust you not to drop me at the nearest tube station so you can get to Poplar sooner.'

'I would never do that,' Derwent protested.

'You've done it before.'

'Only a couple of times.'

'And I should have learned my lesson after the first time.'

He looked amused. 'Thanks, Kerrigan.'

'Any time.' I unlocked the car. 'Now get in. We have places to be.'

3

Five hours after leaving the morgue, I had looked at hundreds of missing persons files on my flickering computer screen. The smudgy images and bland descriptions had all merged into one faceless, anonymous woman. I leaned back in my chair and tipped my chin up, easing the muscles in my neck.

'I can't bear to look at any more. My eyeballs feel like leather. I can't tell if there's something wrong with my screen or my eyes.'

'No luck?' DCI Burt paused by my desk and peered at my notes. 'You've got a shortlist, I see.'

'Of sorts, ma'am.' I straightened up, pulling myself together, because she was the boss after all. 'The trouble is that there are too many women who fit the description of what we've found.'

'We limited it to women who've gone missing in the last month.' Liv was looking pale, I noticed, with dark shadows under her eyes. She was slight and delicate, and six months of pregnancy had left her more exhausted than blooming. It had given her backache, insomnia, heartburn, an insatiable appetite for cake and an obsession with finding the perfect pram which involved endless arguments with her girlfriend over email. I had found her relieved beyond words not to be heading to Poplar, but now I wondered if she was regretting it. Ploughing through missing persons reports was unrewarding to say the least.

'Dr Early thought she was IC1 but we've included other races, just in case she's not white. She could be light-skinned,' I said.

'And we're including females aged thirteen to forty,' Liv added.

'Wise,' Burt said. 'I've seen the pictures from the morgue. They looked as if she could be anything. We probably shouldn't rule too many people out.'

'But that doesn't really help us to narrow it down in any meaningful way,' I explained. 'The volume of mispers is too high. There are too many runaways and domestic violence victims and people skipping out on rent or expired visas, let alone women who might have actually come to harm.'

'Especially since we have to look at mispers from outside the Met too.' Liv sighed. 'There's nothing to say she went missing in London, just because she ended up in that part of the Thames.'

'You're going to have to make some choices about who you include eventually,' Burt said. 'Use your judgement. But remember that you'll make things very hard for yourself if you can't identify her.'

No shit. 'On the bright side, she looked as if she'd been taking care of herself. I'd be very surprised if she was someone who would count as a vulnerable adult,' I said. 'I'm leaving out homeless people, known drug users – anyone who is unlikely to have time for a full wax and manicure every couple of weeks, basically.'

'But what we really need is a DNA match,' Burt said.

'It would be a help.'

'We might have her on our list already but we won't know it until the DNA comes in,' Liv said.

'Assuming someone's reported her missing and we've taken

it seriously enough to put her DNA in the system.' Burt smiled at me and carried on to her office, as if she'd said something helpful.

'Yes, we may never identify her. Thanks so much for your input, boss,' I muttered.

Liv yawned. 'Do you think it's time to knock it on the head for today?'

'Definitely.' I checked the time. 'Shit, I've got to get changed.'

'Going out?'

'I've got a yoga class.'

'*You* are going to yoga. Maeve Kerrigan, going to yoga.'

I stood up and stretched. 'What's so weird about that? It's good for my posture.'

'Yeah, of course it is. But that's not usually a priority.' Liv darted over and yanked open the bottom drawer of my desk before I could stop her. 'What the hell is this?'

'Snacks.'

'Nope. Don't lie. These are not snacks. You used to have snacks in here. There used to be crisps and multipacks of Twixes. Don't try to pretend this is the same.' She started going through the packets. 'Puffed peas – I don't even know what they are. Turkey jerky, gross. Cashew butter protein balls, no thanks. Spicy chickpeas. This is so bleak. Where's the chocolate?'

'There's probably something in there like chocolate.'

She pulled out a bar and inspected it. 'This is carob. *Carob.* I'm going to be sick.'

'I'm being healthy. So what?'

'It's not healthy to eat spiced grit for the sake of feeling virtuous. Baked hemp sticks, for God's sake.' She threw them back into the drawer and shook her head. 'And they say pregnant women are supposed to eat loads of weird stuff. I wouldn't touch any of that.'

'Oh, come on.' I toed the drawer shut. 'Stop giving me a hard time.'

'This is all *his* idea, isn't it?' She meant my boyfriend, Seth Taylor.

I felt the colour rise in my cheeks at her tone. 'Seth did suggest it.'

'And the yoga is his idea too, I bet.'

'I'm meeting him there.'

'Couples yoga? Please tell me you're joking.'

I grinned at her horror. 'It helps my stress levels and my flexibility. It's fun, too. Don't knock it until you've tried it.'

'You've changed.' Liv was looking at me as if she was confused about something. 'I've never known anyone who needed to do yoga as much as you do, but I can't help noticing that you've avoided doing anything healthy for as long as I've known you. You thrive on shit food and too much caffeine. If you're not stressed out of your mind, who even are you?'

'A better person. A happier person.'

'I suppose that's a good thing.' She didn't sound as if she was convinced about it though.

I grabbed my bag from under the desk. 'I'm going to get changed. Help yourself to a snack if you're peckish. I can recommend the kale crisps.'

'No, you can't.'

She was right, I couldn't, but I wanted to get rid of them. 'Try them. Maybe you'll like them.'

'What do they taste like?'

'Indescribable,' I said truthfully.

I'd never actually asked her, but I had a secret suspicion that Liv didn't like Seth much. There was no law that your friends had to like your boyfriend, I reminded myself as I laced up my trainers in the locker room. And Liv was picky about men. Seth was used to winning women over on sight, but his height and build and wide smile had cut no ice with Liv. It was taking him longer than I'd expected to work out how to deal with a woman who wasn't attracted to him, someone he couldn't charm. Their sense of humour was very different, and Seth could come across as arrogant, unless you knew him well. He had a lawyer's need to get the upper hand in arguments and persevered even when I was trying to change the subject, a little beyond the limits of polite conversation. But he could have been Prince Charming and it wouldn't have mattered. She was always going to prefer my old boyfriend, Rob, even though he had broken my heart. There was no one else who would be good enough for her.

I had needed to move on, I told myself. Rob was old news. Besides, Seth cared about me. He was attentive and kind and made me feel as if I was the centre of his world, not an afterthought. As if to prove it, my phone pinged with a message.

Don't forget we have yoga.

I snapped a picture of myself in leggings and sports bra in the mirror and sent it to him.

See you there!

The phone hummed in my hand.

Good girl.

I pulled a face and threw my phone into my bag. 'Good girl' sounded patronising even if he didn't mean it that way. I'd mentioned it before, and hurt his feelings. I wouldn't bother raising it with him again. Compared to everything else I got out of our relationship a throwaway remark was the opposite of important. He was perfect in almost every way and I was fixating on the tiniest of flaws.

He was almost *too* perfect.

I slammed my locker door, irritated with myself. Really, there was something wrong with me if I wanted a boyfriend who was more detached, less keen, harder work. Seth was easy. I was the one who made things difficult. I needed to relax.

Hence the yoga.

'Going out?' Georgia Shaw was unlocking her own locker.

'Exercise class.' I shrugged myself into a hoodie. 'How was Poplar?'

'Grim. Very, very grim. A six-week-old baby. A little girl. Both the parents are distraught, as you can imagine. We had to take the bedclothes, the toys, search everything, ask them loads of questions. The baby was so tiny. Like a doll.' She leaned against the lockers. Her make-up had smudged under her eyes and she'd chewed off her perfect pink lipstick. 'How were the body parts?'

'Inconclusive.' We weren't friends – we might never be friends – but I was trying to make common ground with Georgia where I could. I didn't want her as an enemy. 'Is Derwent back?'

'He stayed in the house.'

'Huh.' I shouldered my bag. 'Interesting.'

'You're really unfair to him, you know.'

I stopped on my way to the door. 'Excuse me?'

'The way you said it was interesting. It wasn't *interesting*. It was kind. He's got a heart of gold.' Her voice sounded strained as if she was on the edge of tears.

'What makes you say that?'

'The last thing I would want to do is stay in that house. We've been there all day, getting in the way, making cups of tea and trying to say something comforting. It was stifling. Mind-numbing. I couldn't wait to get out of there, so I could breathe again. But Josh stayed. He said he'd be there as long as they needed him to be there.'

'I bet they were delighted.'

'They're *grieving*. Of course they weren't delighted. But it's got to be a comfort for them. Josh was so kind. He even carried the baby out to the ambulance when they took it away for the post-mortem.'

I could imagine it quite clearly, I found: the small bundle held with tenderness on her last journey out of the only home she had known in her short life. Derwent would do that well.

'Was she their first child?'

'Yes.'

'What's the age-gap between the parents?'

'She's only seventeen. He's twenty-eight. How did you know there was an age gap?'

I ignored the question. 'Are they close?'

'Very. They were supporting each other through it. Barely left each other's sides all day.'

'Josh isn't staying because he thinks they need his support. He's staying because one of them killed the baby and the other one will tell him the truth.'

Her eyes went wide. 'No way. You didn't see them. They're devoted to each other.'

'Some time tonight, or tomorrow, or the day after, maybe when everyone's supposed to be asleep, one of them will come downstairs because he or she can't stand to share a bed with their child's killer. Guess who will be waiting. He's shown he cares about their child, and about them. He'll have grieved with them. They'll have come to trust him. Even if they don't want to get their partner in trouble, they'll be exhausted by the effort of lying all the time. That'll wear their resistance down until they find themselves telling him the truth.'

'You're so *cold*. Every tragic death isn't a crime, you know, and everyone doesn't lie.'

'No, but—'

'You don't know these people. They're a sweet couple. The nursery was beautiful. And she was a gorgeous little girl. She only started smiling two days ago.' Georgia's bottom lip trembled before she could stop it and there were tears standing in her eyes.

22

'I know Josh Derwent and I know he's not spending the night there because he thinks this was a tragic accident. I've seen him do it before.' I shrugged. 'It doesn't mean he's faking it, you know. He'll be just as upset as you are about the baby. That's where he gets his energy from. He won't give up until they give in.'

'You're wrong. He'd have told me.'

'Nope. He wanted them to think they're going to get away with it. That's more likely if you're sincerely sorry for them.'

'You mean he doesn't trust me.'

'I have no idea whether he trusts you or not.' *But I definitely don't, so . . .*

She lifted her chin, hurt. 'I think you're wrong. You don't know anything about them, or the baby. You're jumping to conclusions.'

'Probably.' I zipped up my top. 'We'll have to wait and see who's right.'

'Enjoy your exercise class.'

I thanked her as if she'd meant it, and left.

Two years earlier

To his great disappointment, he wasn't dead – he just felt that way. A bird had woken him, singing frantically in the tall trees that screened the house from the road, throwing an alarm call into the still silence.

(And how did he know about the trees? It had been dark when they got there, piling out of the car onto the gravel drive, and he had been drunk already. Whose house? Whose idea to go there? Who had been with him in the car, jammed up against his legs, a high-heeled sandal digging into his instep when the girl moved carelessly? Who had stolen the champagne, handing him a bottle that he'd tipped down his front in the dark, on the motorway?)

Waking up properly was slow, a process of adjustments. He had a temperature, but no, he didn't, it was the room that was hot. He felt dreadful. He was ill. No, hungover. The thumping headache, the nausea, the felted surface of his tongue, the burning dryness of his eyeballs: all of that was a hangover. There was someone lying beside him, but no, there wasn't, it was a coverlet rucked up into a ridge that pressed against his thigh companionably. His watch had been stolen – no, he hadn't worn a watch. He had dreamed such a strange, exciting dream, weird and utterly wrong—

Not a dream. He sat up. He *remembered*.

The bird was quiet now, stunned into silence by the heat of the day. The curtains were open, limp in the airless warmth. The sun struck into the room, across the floor. And here came fear, like an unwanted guest swaggering into the room to sit on the edge of the bed and chatter.

The small injuries that told him what he remembered was true. Here, a bruise. There, a bite mark.

white teeth in the dim light grinning as he hissed in pain and pleasure and reached out—

He couldn't get away from the shards of memories that kept slicing into his brain.

Kissing, too aroused to be wary.

The taste, wine edged with tobacco and salt from the sweat that glazed them both.

Full lips, a probing tongue, a tattoo that covered one beautiful arm from shoulder to wrist, a flat stomach, long legs.

He had been clumsy, fumbling with a button. A laugh in his ear that he felt as much as heard, and then a whisper.

'Come on. Let's go somewhere else.'

Which meant that part had been in front of everyone. Anyone could have seen.

Stumbling into the bedroom, kissing already, his clothes coming off, until they were both naked.

We don't have to
I want to
Say if you want to stop
Please
You're hurting me
Oh God

The door had been open. He remembered that. He remembered someone standing, watching them for a while.

What had he done?

4

I couldn't see the river from where I stood, but I knew it was there. The harsh squabbling of seagulls cut through the air, louder than the traffic rumbling past the end of the quiet street. The morning light had a pearly quality, hazy as an impressionist painting, and the breeze carried a faint, dank suggestion of briny water and black mud. I wondered if the woman had been drawn to the river in life as in death – if that was why she had chosen Greenwich as a home, if she had been fascinated by the dark water sliding endlessly towards oblivion in the sea, or if she had had any inkling that one day it would take her too . . .

'Maeve.'

I pulled my mask back up to give myself some protection from the smell before I turned away from the window and faced the room. Liv was making her way towards me carefully, picking her way over boxes and the legs of a crime-scene officer who was lying on the floor, inspecting the area under the kitchen cupboards.

Two tedious days of file-sifting and phone calls and river-dredging had ended with a positive DNA match, the miracle of forensic science coming to our aid with an unarguable answer that should have made my life easier. The woman in the river had a name and a face now, as well as an address and a job: Paige Hargreaves, 28, freelance journalist. I could congratulate myself that she had at least featured in one of the piles of possible victims. I might have tracked her down eventually, without the DNA match, but it would have taken weeks, and it would have been a provisional identification. DNA left no room for doubt.

Being in her home should have given me a proper insight into the murdered woman. In my experience, there was no quicker way to get to know someone than to see where and how they lived. On this occasion, though, I was finding it hard to concentrate, which explained why I was lurking by the window instead of searching. Partly it was the smell: the unemptied bin, the fridge full of sour milk and greenish meat, a bowl of blackened bananas and soft brown grapes complete with orbiting fruit flies. Partly it was the forensic investigators who were tripping over one another in their efforts to examine every inch of the small flat's rooms. Mainly, though, it was the mess that was frustrating me.

Liv made it to my side, swamped in her paper suit. 'This is grim, isn't it? When was she reported missing?'

'Eight days ago.' I flipped through the notes I'd taken when the phone rang that morning. 'Her best friend made the report.'

'Not the neighbour downstairs? Or an employer?'

'Nope. She was a freelancer. No one knew she was gone.'

'And the break-in?'

'That wasn't reported at all.'

Liv looked around. 'I mean, I suppose there was a break-in. This isn't how she lived, is it? No one could live like this.'

I might have been finding it irritating but it was causing Liv acute distress to stand in a room where every surface had disappeared under miscellaneous objects: open letters, piles of books, unframed canvases and stacks of photographs, shoes, clothes, dirty plates and mugs, magazines and newspapers in teetering, disorganised columns, a cascade of empty suitcases in the corner. Everywhere there were notebooks and pens and make-up jumbled together, and headphones tangled up with chargers like mating snakes.

'I think it's *possible* she was burgled,' I said carefully. 'There are chargers everywhere but I haven't found a computer or mobile phone. She was a writer, a journalist – there's no way she didn't have her own computer.'

'She might have had them with her though. If she was out somewhere, working, I mean.'

'Her wallet was here. Her passport.'

'No keys.'

'There's a set of keys behind the door in the hall.'

'They could have been her spare set.'

'They were on the floor as if she'd dropped them there on her way in or out. There was a key for her bike lock on there. You wouldn't have one of those on a spare set, would you?'

Liv shrugged. 'Dunno. Depends on how often you lose your main keys, I imagine. So you think she was taken from here?'

'Maybe.'

'No sign of a struggle.' That was true. The flat was heroically untidy but there were no overturned chairs, no smashed glasses or plates, no damage. No blood, notably. There would have been blood, I thought, unless she hadn't been able to fight back because she was overpowered too quickly, or because she was drugged or drunk.

Two dusty windows looked out over the street. A table stood in front of one, while the other had a small, sagging armchair beside it. There was no television, I noted, thinking of the possible burglary, but then again there was nowhere obvious where it might have stood. The rear wall of the room housed the kitchen, which had seen better days even before everything in it had rotted. The laminate was peeling off the cupboard doors and the cooker was missing two burners. I had already noted the sink was piled high with mugs and glasses; impossible to guess whether Paige had had visitors or if she'd been the sort of person who washed up once a month. A clothes horse was draped with bedsheets and clothes that had dried as stiff as cardboard. I could picture her flinging the damp laundry over it with careless haste.

'Did you look at the bathroom? My pet hate is mildew.' Liv shuddered delicately. 'And underwear everywhere. I suppose everything was *clean*, but . . .'

I shrugged at the thought of the straggling tights looped over the shower curtain rail and the squadron of knickers hanging on the rusting radiator. 'No garden. Nowhere else to dry them. Heaven preserve us from being murdered on laundry day.'

'Amen.' Liv's eyes were solemn above her mask. 'What do you think this place cost her?'

'More than it was worth.' I was looking at the area of black mould that had gathered in one corner of the ceiling, above the fridge. A tongue of it extended down the wall, out of sight, and I didn't like to think what we might uncover when we pulled the fridge out to check behind it. 'Presumably the landlord didn't mind the mess if she didn't complain about the condition of the place.'

I moved across so I could look through the open door into the small bedroom, which had a bed and a bedside table and a clothes rail jammed into the corner. Half of the hangers had shed their dresses and jackets so they puddled on the floor, and the drawers hung open, spilling a waterfall of clothes in bright colours. She had worried about her image in public but behind closed doors she hadn't cared enough to keep her home tidy. Well, everyone had their guilty secrets about which domestic tasks they shirked. Paige had simply chosen to ignore all of them.

The crime scene manager, bulky and red-haired and short-tempered, was lifting a champagne bottle off the bedside table with exquisite care.

'Found anything, Adrian?'

He grunted. 'One set of prints. It's half empty. Looks as if she was drinking in bed.'

'On her own?'

'You'll have to wait for DNA and trace on the bedclothes. My crystal ball isn't working.' He carried the bottle out of the room, holding it in front of him reverently.

'So maybe she was alone and maybe she wasn't.' I rubbed my forehead with the back of my hand, hating the feel of the latex glove against my skin. 'Too early to say. In fact, it's too early to say much about her.'

'She had expensive taste in clothes and shoes.' Liv peered into a knee-high boot. 'Dior. Very nice.'

'I didn't think journalists got paid that well any more.'

'Family money?'

'Or she could have been doing something else on the side to make some cash.'

'Like what?'

'Dealing? Prostitution? Stripping?'

Liv raised her eyebrows. 'Based on what?'

'Nothing? It's a possibility, that's all, and I don't think we should rule it out straight away. Sex work is something young women get drawn into from time to time, and it's high risk. They encounter the kind of men who are used to chopping people up. I'm not judging her – I just think it's worth finding out if she had some extra income to fund her lifestyle.' The photographs I'd seen of her in the missing person file showed a thin woman, tanned and groomed, her eyes heavy-lidded, her nose long, her face narrow. Her hair had been blonde with the kind of sheen that took regular salon appointments to achieve. She had dropped her chin to her chest in all three pictures, peering up at the camera with insouciant sensuality. It looked like a studied pose, practised.

'No boyfriend to get in the way if she did do sex work,' Liv mused. 'Or girlfriend, as far as we know.'

'Which means no main suspect for us to question.' I flipped

30

my notebook shut. 'I'd guess she left here in a hurry, maybe to meet someone, possibly for work given that her computer isn't here.'

'And she never came home.'

'I wonder what she was working on.'

'I'll have a look to see if I can find any notes.' Liv flexed her small hands in her gloves. 'I can't wait to get this place straightened out.'

5

'This is very inconvenient.' Mila Walsh, Paige Hargreaves' downstairs neighbour was forty-four, small of stature, and clearly all heart. Her demeanour was as chilly as the décor in her sparsely furnished home. Unlike the flat upstairs, it was newly decorated and immaculate. 'When are your people going to be finished upstairs?'

'It'll be some time yet, I'm afraid. This is a murder investigation.'

'I understand that. But I'm not used to having people traipsing up and down the stairs. It's very noisy and disruptive. Not to mention waiting for you to finally get around to talking to me.' She checked the gold watch that peeped out from under the cuff of her immaculate white shirt. 'I've had to rearrange several meetings this morning already. My clients are important people.'

'What is it you do?'

'I'm an independent financial advisor. I tell rich people how to look after their money.' She glowered at me from under a millimetre-perfect black fringe. 'You probably think that's not a worthy job.'

'I can think of worse ones.'

A thump from upstairs made her look up; something heavy

32

had fallen to a chorus of cheers and muffled applause. If it turned out to be a breakage, someone would be buying doughnuts for the team.

'They need to be more careful. They'll crack the plaster if they carry on like that.'

'I'm sure it sounded worse than it was,' I lied. 'There isn't a lot of room up there so they've been tripping over each other. But really, they're very good at what they do.'

'I just wish they weren't doing it in my house.'

They weren't technically in Mila's house, I thought, but in the flat above it. Mila's home was a maisonette that occupied the bottom two floors of the house, the one raised slightly above street level and the basement. At some point a separate door and staircase had been installed so the occupant of the top-floor flat had their own entrance, though the partition was paper-thin and every footstep on the stairs echoed through Mila's stark rooms. All the surfaces seemed to be hard, even in the sitting room I could see through an open door. I had not been invited to sit down on the firm-looking sofa so I couldn't say for sure, but it appeared to have the cuddly consistency of a block of granite. At the end of the hall was the main bedroom. Downstairs, she'd explained, were the kitchen, bathroom and a tiny second bedroom.

'Do you know who owns the flat upstairs? I'd like to speak to the landlord.'

She snorted. 'Good luck with that. I have an email address for him but he never seems to check it. He lives in Dubai. The flat belonged to his uncle, I think, and he left it to him when he died. It must have been five or six years ago. He takes absolutely no interest in it. All he does is pocket the rent. We share the freehold but forget trying to get anything fixed.'

'Did Paige find that frustrating?'

'I don't think she noticed.' Mila looked up at the ceiling, her mouth tight, as someone walked over our heads with a heavy tread. 'She used it as a base but she really only slept

33

here, as far as I can tell. She often came home very late – two, three in the morning. The curtains were never open in the morning and I never heard her moving around before I left for work. Speaking of which—'

'I only have a few more questions,' I said quickly. 'Did she have friends over? A boyfriend?'

'Not that I heard. But I'm generally not here at weekends. I spend quite a bit of time out of London. And I really didn't keep track of her comings and goings.' A sigh of disapproval. 'If I'd known it would lead to this . . .'

'Tell me about Paige,' I said, losing the very small amount of patience I'd had for the woman's grievances. 'What was she like?'

'She *seemed* completely normal at first. Pleasant. Warm. I had occasion to talk to her about the state of the flat upstairs after she moved in and she seemed quite considerate.'

'But that changed?'

Mila Walsh gave a tiny shudder. 'She settled in, I suppose. She was terribly absent-minded about her keys. I had her spare keys for a while but I lost count of the number of times I had to let her into her flat in the middle of the night. She had to have the locks changed four or five times when she claimed to have lost her keys altogether, and then of course they would turn up a day or two later, and she would *laugh*. It was exceptionally irritating.'

'Did you complain about her to the landlord?'

She glared at me. 'I thought about it.'

'And decided not to . . . why?'

'I rarely saw her and she was fairly quiet most of the time. She didn't keep the same hours as me. She was out in the evenings, and slept in the mornings, and I was away most weekends, so it suited me that she lived upstairs. She didn't have many visitors. She didn't even cook much. No loud music.' A shrug. 'I don't know. I was afraid I'd end up with someone worse, I suppose.'

'When you say she didn't have visitors, you were out a lot of the time. You wouldn't have known if she had people here.'

'No, I suppose not. We were just neighbours, you know. I tried not to bother her much. This is London, after all. We live here so we don't have to make awkward conversation with strangers,' Mila said tightly. Her nails and lipstick matched, I saw. I was willing to bet her underwear matched too.

'Where do you spend your weekends?'

She looked surprised before her whole face softened. 'With my boyfriend, Harry. Harry Parr.'

She produced the name with the smug air of a poker player revealing their winning hand. If she was waiting for me to recognise the name, she was going to be waiting a long time. I shook my head.

'He's an artist. A sculptor. Very successful. He has a place in Kent, in the middle of nowhere.'

It wasn't a bad life all round, I thought, with her neat little house in a neat little street in pretty Greenwich, her job in the City that paid for the tailored suit and gold watch and the expensive furniture in the artfully bare rooms, and access to a bolthole in Kent. There was quite a contrast between the cluttered upstairs flat and the clean walls and empty space on the floors below.

'Did you ever go up to Paige's part of the house when you had keys?' The change of tack made her jump.

'No.'

'Never?'

'Once or twice – to see if she'd left a tap running.' She gave a tight brittle laugh. 'I'm a worrier. I found it hard to trust her. I didn't like the idea of her doing something careless and causing me problems.'

'We'll need to take your fingerprints and a DNA sample.'

'What? Why?'

'Because you've been in her flat,' I explained patiently. 'It's

35

routine. We need to be able to rule you out as a suspect. It doesn't hurt.'

'I'm aware of that.' She folded her arms defensively. 'But I regard it as an invasion of my privacy.'

'This is a murder investigation. Although you don't seem too worried about that.'

'It's nothing to do with me.' She gave a tut of irritation as footsteps thudded on the stairs going up to Paige's flat. It sounded as if someone was hitting the wall with a hammer. I'd noticed the lack of carpet on the stairs to Paige Hargreaves' flat but I hadn't anticipated how annoying it would be for anyone who lived in the same building. It could almost justify Mila's lack of sympathy for her murdered neighbour.

'You didn't report her missing.'

'Someone else did that. It was nothing to do with me. It wasn't until you lot came round the last time that it all felt real. Since then, of course, I've had to try to disguise the stench of rotting food as best I can.' She wafted a hand over the three-wicked candle on the sideboard behind her that was filling the air with the scent of green figs. 'I suppose everything is going to be left up there once you're finished. It's been horrible, knowing it's empty and full of rubbish.' For the first time, she faltered at the look on my face. 'But I didn't touch anything. I left it as it was, I promise. I haven't gone in since you told me she was missing.'

I was frowning at her, I realised. 'It's not that – you said the last time we came round. Are you saying the police were here before?'

'A detective was here about ten days ago. Of course I spoke to him to find out if he'd heard anything about her. He had a look around to see if she'd left any clues.' Mila looked confused. 'Isn't there a note about this on the file about her disappearance?'

'There should be.' There wasn't, I knew very well. No one had been overly concerned about Paige before parts of her started to wash up on the river shore. She was an adult in full possession of her faculties, without a regular job or dependants and she was able to do whatever she liked. Cutbacks meant there were too many claims on police time to send a detective around to investigate an unexpected absence without any signs of violence. 'What can you tell me about this detective?'

'Nothing much. I was home early that day and I ran into him on the doorstep. He was letting himself into the flat.'

'Did he show you ID?'

'Yes, of course.'

'Do you remember his name? Or what station he was attached to?'

'His name was John Spencer. I have no idea where he came from.'

'What did he look like?'

'Like an estate agent.' She smiled, not pleasantly. 'Or a police detective, I suppose. Cheap suit, ugly shoes, too much aftershave, too much hair gel.'

I ignored the dig. 'How old was he?'

'I didn't ask.' She relented. 'Early thirties?'

'How long was he here?'

'Not long. Ten, fifteen minutes.'

'Did you see him leave?'

She reddened. 'I happened to glance out of the window, yes. I was curious.'

'Did he take anything?'

'Her phone and her laptop, and a lot of paper – files, notebooks, that kind of thing. He put it all in a see-through bag and took it out to his car.'

'Did you see his car?'

'No. I thought he was coming back – he'd said he was going to give me his contact details once he'd put everything in the car. But he never came back.' She checked the time again and sighed irritably. 'Look, why are you asking me all these questions about him? Surely you can look him up and ask him yourself. There must be a register of detectives. A phone book, at the very least.'

'If he really was a detective, I could.'

That broke through the carapace of self-absorption at last. She put a hand to her throat. 'You don't think . . . he wasn't . . . Could he have been the *killer*?'

'I have no idea if he was or not,' I said. 'But look at it this way. You survived.'

6

I was still thinking about what Mila Walsh had told us when I found the address where Paige Hargreaves' friend lived. It was a scruffy purpose-built block in Whitechapel, close to the huddle of soaring glass office buildings that filled the Square Mile but a world away from that money and privilege. I knew that every passer-by who glanced at me as I leaned on the buzzer had identified me on sight as a copper.

I'd left Mila with Liv, who was more sympathetic than me and, importantly, prepared to put up with her hysterics. My main concern was to persuade her to create a photofit of the man who had been in Paige's flat.

'But what if he comes back?' she had called after me as I left, her voice raw with terror. 'What if he tries to hurt me? I *saw* him.'

And he hadn't minded her seeing his face, I thought, puzzling over it. So was the man our killer? Or someone else?

The intercom crackled, bringing me back to where I was. 'Hello?'

'Police,' I said as clearly and quietly as I could. 'Regarding your friend Paige.'

The door clicked and I pushed it open, wondering if the waft of stale urine as I did so was from the doorstep or inside the building. The flat I wanted was, inevitably, on the top floor, and the lift was, also inevitably, broken. I jogged up, trying to read the missing-person report as I went. Someone else had passed on the news that Paige had been found, I knew, and I was glad of it. No one liked delivering death messages, and I was out of practice. It was uniformed officers who got stuck with breaking people's hearts, as a rule, not detectives.

Bianca Drummond had already opened the door to her flat when I reached the top of the stairs. She was small, red-eyed, her face bloated and blotchy from tears, and she was wearing a tracksuit and fluffy socks. No absence of grief here: she looked devastated by the loss of her friend.

'Sorry. It's a long way up.'

I tried to get my breathing under control. 'It's good for me.'

'I had this crazy idea.' She stopped, and rubbed at her eyes with a ratty tissue. 'I thought you might be coming up to say there'd been a mistake and it wasn't Paige in the river. There's no chance you're wrong, is there?'

'None at all, I'm afraid. We matched her DNA.'

I saw the fight – and the hope – die out of Bianca's eyes at that. I understood why she wanted it to be a mistake, and it made me warm to her. She stood aside mutely and watched me walk past her into a small, very warm living room. A blanket was rumpled on the sofa, as if she had been lying there sobbing into the crumpled tissues that littered the floor.

'Sorry, it's not very tidy in here.' She picked up the box of tissues and then put it down again, as if she couldn't think what else to do with it.

'Please, don't worry. It's fine.'

'Cup of tea?'

No matter how awkward the social occasion, there was always tea. 'No, thanks. I won't stay long. I just have a few questions for you about Paige.'

She sniffed as she drew her hair into a ponytail, visibly

pulling herself together at the same time. 'I can't believe she's gone.'

'It must be a shock.'

'I mean, I was worried about her. You know I was, I reported her missing, for God's sake. But I never thought . . .' She took a deep, quavering breath, trying to hold back her emotion. 'They said she was in the river.'

'That's right.'

'Was she strangled? Or . . .'

'We're still working out exactly how she died,' I said truthfully. If Bianca didn't know the details, I wasn't keen to tell her.

'Do you know when it might have been? Was she already dead when I reported her missing? Was she kept somewhere? Or did they kill her straight away?'

'They?' I repeated.

'Whoever did this.' She took refuge in a tissue, but I had noticed the flicker of her eyelids as she registered she'd said more than she intended to. Because she knew something?

'We don't know yet. This is a very early stage in the investigation, though. We only identified her this morning.' I paused for a beat. 'The best way you can help to find the person or people who did this is to tell me everything you can about Paige and anyone who might have wanted to harm her.'

'I've been trying to think.' She sniffed. 'I want to help.'

'Let's start by talking about Paige. How long have you known her?'

'We were at university together. Same course. We met on the first day and just clicked.'

'Would you say you were one of her closest friends?'

Bianca nodded. 'She didn't have many friends, you know. She had loads of acquaintances but it took a long time to get to know her. She was . . . self-contained. She didn't need to be around people all the time. She didn't want to be, either.'

'Did she have a boyfriend or girlfriend?'

41

'She dated men, but she'd drop them as soon as they got too serious. She didn't want to let people into her life. I was in her flat twice, I think, and she lived there for four years.'

'Can you tell me about her family?'

'She didn't have one. She was an only child and her parents died when she was twenty. They got food poisoning on holiday in Egypt in some dodgy resort that got closed down over it. You'd never expect that food poisoning would kill you, but they died a day or two after they got sick. Paige was devastated.'

'I can imagine.'

'It was really awful. Especially when it turned out that there wasn't any money. They'd sent her to expensive schools and they were dead posh, but they were actually living way beyond their means. They'd borrowed money for their business, but the business wasn't going well. When they died they were months behind with their mortgage, they had loads of credit card debts and basically everything had to be sold off. Paige was supposed to get compensation from the holiday company but they went bankrupt. She ended up with very little to live on. As long as I've known her, she's worked. I've never known anyone so driven.'

'She had a lot of expensive clothes in her flat – designer stuff.'

Bianca nodded. 'That's a perfect example of what I mean. She started out as a fashion journalist. She was able to put together a really impressive wardrobe because she got invited to sample sales and she made friends with fashion PRs so she got huge discounts or freebies. I don't think she ever paid full price for anything.'

'You said she started out in fashion. Was that still what interested her?'

Bianca laughed. 'It never interested her. It was useful because of the lifestyle and she was good at it, but it bored her. She wanted to be a proper investigative journalist, digging into the dark side of life, uncovering the truth. But no one took her seriously. She couldn't persuade anyone to give her a job in that area. They wanted her to write colour stuff, fashion, celebrity news. It drove her mad. She really knew what she was doing – all she needed was someone to give her a break. But she was determined and I felt she was going to succeed one way or another. She went freelance so she could work on the stories she wanted to tell.'

'Why were you worried about her when you couldn't get hold of her? She liked her own space, from what you said. She liked to be on her own. She worked alone. Why did you assume something had happened to her?'

'I just had a feeling.' Bianca shifted uneasily as she concentrated on fraying the tissue she was holding.

'A feeling?' I leaned back in my chair and waited. When the silence became unbearable, she sighed.

'Look, she was working on something big. I thought she'd run into trouble.'

'What was the story?'

'I don't know.' She flinched at the sceptical look on my face. 'I don't, OK? She kept it to herself. She was worried someone would scoop her.'

'Even you? Her best friend?'

Bianca fidgeted. 'She didn't trust anyone. I didn't take it personally.'

That was a lie, I thought, but one I could understand. 'So she didn't talk to you about it?'

'She wouldn't even tell me what it was or where she was going. But I know she was excited about it.'

'How can we find out what the story was?'

'There must be notes on her computer.'

I didn't want to tell her the computer was missing. 'Who else would know about it?'

'She'd pitched it to a few editors.'

'Without success?'

'As far as I know.' She read the doubt on my face. 'That doesn't mean she was barking up the wrong tree. Mostly we don't get commissioned on an idea. You really need to be sure of what you've got before they take an interest. She'd been working on it for a couple of months.'

'But she had no guarantee it would be published.'

Bianca shrugged. 'That's how it is. And the worst part is that you're on your own. In the old days, your editor knew where you were and what you were doing. Now we have no protection. No one knows what we do or where we are. It's risky for all of us but the young female journalists have the hardest time with it. I suppose that was in the back of my mind all the time. That's why I panicked when I couldn't get hold of her.'

'Can you write me a list of editors she might have approached?' I slid my notebook and pen across the coffee table to her. Instead of picking them up, she stared at them, wordlessly plucking at the tissue. I wondered if I was unaware of some professional etiquette that might account for her reluctance. 'I can get the list from someone else if you prefer.'

'No, no. It's fine.' She leaned forward and wrote down five names and publications. 'This is where I'd start if I were you. I don't know for sure that she approached them, but I know she wanted to be published by them.'

As she slid the notebook across to me, a rattle at the door made me look around. Bianca jumped up.

'That's my boyfriend. He's not supposed to be home yet.'

'I think I'm finished anyway.' I stood up too, gathering my things. 'I'll get out of your hair now.'

Bianca rushed into the hall and I heard her hiss, 'What are you doing here?'

'I got off early.' A rustle. 'These are for you.'

Bianca whispered something in return. I checked I hadn't left anything behind before I followed her into the flat's tiny hall. It was mainly filled with flowers, at first glance. The boyfriend had arrived with an armful of peachy, close-petalled round blooms.

'They're beautiful.'

'Ranunculus. Favourites of mine. Thought they might cheer Bianca up.' The boyfriend was in green from head to toe, wearing the fleece and utility trousers of a professional gardener. He smiled at me and stuck his hand out. 'Sam Williams.'

'Maeve Kerrigan.'

'She's a police officer. She's here about Paige.' There was a strained quality to Bianca's voice.

'I'm so sorry, love.' He pulled her into his arms for a quick hug. Bianca fought free, grief shading to irritation. It could take people that way, I knew, but Sam looked hurt.

'I'm just going,' I said quickly. 'Thanks for your help, Bianca.'

'Is that everything?'

'For now.' I handed her my card. 'Call me if you think of anything that might help. And Bianca, I'd appreciate it if you kept the details of the investigation to yourself. I don't want to open the paper tomorrow and find this is a double-page feature.'

'I wouldn't do that.' She sniffed, hurt.

It was the second thing she'd said that I knew for sure was a lie.

Two years earlier

He ran his hands through his hair so it stood on end. There was nothing in the room apart from the bed and a dusty chandelier that looked too heavy for the cracked, peeling plaster of the ceiling. A champagne bottle lay on its side on the floor, empty. The smell was bad – someone had been sick, he thought. Or worse. There was a crumpled heap in the corner that looked like a T-shirt. It was smudged with brownish liquid – red wine vomit, shit, blood, he didn't know. But it stank. *He* stank.

He swung his legs off the bed and pressed his feet into the floor, which was veiled in grit. His chest was a dusty birdcage, his heart fluttering weakly like a dying canary. He coughed as he pulled his shirt on, the sound echoing off the bare walls.

The house had seemed so grand the previous night, when he had been hopelessly drunk and it had been dark.

White candles wedged in the neck of old bottles, the light wavering.

Wine, so much of it.

Music, the thump of the bass in the pit of his stomach teaching his heart how to beat.

The tremendous heat, and how it had pressed against every inch of his skin, relentless. The sweat on his back, on his neck. The taste of salt.

The unfamiliar roughness, demanding, determined.

It wasn't *him*, he told himself. He had only been doing what he was asked to do.

The throat offered up to his hand, the head tilted back in supplication and abandon, eyes closed, mouth slack. He had never felt so much like a man, so in control, so commanding.

What a *joke*.

7

I was on the fifth fruitless phone call to the editors on Bianca's list before I struck gold, and that was by pure chance.

'Definitely not someone on my radar.'

I drew a line through his name and sighed. 'No one else I've spoken to knows anything either.'

'Who else have you called?'

I read through my list.

'Where did you get this list from?' I recognised the sharpened professional interest in his voice.

'Another journalist, a friend of Paige Hargreaves.'

'I can't think why they've left Adelia Munroe out. She's the obvious place to start.'

I wondered if Bianca had left her off the list in the hope that I wouldn't know enough to ask her. She had seemed helpful, but I didn't altogether trust her to tell me everything she knew. A good journalist would go a long way for a good story and from what Paige had hinted, this was a good story. I suspected Bianca wouldn't want me blundering into the middle of it if she could help it. An innocent explanation, yet it still bothered me that she might have left a key detail out deliberately. Sometimes the things people didn't tell you were as important as the things they said. I drew a box around Bianca's name in my notebook and shaded in the edges. 'I'm afraid she wasn't obvious to me.'

The editor chuckled. 'No. But you do know who Adelia is, don't you?'

I did, in fact, because Adelia had edited *Insight* magazine throughout its twenty-year history and was a regular on television and radio. I knew enough about her to be intimidated at the thought of asking her questions.

'I do.'

'Give her a call. She's not as scary as she seems,' he added, and I thanked him. Not scary if you were another editor, maybe, but quite terrifying for me. I tried to sound confident as I called her office and after a short time I found myself speaking to Adelia herself.

'Oh yes, I spoke to Paige Hargreaves about a story. It wasn't for us, unfortunately, but I was intrigued by it.' The voice on the other end of the line was cultured and had the measured quality of someone who is used to being listened to. I could imagine her disapproving expression; her hawk-like features were familiar from frequent appearances on television as a forthright talking head.

'What was the story?'

'I spoke to her some months ago. Let me try to recall the exact details of what we discussed.' She fell silent for a few moments, long enough that I started to fidget at my desk. 'Yes. That was it. She wanted to investigate the Chiron Club. C-H-I-R-O-N.' She pronounced it *Ky*-ron.

'What's the Chiron Club? I've never heard of it,' I confessed as I wrote down the name. It was better to admit ignorance than bluff.

She chuckled. 'You wouldn't have. It's not for the likes of us. Strictly boys only, and by invitation. It's a social club, or at least that's what it pretends to be. They have fundraising events for charity – balls, dinners, boxing matches. That's the only time they look for publicity, and that's all most people know about them.'

'If it's not just a social club, what is it?'

'Well might you ask. There's a culture of silence about them and no one has ever succeeded in breaking it. The membership is small and extremely wealthy. These men are politicians, businessmen, bankers, judges – the elite. They are powerful men, and they largely recruit their new members from the children and grandchildren of previous members. It's all deeply secret and a little bit silly, if you ask me, but Paige was convinced there was something sinister going on there.'

'Sinister,' I repeated. 'Such as?'

'She wasn't prepared to say unless I commissioned her, and as I said, I didn't feel it was for us. There was something grubby about the story.' Adelia paused. 'You know, the members are powerful men. I had to weigh the importance of getting the story against what we might lose in access to these people. I have spent a long time building up the reputation of this magazine. I didn't want to lose that over a story that might be more suitable for a tabloid newspaper's exposé.'

Ouch. 'Did you say this to Paige?'

'I was kind to her about it. She had potential as a writer. I wanted her to take her time and develop her work instead of starting out by bringing down the establishment, or whatever she was planning to do.' A pause. 'Is it possible this story had something to do with her death?'

'I don't know yet,' I said. 'But it's somewhere to start.'

After I got off the phone, I looked up the Chiron Club on the internet and got a handful of news stories about fund-raising events, as Adelia had predicted. They had a website, which surprised me given their apparent obsession with secrecy, but when I clicked through to it I found it was blandly uninformative. The landing page was a black screen with a login window for members. There was no further information – not even an email address for enquiries. You were in the gang or you weren't welcome, I gathered. A further dive into Google earned me an address, at least.

'What's that?' Liv leaned over my shoulder to look at the street-view I'd called up of the ornate, heavily pillared frontage of the club's home. 'Amazing building.'

'It's the headquarters of a secret club, believe it or not.' I rotated the view. 'It's beside Blackfriars Bridge overlooking the river.'

'I knew I recognised it. I love that building. I never knew what it was.'

'They keep it quiet. No sign outside.'

'The Chiron Club,' Liv read off my notes. 'Are you planning to join?'

'Not eligible.' I explained to her why I was looking at it and saw her interest kick up a gear.

'Do you want me to have a nose around and see what I can find out?'

'That would be brilliant. I want to try to speak to someone there about Paige. The more I know beforehand the better.'

'Consider it done,' Liv said, and disappeared to her own desk. She had a background in financial investigation and I knew she had contacts who would speak to her off the record about the Chiron Club and its members. I turned my attention to Paige, double-checking the information I'd got from Bianca about her family and background. It was boring but necessary work – necessary, because in spite of Bianca's deep and sincere grief for her friend, I didn't trust her fully. I'd learned that lesson the hard way.

I flicked through my notebook to the interview with Mila and read the notes I'd taken again, wondering about the fake police officer. I looked at Mila's website, as crisp and uninformative as she was in person. I even searched for Harry Parr, as if he might be relevant. At the start of any investigation, it was impossible to tell what mattered and what didn't. Hunting down the details was what I did best, I assured myself, and it wasn't just human curiosity about what attracted Harry (a silver fox if ever I'd seen one, as well as being actually famous for his sculptures) to Mila. A colour magazine profile (that included a picture of him in his studio, all blue eyes and muscled arms) told me that he'd moved to Kent for the sake of his health after he suffered a life-threatening auto-immune disease that he linked to the house in London. That explained why they lived apart, although I thought I'd have been more likely to become allergic to Mila herself. The pictures of his low bungalow by the sea in Kent made me want to give up living in London. I was in the middle of a thoroughly enjoyable daydream about it when the door to the office swung open and banged against the wall: Josh Derwent, making an entrance. The top button of his collar was undone and his tie was askew, as if he'd loosened it in a hurry. He was pale and his hair was ruffled but his eyes were bright.

'Who's coming for a drink?' He scanned the room, squinting a little. With a sinking feeling I recognised that look as exhaustion. He was running on adrenalin and not much more. 'Come on. Georgia's in. Chris?'

Pettifer nodded. 'Give me five minutes.'

'Five minutes is all you're getting. Who else? Liv?'

'I would kill for a glass of red wine.' She smiled at him. 'I'll settle for sparkling water.'

His eyes tracked around to me. 'Kerrigan. Drink?'

'What's the occasion?'

'We made an arrest in the Poplar case.' Georgia had come in behind Derwent. She put a file on her desk, moving slowly as if she was completely drained of energy. 'The dad's been charged with murder and remanded to prison. His girlfriend is giving evidence against him.'

'Worth celebrating, isn't it?' Derwent had wandered over to my desk so he could pick up and examine everything on it. 'Good news all round. Except that the baby's dead and the mum's heartbroken. But still definitely worth a drink.'

I took my favourite pen out of his hands gently and put it back in the pot where it lived. 'Leave my stuff alone.'

'Come for a drink.' He dropped the swagger as he met my eyes, and when he spoke again his voice was so quiet only I would have heard him. 'Please.'

He couldn't go home yet, I recognised. He couldn't take that dark, boiling anger and frustration home to his girlfriend and her son. He couldn't risk letting it spill over unless he was with the people who understood how he felt without having to ask.

'Why not.' I stood up and pulled my jacket on. 'I wasn't doing anything else.'

As usual, it took considerably longer than five minutes to round up everyone who was going. It was more like half an hour before we were all ready. I found myself standing by the lift with Georgia as we waited for the others to gather their things.

'Are you OK?'

'Yeah.' She shivered. 'You were right.'

'I wasn't going to say that.'

'He handled it really well.' The two of us looked back into the office where Derwent was spinning around on a chair, saying something that made Pete Belcott redden and the other members of the team laugh. 'He was so good with the mum. I didn't know he had it in him.'

'Now you do,' I said simply. 'He's better at this than people know. But it takes its toll.'

She nodded and blinked furiously, clawing for composure. 'Make sure you talk to someone about how you're feeling.'

'That's what Josh said.'

Josh. I hated that Georgia was working with him, but I was determined not to show it. 'That's good. Not that he would ever have counselling himself, of course, but you should.'

She nodded, taking it on board. 'Do you?'

'Sometimes.'

The rest of the party finally tore themselves away from their desks and we piled into the lift, like a rowdy group of kids let out of school for the day. When we reached the ground floor, Derwent stood inside the lift and counted us out into the lobby. I hung back so I was the last in the group and paused before I stepped out of the lift.

'Shitty case. Are you all right?'

'I will be.' He dropped an arm around my shoulders and I hugged him, leaning into his warmth for a moment before he steered me out of the lift. 'I'm glad you're coming out.'

'No problem.' Even as I said the words my brain was starting to process the very real problem that was stepping forward, to my total surprise.

'Seth?'

He was wearing one of his impeccable three-piece suits with a blue silk tie and looked as if he had come straight from work. Everyone in the lobby was staring at him, which he was used to, because he was that sort of handsome. This time, though, not everyone was admiring him.

'Hey, Maeve. I was about to call you.'

'Well, this is a nice surprise,' Derwent drawled. He took his arm away from me, but slowly. 'Are you coming to the pub too?'

'I'm taking Maeve out to dinner.'

'But, Seth, we didn't have plans.' Even as I said it, I was wondering if I could have forgotten something. 'Did we?'

'No, we didn't.' He gave me an uncertain smile. 'I didn't know I needed to make an appointment. It was a spur-of-the-moment thing.'

'I texted you to tell you I was going out. Didn't you get it?'

'Yeah, but it only came through a minute ago. I was already on my way here when you sent your message. No reception on the Tube.' He waggled his phone at me apologetically.

'Oh.' I looked at Derwent and then at Seth. 'Well. I said I'd go for a drink with the team.' I slightly stressed the last two words, as if that would help. The others had moved away, though I knew everyone was watching this little stand-off.

Seth nodded. 'Right.'

'I didn't know about dinner.'

'No, of course you didn't.'

'You could come to the pub with us, Seth,' Derwent said. I looked at him, wary, noting the glint in his eye that was pure trouble. He was still on edge, and volatile as a result. What he would like more than anything else was a fight, I thought uneasily. But he sounded pleasant enough. 'If you wanted to join us, that is.'

'I don't think so, mate.'

'Mate?' Derwent laughed. 'OK.'

I stepped between them and turned to face Derwent, my temper rising. 'I know you've had a tough day, but don't take it out on him.'

'It's OK, Maeve.' Seth put his hand on my arm and gave it a quick, reassuring squeeze. 'If you want to go out with your team, go. You can call me later to let me know you've got home.'

'There you go. You've got permission now,' Derwent said and I caught my breath.

'I wasn't waiting for permission and I'm not going anywhere with you. As if I would, after that.'

His eyes narrowed. 'After what, exactly?'

If he wanted a row, he could have one with me. 'After you behaved like a complete twat.'

'Language.' He raised his eyebrows. 'I must say, it's good to know where your loyalties lie.'

'Are you really surprised that I'd rather go out for dinner with my boyfriend and have a nice time than go to the pub and listen to you sneering at me for a few hours?'

Derwent shook his head. 'If you want to make bad choices, I'm not going to stop you.'

'As if you could.' I was trembling from sheer rage.

'I'm not sure I like being called a bad choice,' Seth said from behind me.

'I'm not sure there's a word to describe how little I care about what you like,' Derwent snapped without breaking my gaze.

Thanks for making this easy for me, I thought, and stepped away from him towards Seth. 'Dinner would be lovely.' To Derwent, I said, 'You lot will have to manage without me.'

He was walking away already, beckoning to the rest of the team as he went, hurt filling the air around him like smoke. 'Let's go.'

The lobby seemed very big and very empty after they'd gone. Seth looked at me.

'I'm sorry.'

'Why should you apologise? It wasn't your fault.'

'I shouldn't have come here.'

'I'm glad you did.' I stepped closer to him and he put his arms around me. 'Let's just go home.'

'Sure? What about dinner?'

'I don't really feel like it.'

'We can get a takeaway.'

I was far too upset to eat anything, but I nodded, and smiled, and kissed him. It was so like him to be kind about it, when my anger was choking me. Not for the first time, I had the feeling that he was far too good for me.

8

'How did you get here?'

How did I get here? The question floored me because it was so familiar. It was the phrase that had been repeating in my head ever since the previous evening: all the way to Seth's flat on a rattling Tube train, and for endless hours where I tried to put the argument with Derwent out of my head, and then later as I waited hopelessly for sleep while Seth snored beside me. I would have been the subject of conversation in the pub, I knew, and hated it. Speculation about the state of my relationship. Liv delivering her opinion of my boyfriend in short, trenchant sentences. Derwent, scathing about how biddable I'd been, exorcising his anger about the poor dead baby by sneering at me. There would have been laughter at how I'd sprung to Seth's defence, at how touchy I was, how easily Derwent had got under my skin.

But I should have been happier to be with Seth than with them, and I didn't feel that way at all as I stared into the darkness of Seth's bedroom.

It was ridiculous to be irritated that he was so attentive to me. What sort of girlfriend complained that her boyfriend wanted to spend the evening with her? What sort of person was so ungrateful for love and devotion? I felt overwhelmed, but that was my fault, not his. I was bad at allowing myself to be loved, I remembered. I had messed up one relationship by thinking my independence mattered more than being there for someone who was perfect for me in every way. I'd only realised too late how much I cared.

Seth couldn't have been more perfect as a boyfriend. He was clever and handsome and he told me I was wonderful pretty much every day. He was just . . . keen. It was utterly insane to object to that.

I wasn't going to ruin things again.

The person who had asked me the question in real life was waiting for an answer, I realised, his eyebrows politely raised.

'I walked.'

'You *walked*. Fascinating.'

'Is it?'

'It is to me.' He sat in a fat, squat leather armchair. The leather was sandy with wear along the back and arms in a way that shouted money far louder than if it had been shiny and new. Not that it needed to shout, or that shouting would have been permitted in the elegant surroundings of the Chiron Club. Everything from the dull silk curtains to the gilt-framed mirrors and the heavy marble fireplaces spoke of wealth, and culture, and privilege. The bronze lamp beside the armchair was shaped like a slave girl holding a torch, her head bent, her breasts bare, the robe swathed around her hips picked out in gold. I thought it was hideous.

'It's a nice day for a walk. I was only coming from Westminster.'

Sir Marcus Gley beamed at me. He was a small, round man with bright eyes and a voice full of good humour. 'It's a little interest of mine. Much more telling than you might imagine. Most people don't walk. If they come by car, it means they have a driver, because there is nowhere to park a car around here. If they come by taxi, it means they don't mind spending money – or their employer's money, I suppose. We're slap bang beside Blackfriars Station. There is no need to take a taxi here. Then again, if they come on public transport, they are humble but also mundane and not striving for originality. There is room in life for people who take the obvious route, but one must have originality too. If they cycle, they are independent and bloody-minded and possibly a little bit stupid. I wouldn't cycle in London for love or money and I care a lot about both.'

It was my turn to raise my eyebrows. 'And if they walk?'

'Then they aren't in a hurry. Their mind may not be entirely on their job.'

I felt myself blushing and hoped the lighting was dim enough to hide it. 'Or it's just a nice day for a walk by the river.'

'Indeed it is. I quite envy you.' He twinkled at me sweetly.

'Thank you for agreeing to see me, Sir Marcus. I appreciate it.'

He waved a hand. 'I was interested. And aside from the Club and a handful of boards, I am retired. I can't pretend to be busy.'

'All the same, I wasn't expecting to be allowed in here so easily. I'd heard it was a secret organisation.'

He chuckled. 'Like something from a Bond film? I'm so sorry to disappoint you. We do allow visitors, from time to time. Of course, if you wanted to ramble all around the building, I might have to be more . . . stern.'

'This will do for now,' I said, holding his gaze. I could cope with being patronised all day and all night by the charming old rogue.

'I must admit I'm hazy on what we might be able to do for you here. You mentioned something about an investigation. I'm on good terms with a number of retired police officers – even a couple of the Met's commissioners. They can vouch for me.'

I had been deliberately vague, and now I smiled. 'It's not clear yet how the Chiron Club might be of interest, but as I said it's a murder investigation.'

'Thrilling,' he said, sitting forward as if he was watching a particularly gripping film. 'Who is dead?'

'A journalist.'

'My goodness, it really is cloak-and-dagger stuff, this. I assure you, we haven't offed any journalists here. What was his name?'

I registered the pronoun and wondered if it was deliberate. 'Her name was Paige Hargreaves.'

'Hargreaves.' He thought for a second. 'No, I don't remember anyone of that name. How did she die?'

'That's an excellent question. She didn't try to contact you?'

'No. No, I'm sure of it. What made you think she had?'

'She was working on a story that might have been about the Club.'

'Might have been,' he repeated. 'Don't you know?'

'We're at an early stage of the investigation.'

'You certainly must be if you don't know something so basic.' He shook his head, smiling, baffled. 'I can't see how we could have been of interest to her or how we might help the police now. We have nothing to hide.'

'Even though you are so secretive about your membership and what goes on here?'

'Where you see secrecy, we see privacy.'

'What can you tell me about the Chiron Club? I've found it very hard to get much information about the way the club works or what it does.'

'That's quite deliberate, but not for any sinister reason. The details are only of interest to members, and one cannot apply for membership. Prospective members are selected with great care. They are approached and offered the opportunity to be a part of this organisation. We don't want to attract attention from those who would be . . . let's say *unsuitable*.'

'How many members are there?'

'Hard to say. Some are involved very little. They are members in name only. Others are here every day.' He spread his hands helplessly. 'You make me feel I'm being quite vague. I promise, I'm not doing it deliberately.'

'What makes a suitable member?'

'Financial stability. Fees are somewhat steep but buildings like this don't maintain themselves, unfortunately.' He waved a cheery hand at the room as I wondered what 'somewhat steep' meant in these surroundings. Fifty thousand a year? A hundred? 'Everyone pays the amount they can afford, which is fair. And they have to be the right type of person. Someone with prospects. Brilliant, of course, and successful, with potential. Most of our new members are in their twenties. We don't want to become a collection of OAPs rattling our walking sticks at one another.'

'All male, I gather.'

He looked mildly disconcerted. 'Well, yes.'

'Could there ever be a female member of the Chiron Club?'

'Difficult to say.' He laced his fingers under his chin and twinkled at me. 'It's never arisen. One of the issues, you see, is that we are not altogether keen on the feminist movement, which seems designed to reward the less able simply by virtue of their sex. Either women are our equals and don't need special treatment, or they are fragile and require opportunities to be created for them, and quotas, and so forth. Feminists seem to be promoting a most confused and illogical ideology that is much more about making trouble than anything else. And of course, they aren't good company, these people. In short, any woman who would wish to be a member of the Club would find that they were unsuitable, simply by virtue of expressing that wish.'

I almost admired the neatness of it.

'Are women ever allowed in the Club as guests? Or to work?' I found myself giving it a capital letter in my head, as Sir Marcus so clearly did. I hadn't seen another woman so far. A large, tough-looking man had welcomed me, introducing himself as Carl Hooper, the head of security. He had ushered me through the black-and-white-tiled hall to the side room where Sir Marcus had been waiting for me, cheerful in pinstripes. A couple of members had glanced in my direction as I passed through the hall, their expressions studiously neutral, but women were clearly an unusual sight.

'There are administrative staff on the top floor and I think we have two ladies in the kitchen at present.'

'What about social occasions?'

'It depends on the occasion. Some of them are for members only. For others – our Christmas party and our summer ball, notably – we are very happy to welcome wives, girlfriends and so forth. We bring in temporary hospitality staff for events and there can be waitresses. But women aren't allowed in the Club dining room or bars as guests.'

I flipped open my file. 'Here's a photograph of Paige Hargreaves. Does she look familiar?'

He took it from me and stared at it earnestly. 'No. Striking girl. I don't have much of an eye for faces but I'm sure I would have remembered if I'd met her.'

'Can I have a list of members?'

'Absolutely not.' A twinkle that had no warmth in it at all. 'It's against the Club rules to share that kind of information with outsiders.'

'Can I speak to the administrators on the second floor?'

'They're much too busy. I can pass on any questions, if you like.'

'I ask my own questions.'

'Not on this occasion, I think.' He was still smiling but I could see the power of the man for the first time. I could keep pushing but I would get nowhere. 'Now, I'm afraid I must bring this fascinating conversation to a close. I have another appointment.'

'May I have the photograph?'

He tucked it into his inside breast pocket as he stood up. 'I thought it might be useful if I kept it. I can show it around and so forth. Try to find out if this young lady was here behind my back, in some capacity.' He looked bewildered for a moment. 'I do try to stay on top of these things but I don't always succeed.'

I did not think it would be useful at all, but there was nothing I could do short of pinning him down and ripping it out of his suit. I shook his hand instead and thanked him (for nothing). He had told me very little I hadn't known or suspected already.

The sunlight was still glittering invitingly on the waters of the Thames under a clear blue sky, but I trudged down the steps to the grim underpass that cut under the road and led to the station. I would take a humble, unoriginal underground train to the office, proving once and for all that I knew my place.

Two years earlier

The hallway was empty, doors standing open to offer him a view of deserted rooms. A single shoe lay capsized on the floor: a woman's, black, suede, fragile. No sign of his. He couldn't remember taking them off, or his socks, or his phone – that had gone earlier in the evening, he recalled, and cursed himself. His shirt gaped open, half of the buttons gone.

The stairs creaked under him and he caught his breath. Someone would hear.

So what? He wasn't doing anything wrong. And if he'd learned anything at all at school, it was that people took their cue from him. If he acted as if he'd done something dreadful, that's what people would think had happened. If he pretended there was nothing to be ashamed of, it would convince ninety-nine out of a hundred people.

He jogged down the stairs, whistling, making enough noise to raise the dead.

No one came, dead or not.

They'd gone and left him behind. They'd *gone*. They'd left him behind! They'd *actually gone* . . . the thought kept bouncing off the inside of his aching skull as he trailed through room after room, the slap of his steps echoing on the bare boards. There was hardly any furniture – a stained sofa in a room big enough to be a ballroom, a broken armchair surrounded by empty shelves in what must have been the library. He stepped through an open French window on to a terrace that was shimmering with heat. It had been grand, once upon a time, and last night it had been heaven. Pots stood at regular intervals along it, holding the parched remains of ornamental trees. Two pouting cherubs held up empty basins on either side of the steps that led to the garden. Cigarette butts and corks littered the flagstones. An army of empty bottles marched along the terrace and down the steps to the bleached, dusty lawn. Someone had spilled red wine; it had run between the stones and stained the ground like blood. A pair of deckchairs stood at careless angles to one another and prompted him to remember lounging in one, cigarette caught between his fingers, the smoke spiralling up into the starry night.

Crickets rasped in the garden, a dry, sharp sound that scraped his nerves raw. He stumbled down the steps. The brittle lawn was alive with ants, some burdened with huge wings that they dragged after them as they moved through the grass. Why they didn't fly was a mystery, like so much else . . . But maybe the air was too dense for them, too hot. The sky was cloudless, glaring like white metal. There were the trees he'd remembered; daylight showed that the summer heat had withered the leaves already. He broke into a shambling run that took him around the corner of the house. There was a tall hedge blocking his path, with a gap about halfway along. He plunged towards it, shooting through the gap and out into the sunlight on the other side where he stopped, his toes digging into the ground. His arms windmilled as he teetered on the edge of the swimming pool that he remembered the moment he saw it and not before.

The water was dirty. Green algae clung to the sides. Black mould clogged the tiles, and a scurf of drowned insects and dead leaves coated the water. A single wine glass lay at the bottom of the pool, swaying back and forth at the whim of an unseen current. The pool house was a low building styled like a Greek temple, squatting to the left of where he stood. It was empty, like the house. Deserted. Nothing human lived here except for him. It was like a curse, or a fable. The last man standing.

He became aware that something cold was touching his foot and looked down to see a condom draped over the edge of the pool.

'Fuck.' He kicked it away, disgusted, and a cloud of fat greenish-black flies rose up from the water, peevish at being disturbed. His eyes fell on something he hadn't noticed, right at his feet. It was under the raised lip at the edge of the pool, in the shadows. A shape.

A body.

He stared at it – the back just breaking the surface of the water, the hair swaying, the hands hanging with loosely curled fingers, the white flash of untanned skin on the buttocks. A graze, bloodless, that ran across the spine. A tattoo that covered one arm from shoulder to wrist: blue clouds blooming over the upper arm and a dragon that curved around the elbow to blow fire across the soft skin inside the joint.

What does it mean?

It's a scene from Chinese mythology.

Are you into Chinese mythology?

Not really.

They had laughed.

He turned away from the pool to vomit, thin bitter bile that splattered his trousers and his feet.

This couldn't be happening.

9

It was seven days since Kim Weldon had found Paige Hargreaves' hand by the Thames and I was no nearer to finding out who had put it there. The fair wind that had given me one lead after another at the start of the investigation seemed to have dropped, and it had left me marooned. The Thames had given up two more pieces of the dead woman – a foot and part of a thigh – but the fragments had told us nothing we didn't know already and the Marine Unit were muttering discouragingly about the likelihood of finding anything else. I had no suspects, no real motives and no ideas.

The Chiron Club had seemed like a promising place to start looking for a killer, but I'd uncovered nothing there. I was beginning to think there was nothing to find, despite Paige's excitement over her story. My interview with Sir Marcus Gley gave me the impression it was nothing more than a collection of over-privileged men making opportunities for one another, which wasn't exactly a scandal. That was how the world worked, after all. Maybe it had come as a shock to Paige. I was all too used to it.

The analysts had pored over Paige's bank statements and phone records, but what they'd given me didn't look suspicious in any way. There were no large payments in or out of her account, she hadn't used cash to hide any purchases that I could see and her spending had matched what I'd expect from a reasonably frugal single woman in one of the most expensive cities in the world.

I sat at my desk staring into space, waiting for inspiration to strike. The office was quiet, the early buzz dwindling mid-morning as detectives went out to crime scenes and interviews and court. I noticed familiar footsteps approaching without expecting them to stop by my desk, so it wasn't until Derwent cleared his throat that I looked up.

'Oh, it's you.'

'Obviously.' He had adopted his usual wide stance, looming over me with his hands in his pockets, but the arrogance was a reflex, I thought. He looked wary – almost apologetic, if he was capable of that. It was the first time we'd spoken since the confrontation with Seth. I'd been avoiding him and he had been ignoring me, because we were both grown-ups.

'What can I do for you?' I couldn't quite manage to sound enthusiastic about it but I was civil.

'I was an idiot the other night.'

Not what I had expected. I blinked. 'I'm aware of that.'

'Yeah. Well. It was a bad day.'

'I'm aware of that too. You shouldn't have taken it out on Seth.'

Derwent made a noise in the back of his throat that definitely didn't sound as if he was agreeing with me, but he couldn't meet my eyes. 'It upset you.'

'Yeah, it did.' I folded my arms. 'Just to be clear, are you actually going to apologise or is this your way of making sure your recollection of events matches mine?'

He looked at me as if I was insane. 'I'm not here to *apologise*.'

'Of course not. Why would you?' So far, so normal. 'What *do* you want?'

'Do you like him?' The question was abrupt.

'Yes. Of course I do. He's my boyfriend.'

'I don't trust him.'

My face was hot. 'I don't remember asking for your opinion.'

'You're getting it anyway. I think he's trying too hard.'

'Trying too hard,' I repeated. 'You're right, I should dump him.'

'Dump him or don't. I don't care. But pay attention to what he's doing.'

'And what's that exactly?'

'He's taken over your life. You had decided what you were going to do the other night but as soon as he turned up, you changed your plans. You left your friends to spend the evening with him.'

'The reason that happened was because your behaviour was inexcusable. It was nothing to do with Seth.'

'No?' he said unpleasantly. 'That's how you saw it, is it?'

'That's how it was.'

'When was the last time you went out without him? Or with friends?'

I opened my mouth to tell him, then shut it again. I couldn't remember, off-hand. He pressed home his advantage.

'You've changed since you've been seeing him. Everyone's noticed it. The way you eat. The things you do in your spare time. The way you are.'

'You've been talking to Liv,' I said accusingly.

'So what? We both noticed it.'

'You're being ridiculous. This is what happens when you're in a relationship – you spend time with your boyfriend and you start doing things differently. You make room for the other person in your life and your friends and family may have to shuffle over too. I'm sure I have changed, and I'm glad about it. Let's face it, the main difference between how I was before Seth and how I am now is that I'm happy.'

He dropped the hostility from one second to the next, his eyes softening in that way I found so disarming. 'If you're happy, that's all that matters.'

'Well, I am,' I said, still suspicious because I knew him too well to relax.

'It's just that he's making you into a different person.'

'So?'

'I liked the old one.' He walked off without waiting for me to respond and I sat at my desk stewing, thinking of a hundred different things I could have replied if I'd been quick enough to keep him from having the last word.

It was Liv's turn to stop beside my desk a few minutes later. 'Are you OK?'

'Absolutely fine,' I said, deciding on the spot that I could do without another conversation about my current relationship. 'I'm trying to work out where I've gone wrong with the Paige Hargreaves case.'

She borrowed a chair from the next desk and sat down with a wince, leaning back to make space for her bump. 'What makes you think you've gone wrong? You've been doing a great job.'

'I've done such a great job that I have no leads and no ideas.'

'What about the Chiron Club?'

I shook my head. 'Dead end, as far as I can see. Just because she was working on a story about them that doesn't mean it connects with her murder. And I have no idea what the story is. I still haven't found her phone or her laptop. We haven't identified the fake police officer. We don't even know how she got into the river.'

'The club is right on the riverfront, isn't it? Doesn't that seem suspicious to you?'

'Sort of, but it doesn't help. The Marine Unit officers told me there's no way to tell where her body was dumped from where the pieces turned up, and we still don't know when they put her in the river. I need a clue, a witness – something to narrow down the time of her death and the window for her body to be disposed of. Then I can call in CCTV from

70

the right area and the right time. If I guess, we'll find ourselves with hundreds and hundreds of hours of footage to review and no guarantee of spotting anything useful.'

'We could start with the cameras around Blackfriars Bridge. Given that we have to start somewhere,' Liv said hesitantly.

'Covering what period of time?'

'Before she was reported missing, up to the day before the mudlarker found her hand.'

I sighed. 'Even if we only have a few cameras, that'll be a lot of CCTV to review.'

'Get Colin to do it. He loves a challenge.' She was right, Colin Vale lived for the kind of tedious CCTV reviewing that made me want to lie on the floor and howl.

'What we really need is to find out where her body was cut up. It must have been messy. Think what Kev Cox could do with a scene like that.' Kev was my favourite crime scene manager, a gifted and intuitive scientist with a perpetually cheerful approach to life despite spending most days up to his elbows in death.

'If we find something on CCTV that suggests suspicious activity near Blackfriars Bridge, we might be able to turn that into a search warrant for the club.'

'Sir Marcus Gley promised me they weren't hiding anything, but he wouldn't let me get beyond the hall,' I said thoughtfully. 'In an ideal world I'd search that place from the attic to the cellars. All I need is a reason.'

'It would really help if we knew what Paige's story was about, wouldn't it? I didn't find anything useful in her flat.'

I hesitated, wary of offending her. 'I thought I might take another look in case we missed something.'

'In case *I* missed something, you mean.' She was grinning, though. 'I knew you couldn't stand to leave it up to me. There's nothing there, I promise. But be my guest.'

71

10

I slit the police tape that was strung across Paige Hargreaves'
front door and let myself in. As the door closed behind me
with a click and a thud, I shivered. The last time I'd been there,
the flat had been humming with activity. I had been focused
on finding evidence. More than that, I had thought of Paige
as a conundrum to be solved rather than a real person. But
standing in the small white-painted hallway with the bare
wooden stairs stretching ahead of me, the distinctive sound of
the door closing still echoing in my head, I thought of her for
what felt like the first time. She had drawn the door closed
behind her countless times. She had hung her coat on the
wall-hooks beside me. She had leafed through her post where
I stood, hoping for good news rather than bills. She had kept
her home to herself, so maybe it had been her retreat from
the world, her safe space. She had trudged up the steps the
same way as me, her hand on the wooden rail that ran up
one side of the narrow space. One day she had gone up the
stairs for the last time, without knowing it. She had lived in
this space, and now I was walking in her footsteps to find out
how she had died.

When I stepped into the kitchen at the top of the stairs,
the first thing I noticed was that someone had dealt with the

smell. The fridge stood open, switched off but thoroughly cleaned. It would take more than a little bleach to get rid of the mould on the wall, though. One of the sash windows had been lowered a couple of inches, enough to take the edge off the stale atmosphere. The rooms were tidier, too: the same items I'd noticed before, but arranged in a logical way. That would be Liv's work. I felt more optimistic about my chances of coming across something useful as I lugged a stack of newspapers and magazines over to the armchair by the window. There would be something here, caught between the pages or scribbled in a margin. There had to be. All I had to do was find it.

Three hours later, I was not feeling so positive. I stretched my neck with a wince, easing tight, tired muscles. A half-moon area around my chair was completely covered in stacks of paper, organised by type and date. It was looking more and more like busywork rather than useful research. I had found nothing that related to any current work that Paige had been doing – no notes, no printouts, no folders of research. I had found Paige's personal archive of published stories though, and read through it, noting that she had a wry turn of phrase. The earlier pieces were showy, heavy on the adjectives and self-consciously clever. As she got more experience, she settled into a style that was all her own: caustic humour, a questioning eye, intriguing opening paragraphs and a neat way with endings, a fearless ability to puncture overblown privilege. In among the fashion and the lifestyle pieces, there were some articles on homelessness and drug abuse that stood out: she had cared about these pieces, I thought, and it showed. On the whole, I felt – slightly to my surprise – that I would have liked Paige if I'd known her.

I stood up and stretched. The chair had never been particularly supportive, but over the hours I'd been sitting there it had turned into a proper instrument of torture. The springs were poking up through the seat, and the wooden frame had won the battle with the stuffing that was supposed to pad it. I couldn't imagine Paige sitting in it while she worked. The table had been so thoroughly covered in the debris of her life that I doubted she could have found a space to write there either. The two upright chairs that stood at the table had been tucked in between the table and the window, out of the way unless they were needed. The attic flat was a small space. Choices had to be made about what furniture you kept and how you used it, and I couldn't see anywhere that Paige could have made into a working area.

I stepped through the stacks of paper on the floor to get to the bedroom. It wasn't a particularly pleasant room, relying on a narrow skylight for natural light. We had imagined her lying in bed drinking champagne from the bottle, alone or with a friend, because of what we'd found on the bedside table, but I doubted she could have worked in bed. The mattress and bedding were gone now, taken away by the forensic scientists for analysis, but I could recall the scene as it had been: two limp pillows that offered no support, and a low wooden bed-head. It would have been uncomfortable to try to work there. I turned in a circle, scanning the small flat, reading the black-and-white poster on the wall at the end: *Be Your Own Hero*. There was nowhere else to work, unless she'd put her laptop on the kitchen counter and stood up to write. That seemed unlikely to me, especially given how untidy the kitchen had been when we looked at it before.

So if she hadn't worked at home, she had to have gone somewhere else. I frowned, trying to remember. I'd read something she'd written, hadn't I, about the neighbourhood . . . I crouched beside the stacked pages, searching for the right article. It had been a stray reference among a few others, and I had skimmed over it without thinking. Something about places to eat in Greenwich.

I almost missed the article as I flicked, recognising the

photograph by chance when it flashed past. With an exclamation I pulled it out and scanned it.

. . . but it's all too cute and self-conscious for me. Give me proper plates, not fish and chips served with a pretentious bucket and spade. If your hipster allergies are playing up too and you want a more authentic experience, a few doors down you'll find Carlo's, a friendly, family-run café that hasn't changed since the 1960s. The current owner, Carlo Jr, doesn't mind you sitting for hours over a cup of tea and a fried egg sandwich while you race to meet a deadline. At least, he doesn't if you're me, but then I *am* in there practically every day . . .

I checked the address. It was two minutes from the flat. I would pop in, I decided, and not just because I was drooling at the thought of a proper fried-egg sandwich.

From the outside, Carlo's looked like a typical London greasy spoon. The lower third of the wall outside was tiled with pink and white tiles, some cracked or broken. The window was fogged with dirt. I peered through the glass, and saw a handful of booths, all occupied. It was a good sign if it was popular with the locals. When I pushed open the door I encountered a gust of warm air that was scented with a heady mix of coffee, frying bacon and toast.

At the counter, there was no sign of Carlo. A small woman with dyed black hair and darting, nervous eyes took my order and told me that Carlo was out for half an hour.

'You speak to him when he comes? Or I could call him . . .' she trailed off, uncertain.

'There's no hurry.'

She nodded at me, looking relieved. The police often made people nervous but I felt her edginess was habitual, that she was always operating at the limits of her capacity.

I went and found a seat in the window and the food arrived almost before I'd finished taking off my coat. The egg sandwich oozed golden yolk all over the plate and was as good as Paige had promised. I wondered if she had sat where I was sitting, watching the people hurry past, heads down against the spring breeze. The tea was strong enough to satisfy even me. I gave myself permission to enjoy it, and the unaccustomed break from dashing around. I was almost disappointed when a stocky, dark-haired man swung into the café and ducked behind the counter with a nod to the regulars. I gathered my things slowly, giving the woman time to tell him who I was in a low voice that I couldn't hear over the hum of conversation in the café.

He was waiting for me when I arrived at the counter, his face open and friendly with an undertone of concern.

'You're here about Paige? Is she OK? She hasn't been in for a while.'

'I'm so sorry,' I said, and told him the bare outlines of what he needed to know: that she was dead, and we were treating it as murder.

'My God.' He fell back against the counter behind him, one hand to his head. 'I had no idea. I thought – God. Do you know who did it?'

'Not yet. We're pursuing a few different lines of enquiry.' There were times I loved police jargon, which allowed you to say everything and nothing at the same time. 'You said she hadn't been here for a while?'

'Not for a few weeks.'

'She was reported missing a month ago.'

'That would fit. Marta, Paige hasn't been here for a month, has she?'

The woman gave a complicated, wordless nod and shrug which managed to convey it was possible, but she couldn't say for sure.

'Did you know her well?'

'Sort of. We get to know our regulars. If I saw her in the street, I'd stop and chat, you know what I mean? She liked a bit of banter when she was in. But I don't know if you could say I knew her well.'

'Did she come in here with anyone?'

He shook his head. 'Always alone. She loved working in here because we don't have the internet so there were no distractions. She'd sit there tapping away, headphones on. Mind you, she knew what was going on all the time – she never missed anything. And she was kind. When she had a bit of extra cash she'd pay for some of the older customers – the ones who come in here for a chat and to get warm. Never told them she'd done it and wouldn't let me tell them either.'

'Before she disappeared, how did she seem to you? Same as usual? Or was she worried about anything?'

He blew out a lungful of air, considering it. 'I dunno, darling. Now that you're asking me, I'm thinking maybe she was a bit low, but not so much I'd ask her about it. She was quiet, the last few times she came in. There were days when she was up for a chat and days when she wanted to work.'

'Do you know what she was working on?'

'She never talked to me about it. We used to talk about food. She gave me a cookbook, once, because I'd mentioned it.' He ran a hand over his head, embarrassed. 'This is my dad's place. I always wanted to be a proper chef but I ended up in here. Don't get me wrong, I'm proud of it, but I know there's more I could be doing. Paige encouraged me.'

I let him talk for a little longer, appreciating the insight I was getting into her. It was comforting to know that Paige would be genuinely mourned and missed. She had probably had no idea how much she had meant to the friends and acquaintances she kept at arm's length. At first glance she was an airhead – a fashion-conscious glamour girl who liked the idea of being an investigative journalist, who lived in semi-squalor that she hid – but there was more to her than that, and I was glad of it.

'We're still looking for Paige's laptop and phone, and we still don't know exactly what she was working on. I don't suppose she left anything here? Notes, or her computer . . .' It was a vain hope, I knew, but I thought I might as well ask.

'No, nothing like that.' Marta nudged Carlo and muttered something. He smacked his head and twisted to look behind him. 'Wait, there is this.'

There was a book on the shelf below the cash register: a thin book, navy blue with the title picked out in gold foil. Carlo handed it to me. 'That was Paige's. She left it in here the last time she was in.'

I turned it so I could see the spine, where a single word jumped out at me: GLEY. The book was a short biography of Marcus Gley, I saw, turning it over. Privately printed, in a limited edition, in honour of his twentieth year as president of the Chiron Club.

'Can I take this?'

'Be my guest.'

I was halfway out of the café when another thought occurred to me. 'Carlo, when you say she left it here, was it an accident? Did she leave it behind by mistake?'

'No. She asked me to keep it for her. Keep it safe.' He looked worried. 'Does that mean it's important?'

'I hope so.'

I headed out with a new spring in my step.

If Paige had wanted to keep it safe, maybe she'd known she was in danger. And maybe I'd find the reason she died between the navy-blue covers of the book in my hand.

Two years earlier

He was inside the pool house, he came to realise, standing in the bathroom. He was shivering, unwell. Thank God, there was a toilet and a tap that worked. He used the toilet, his guts liquid. Then he ran water into his cupped palms and splashed his face, drinking a few mouthfuls before he straightened up. His stomach lurched, a warning to move carefully, slowly.

Outside, the pool was still. The water was grey, the air oddly dim so he had to strain his eyes to see what he knew was there: abandoned wine glasses, the dress hanging limp on the lounger, the body . . . He glanced up and understood why the light had changed: heavy, blue-black clouds boiled overhead now, swollen with rain.

How could he hide this?

The body was in water which would wash away any traces of his sweat and his – his saliva. But if his—

He stopped. Balked. Remade the thought so it was bearable. If his *DNA* was *inside* it—

you don't need a condom I promise it's fine
do it now

His DNA was inside the body. That was a fact. They would find it, when they did a post-mortem. He wasn't the sort to get arrested; his DNA wouldn't be on file. But if the police traced him somehow and tested him, they would match it. Then he wouldn't be able to deny that they'd had sex.

Which was a problem on so many levels, he couldn't even form the words to list them.

He couldn't hide the body. He couldn't bury it. There was no way he could lift it out of the water on his own, even if he was prepared to touch it, which he wasn't. He couldn't burn it: the thing was waterlogged. Even in this heat it would barely smoulder.

He couldn't do anything but hope no one found the body for a while, long enough for it to decompose. The flies were already at work. A few days should be enough. A week would be better.

He had no idea if he had minutes or months before someone came looking.

He cleaned up the pool house, wiping down everything he might have touched. When he walked outside the air felt even hotter, charged with electricity. A low growl of thunder echoed on the right. Rain would come, sooner or later. Rain that would wash away his vomit, that would disperse all the traces of him from the poolside.

The body was a shadow in the water, still and horrible. He went through the gap in the hedge and trudged around the side of the house again. Something moved on the terrace as he came level with it and he flinched before he realised what it was: a magpie strutting along the balustrade, watching him. The house's blank windows stared at him too as he stumbled across the wide expanse of straw-like lawn, his only thought to get away.

11

My feeling that I'd found something important faded as soon as I started actually trying to read the biography of Sir Marcus Gley. It was set in tiny print with very narrow margins, and it was indescribably tedious. The biography started off with Sir Marcus's early years, a predictable history of prizes and accomplishments at one exclusive school after another. I skipped forward, past his academic and sporting triumphs at Cambridge and his glittering career in the legal profession before taking up a new role in the City. One company name followed another, successes, record profits, blah blah blah. The words danced before my eyes and I found myself stifling a yawn. If I wasn't very careful, I would wind up sleeping at my desk.

I gave up on reading for the time being and flicked through the pages, scanning the close-set type for any underlining or marginal comments that Paige might have left. I needed something – anything – to confirm that this book was important to her. A little voice in my head whispered that maybe it wasn't. Maybe she had been going out and hadn't wanted to take a hardback book with her. Maybe Carlo had completely misunderstood her when she told him to look after it. I'd expected to find a chapter at the very least on the Chiron

Club, given that it was published in celebration of his presidency. The Club, though, was only mentioned in passing in a few places, almost as if nothing needed to be said. The book was for Chiron Club members, I reminded myself. They already knew it all.

I sighed and turned to the end of the book, looking for an index that I could skim through for familiar names, or anything that could be of interest. I'd have to read the whole bloody thing anyway, I knew, because I couldn't bear to think I'd miss something. *Keep it safe*, she had said, and left it with someone she trusted. And there wasn't so much as a sheet of paper elsewhere to tell us what she had been writing, or why, so this was my only lead currently.

That in itself suggested that I was on the right track to pursue the Chiron Club angle. Someone had cleaned up. Someone had erased every trace of her research. That couldn't have been by chance. They must have had a good reason. They must—

I stopped. There was no index. But written in faint pencil on the inside of the back cover was a name. Beneath it, there was a telephone number.

And they were both in Paige's handwriting.

'Roderick Asquith.' Liv grinned at me. 'He doesn't sound posh at all.'

'I bet you a fiver he calls himself Roddy,' I whispered, and rapped the knocker on the peeling blue door. The house was in Fulham, a part of London that was generally well-heeled and mainly residential, a warren of Victorian terraced streets. Roderick Asquith's home was halfway along a street of similar houses, but it was not the best kept by any means. In contrast with the neighbours' gardens that flanked it, the front featured a large bike shed beside some overflowing bins and a spindly, unkempt hedge. At a glance, the recycling was largely composed of beer cans and wine bottles.

'Big drinker.' Liv was eyeing it too. 'Does he live here on his own?'

'He's got two housemates. Even so, if that's a week's worth of booze I'm worried for their livers.' I was peering in through the shutters. From what I could see, the sitting room was dominated by a giant TV and every variety of games console imaginable. 'Typical boys' house.'

I'd done my research, as far as that was practical. I had an aversion to turning up on someone's doorstep without knowing what to expect. If there was someone there who had a habit of being violent with the police, or who had arrests for carrying concealed weapons, I wanted to know about it before I knocked on the door. There weren't any red flags for this address.

'He does know we're coming.' It wasn't quite a question.

'I called him. He said he'd be here at five and it's ten past.' I sighed. 'Maybe he's not home from work yet.'

'Where does he work?'

'Holborn.'

'We could have met him at his office. It would have been more convenient for us too.'

'He didn't want me in his office or anywhere near work. He said his two housemates wouldn't be home if we met at five.'

Even as I said it, the door opened.

'Roderick Asquith?'

'Roddy,' he said automatically, and I felt Liv quiver with amusement beside me.

'Maeve Kerrigan. We spoke on the phone.' I held up my warrant card, aware that Liv was doing the same. 'Can we come in?'

Roddy Asquith looked about twenty-five, but his fair hair was already thinning noticeably. He had a pink-and-white complexion that gave away his every emotion. At the moment he was flushed and definitely unhappy. His face was rounded, as if he had puppy fat left to lose. His shirt had pulled out from one side of his suit trousers and his tie was crooked.

'Hi. Yes. The thing is, I don't actually want to talk to you so I'm going to have to say no. Sorry.' He started to close the door and I put out my hand to hold it open, using enough force to stop him.

'Mr Asquith, as I explained to you on the phone, this is a murder investigation.'

'I know. I know. I should have said no when you called me but I was at work and I wanted to get off the phone.' He swallowed, embarrassed. 'I'd like to help. Really, I would. But I think it's best if I don't say anything.'

'I'd rather talk to you here than at the local police station,' I said. 'But if you'd prefer to accompany us there—'

'Oh God. Oh, no.' He ran a hand over his head, panicking. This wasn't playing out the way he'd imagined it. 'I don't know what to say. I don't know why you won't take no for an answer.'

'Because I am trying to find the person who killed Paige Hargreaves and disposed of her body in a particularly grotesque way. Do you know anything about that?'

'About Paige? No, of course not. I heard she was dead.' He was sweating now, his upper lip shining. He dabbed at it with the back of his hand. 'I saw it in the paper.'

'How did you know her?'

'I didn't.'

I tilted my head to one side. 'That's not true, is it?'

'What makes you say that?'

The way he was behaving. The fact he had used her first name when he talked about her, unthinkingly. The fact that he had noticed the newspaper reports about her death, which had been light on detail because we wanted to keep some of it to ourselves. I knew he was lying to me, and fortunately I could prove it.

'We found your name and telephone number among Paige's

possessions, handwritten by Paige herself. If we check your phone records, we'll know the truth.'

'You can't take my phone without a warrant.'

'I don't need to. I can get a court order to check the records through your service provider. To be honest, I'd do that anyway. It's useful for us because you won't be able to delete any calls or messages by clearing your phone.'

'I – I wouldn't do that.'

I raised an eyebrow and he blushed more deeply. 'Look, I just want you to leave me alone.'

'That's not an option, I'm afraid.'

'Can we come in?' Liv pushed her coat back and patted her bump, shamelessly playing the pregnancy card. 'I'd really love to sit down for a bit. You know how it is.'

He took a deep breath, bracing himself. 'No. No, I'm afraid you can't. I don't want you in here. If you want to talk to me, you'll have to arrest me.'

'I can't arrest you if you haven't done anything wrong,' I said. 'And I don't want to. I want to know why you were in contact with Paige and if it has anything to do with her investigation into the Chiron Club.'

I thought he was going to be sick then and there. The colour drained out of his face. 'You can't ask me about that.'

'Are you a member?' Liv asked.

'I'm not supposed to talk about it.'

'But you did talk about it, didn't you?' I said it gently. 'You talked to Paige.'

'I didn't think it mattered. But I shouldn't have – I wasn't supposed to—' The words burst out of him before he'd considered the implications of saying them. 'Oh God.'

'Mr Asquith—'

'No.' He shoved the door, hard, and I couldn't hold it open. The door slammed home and I took a step away, wincing. The movement had jarred my shoulder painfully. More than that, though, I was upset with myself for assuming he wouldn't force the door closed, but panic had overcome his social conditioning. Panic caused by my mentioning the Chiron Club, I thought.

Liv bent and pushed open the letterbox. 'Thank you for your help, Mr Asquith. We'll come back for a chat soon. You have a think about what you know in the meantime and maybe you can be more helpful to us than you have been up to now.'

We headed to the car in silence. It wasn't until the doors were closed and I was sure we couldn't be overheard that I turned to Liv.

'Search warrant?'

She gave me a small, wicked smile. 'Search warrant.'

12

Getting a search warrant was routine, a matter of finding a magistrate who was at home and prepared to sign the papers since it was outside court hours.

'Do we suspect there's evidence of an offence in there?' Liv asked me as she filled in the form.

'From the way Roddy wouldn't let us into the house? Definitely.' I sounded sure. In truth, though, my main reason for wanting to get into his house wasn't so much recovering evidence as it was a way of reminding him that we were waiting for him to talk to us, and we weren't going to give up until he told us everything he knew. If his housemates were inconvenienced in the process, that was a bit of extra pressure to pile on him.

'You – you can't do this,' Roddy said helplessly as a search team marched into the hallway of his house carrying an array of containers for any evidence we might find. There was a theatrical element to it and I hid a smile. I'd told them to make a big entrance and they'd done me proud. 'You can't just come in here,' he blustered.

'This piece of paper says we can.' Liv handed it to him.

'Now I might have that sit-down, since I've got in here at last.'

'I'm sorry about leaving you on the doorstep. I'm sorry about all of this.' He looked as if he was on the verge of tears. 'Do you have to do this? Really?'

'We wouldn't be here otherwise,' I said briskly.

'You only wanted to talk before. You didn't say anything about searching the house.'

'That's right. But the circumstances have changed.'

'What do you mean? I don't know what happened to Paige. I don't know anything about how she died or who killed her. You have to believe me.'

'Mate.' A figure appeared in the doorway behind him, a dark-haired man about the same age as Roddy, but otherwise as different as it was possible to be. He was thin, with the leanness of a keen runner, and close-cropped hair. His suit was impeccably tailored, unlike his housemate's. His skin was sallow and his light-brown eyes were shrewd under straight black brows. 'You don't have to say anything, Roddy. Not a thing.'

'I don't think we've been introduced,' I said. 'Detective Sergeant Maeve Kerrigan.'

'Orlando Hawkes.' He held out a slim hand and gave me a handshake that was so firm it very nearly qualified as assault on a police officer.

'Do you live here, Mr Hawkes? Which is your room?'

'The big bedroom at the front.' As he said it, footsteps overhead told me that the search team had entered his room. He grimaced. 'Do you have to search it?'

'I'm afraid so.'

'Lando, I'm so sorry. I'm so sorry.' Roddy was babbling, now, distressed. His friend stopped glowering at me for a moment.

'It's OK. It'll be fine. Sit tight. This is all a game.'

'It's very much not a game,' I said tightly. 'A woman died.'

'Nothing to do with us.' Orlando leaned against the doorway and folded his arms, trying to look as if he was unconcerned though I felt his attention was on the movements we could hear from above us. 'You're wasting your time.'

'Are you a member of the Chiron Club too?'

His eyelids flickered, a reaction he wasn't quite quick enough to conceal. 'I don't need to answer your questions either.'

'I think you just did.' I smiled at him. 'And where's the third musketeer?'

'Luke's away.' Roddy looked at Orlando. 'It's OK to tell her that, isn't it?'

His housemate shrugged. 'I wouldn't say another word, mate. Let her figure it out for herself.'

'Fortunately, I'm good at that.' I pulled my search gloves out of my pocket and started to draw them on. 'Thank you for your help, gentlemen.'

I'd expected the house to be both untidy and in need of a good clean, given that three men in their twenties lived there, but the living room was immaculate and so was the kitchen.

'We have a cleaner,' Orlando drawled when I commented on it. He was sitting at the kitchen table, watching me search, tilting his chair at a dangerous angle. 'She pops in twice a week.'

'She does our ironing too.' Roddy now blushed every time I looked at him, something that I was starting to find irritating. 'Well, mine and Lando's. She doesn't do Luke's.'

'Why not?'

'Luke does his own cleaning and ironing.' Orlando rolled his eyes, as if the very idea was bizarre. 'He didn't see the point in spending money on a cleaner. But, you know, Maggie's got to have some dosh to send home to Poland and I don't want to spend the weekend pushing the vacuum cleaner around so it all works out.'

Roddy made a swift movement to quell his friend, obviously

uneasy about how he was speaking to me. It didn't bother me, though. If anything, Orlando was overdoing the drawling privilege, which meant he was trying to distract me, which meant there was something in the house for me to find. I smiled at both of them sunnily and headed up the stairs to find out how the search was progressing up there.

Liv emerged on to the landing from the bedroom at the back that I knew belonged to Roddy. I glanced through the door. A signed England rugby shirt was framed on one wall and the bedclothes were Union Jack themed.

'Nothing in bedroom one,' she announced.

'Nothing you wouldn't expect to find, anyway.'

'He's not exactly challenging the stereotypes,' she whispered with a grin. 'Anyway, they're still working through bedroom two. We haven't started on bedroom three, the one belonging to the missing housemate.'

Bedroom three was the smallest, more of a box room than a bedroom. 'I'll take a look,' I said. 'It looks like a one-person space.'

Liv considered it. 'You might just fit two people in there, but you'd have to be really good friends. And there definitely isn't room for me in my current condition.'

I edged in, pushing the door open as far as it would go to make the most of the space. In fairness to self-sufficient Luke, he kept his part of the house neat and tidy, though the room was so small that even one thing out of place would have made it feel messy. There was nothing in it but a narrow wardrobe, a small chest of drawers and a single bed made up with plain white cotton bedlinen. A square mirror hung over the chest of drawers; it was the only thing that you could describe as remotely decorative. There were no pictures or posters on the walls. The only colour came from a tier of wall-mounted shelves at the foot of the bed which were loaded with books arranged by subject, and – I looked closer – further categorised in alphabetical order. So Luke was orderly in his habits and tidy, as well as frugal and absent, and favoured non-fiction over fiction.

I started with the drawers, working through them methodically and finding nothing too remarkable. Considering the single bed, he was well supplied with condoms, I thought, moving a second box of twelve aside to get at the passport underneath it. I flicked to the picture page and raised my eyebrows: floppy brown hair, blue eyes, cheekbones that could cut glass and a mouth made for trouble. He was twenty-five and not even the rigorous requirements of the passport office could hide the fact that he was outrageously handsome.

'Too young,' I murmured, taking one last look.

'What did you say?' Liv poked her head into the room.

'Nothing.' I waved the passport at her. 'Taking a look at Luke.'

She twitched the passport out of my hand and frowned at it. 'Pretty boy. Luke Gibson. You know, something about him is really familiar.'

'Do you think so?' But even as I said it, I was wondering if I'd seen him somewhere before. I should remember him if I'd met him, I thought; he had the sort of face that was hard to forget. I slid the passport back into its place and carried on, checking the pockets of the three suits hanging in the tiny wardrobe. He didn't have much in the way of casual clothes and I guessed he'd packed most of them for his break. Orlando had yawned his way through telling me that Luke had had a few days off work and was visiting a sort-of girlfriend in Edinburgh, though he was due home the next day.

'She's rich as sin, gorgeous, absolutely filthy, and thinks he can do no wrong.'

'She sounds lovely,' I said sincerely. 'So why is she only a sort-of girlfriend?'

'Luke likes to keep his options open.' Roddy, wide-eyed and pink as ever. He sounded reverent when he talked about Luke. Poor Roddy, plain and rich and shy, saddled with two housemates who were far more attractive and confident than him. Maybe he had wanted to impress Paige, I thought, rolling a couple of dumbbells out from under the bed with some difficulty so I could check there was nothing hiding behind them. Maybe she had coaxed him into talking out of turn, and he'd regretted it as soon as he opened his mouth. Maybe I could charm him into telling me what he'd told her, though I didn't want to play that kind of game with him. It felt manipulative.

I was about to announce that Luke's room was clear when it occurred to me to check behind the door. A plain backpack was squashed against the wall: black nylon, unmarked, unremarkable in every way. It was well-used, though, the material shiny in places from wear and tear. I picked it up to make sure it was empty, more out of habit than anything else. Nothing inside the main compartment. Nothing in the big pocket on the front. I unzipped the smaller pocket above it, noticing a sweet smell as I did so. Perfume, heavy on the roses. Could the bag belong to the Edinburgh girlfriend? Or someone else who didn't mind the single bed if she was sharing it with Luke?

There was nothing in the small pocket but a few coins and a white card the size and shape of a business card. I pulled it out and glanced at it casually, then looked again, with my full attention this time. Not a business card; a loyalty card that was almost complete. Nine stamps were filled in. The tenth would secure a free coffee from Carlo's, Royal Hill, Greenwich, a long way from where I was standing in Fulham.

I spread out an evidence bag and turned the whole backpack inside out.

'What have you got?' Liv peered over my shoulder.

I unzipped the small secret pocket right down at the bottom of the backpack and pulled out a credit card wrapped in paper secured with a rubber band. Scrawled across it in pen, in straggling capitals, were the words: EMERGENCY USE ONLY.

'Whose is that?'

I snapped the rubber band off and slid the card out of its paper covering. She read the name on the front of it.

'Paige Hargreaves. That's her card?'

'And her bag.' I folded it into a second evidence bag, careful to include the one I'd flattened out in case I'd shed any trace evidence. 'I think Mr Gibson has some explaining to do.'

Two years earlier

Humans are good at being scared, but not for long. He had been sick with fear, sobbing, a gibbering wreck when the car pulled up beside him, after endless wandering through horrible fields and withered woodland. The rain had come at last and soaked through his clothes, slicking his unruly hair down, making him look eccentric rather than desperate despite his bare feet. And then he had arrived in the most perfect English village, complete with a Norman church and an immaculate green surrounded by cottages with roses tumbling around the doors. The sort of place to have a proper phone box still, unvandalised. The sort of place where the police station had fallen victim to budget cuts, so the curtain-twitching inhabitants couldn't summon up the cops to question the dishevelled stranger in their midst.

He had called for help and help had come. He had got into the car and burst into tears, which he wasn't proud of. He had sobbed on and off all the way to London, and on and off for the next week. Pieces of the night came to him unexpectedly when he wasn't even thinking about it: snatches of conversation, images, faces in the dark, a woman dancing, her dress askew.

He threw away his shirt and the trousers, stuffing them

into a public bin miles from his house after he'd washed them on the hottest setting his washing machine could manage.

He shaved off his beard and got a haircut.

He went to a library and stood by the Ordnance Survey maps, trying to puzzle out where he had been. The village was easy enough to find; the house wasn't. He had wandered, half-delirious, and what he remembered of the topography didn't match the maps. A mystery, he decided, and wadded the last map back onto the shelf.

He steeled himself and rang a friend who had been with him when they arrived at the house.

'Mate, where did you go? We were looking for you everywhere. That was a weird party.'

'How long were we there?' he made himself ask.

'We left after an hour? Something like that. Zibby told us his folks lived nearby so we piled into the car and let me tell you, it was not nearby. Plus we got lost. Zibby is an arsehole.'

'I don't know him.'

'Yeah, don't bother is my advice. He's a twat.' There was a pause. 'Sorry for leaving you behind, mate. If I'd seen you—'

'No, no. Don't worry.' He was weak with relief. They had left, before he— before any of it had happened. No one had seen him. The police didn't knock on his door. The news didn't mention the discovery of a dead body at a country mansion. The heatwave didn't break either: every day seemed hotter than the last, every thunderstorm a false promise of cooler weather.

He gave up drinking for a while.

He gave up doing coke for good.

He cut down on cigarettes, red meat, caffeine, sugar and wheat until he was too bored to persevere with it.

He went to a handful of interviews for real jobs, the sort that would set him on a 'career path', something which had never seemed very important before.

He woke up in a panic at least once a night, until he didn't any more.

The world hadn't ended, after all.

Everything was going to be all right.

13

The next day I stood on the concourse at King's Cross, watching the arrivals board for the Edinburgh train that was due at midday. Somewhere on it was Luke Gibson, returning to London, hopefully oblivious to the fact that I was waiting to talk to him. I'd taken care to give his housemates the impression that we hadn't found anything of interest and had other lines of enquiry that were more promising. There was a record of the items I'd removed from their house that I was supposed to leave with them, but I'd elected to post it to them rather than filling it out before I left. Somehow, I hadn't got around to posting it yet. By the time it arrived, they would know all about the bag and its contents. More to the point, so would I.

There were too many people on the concourse and too many exits for my liking, even though I'd called in British Transport Police support to make sure I didn't miss Luke. They had confirmed with the guard that someone who matched Luke's description was sitting in the seat he'd reserved on the Edinburgh train. A vast group of Spanish students swarmed past me, chattering and laughing, and I scowled at the noise. I moved a few paces to my right so I could keep platform 4 in my line of sight as they passed.

The platform was currently deserted, apart from the officers strung along it, waiting.

'Don't worry, we won't miss him.'

I smiled at the big BTP sergeant who was standing beside me. 'I have faith in you.'

'We know which train he's coming in on, and we've got a good recent description of him. We'll pick him up.' He listened to his earpiece. 'The Edinburgh train has left Stevenage. It should be here in twenty-two minutes.'

'Give or take thirty seconds.'

'It's usually on time.' He was an older officer and serious to his very bones. He nodded up at the clock above us. 'It'll be bang on. You wait and see.'

I'll have to, I thought. I had nothing better to do.

The sergeant yawned widely, and excused himself. 'I was on earlies today. Up at half past four. It catches up with you.'

'I can imagine.'

'I need a coffee. Can I get you one? You've still got time before the train gets in.'

'White, please. No sugar.'

He headed off to get it from one of the cafés on the concourse. Seth would have scolded me for drinking it when I'd already had coffee that morning. He would have insisted on herbal tea, or decaf. What was the point in decaf if you didn't *have* to drink it, Derwent's voice sneered in my head. On the other hand, I wasn't sure more caffeine was such a good idea. I found myself flinching as a pigeon swept low over my head to investigate a crumb on the floor. It wasn't as if I needed to be any more jittery.

I'd have felt calmer if Derwent was with me, oddly; I trusted him to get his man. But he was all the way down in suburban Sutton with his girlfriend, Melissa, and her little boy Thomas, taking a day off after his efforts in the Poplar case. There was a time he'd have turned down extra time off, but he had more reasons to stay away from work these days. Nothing had changed him like getting together with Melissa and taking on responsibility for Thomas. He had become a father to the boy, and that had mellowed him, which should have made him easier to deal with. It made him more vulnerable, though, and miserably aware of it. These days the tough cases were more likely to get under his skin. I thought of him carrying the tiny body of the baby out of the house where she had lived her brief life, and how he must have felt about it. That was the sort of job that left a mark on your soul even if you managed to make an arrest. I should call him to see if he was all right, and I would have if we hadn't been bickering about Seth. And Seth was irrelevant, when it came down to it, because this was about work and being there for your colleague.

Be the better person, Maeve.

The BTP officer returned with something that at least looked like coffee. It was hot, and strong enough to make me stand up a little straighter, and entirely welcome. I drank it fast, feeling the caffeine hit my bloodstream. *Decaf indeed . . .*

The sergeant nudged me sooner than I had expected. 'Two minutes.'

The clock said 11.58. I alternated between staring at it and looking down the tracks, trying to pick out the approaching train's headlight.

'There.' He pointed at a glimmer in the distance. 'See it? Another sixty seconds and the passengers will be disembarking.'

The train slid into the station and came to a stop. All down the empty platform, the officers had taken up their positions, arms folded. They were big, solid men, so if Luke Gibson tried to cause me any problems I had plenty of muscle to call on.

'According to his reservation he's in Coach G.' The officer guided me to a different position, to one side of the platform so I could see the length of the train. 'Here they come.'

The passengers spilled out when the doors finally slid open, a surge of humanity in all shapes and sizes, ages and classes. They hurried towards the taxi ranks and the entrance to the underground, rushing because life was a competition, especially in London. The platform went from deserted to Oxford-Street-on-Christmas-Eve crowded in the time it took to take a breath. I scanned the faces, hunting my target, afraid to blink in case I missed him.

'Is that him? IC1 male, blue hoodie, bag on left shoulder, beard—'

'No.' I had seen him at last and already started to move, sure of myself now that I'd found him. 'Navy polo shirt, carrying a brown leather holdall in his right hand. His hair is shorter and lighter than in the passport picture.'

'Got him.' My BTP sergeant muttered something into his radio.

The officers began to converge on Luke Gibson as he walked up the platform, still unaware that anyone was watching him. He looked tired, his eyes shadowed in the harsh station lights. He was taller than I had expected, and broader – he'd put on muscle since his passport photograph was taken. The boyish good looks had settled, becoming more interesting. He swung his bag up to his shoulder as I watched and something about the movement looked familiar to me, an echo that I couldn't quite trace to its source. There was something about him . . .

I shook off the feeling as my path converged with his. *Concentrate.* He hadn't noticed me approaching. I waited to speak until he was close enough to touch, in case he ran. 'Luke Gibson?'

He frowned at me, confused. 'Sorry?'

'Are you Luke Gibson?'

'Yeah.' He looked down at the ID in my hand, and back up at me, and then at the little ring of uniformed officers that had gathered around him. 'What's going on?' Then, with sudden tearing anxiety, 'It's not Mum, is it?'

'Nothing like that.' I couldn't quite manage to smile at him, though, as I usually would, to reassure him. Everyone feared the police for the bad news they might bring, if nothing else. But I was there because of a murdered woman, and at the thought of her I found I was all out of smiles. 'We need to speak to you regarding the death of Paige Hargreaves.'

'Who?' His expression was absolutely blank. Too blank?

'Paige Hargreaves,' I repeated clearly. 'She was a journalist.'

'Oh!' He blinked. 'Yeah, I remember her. Did you say she's *dead*?'

'You didn't know?'

I'd allowed an edge of sarcasm into my voice but he answered as if I'd been straight with him. 'No, I didn't. I had no idea. When did this happen?'

'We're still trying to establish the facts of the case.' Police-speak at its best, telling him absolutely nothing.

'Right. Sorry, why do you need to speak to me?' He was looking baffled. 'I barely knew her. I think I met her twice.'

'We found some personal items of hers in your house.'

'Personal items?' He frowned. 'What do you mean by that? What sort of thing? And what does that have to do with me?'

'We'll discuss it in interview.' I nodded to the officers on either side of him. 'We need to search you—'

That got through to him. 'Search me? Like hell. I haven't done anything wrong.' His voice had risen but he caught hold of his temper before I had the chance to tell him to calm down. He took a moment to collect himself, then said more quietly, 'You have no reason to search me.'

'We can't transport you to my office without searching you. It's for your own safety and for the safety of the officers who are taking you there. It's routine,' I added, which was true.

'This is crazy.' He looked past me and flushed, aware for the first time that everyone who passed us was staring and undoubtedly speculating on why he was being stopped. 'I have no idea what's going on.'

'I'll explain everything when we're at the office, OK?' I

101

touched his arm to get his attention back on me. 'Let's get this done quickly. I don't want to keep you standing here for any longer than you have to be.'

I could see him thinking through what I'd said to him so far, considering his options, puzzling through the situation he'd found himself in. Anyone would have been rattled to be stopped like that in public, but he was more self-possessed than most, I thought. After a beat he nodded and bent to put his bag down. 'Fine.'

'Arms out,' a BTP officer behind him said briskly. 'Are you carrying anything you shouldn't have on you? Anything sharp in your pockets? Anything that could hurt me when I'm searching you?'

'Nothing.' He looked up and kept his eyes fixed on mine as the officer patted him down, assessing me in the same way I was contemplating him. I couldn't guess what conclusions he was coming to, but I had the impression of a sharp intelligence at work: not just a pretty face. And he had the sense to go quiet, which nine out of ten people wouldn't have managed. He didn't speak again until we started to move towards the exit, where the transport van I'd requested was waiting on double-yellow lines with its hazard lights flashing.

'Are you arresting me?'

'This is only a conversation,' I said smoothly, sidestepping the question of whether arrest was a possibility.

'Do I need a lawyer?'

'You know that better than I do.'

'I don't know anything at all.'

I shrugged. 'It's up to you, then.'

He didn't say anything else – not then, nor in the van, nor when we arrived at the office, which made me wary. If he was quiet, he was thinking.

I would have given a lot to know what was on his mind.

14

I was in no hurry to interview Luke Gibson. Instead, I went to find Liv. I needed to find out what I'd missed.

'Absolutely nothing.' She was dunking a herbal teabag in hot water unenthusiastically. I didn't blame her; the smell that rose up from it was the opposite of appetising. 'After you let us know you'd got Luke, we picked up Orlando Hawkes and Roddy Asquith at their offices.'

'Did they argue with you?'

'No. I don't think they were expecting it, but they came quietly. Maybe they didn't want to draw attention to what was happening.'

'Sensible,' I commented. 'That's unusual.'

'It was a bit like they'd been advised on what to do if the police came calling.' Liv raised her eyebrows at me meaningfully. 'They both asked for their lawyers. We can't interview them until the lawyers are ready.'

'And are the lawyers here?'

'Orlando Hawkes is with his brief as we speak.'

'He's preparing a statement.' Pete Belcott gave a bubbling sniff that made me wince. He was pale and sweaty.

'Jesus. You look awful.'

'It's only a cold,' he croaked, 'but it's kicking my arse.'

'I keep telling him he should be at home.' Liv was as far away from him as it was possible for her to be. 'You're going to give it to the rest of us.'

He looked at me, his eyes threaded with red veins and watery. 'Is that OK?'

'Please, go.' I always forgot I was senior to Belcott now. He never forgot it, which said everything about how he felt about it. I knew he had told everyone that I'd only been promoted because I was a woman, as a box-ticking exercise. The trouble was, as he and I both knew, I'd earned my promotion and he'd failed his sergeant's exams. That should have been the end of that, but Belcott had never met a grudge he didn't want to cherish.

'If you're sure you don't need me, I'll head off.' He dragged himself out of the kitchen and I heard him coughing his way down the hallway.

Liv shuddered delicately. 'Health hazard.'

'At the best of times,' I murmured. 'But I do feel sorry for him.'

'He lives on his own, doesn't he? It's miserable being sick when you're alone.' Liv had Joanne to make her lemon and honey drinks and tuck her into bed with a hot-water bottle, and I had Seth to do the same, even though it would come with a lecture about improving my immune system and herbal tinctures that I was guiltily aware I deserved. I gave a tiny sigh. It was amazing I'd managed to survive for so long.

'And you picked up Gibson without too much trouble?'

'He's in room three,' I said.

'Asquith is in two, Hawkes is in one.' Liv sipped her drink and pulled a face. 'Disgusting. I'm hoping it kills off the cold germs before it kills me.'

'Who else is here?' The office was quiet, for once.

'Georgia.'

'Great.'

Liv snorted. 'I can see you're delighted.'

'Oh, she's fine. Look, you don't need to stay. Even Georgia can't make a mess of babysitting a couple of interviews.'

She shook her head. 'I want to hear what Hawkes has to say.'

'Then you're in luck.' Georgia appeared in the open doorway and I tried to remember what I'd been saying about her, wondering how offensive it might have sounded and deciding the answer was very. 'Mr Hawkes is ready to share his statement with us.'

Technically it wasn't Mr Hawkes who shared his statement with me and Liv and the tape machine, but his lawyer.

'Jeremy Fallon.' He held out his hand to shake mine and I felt the heavy signet ring on his little finger press into my skin. He was a large man wearing a very expensive suit that had been tailored to give him wide shoulders and a waist he might otherwise have lacked. An orange and blue tie lurked under his chins. It had the soft sheen of silk and was covered in interlocking Hs: the sort of tie that didn't come cheap for the sort of lawyer whose hourly rate would pay for a handful of them. Fallon had a jolly smile and eyes that were colder than the rings of Saturn.

'I'm here at Mr Hawkes' request to read you a statement that he's prepared about his involvement with Miss Paige Hargreaves. Or rather, his lack of involvement with her.'

I looked at Orlando Hawkes. 'Are you prepared to answer some questions after we've heard your statement?'

'Mr Hawkes is not,' Fallon said smoothly, before Orlando could even react. 'Although he wishes of course to be helpful, he can't add anything to what I am about to read.'

'Can't or won't?'

Fallon reared back, hurt. 'My client would be perfectly within his rights to refuse to say anything at all.'

I put my pen down on my notebook and folded my arms. 'Please, go ahead.'

Orlando Hawkes' face was completely impassive as his lawyer held up the single sheet of paper that had taken them two hours to write.

'This statement has been prepared on behalf of Orlando Edgar Hawkes, currently resident of 23 Garsington Road, Fulham.' He cleared his throat. '"I am aware of the very sad death of Paige Hargreaves and wish to assist the police in their enquiries to the best of my abilities. I knew her socially because we moved in the same circles and had friends in common, but I did not have a close friendship with her. I met her a number of times at bars and informal gatherings and on one occasion she visited my home in the company of other friends. It was a casual visit following a night out at a bar. At no time was I alone with her and I did not have any meaningful conversation with her then or at any other time. I was not aware that she had left any personal items in my home. I do not know when she might have left her possessions in my home but I suggest it might have been on that occasion. It is the sole occasion that I can remember Miss Hargreaves being in my home. I do not know which rooms she visited on that occasion. She would not have been restricted to rooms on the ground floor and may have been in the bathroom and bedrooms.

"I am aware that Miss Hargreaves was an investigative journalist. I did not speak to her regarding her work. Nor did she ever interview me, formally or informally, regarding her work.

"This statement is my full and complete account of my interactions with Paige Hargreaves. I am not aware of any other information which may be of use to the police in their investigation."'

The lawyer laid it on the table delicately and slid it across to me. 'It's signed, as you can see, by Mr Hawkes, and dated with today's date.'

It was a clever enough statement, I thought. Hawkes had been told that we'd found some of Paige's belongings in the house, but not what we'd found, nor what that might imply, nor how we had identified anything that belonged to her. He hadn't made the mistake of knowing too much: the very vagueness of what he said made it hard to question him. What he was really saying was that there was no significance to anything we had found. Moreover, if we found Paige's DNA in the house – just about anywhere – he had established that there was an innocent reason for it to be there so it had no evidential value for us. He had admitted to knowing Paige, so if we encountered some of their mutual friends there was nothing they could say that would contradict him. However, he was the only one who knew how close his relationship with Paige had been, or if he had talked to her about the Club. If he said they were vague acquaintances, who could say that was wrong?

'Is that it?' I asked.

'That's all we have to say. Now, I think my client would like to go.' Fallon looked to Orlando, who nodded sombrely.

'Before you do, can I ask you what job you do, Mr Hawkes?'

Fallon's eyes narrowed but his client didn't see a trap in the question. 'I'm a trainee at the London branch of a US management consultancy firm.'

'Does that pay well?'

He shrugged. 'I don't know. I don't know what you'd consider a decent salary. It probably pays a bit more than you get.'

Fallon cleared his throat and Orlando slumped in his chair, obviously irritated at being told off. Irritated was useful for my purposes.

'What I'm wondering,' I said slowly, 'is how can you afford to have Mr Fallon here represent you.'

'You don't need to say anything about that.' Fallon pushed his chair back. 'This interview is over.'

'Were you retained by the Chiron Club, Mr Fallon, on Mr Hawkes' behalf?'

The question was for the lawyer but I was watching Orlando Hawkes. He had a long way to go before he could risk playing poker: that I'd hit the mark was written all over his face.

'I don't need to explain how I'm being paid.' Fallon nudged his client. 'Come on. We're finished. Turn off the recorder.'

'Interview concluded at 1.28 p.m.,' Liv said into the machine and switched it off.

'There really are advantages to being a member of the Chiron Club. I wonder what the disadvantages are.'

I said it idly, unthinkingly. Hawkes looked hollow with terror. He had been pushing his chair into place at the table, but he faltered, suddenly clumsy. When he took his hands away, his fingers left sweaty marks on the chair.

'It's been a pleasure, Sergeant Kerrigan.' Fallon nodded at me, his eyes like chips of ice, and I thought he would know me again, if our paths ever crossed. He ushered Hawkes out of the room, one plump hand on his shoulder, steering him away from me so there couldn't be any more casual chitchat. Liv followed to escort them out and I sat for a few minutes longer, considering what Hawkes had told me deliberately and without intending to. The caffeine had worn off and I was tired. I wanted a break, but I had to deal with Roddy Asquith before I could start to work on Luke Gibson.

As it turned out, I needn't have worried. On the advice of his lawyer, a well-spoken woman with naturally grey hair and a steely, unsmiling manner, Roddy gave a no-comment interview. From start to finish, he didn't answer a single question, and at the end of it I was truly fed up.

'This means we're going to have to ask you the same questions another time. Wouldn't you rather deal with it now?'

Somewhere around the third question he had settled on staring over my right shoulder. I wasn't even sure he was listening to me. He barely blinked as he replied, 'No comment.'

'She was your friend. You knew her. She was in your house.

Don't you want to help us find the person or people who killed her?'

'No comment.'

'Don't you care?'

'No comment.' He said it with all the feeling of a robot. I couldn't even get him to blush. With disgust, I gave up on him altogether and ended the interview.

'Frustrating,' Georgia said happily, swinging into the room after he had departed.

'I meant what I said. I'll be speaking to him again. This is not over.'

'Well, it's over for now. And you didn't get anywhere.' She wasn't quite gloating, but she wasn't far off it.

'I've still got Luke Gibson to go.'

'Can I sit in on that one too?'

'If you want.' I yawned so widely my jaw creaked in protest. 'It'll probably be just as interesting as the last one.'

'I saw Gibson when you brought him in.' She grinned. 'I don't think I'm going to be bored.'

15

Luke Gibson wasn't behaving as if he had a guilty conscience. When I opened the door to his interview room he was fast asleep, his head pillowed on his arms, the picture of innocence.

'Aww,' Georgia whispered from behind me as I drew the door shut quietly. 'He's out for the count.'

'He's probably knackered after his week away. From what his housemates said, he wasn't planning on doing much sleeping.'

'Are you waiting for his lawyer?'

'He hasn't asked for one.'

'That's stupid of him.'

'But useful. You could make him a cup of tea,' I suggested. 'That might help to wake him up.'

'Do you want some tea?'

'I'm all right, actually. But thanks,' I said, surprised that she'd offered. 'You'd better put two sugars in Mr Gibson's. He'll need the energy.'

Her eyes danced. 'Why? What are you going to do to him?'

I grinned. 'Only ask a few questions. Nothing too strenuous.'

'Shame.' She bounced off towards the kitchen. There were brief moments where I thought we might actually end up getting on quite well. Then I would put my foot in it, or she would say something horrible, and we would end up where we'd started. She had probably been planning to spit in my tea, I thought, and part of me felt that was fair enough. I should apologise for what I'd said to Liv about her.

I *should* apologise, but I knew I wouldn't.

The second time I went into the interview room I let the door thud home behind me. Luke raised his head with a start.

'Christ.' He blinked and rubbed his eyes. 'Sorry, I was just . . . sleeping.'

'Most people probably wouldn't be able to sleep in these circumstances.'

'I can drop off anywhere. Even if I probably shouldn't.'

'There isn't much else to do in here. Anyway, someone's sorting you out a cup of tea.'

'Thanks, that'll help.' He shook himself and sat up straight. 'I'm awake now.'

'We'll get started with your interview when my colleague comes back.'

He checked his watch. 'What was the hold-up?'

'There were a couple of other people I needed to speak to.'

'Roddy and Orlando?'

I'd already reached the conclusion that he was clever but the question still surprised me. 'Now why would you ask me that?'

'Because you said you'd found personal items belonging to Paige in our house. I can't think why you'd have singled me out to interview since I barely knew her. I assumed you'd want to talk to all three of us.' He raised his eyebrows. 'Am I right?'

I started to fiddle with the tape machine instead of answering, knowing that I might as well have told him he was on the money. He was managing not to look smug when I glanced at him, but only just.

Well, you can have that one. If you think you're cleverer than me, you'll relax. And then maybe you'll make a mistake.

When Georgia came in with his tea, he beamed at her.

'Thanks. That's really kind.'

'Not a problem.' She was blushing, I was amused to see. His eyes followed her as she walked all the way around the table to her seat, and again I had the jarring feeling I'd seen him somewhere before, or someone very like him . . .

'Shall we get started?' Georgia had her hand on the recorder, ready to go. I nodded, and during the preamble and opening questions establishing who he was I did my best to pull myself together and concentrate. He worked in a bank, he said, in the City.

'Is that where you met your housemates?'

'I was at university with Orlando.'

'Which university?'

'Cambridge,' he said shortly, looking down at his tea instead of at me, as if he knew it would colour my opinion of him. It was one word but it invited me to make a whole host of assumptions about privilege and intellectual arrogance, and that obviously bothered him.

Or he knew I was making assumptions about his privilege and intellectual arrogance and he wanted to persuade me it was unjustified.

'Was Roddy at Cambridge too?' I asked, offering him safer ground.

'No, he went to Leeds. Orlando and Roddy were in school together. We were all looking for somewhere to live in London at the same time and Orlando suggested sharing a house.'

'Have you lived with them for long?'

'Three years, something like that.'

'Any arguments?'

'We get on fine.'

'Even though you have the smallest room?'

He grinned. 'I'm used to it. And I pay less rent than the other two.'

'And you do your own cleaning and ironing. I'd have thought you didn't need to watch the pennies, given your job.'

'I don't have the same background as the other two. My mum brought me up on her own and there wasn't a lot of money for extras. I don't have anyone to dig me out if I run out of cash, so I make sure I don't run out.' The way he said it was matter-of-fact. He wasn't ashamed of his past, I thought, and liked him for it.

'Are you a member of the Chiron Club?'

'Me? No. They wouldn't want someone like me.'

'What do you mean, someone like you?'

'I'm not connected. I don't have rich parents. They like people who are like them.'

'Like your housemates.'

He shrugged. 'I suppose so.'

'What else do you know about it?'

'Nothing, really. As far as I can see, membership mainly involves going to parties.'

And getting decent legal representation if there was the faintest whiff of trouble in the air, I thought. And something that had made Orlando Hawkes go pale when I hinted at it, something that had made Roddy Asquith too scared to speak to us at his home or in interview.

'Tell me about Paige Hargreaves. How did you know her?'

'I didn't.' He saw my frown. 'She was a friend of a friend of a friend. I ran across her a couple of times when we were out. I knew her well enough to say hello, not enough to have a conversation.'

'Was she ever in your house?'

'Not that I recall.' He thought about it. 'Maybe when I wasn't there. Sometimes I sleep . . . elsewhere.'

'Elsewhere?'

'You've seen my bedroom. It's on the small side. I usually persuade girls to invite me to their place because it's more comfortable.'

'Does that happen often?'

The eyebrows went up again. 'That's a very personal question.'

I laughed in spite of myself. 'It's not meant to be. I'd still like you to answer it.'

He drank some of his tea before he answered, taking his time while he thought through why I might be asking. 'Often enough. Are you hoping I can narrow it down to a specific date because you don't know when Paige was in the house?'

Basically, yes. 'We're still at the start of our enquiries,' I said. 'We're trying to put together what happened and when. Any details help.'

'I can't tell you anything more than I've said already, I'm afraid. I never saw her in the house. No one ever mentioned she'd been there. And no one ever told me she was dead.' He frowned. 'That's something I've been thinking about. How did she die?'

'We don't know yet.'

'You haven't done a post-mortem?'

'It was inconclusive.'

'So it could have been natural causes?'

I shook my head. 'Not from the way her body was treated after she died.'

'What does that mean?'

'She was dismembered,' I said coolly.

'Jesus.' He looked genuinely shocked, the colour leaching from his skin. It took him a moment to recover his composure. 'I'm sorry to hear it, obviously, but I barely knew her. I didn't even recognise her name when you asked me about her at King's Cross.'

I opened my folder and took out a picture of the bag. 'Do you recognise this?'

'No.' He sounded definite.

'It was in your bedroom.'

'Where?'

'Behind the door.'

He shook his head. 'There was nothing behind the door.'

'This bag was there when I searched your room.' I tapped

the picture with the end of my pen. 'Look at it again. Are you sure you don't recognise it?'

'I've never seen it before.' He looked at me. 'I'm telling you the truth. Someone must have put it in my room, and recently. It wasn't there when I was packing for Scotland.'

'Who would put something in your room?'

'I don't know. One of my housemates? One of their mates? Maggie, the cleaner, if she thought it was mine?' He shrugged. 'I don't know who did it, I'm afraid.'

'When you say Paige was a friend of a friend of a friend, who's your friend in that list?'

'Roddy, I suppose,' he said reluctantly. 'He had a pal at university who ended up working for a production company that made documentaries. He knew Paige through his mate.'

'And did they socialise much?'

'You'll have to ask Roddy.'

I had, and hadn't got anywhere.

'Do you remember Roddy's friend's name?' Georgia asked.

'Jonny Gough.' He spelled it for her. 'She's a girl. No idea what it's short for. Jonquil, probably.'

'Do you know the name of the company she works for?'

'No . . . but I do have her number in my phone.'

'I thought she was Roddy's friend,' I said, amused.

'Jonny and I – we're not exactly friends. We had a bit of a thing for a while.' The corners of his mouth curved up irresistibly and I stared at him, mesmerised. It was *too* familiar; where had I seen that smirk before?

Georgia shifted in her chair and knocked against the table leg, which jarred the table and made tea slop over the side of Luke's mug. He lifted it with a sharp, 'Careful.'

'Sorry. I'll clean it up.' She jumped up and hurried out of the room. I leaned across and suspended the interview. It was going to look really good on the transcript. I hoped I didn't have to read it out in court. More than that, I hoped I wasn't going to need to read it out. I'd been prepared to treat Luke as a suspect, and he wasn't out of the woods yet, but I'd be sorry to arrest him. I was as sure as I could be that he had been honest with us so far.

Luke had lifted my notebook out of the danger zone while I was dealing with the tape machine. He handed it to me. 'You don't want to get it on your notes.'

'We might as well take a break since we've had to stop.'

His eyes darkened with disappointment. 'I was hoping I could leave. I'm sorry if I haven't been helpful but it's not deliberate. I've told you everything I know.'

I thought he probably had, but I wanted to ask him what else he knew about the Chiron Club before I let him go. 'I'll try to wrap this up as quickly as I can.'

'OK.' He hesitated. 'It's just there's someone waiting for me.'

Of course there was. 'Waiting here? In the office?'

'I was supposed to see her when I got back from Edinburgh. I had to call her to let her know where I was.'

He certainly didn't waste any time in moving on from the Edinburgh girl, I thought, but I kept that to myself. 'I'll see what I can do.'

'Thank you. I appreciate it.'

Georgia returned with handfuls of paper towels and started mopping the table. As I headed for the door, he said something to her in an undertone. It made her laugh out loud. I glanced over my shoulder to see him looking up at her, his face full of mischief. I had seen that look before, I knew it.

I still couldn't place him and it was driving me mad.

16

I'd planned to spend a few minutes going through my notes before returning to the interview room, but Liv was waiting for me outside.

'All done?'

'No, having a break because Georgia spilled tea all over the table.'

Liv grinned. 'And you thought she couldn't mess up an interview.'

'What's up?'

'I didn't want to interrupt you while you were interviewing him but there's a lady in reception waiting for Luke Gibson. Any idea what time you might be finished?'

'Soon, I think. He did tell me someone was waiting for him. I'm wrapping things up.'

'Oh good, I'll tell her. Poor thing, she looks absolutely terrified.'

'Terrified? Why?'

'It's natural, isn't it? It must be awful to know your son is being questioned in a murder investigation.'

Understanding dawned on me. 'His mother is waiting for him? I assumed it was yet another girlfriend.'

'Nope. His poor devoted mum.' Liv stretched her back and winced. 'I'll go and tell her he'll be a while longer.'

'I can go. You look shattered. Go and put your feet up.'

'Are you sure?'

'It'll take me five minutes. Honestly, go.'

I headed off down the corridor, reflecting that I'd misjudged Luke Gibson. Then again, given the way he'd been flirting with Georgia, maybe I hadn't. But it wasn't a crime to have a gaggle of girlfriends at the same time, and Georgia could presumably look after herself . . .

The only person in reception was a small, slim woman with black hair who was facing away from me. She rocked back and forth as she sat there: the tension that gripped her was obvious a mile away.

'Mrs Gibson?'

She looked around at the sound of my voice. 'Oh, no, I'm not. I mean, I am Luke's mother if that's who you're looking for, but we don't have the same surname. My name is—'

'Claire Naylor.' I'd recognised her straight away. If I sounded calm it was because I was experiencing the numbness of pure shock. 'We've met before. Years ago.' It had been so long ago that I'd forgotten all about her, and now I was wondering how I'd managed that.

She frowned. 'You do look familiar. I'm sorry, I can't remember your name.'

'Maeve Kerrigan.'

She got to her feet and turned to face me properly. She looked surprised, as well she might, I thought. Pretty features, a pale complexion, dyed hair that was a couple of shades too harsh for her skin, bags under her eyes. The overall impression was of an attractive woman who possibly lived on her nerves too much.

'That's right. Maeve. It was on the tip of my tongue. You came to my house to interview me about my friend being killed when she was a teenager. You worked with Josh Derwent.'

Josh Derwent, who had been the boyfriend of the murdered girl and the prime suspect in the case until an unbreakable alibi cleared his name. Josh Derwent, who had left home because of the scandal and cut himself off from friends and family. Josh Derwent, who had never really recovered.

'I still work with him.'

The smile died on her face, replaced by absolute horror. 'He's not here, is he?'

'He's off today. And he's not working on this case,' I added quickly.

'So he hasn't met Luke?'

I shook my head. 'He doesn't know anything about him.'

'And you haven't said anything about – what you found out?'

About the fact that Derwent had unwittingly fathered a child during a one-off fling with Claire, his childhood friend, when they were both sixteen? That he had a grown-up son he didn't even know about, who I'd just realised was currently sitting in our interview room? No, I hadn't found myself launching into that particular conversation. 'I wouldn't know how to start. Besides, it's none of my business.'

Relief made her pretty for a moment, the colour sweeping into her face and her eyes bright. 'Thank God. It's – well, it's complicated.'

'Very.' The word came out with a lot more emphasis than I'd intended. I moved to sit on a chair, feeling distinctly shaken. 'I thought Luke reminded me of someone. I didn't realise – he's very like Josh, isn't he?'

'Is he? I don't really remember.' She sat down opposite me. 'It was a long time ago.'

'They're so alike. The way they carry themselves . . .' I trailed off. *The way they look at women* . . . but I couldn't say that to his *mother* . . .

'He's just Luke to me. All that is him. No one else.' It was as if she was challenging me to say Derwent had given him

119

any of his looks or his charm or his brains. Maybe he hadn't but he had given him *something,* even if it was only a glint in his eye and the way he moved – that wholly masculine kind of grace that was all controlled power and economy of effort.

'Why don't you have the same surname as your son?' That would have given me a fighting chance of realising who he was, I felt. Someone wasn't playing fair here.

'Luke had a falling out with my dad. He decided to take my mother's maiden name instead.' She pulled a face. 'My dad isn't the easiest to get along with at the best of times. When Luke got into Cambridge, he should have been proud but he came down on him like a ton of bricks. Said he was getting above himself and he'd never be happy. Said his new friends wouldn't want to know him when they knew where he came from. Luke put up with it for as long as he could but when my dad was rude to a girl Luke brought home, that was it. They had a big row and now they don't speak. Luke decided he'd rather be a Gibson than a Naylor.'

'Tough on you.'

She laughed. 'My dad deserved it. He needs someone to stand up to him. Luke doesn't take shit from anyone.'

I knew someone else like that, I thought, and sat on the comment because if Claire Naylor wanted to pretend her son was the product of the second attempt at the Virgin Birth, who was I to disagree? Except that I didn't think it was fair to Derwent. I couldn't live with myself if I passed up the opportunity to convince Claire she needed to give him a chance.

'Does Luke know who his dad is?'

'No. Absolutely not.' Her hand shot out to grab my knee, gripping me hard enough to leave a mark. 'You can't tell him.'

'I wouldn't do that!' She let go of me, satisfied, but I was puzzled. 'Isn't he curious? Doesn't he ask you about his father?'

'He used to, from time to time. Not so much any more.

He doesn't need a dad, though. He has me.' She was sitting very straight now, daring me to argue with her.

'Josh has changed a lot since I met you before,' I said tentatively. 'He's different. I think if he knew about Luke—'

'He's never going to know. You can't tell Josh anything about Luke either. Not even a hint. *Promise me.*' Her eyes were fixed on my face. 'You haven't said anything to him up to now. Why don't you keep saying nothing? Forget you even met Luke.'

Because I *had* met him now, I thought unhappily. It was one thing for him to be a theoretical child, a stranger I could assume had nothing in common with his accidental sperm donor. I had managed to forget about the Luke I'd imagined quite easily – the academic son of a single mother who had nothing in common with his father. The Luke I'd talked to, laughed with – *liked* – was a different proposition.

'But he'd be so proud of him,' I said lamely.

'No.' She shook her head. 'He doesn't get to be proud of him. He had nothing to do with what Luke has become.'

'He didn't have a chance to be there for him. You don't know what kind of dad he might have been if you'd told him about Luke.'

'Trust me, I do know.' She gave me a bitter little half-smile. 'I was his friend, remember. You didn't know him then. He would have been head over heels in love with Luke, and then bored, and then he'd have fucked off to do whatever he wanted to do with his life. As indeed he did. We wouldn't have seen him for dust once the novelty had worn off.'

I winced, recognising the Derwent I'd met when we started working together: arrogant, unprincipled, self-indulgent and irresponsible. He was still arrogant, if it came to that, but otherwise I thought he was much improved. Most of the time.

'Luke and I would have been on our own anyway,' Claire went on. 'We didn't need someone coming and going whenever they felt like it. Luke was better off without him when he

121

was a kid, and he definitely doesn't need him now that he's an adult.'

'I understand what you're saying – believe me, I do – but please think about telling him. Tell them both. You said it yourself: Luke's an adult. He has a right to make up his own mind about Josh.'

If anything, she looked more determined not to give in. So much for my persuasive arguments.

'When are you going to tell Luke he can leave?' she asked.

'Soon. We're almost finished for today.'

'I don't understand why you wanted to talk to him. He said it was about this woman he didn't even know. He's not a suspect, is he?'

Which was a question I didn't want to answer. 'It's hard to explain. I can't really tell you any details about the case at the moment. But Luke has been very helpful.'

'You need to let him go.' She pulled her sleeves down over her hands nervously. 'What if Josh comes in and finds him here?'

'No chance. He has a day off. He never comes in on his day off any more.'

'Any more?' She tilted her head, interested, and I found myself wondering if Luke had got his brains from his mother. Like him, she missed nothing. 'What's changed?'

'He's settled down a lot in the last year.'

'Family?'

'Sort of. His girlfriend has a son. They live with him now.' *And he's a great father figure – even if he doesn't have a huge amount of competition in that particular boy's life.*

'How old?'

'Thomas is six.'

Claire hugged herself, considering it. 'That's a nice age.'

'Josh would do anything for him.'

She understood what I was hinting at immediately and was having none of it. 'You're not going to convince me he's changed by telling me about him playing happy families with someone else's child. Why doesn't he have kids of his own if he's such a great father? Because he doesn't want the responsibility, that's why.'

'I'm not sure if that's it,' I said carefully. 'I mean, we haven't discussed it. But I think he's waiting for the right time. I don't know if he and Melissa are trying, or—'

'Melissa. Is she pretty?' Claire laughed. 'I don't even know why I'm asking. Of course she is. And of course it doesn't matter. Josh and I were never . . . Not properly, I mean. It was only once.'

'I get the impression he'd like to have children, for what it's worth.'

'It's worth nothing. He must never know. Never.' She leaned forward. 'Can't you let Luke go, now that you know who he is?'

'It doesn't work like that. I have to finish interviewing him. But I promise I'll make it as quick as I can.'

'And then you can forget all about Luke.'

There was absolutely no chance of that, but I smiled, and said goodbye to her, and hoped like hell I wouldn't need to arrest him somewhere down the line.

Two years earlier

The envelope was lying on the mat when he got home from the gym. No stamp: hand-delivered. His name in neat letters, the kind of handwriting that's unsettlingly regular and characterless. And in capitals across the top, PRIVATE.

He should have been wary – his heart should have jumped in his chest. But it had been *months*. He had honestly forgotten about the house, the party, the body. He ripped open the envelope and shook the contents into his hand. Photographs, eight by ten, big enough that you could see the detail in them. Professionally taken, he thought. Pin sharp.

Each one worse than the last.

His drunken idiot face, his eyelids drooping, a bow tie undone and hanging around his neck.

Barefoot and bony-ankled, balancing on the balustrade, one elbow on the cherub's bowl, his eyes narrowed against the smoke from the cigarette that dangled from his mouth.

A dark corner of the terrace, sitting on the balustrade now with his legs apart, kissing—

His hands tracing patterns on skin—

Leaning in, eyes closed, lost in desire—

Lost in desire for the stranger who stood between his

knees, whose tattoo showed so clearly in the picture, he could make out the dragon's tail looping around one narrow elbow.

The next picture was worse.

And the next.

He dropped them on the kitchen counter and walked away, clutching his head. What the *fuck*. Who could have done this?

He wouldn't look at any more.

He had to look at them. Quickly, he cycled through them: up against a wall, on a bed, both of them naked, no question what he was doing or that he was in charge. That was the pool house, that was the pool, *Christ*, they had been in the pool – he had no memory of it but there he was, swimming naked in the filthy water.

And there was the stranger he'd screwed blind, fit and alive, tattooed and pretty, eyelashes starry from the water, eyes like jewels. Unharmed, he pointed out to an imaginary police officer tapping the glossy surface of the print.

You were in the swimming pool together, and the body was found in the swimming pool, floating face down.

I can't explain it. I can't explain any of it. My drink was spiked, I think.

Then, pleading with his family. *It wasn't me. I'd never. I'm not. I didn't. I know it looks—*

Please, you have to believe me.

They might believe him, though they would take a while to get over it. He was an only child, adored, indulged. Sex was no big deal. He would be forgiven for that, especially if they didn't actually see the pictures.

But the police didn't have to believe him, and a jury wouldn't. They could look at the photographs and follow the story of what had happened.

One of them had lived and one of them had died and he couldn't remember how it had happened, or what he had done. He would be the chief and only suspect, and he couldn't begin to defend himself.

All he knew was that he would do just about anything to keep what had happened a secret.

17

I was waiting for Una Burt when she got into work the following morning, watching the door. As soon as she arrived I shot out of my seat.

'Ma'am?'

'What's up?' She didn't break her stride on her way to her office. In fairness she was weighed down with a thermos of coffee (made at home because she didn't believe in spending money on takeaway coffee), her breakfast in a Tupperware container, her sensible raincoat and a bag-for-life full of paperwork. Contrary to its promises, the bag was threatening to split.

'It's just – could I have a word?'

'If you're quick about it. I have a meeting in five minutes.' She dumped everything on her desk and started to fuss with the thermos. 'Come on, come in. Sit down.'

I shut the door even though there was no one else at work yet and perched on the edge of the chair opposite her desk.

'Let me guess. You're leaving.'

'No.' I felt a wave of irritation sweep over me. 'Why would you say that?'

'The Met is a big organisation. You have other options than

this team. You'd be very silly not to consider them.' She sat down and folded her hands, adopting what I thought of as her listening pose. 'But of course I'm glad if that's not it.'

Of course.

'It's a little bit awkward,' I began, and stopped. I'd spent all night worrying about whether I should say anything at all, to her or anyone else. It would be easy enough to tell Derwent and let him decide what to do about it, if anything, but there were complications to that approach, not least the *timing* . . . And if Burt asked him to work on the case, I'd have to tell her anyway, and she'd have to tell Derwent there was a conflict of interest, and then I'd have to say why. It was better to tell Burt, not least because she was in a position to give me proper advice. She would be able to look at the situation objectively, without her feelings for Derwent affecting her thinking. Not that I had *feelings* for Derwent.

Una Burt was starting to fidget. 'You're having a baby as well? Honestly, there are times I think it must be contagious. One member of a team gets pregnant and suddenly all the women go on maternity leave.'

'No! Absolutely not. But it is sort of about a baby. Only he's not a baby any more. And definitely not mine.'

Her eyebrows were hovering around her hairline. She poured coffee into the lid of her thermos and blew on it. 'I don't mean to hurry you, but I do have that meeting.'

'Right.' I took a deep breath. 'Well, you might remember a few years ago there was a case where Josh Derwent was a suspect. His girlfriend was murdered when he was a teenager and her death had elements in common with the series we were investigating.'

'I remember. He was in a lot of trouble for a while. You got him out of it, as I recall.' Her voice was entirely colourless but I knew she was far from Derwent's biggest fan. She had been almost disappointed to find out that he wasn't a killer. From that point on she had taken the view that I was on his side rather than hers, and held me responsible for his worst behaviour whether that was fair or not.

'Well, during that case I interviewed a woman named Claire Naylor. She was an old friend of the victim, and of Josh. She's a single mother. From what she told me then, and from pictures I saw in her house, I worked out that Josh was the father of her son.'

'Right,' she said slowly.

'And he didn't know about it.'

'Right,' she said again, but this time with more understanding. She placed her cup on a coaster and cleared her throat. 'And you didn't tell him.'

'I tried to convince Claire Naylor to tell him herself.' I fidgeted. 'Maybe I should have tried harder to persuade her, or taken matters into my own hands and blurted it out. It seemed easier to put it to the back of my mind. I thought if he didn't know, it didn't matter. But since he found Thomas . . .'

'He's changed.'

I nodded miserably. 'Now I think he would have wanted to know and I should have told him straight away.'

'Tricky situation.' She turned the cup through ninety degrees, considering it. 'But I think your instincts were correct. Presumably this Naylor woman had her reasons for not telling him he'd fathered a child.'

'She felt he might be an unreliable parent and they were better off without him.'

'Sensible woman.' She looked up at me. 'Why is this upsetting you now?'

'I brought the son in for questioning yesterday in the Paige Hargreaves case.'

'Oh shit,' she muttered, and it wasn't like her to swear. On this occasion I felt it was more than justified.

'Yeah, that's what I feel about it.'

'Is he a suspect?'

'I was up all night wondering about that. I don't think so,

but maybe I don't want him to be. I liked him, even before I knew who he was. And I thought he was honest with us.'

'Why was he brought in?'

I explained about the bag and she listened, frowning. 'Well, at least one of the three of them is lying to you.'

'Or maybe all three of them are. The prepared statement that we got from Orlando Hawkes is basically arse-covering in case we find anything in the house that ties in with Paige Hargreaves. I don't know if it's a prudent way of getting his excuses in first or if he genuinely has something to hide. Roddy Asquith refused to say anything at all. I don't think he's the sharpest tool in the shed and he seemed to be afraid he'd say the wrong thing even in a prepared statement. But the only link I can make between Paige and Luke is the bag, and that was shoved into his room behind the door, more or less in plain sight once you looked. If he'd wanted to hide it, he'd have done a better job, I think.'

'It could have been one of the other two who left it there.'

'That's what I thought. The one thing we do know is that there's a definite connection between Paige and Roddy Asquith because Paige herself wrote his name and phone number in the book I found. I think he was helping her with her Chiron Club story and now he's terrified he'll be kicked out of the club at the very least. Before he went no-comment on me, he more or less admitted he'd been talking to Paige about her story.'

'And now he's clammed up.' Burt seemed to have forgotten all about her important meeting, or she'd decided this was more urgent after all. She leaned on the desk and ran her hands through her hair. 'What a mess.'

'Josh wasn't in yesterday – he had a day off. If I have to bring Luke in again and he sees him—'

'It could be awkward.'

'He probably wouldn't recognise him. He's never seen him before.'

She pressed her fingertips against her forehead for a few moments, then dropped them to the desk. 'I think you should tell him though.'

Not what I wanted to hear. 'But I promised Claire I wouldn't.'

'Ordinarily, I would say you should respect her confidence. But did she tell you about Luke, or did you find out for yourself?'

'She tried to hide it. I worked it out. Luke looked very like Josh when he was little, and Claire took his pictures down so I wouldn't see them.' The corners of my mouth turned up at the thought of him. 'He still looks quite like Josh, if it comes to that, but I might not have made the connection now that he's an adult.'

'She didn't trust you with any information; you worked it out. What you do with what you learned is up to you.'

'But she begged me not to tell him or Luke.'

'Claire knew Josh when he was sixteen. You know him now. What do you think you should do?'

'Tell him.'

'You'd want to know, if it was possible for you to be in his shoes.'

'But then I have to think of a way to explain why I've known about Luke for so long and haven't said a word about it. He won't be pleased.'

'I can't help you with that, but I feel sure you'll be able to work out how to break the news diplomatically.' She actually looked sympathetic for once. 'It might take him a while to get over it.'

'Oh, he'll blame me. That's one reason why I was hoping you'd say I should keep quiet.'

She shook her head slowly. 'Sorry.'

'I know it's the right thing to do. But I don't think I should tell him now. I want to be sure that Luke's in the clear first.'

'Agreed.' Burt glanced at her watch. 'Crikey, I need to go. They'll have started without me.'

131

I stood up and held the door open for her as she gathered her files for the meeting. The desks in the main office were still empty, I was glad to see. As she passed me, she said, 'I'll try to find something for Josh to do that will keep him out of your way. There'll be a case somewhere that needs his attention, urgently.'

'Thanks, I appreciate it.'

She stopped. 'You know, he's lucky to have you. It's not every colleague who would be so sensitive about telling a man he had a secret lovechild.'

'A secret lovechild who is all of twenty-five and about six foot two,' I said drily.

'And looks like Josh?' She whistled. 'I bet this Luke is trouble.'

'He was on his best behaviour yesterday but I'd say so. He has a definite glint in his eye.'

Una Burt chuckled. 'If you do have to bring him in again, let me know. I'd like to have a look at him.'

I returned to my desk feeling marginally better about the situation. Obviously, telling Derwent would give rise to a whole new set of problems, but it was honest. He prized honesty above all other things, even if he was capable of lying on a spectacular scale when he thought it was justified. And because I'd been hiding Luke, I hadn't been honest with him for years. He'd forgive me, though, eventually.

At least, I hoped he would.

The door banged closed behind Una Burt and I smiled to myself: who would have thought she would be so human about it? But she had been kind, almost as if she really cared . . .

My train of thought sputtered into silence as Georgia straightened up from behind her desk and stared at me, her eyes wide.

'I didn't know you were here,' I said. Then, with growing anger, 'Were you *hiding*?'

'I was changing my shoes. I cycled to work this morning so I was wearing my trainers.' She held them up for me to see, as if I cared. 'I can't cycle in heels.'

'What did you hear?'

'Only what the boss said to you as you were leaving her office?' It came out as a question: if I was horrified, Georgia was too.

'Which was?'

'Luke Gibson is Josh Derwent's son and he doesn't know it and you want to keep him from finding out.'

'So, everything. *Fuck.*' I covered my face with my hands. I couldn't even look at her.

'I'm sorry, I really wasn't trying to listen!' She sounded as if she was about to cry. 'I won't say anything.'

'You'd better not. Not to anyone. No one knows apart from you, me and Burt.'

'I promise.'

I put my hands flat on the desk and glowered at her. 'I'm going to tell him.'

'Of course.'

'I just need to wait for the right moment.'

'I understand.' She was blushing. 'I can't believe Luke is actually Josh Derwent's son. I had no idea. None. I mean, I was *flirting* with him.'

It was on the tip of my tongue to point out that it was hardly unusual for Georgia to flirt, but I stopped myself. If I was ever going to be nice to her, now was the ideal time.

'Look, the main thing is to rule Luke out as a suspect. Then I'll talk to Josh about him. In the meantime, do your best to forget you heard anything.'

'I will, I swear it. You can trust me.'

The door banged and two of the other detectives came in, talking about football. Georgia blinked at me meaningfully and got up.

'Tea? Coffee?'

'Neither, thanks.'

She teetered away to the kitchen and I tried not to dwell on the thought that it was really only the least reliable people who felt they needed to tell you that you could trust them.

Two years earlier

The fifth or possibly the sixth time he looked through the photographs, he thought to turn them over and look at the other side. Unbranded paper, no photographer's stamp. No clues there. But on the last picture (tangle of limbs, his face twisted with effort, one of the worst, actually, if you were ranking them), in faintest pencil, there was something. A telephone number in the same writing that had been on the envelope.

He didn't call it straight away. He wasn't stupid.

He went across London, to a busy and impoverished area where he found a cramped internet café full of Chinese students playing games, headsets on. He chose a seat where no one would be able to see his screen. First he looked up the number and found nothing: it was a mobile but not connected to any business or named individual.

Then he tried searching every variant on 'body in swimming pool' he could think of. There were high-profile cases, celebrities, rumours. Nothing that matched what had happened to him. No mystery twenty-something with blue eyes, fair hair, a tattoo that covered one arm. No missing person appeal. It would have helped if he'd had a name to search for but they hadn't swapped names, had they? They hadn't said much.

We don't have to
I want to
Say if you want to stop

He leaned back in his chair and pressed his hands against his face. *I want to stop. Make it stop.*

The voice at the other end of the phone was cool, female and neutral.

'I'm pleased to inform you that situation has been resolved.'

'What do you want from me? Is this blackmail? Because I don't have money.' The cheap pay-as-you-go phone slipped in his hand. He was sweating as if he was in a sauna. He turned in a circle, checking that no one was within a few hundred yards of the spot he'd chosen on Hampstead Heath, with all of London spread out in the distance and the illusion of privacy.

At the other end of the line the woman laughed, and told him who she worked for, and everything made a horrible kind of sense.

'So what do you want?'

'Think of this as a mutually beneficial arrangement.'

'What does that mean?'

There might have been a hint of pity in her voice, or condescension. 'When we need your assistance we'll let you know.'

18

I was braced for impending doom but when my phone rang at ten past eleven I didn't realise the moment had arrived.

'Is that DS Maeve Kerrigan?'

'Speaking.'

'My name is Paul Varley. I'm a police constable in Swindon. I believe you're investigating the murder of Paige Hargreaves.'

I sat bolt upright. 'I am. What can I do for you?'

'Well, I hope it's what I can do for you.' He had a mellow, measured voice with a pleasant country burr, and sounded as if retirement couldn't be too far off. 'I don't know if it's any use to you but I thought I should get in touch regarding a conversation I had with this Miss Hargreaves about two weeks before her body was found, regarding an investigation she was doing into some private club in London.'

I pulled my notebook towards me, hope tingling down my spine. 'That could be very useful. What did she want to know?'

'Well, it was a backwards kind of conversation. Miss Hargreaves was convinced that there'd been a murder near a village called Standen Fitzallen coming up on two years ago. She wasn't sure of the address where this crime had taken place or who had been killed, but she knew the date – the night of the twenty-second of July.'

'She didn't know much, did she?'

'Very little. She said someone had told her they'd picked up a friend from the middle of Standen Fitzallen on the twenty-third of July, about four p.m., and he'd been hysterical. He said something about a dead body in a big old country house, in the swimming pool. He'd walked to the village from the house. Miss Hargreaves was wondering if she could match it up with a murder investigation in that general area, around that time.'

'Could you?'

'Absolutely not.' I heard the smile in his voice. 'You probably deal with murders all the time but it's not the kind of thing we'd forget. There was nothing of that sort within thirty miles of Standen Fitzallen in July or August that year. And nothing since, either.'

'But she was sure about the location where the car picked up this person who claimed there'd been a murder?'

'She was. And I did recall one thing: on that Saturday we had a few phone calls from concerned residents about a young man who was behaving strangely in the village. It's the sort of place where you can't cough without someone noticing. Quiet little spot.'

'What sort of strange behaviour did they notice?'

'He was barefoot and dishevelled. One or two people tried to talk to him but got no sense out of him. They were concerned he'd escaped from some institution or other. I wasn't too busy so I went over to the village to check it out, but by the time I got there he'd been picked up.'

'And no one got the car's number plate.'

'Oh no, they did.' He was smiling again, I could tell. 'Told you, they miss nothing around there. I didn't take it any further because the young man had gone, so as far as I was concerned the situation was resolved. I didn't know anything about a connection with a murder at the time – not that I know any more about it now than I did two years ago, but regardless, I might have followed it up if I'd had a reason to.'

138

'You don't have the number to hand now, do you?'

'Right here.' He dictated it to me. 'A 2009-plate blue VW Polo.'

'Amazing. I'll follow it up.' I hesitated. 'I suppose she didn't happen to mention how this tied in with her investigation into the Chiron Club.'

'The what? Oh, this private club. No, all she said was that some of the people involved were members and she believed the murder was an initiation thing. But there was no murder. No reports of missing people.'

'What sort of area is it?'

'Small villages, well spread out. Heart of the horse-racing industry. The Downs. Farmland, managed woods, that kind of thing.'

'Lots of big old country houses?'

'Tons of them,' he said cheerfully. 'Many with swimming pools. I did try to work it out but without more information I'm stuck, I'm afraid.'

'If I find out anything at my end, I'll let you know, I promise.'

'Mind if I say I hope you don't? Nothing personal but I prefer a quiet life.'

'Don't we all,' I said, with feeling.

Calling the DVLA was my next step, and they were as efficient as ever in matching up the registration of the car with its registered keeper. It was a matter of minutes before I had a name and an address. I made sure I'd ended the call before I gave vent to my feelings.

'Fuck everything sideways.'

The second time Luke Gibson came in for interview, late that afternoon, he walked in by himself. This time his mood was distinctly cooler.

'I don't know why you've had to call me in again. I thought we'd covered everything yesterday.'

'So did I. Some new information has come to light and I wanted to ask you about it.'

'What sort of information? About Paige?' He was frowning at me and now that I knew who he was it might as well have been Derwent sitting on the other side of the table. The hostility was identical.

'Do you have a car, Mr Gibson?'

'Yeah.' The frown deepened. 'So?'

'Is it a VW Polo?'

'Yes. It's parked outside the house. I hardly ever use it these days. Weekends, sometimes. The supermarket. IKEA trips. That's about it.'

'How long have you owned it?'

'Since university.'

'Does anyone else drive it?'

'No.'

'Where do you keep the keys?'

'In my room, in a drawer.' He looked mystified. 'What's this about?'

'Have you ever been to Standen Fitzallen?'

'Where?'

'It's near Swindon.'

'Not as far as I remember.'

'What about the twenty-third of July the year before last?'

He laughed. 'You're joking, aren't you? How do you expect me to remember that?'

'A car matching your car's make and model, with licence plates that matched your vehicle, was seen in Standen Fitzallen on that day.'

'Seen? By whom? Why does that matter?' He shook his head. 'Look, I'm sorry, I don't understand what you're asking me or why.'

'Someone driving that car picked up a man who was behaving in an unusual way in the village. Paige Hargreaves contacted the local police there shortly before she died to find out more about that incident. She claimed it was connected with a murder at a country house near Standen Fitzallen.'

'A murder? Who died?'

'That's something we still need to clarify.'

'Two years ago.' He looked thoughtful all of a sudden. 'Can I check something on my phone?'

'Be my guest.'

He took it out and checked the calendar, thumbing through the months. 'What date did you say?'

'The twenty-third of July. Mid-afternoon.'

'Maybe my car was there, but I wasn't. I couldn't have been the one who was driving. I was hiking the route to Machu Picchu that day.'

Relief made me sag in my chair for an instant. If he wasn't involved, my life was about to get much simpler. 'Can you prove it?'

'Probably. I was with a girlfriend. We hiked in and out. Took us a couple of weeks. I think she put the whole trip on Facebook.' He paused for a second as his phone loaded, then started scrolling through images. 'Yeah. There you go. They're all dated. She put them up when we came home.'

I took the phone from him and skimmed through pictures of Luke grinning as rain dripped off his hat, squinting up at the camera as he held it so the ruins were visible in the background, a pretty girl draped around him. The dates tallied with what he'd told me. I gave him the phone. 'That's really helpful.'

'You're not kidding.' The tension had ebbed away from him, taking the scowl along with it. 'I must give Lily a call and thank her for getting me off the hook. I can't honestly remember why we broke up.'

'You're not completely in the clear yet. If you weren't driving your car, someone else had to be.'

He froze in the act of putting his phone away. 'Ah.'

'Any idea who that might have been?'

141

'No.'

'What about Roddy?'

'Roddy can't drive. He has epilepsy. He's never learned.' He said it as if his mind was somewhere else. I watched him think, and saw the exact moment something clicked. His eyes widened for an instant, before he looked up at me and shook his head. 'I'd like to help.'

'Then tell me who was driving.'

'I don't know.'

'But you have some idea.'

He groaned. 'Do I have to say?'

'No, I suppose you don't. I can't compel you to.' I folded my arms. 'I don't know how Paige Hargreaves died, but from the manner of disposal of her body I would guess it wasn't pleasant. I currently have no suspects and no motive for her death. If I'm going to work out what happened to her, and why, and who did it, I need as much help as I can get. I know it might put you in a difficult position if you want to be loyal to your friends, but Paige deserves some loyalty too. Someone ended her life, quite brutally, and I want to bring them to justice.'

His mouth thinned to a grim line. 'Yeah. I get it.'

'Paige seems to have believed that someone was murdered near to Standen Fitzallen and it had something to do with the Chiron Club. Your housemates are members of the club. As far as I can tell, Roddy was helping her with this story she was working on, but he's not being very helpful to me at the moment. Now, from what you're saying it couldn't have been him who was driving because of his epilepsy, but he could have been the man in the village.'

'Roddy wouldn't have hurt anyone. He's not that sort of person. I don't think I've ever even seen him lose his temper.' Luke's forehead was creased with worry. 'Can't you ask him?'

'I can and I will, but the more I know in advance, the better chance I have of getting a proper answer out of him.'

'There's a guy who's a friend of Roddy's,' Luke said slowly. 'Ash. He borrowed the car a couple of times when Roddy needed driving somewhere. I'd completely forgotten but he was insured on the car for a few months. Roddy paid for it. Both of them knew where the keys were. If Roddy needed picking up – or if someone else did – he might have asked Ash to do it. I haven't seen him for ages.' He frowned. 'Thinking about it, I don't think I've seen him since that trip to Peru. Roddy never mentioned him to me.'

'Where does Ash live?'

'I don't know.'

'What's his surname?'

'I don't know that either.'

'Do you have a number for him?'

'No, sorry. He was never a friend of mine. I just let Roddy sort out the car when he needed it and Ash did the driving.'

'How do they know each other?'

Luke shrugged. 'School? University? I do know Ash is a member of the Chiron Club too. They went to events there together.'

I started at the beginning again, asking the same questions in a different way, the best method to identify the places where he might be lying. As before he answered carefully and precisely, and I believed him. Once I was satisfied he'd told me all he knew, I ended the interview.

'Right. That's it. You're done.'

He rubbed his face. 'I feel like shit for dropping Roddy in it. And Ash. I don't even know if they did anything wrong.'

'That's for me to find out. But if they were involved in something illegal, they used your car to do it, without your knowledge. If you hadn't been able to prove you were out of the country I could have arrested you by now.'

He ran his thumb over his knuckles edgily, not looking at me. 'They probably didn't realise I could be implicated.'

'Or they were prepared to take the risk.'

'Roddy wouldn't have wanted to get me in trouble.' He sounded certain but his eyes were shadowy with hurt. He knew as well as I did that someone had decided it didn't matter either way. As far as they were concerned, he was dispensable.

If I'd been Luke, I'd have been thinking about acquiring some better friends.

19

It was well after seven by the time I was finished with Luke Gibson and prepared to let him go.

'Before you leave, can I remind you not to say anything to Roddy Asquith about what we've been discussing?'

He sighed. 'I'd rather be straight with him.'

'Roddy came here yesterday and gave me a no-comment interview, which means that he said nothing. I know you think he couldn't have done anything wrong, and I'd like to believe that too, but it's my job to persuade him to tell me what he knows. Anything that gives me an advantage is important and at the moment all I have is that I know a tiny bit more than he thinks I do.'

Luke's mouth curved. 'I'm sure you'll persuade him to talk. You're good at this.'

'I should be. I do it for a living,' I said crisply. 'Look, I specifically don't want you to mention Ash to Roddy, or anything else that we discussed about the car, but if you happen to remember anything about Ash – his surname, ideally, but anything at all that comes back to you – can you let me have it? You've got my card. Drop me an email or call me.'

'Sure.' He got up and stretched, filling the room and I hid a smile. He had inherited his father's trick of physically dominating any space he was in, but unlike Derwent he didn't use it as a weapon. 'So that's it? We're really done?'

'We're done. Thanks for coming in to talk to me.'

'I want to help.' He looked down at me, serious now. 'I don't like to think of Paige suffering. My mum said I shouldn't come in for interview again, but it never occurred to me to say no. She told me I should get a solicitor to come with me.'

'It can be a good idea.' I held the door open for him.

'Waste of money, though. I knew I hadn't done anything wrong.'

I started to walk towards reception with him. 'Yeah, it should work that way.'

'It doesn't?'

'Put it this way, I've never locked anyone up who didn't deserve to be behind bars.'

He considered it. 'That's sort of reassuring and sort of not.'

I laughed. 'I'm doing my best. There's a reason solicitors exist, I suppose. And we don't assume that if you come in with one, you're hiding something.' *Not necessarily, anyway.*

We turned the corner to reception and Luke looked surprised. 'Mum? What are you doing here?'

'I was worried about you.' She stood up, a slight figure in a raincoat, her eyes worried. She turned to me. 'Is everything OK?'

'Absolutely fine,' I said firmly, trying to convey I-haven't-said-anything from my expression alone.

'You'd swear I was fifteen or – or mentally challenged.' Luke glowered at his mother, his jaw tight with anger. 'I can look after myself. I don't know why you do this. You're so over-protective.'

'You don't listen, that's why. I told you to get a solicitor.'

'I didn't need one.' He took a deep breath and when he spoke again, his tone was soothing instead of angry. 'Everything's sorted. Really. Sergeant Kerrigan needed to check a few things with me, and I was able to answer her questions. She's happy, I'm happy. OK?'

Claire Naylor nodded, on the verge of tears. 'It's just . . . I don't like this.'

'Course you don't.' He pulled her into his arms and hugged her, tucking his face into her neck. 'But I'm not a kid. I can handle this.'

'Sorry.'

'Let's go and get something to eat.' Luke turned to me. 'Thanks again. I promise I won't say anything I shouldn't.'

'I appreciate it,' I said, and started to steer them towards the door. It was raining, and I was about to make some remark about it when Derwent pushed through the revolving door and stopped to brush the water from his hair.

'It's brutal out there.' A frown for me, along with a quick up-and-down that took in my thin silk shirt and total lack of a jacket or coat or umbrella. 'You're not going out like that, are you?'

'No.' I managed not to look around at Claire or Luke. 'Seeing some people out.'

He looked past me to see who I meant because his curiosity was constant and insatiable. Neither of them held his attention for long. 'Right. Coming up to the office?'

'In a bit. Don't wait for me.'

'Who said I was going to?' He grinned, though, to take the sting out of his words, and sauntered over to the stairs, shaking the raindrops from his jacket as he went. I held my breath as he ran up the steps two at a time, disappearing from view. When I was sure he was gone, I turned to the pair behind me. Claire was white and trembling. Luke, oblivious, peered out at the rain.

'I think we should wait a few minutes. I bet it's only a shower.'

Ordinarily I would have agreed with him, but I wanted them gone. 'It looks to me as if it's set in for the night. I'd go before it gets any worse, if I were you.'

'Really? Do you think so?'

The lift pinged behind him, and the doors opened, and Derwent stepped out into the lobby with a frown on his face. He walked across to us and there was something tentative in how he moved.

'Sorry – I just thought – Claire?'

'Josh.' She tried to smile, her mouth quivering. 'I thought that was you.'

'Claire Naylor, my God.' He gave her a quick hug, then held her at arm's length to look at her. 'It's been years. Decades.'

'I'm surprised you recognised me.'

He smiled down at her. 'How could I forget you? Anyway, you haven't changed.'

Her hand went to her hair, but her smile this time was genuine. 'You were always good at saying the right thing, even if it wasn't true.'

I risked a glance at Luke, who was looking bemused. He put his hand out.

'Luke Gibson. I'm Claire's son.'

'Josh Derwent.' He gave Luke an assessing look as he shook hands but there was no recognition in it, no hint of suspicion, and I let myself start to breathe again: OK, yes, this was bad and had the potential to be *very* bad, but there was also a good chance we would all be going our separate ways after a brief session of do-you-remembers and there would be no harm done.

'I'm guessing you two used to know each other,' Luke said.

'We were best mates when we were kids,' Derwent explained. 'There was a gang of us who hung round together all the time. Your mum and your uncle Vinny were part of it, and a couple of other people. We did everything together.'

'Shame you lost touch,' Luke said lightly.

'Yes, it was.' A shadow passed over Derwent's face before he turned back to Claire. 'I missed you, you know.'

'Of course. We missed you too.' It came out as a whisper. All of a sudden she couldn't look him in the eye.

I resisted the urge to kick her in the ankle. *Stop acting as if you feel guilty about something or he'll guess you have something to feel guilty about.*

'But what are you doing here?' Derwent asked her. 'Is anything wrong?'

'I had to interview Luke,' I said briskly. 'We're finished. In fact, Luke and his mother were just leaving.'

'Lucky I caught you.' He was staring at Claire again, mesmerised. 'I knew I recognised you. I was trying to work it out the whole way up the stairs.'

'You never forget a face, do you?' I took a step away from them, towards the door. 'Thanks again for coming in, Luke.'

'Yeah, we should go.' He nudged Claire. 'Come on, Mum. Swap numbers or whatever and then we'll get going.'

Claire came to life. 'Oh, I don't think there's any need for that.'

Derwent had had his phone in his hand. He slid it into his pocket as his expression went from surprised to wounded before he gained control of himself. A bored, distant look came over his face like a mask. 'No point in pretending it's worth trying to go back, is there?'

'It was a long time ago.' Claire stared down at the floor.

'Yeah.' Derwent cleared his throat, the tenderness breaking through despite himself. 'It was good to see you again, though.'

She nodded, her face flaming.

He stepped forward and dropped a kiss onto her cheek. I heard him murmur, 'If you ever want to catch up, you know where to find me.'

The revolving door hissed and a little group hurried in, talking and laughing and shaking out umbrellas. Last of all was Georgia. She looked from Luke to Derwent and beamed.

'Wow, a family reunion! When the two of you are side by side you can really see the similarities.'

'*Georgia!*' I didn't recognise my own voice as I moved towards her. 'Can I have a word?'

She sidestepped me, all her attention on Luke and Derwent. I could smell alcohol on her breath and guessed she'd been to the pub for a few post-work drinks before she came back to get changed so she could cycle home. No wonder she was failing to read the situation.

'This must be so weird for all of you. Especially you, guv. Maeve has been stressing about when she should tell you.'

'Tell me?' Derwent looked wary, and flicked a glance at me. 'What did she have to tell me?'

'Congratulations, *Daddy*.' Georgia lunged forward to pat his arm. 'You should be really proud of him. And Luke, *you* can be proud of having a dad like Josh. He's lovely.'

Luke was standing completely still, as if he had been turned to stone. Claire pulled at him, desperate.

'Come on. Let's go. Luke, come on.'

'Wait.' Derwent put out a hand. 'Hold it, Claire, for a second. Georgia, what are you saying?'

'You're Luke's dad.' She looked at him and blinked, swaying where she stood. 'Didn't you know? I thought Maeve would have told you by now.'

'She hadn't mentioned it.'

Georgia smiled at him fuzzily and I could already have cheerfully shoved her under a bus even before she added the unforgivable part. 'That's so strange. Maeve has known you were Luke's dad for years. Since she met his mother the first time.'

'You *promised* me.' Claire's voice was ragged with anger and fear. She pointed a shaking finger at me. 'You *promised* you wouldn't tell anyone. I should have known I couldn't trust you.'

Derwent turned slowly to face me, and I felt some part of myself die of shame at the look of betrayal in his eyes.

Now

He couldn't truthfully say he'd forgotten all about it, but these days he never thought about the *incident,* as he'd come to name it. He accepted that it had happened; he had moved on. The repercussions had been manageable. (Useful, even, at times.) It had proved to be a turning point of sorts. He was a better person than the boy who had run away crying from the corpse in the swimming pool. If it wasn't tasteless to say this about murder, it had been the making of him.

Now he had the uneasy feeling it might be the unmaking of him. It had seeped out of his past like some horrific virus released from the melting Arctic permafrost to taint his future with long-forgotten malignancy. That was unacceptable. He had been promised there would be no trouble.

Promised.

But when it came down to it, you couldn't trust anyone to look out for your interests, no matter how they swore they would, no matter how often they promised to say nothing at all. Well, if it was to be every man for himself, he'd have to take matters into his own hands, because he couldn't be absolutely sure that people had listened to him and heeded his warnings. They'd have to understand there were consequences to insisting on knowing the truth. It was human nature to put yourself first. He knew it, and they knew it, and it was only a question of which of them decided to do that first. He would take the guesswork out of it and take control. That was what he was good at, after all.

Every question the police asked told him they were closing in on the truth, even if they didn't know it yet. Sooner or later they would find out enough to terrify people into speaking up, to defend themselves, and what they knew was enough to get him locked up for a very long time.

He stared at himself in the mirror, his jaw tight, his face drained of colour. Maybe he didn't remember exactly what had happened the first time, but he had done this before. He could do it again.

He had to.

It was the only way he could be sure he was safe.

20

'Are you going to be like this all night?'

'Like what?'

Seth raised his eyebrows. 'I was going to say miserable, but let's go for snappy and miserable.'

'I'm not being snappy.'

'Then how would you describe your tone? It sounds distinctly snappy to me.'

'Sorry.' I picked at my food unenthusiastically. 'I had a bad day.'

'I know. And yesterday was a bad day too. You mentioned that.'

'Sorry,' I said again, and leaned my head on my hand. 'I can't seem to stop thinking about it.'

'Or talking about it.'

I tried to look more cheerful; Seth had had a long day in court, after all. He'd decided we should try out the new Chinese restaurant that had opened near his flat. It was kind of him to take me out for dinner, when I would otherwise have been too tired to cook. The least I could do was be pleasant. 'What would you like to talk about?'

'I don't know. The news. Politics. Something light-hearted. This restaurant. Do you like it?'

'Yeah, it's nice.' I looked around, trying to think of something to say about it. The restaurant was painted red with black accents and every table had a tiny spotlight directed at it instead of proper lighting. The effect was like dining inside a poorly lit stomach. 'It's very . . . intimate.'

'What do you think of the food?'

'It's nice too.'

'Nice. Is that the only adjective you know?'

I felt a wave of absolute exhaustion sweep over me. I really didn't want a fight. 'No. The restaurant is really . . . atmospheric. And the food is delicious.'

'I'm surprised to hear that. You haven't eaten much of it.'

I stared at the glutinous Szechuan chicken I'd ordered because I couldn't be bothered to read through the whole menu. It was looking less and less appetising as it cooled on my plate. 'Look, Seth, leave it. I'm not in the mood.'

'Because your dickhead colleague isn't talking to you.'

'It's upsetting.' A tear slid down the side of my nose and Seth threw down his chopsticks.

'This is ridiculous. I'm getting the bill.'

I sat back in my chair, glad of the Stygian gloom since it meant none of the other diners could see me crying. I needed to pull myself together, or Seth would be completely justified in dumping me. Besides, I couldn't spend another sleepless night worrying about whether Derwent would ever forgive me.

After Georgia dropped her bombshell, she had staggered off to the lift, oblivious to the strained silence she'd left behind her. Claire bundled Luke out through the revolving door, showing considerably more physical strength than I would have anticipated, and the two of them disappeared into the night.

That left me and Derwent.

'Do you want to talk about it?' I faltered.

'I think we should.'

The lobby suddenly felt like a very public space.

'Interview room?'

He nodded and gestured that I should go first. I listened to the sound of his footsteps following me and tried to work out how he was feeling. Shocked? Probably. Hurt? More than likely. Murderously angry? That was a distinct possibility.

I led the way into the interview room I'd just left, and stood by the table. He closed the door gently, as if to emphasise how reasonable he was being. It struck me that he wasn't using any of the usual tricks that indicated he was angry with me. He was almost being too courteous. Instead of crowding me, he stayed on the other side of the room.

'When exactly did you find out?'

'When I interviewed her about Angela Poole.'

His eyes narrowed for a moment at the mention of his dead ex-girlfriend, but he continued in the same level tone of voice. 'And she told you.'

'She didn't *tell* me. I worked it out.'

'How?'

'She hid his pictures the first time I went to see her. She was obviously proud of him.' I was trembling; that was pure shock making itself felt. 'She told me all about him but there weren't any pictures in her living room – she'd taken them down and shoved them in a drawer before she let me in. Then I started wondering why she'd be happy for me to know he existed, but worried about letting me *see* him. She knew I worked with you – she asked me quite a lot about you. But she wouldn't hear of getting in touch with you herself. When the case was over I went round again without warning her, so she didn't have time to hide anything, and there were photographs of him everywhere.'

'And?'

'He looked exactly like you when he was little. I could see it straight away.'

Derwent's eyes were inky black, like an animal in pain. 'That proves nothing.'

'When I asked her directly, she admitted it. She said – the two of you – she said it was a one-off.'

'It was.' He was looking at me but I had the impression he didn't see me at all. 'I'd forgotten. Not that it didn't mean anything at the time. I suppose I'd put it out of my mind.'

'Well, you didn't realise it was significant.'

'Why didn't she tell me she was pregnant?'

'I mean, I think you should talk to her about all of this.' *And leave me out of it.*

'Maybe I should, but I'm talking to you.'

'Right. Well, I think she wanted to handle it on her own. It was complicated.' *Remember, everyone else thought you were a murderer at the time . . .* I cleared my throat. 'You know, I think you'd already left town when she found out she was pregnant. She was able to pretend she'd slept with someone else, a stranger. It was easier that way, from what she said.'

'Easier?' His face was bleak. 'Was she that ashamed of me?'

'I don't think that was a factor,' I said feebly. 'I really think you need to talk to her, though. I can't tell you exactly what she was feeling or thinking. She was very young, after all. You both were.'

'Why didn't she want me to know about him later? He must have been an adult by the time you found out about him.'

'He was at Cambridge. She didn't want to upset him, I think. She didn't say he'd been asking about his dad but I assume—' I broke off because at the words 'his dad' Derwent had pulled a chair towards him and sat down abruptly. 'Are you OK?'

'Not exactly.' He leaned forward and dropped his head into his hands so he didn't have to look at me. 'Go on.'

'I assume the question had come up from time to time. I mean, Luke is bright. He would have wondered where he came from and what she knew about his . . . his father.' I held myself very still because I really wanted to go over and put my arms around him, but I didn't think it would be welcome. 'I tried to persuade her to talk to you. I left her my card. She never called me.'

'You left her your card,' he repeated. 'Great.'

'What else could I do?'

It was a stupid question to ask, I realised as soon as I said it.

'A lot of things.' He looked up at me then. 'You could have *told* me for one thing.'

'I – I promised her.'

'Someone you didn't know at all. Someone you'd met . . . twice, was it?'

I nodded.

'I would have thought,' Derwent said evenly, 'that you might have thought it was more important to tell me what you'd found out. Since you know me quite well.'

I knew my face was flaming. 'At the time—'

'What? You didn't think I deserved to know?'

'I didn't think you'd care.'

The silence that fell was as dense as a wall. He got to his feet and walked from one side of the room to the other, as if he couldn't bear to stay still but had nowhere to go.

'I – I'm sorry. I didn't think—' He seemed completely unreachable, as if nothing I could do or say would draw him back. 'At the time you didn't seem to be interested in being a dad. It was a couple of years ago, remember. You were different then. Once you became involved with Melissa and started to spend time with Thomas, I could see things had changed. You changed.'

'But you still didn't say anything.' His calmness was worse than anger, colder.

'I didn't think I should. It wasn't my secret to share with you. It was between you and Claire.'

'I might never have known about him. I might never—' He stopped, facing away from me. 'What was he doing here today?'

157

'I asked him to come in again to explain why his car was seen at a particular place two years ago. He was abroad at the time. Nothing to do with him. He's not in trouble,' I added quickly. 'You don't need to worry.'

'Was that the first time you'd met him?'

'The second. He was in yesterday. That's when I realised who he was.'

'But you didn't think of telling me, even though you knew he was going to be in the office this afternoon.' His voice had a note in it that I'd never heard before.

'I was waiting,' I said lamely. 'I wanted to make sure he wasn't involved in my murder. Then I was going to tell you, I swear. Una Burt told me I should.'

He swung around, his face white, his eyes glittering with pure rage. 'Who else did you tell? For someone who's so devoted to keeping secrets you seem to have spread this one far and wide.'

'I told Burt because I was worried about this exact thing happening. I didn't want you to find out this way. I needed her help to keep you away from the case altogether. I had to tell her. And she told me to tell you, for what it's worth. She thought you should know.'

'Kind of her. And Georgia?'

'Georgia overheard us talking. No one else knows, I swear. Not Liv, not *anyone*.'

He turned away again, as if he couldn't bear to look at me.

'I'm sorry, Josh. I didn't mean to hurt you. If I could turn the clock back, I would. You should never have found out that way. I know you would have been a brilliant dad to Luke. I tried to convince Claire of that. I wasn't going to leave it this time. If she hadn't told you I really would have told you myself.' I fell silent again, waiting for him to answer, but when he spoke again it was with a question that he ground out, as if he couldn't bear not to ask it.

'What's he like?'

'He's brilliant.' I cleared my throat, fighting to keep my composure. 'He's clever and funny and kind. He's exactly what you'd want him to be.'

He shook his head, still facing away from me. 'You should have told me.'

'Look, I—'

He held up a hand. 'There's nothing you can say to make what you did all right. Just . . . go, before I tell you what I think of you.'

'Josh,' I said, appalled.

'Go.'

And I had gone. I'd left him shut in the little airless interview room with his regrets and his unbearable sorrow. I had let him focus his anger on me because after all, why shouldn't he? And I had hoped he would calm down, if I left him for long enough. I hoped he might understand that I'd been in an impossible position.

Based on the day I had endured, that wasn't going to happen any time soon. He had rebuffed any attempt I'd made to talk to him. He had got up and left the kitchen as soon as I walked in. I had seen him pacing in Una Burt's office with the door closed, as she sat at her desk with a remote expression on her face, and could only guess at their conversation. I had endured meetings, trying not to stare at the back of his head. I had pretended to concentrate on my work when all of my attention had been on him and whether he was coming over to talk to me or stalking past.

Claire hadn't called me, and neither had Luke. Whatever I was going through, I reminded myself, it was nothing compared to the principal actors in this sorry little soap opera. I was collateral damage at best.

But it hurt.

I came back to myself when Seth tossed his card on the table as the waiter hovered with the machine. I scrambled for my bag. 'Let me go halves.'

'If you want.'

The manager appeared as I got up after paying. 'Was everything all right with your meal?'

'It was fine except for the company.' Seth turned on his heel and walked out, leaving me to stammer my thanks and congratulations on the new restaurant and to promise that yes, we would return, very soon, lovely place, lovely food, thank you so much . . .

I found him outside, looking at his phone. 'Thanks for that.'

'You ruined my evening.' He started to walk away and I hurried after him, cursing the shoes I was wearing, shoes that I had only put on because he liked me in heels.

'I'm sorry, I wasn't in good form.'

'You spend enough time with him at work,' he said, enunciating clearly. 'You even live in his flat, for God's sake. When you spend an evening with me, I don't expect you to talk about him. I don't want to hear what he said or didn't say or how that made you feel. I want you to leave work behind when we're together. I expect you to be interested in me, and interesting, and for the time we have together to mean something. Is that too much to ask?'

'No, of course not. Look, it's been a bad week.' I had left my jacket in Seth's flat because the evening had seemed warm, but there was a definite chill in the air now, and not only because of his manner. I rubbed my arms, shivering. 'I can't help being upset. I know you don't like him but I've worked with him for a long time. We work well together and I'm worried this horrible situation will damage our *professional* relationship and can you slow down a bit, please?'

'Sorry.' He didn't sound it. He turned the next corner abruptly and I trotted after him, cursing my shoes and my luck with equal fluency.

'Seth, wait.'

I really hadn't expected that he would, but I ran straight into him. He grabbed me by the shoulders and pushed me up against the wall so hard that my head hit the bricks and I saw stars.

'I can't do this. I can't even look at you.' His anger was burning hot and I recalled with some alarm that he had a serious temper even if he rarely gave in to it. 'Take the hint, love. If you don't leave me alone I'm going to say or do something I regret.'

'Seth—'

'Leave me alone.' He turned and strode away, not looking back as I lost my balance and fell, the pavement rushing towards me. Pain blossomed in my knee, my hands and my right elbow as I clattered to the ground.

It took me a second to realise that Seth was really gone.

It took me a minute to get to my feet and assess the damage I'd sustained: grazes from the wall and the pavement, bruises, nothing broken, dignity in tatters.

It took half an hour of shivering outside a minicab office, my feet aching from my shoes, to get a taxi to take me to London Fields in all my mascara-streaked misery.

It took forever to drive there while the Italian driver talked to me incessantly about his crazy girlfriend. 'I say to her, you look like an angel and you talk like a woman from a fish market in a town that God forgot, and she *scream* at me but what can I do, I love her, I need to be with her . . .'

It took me four attempts to get my key in the door when I finally got home, the silence humming against my ears once I was alone.

It took me two and a half hours to stop crying for long enough that I could finally go to sleep. I had done it again, I thought dismally. I had taken a good man and turned him into my worst enemy because I was too consumed with work to make him feel as if he was important to me. I was alone, and I deserved to be. If Seth ever spoke to me again, I'd have to try to find the words to apologise, or I'd lose him the same way I'd lost everyone else who tried to care for me.

21

The day began, as it so often did, with a phone call. I fumbled for the phone, squinting against the morning sun that had found a gap in the curtains. The light speared through my head, pinning me to the pillow.

'Maeve? You busy?' Chris Pettifer was two shades too loud for me at the best of times, and this was certainly not the best of times.

'Not as such. What time is it?'

'Coming up on six.'

I didn't want to work out how much sleep I'd had: not enough, anyway. My eyes felt gritty, the skin around them puffy and tender, and all I wanted to do was phone in sick and go back to sleep. That had been my plan but Chris had got in first. He was on call, I remembered, so if he was on the phone it was because he needed to be.

'What's up?' I had enough practice at waking up instantly to sound as if I was alert even if that was far from the case.

'Hampshire Police have been on. They've got a body they wanted you to know about.'

'That's kind of them but I've got plenty of my own to worry about.'

'This *is* one of yours.' Chris really needed to tone down

the heartiness, I thought. He sounded altogether too cheerful for that time of day.

'What do you mean, mine?'

'He's got your card in his wallet.'

'Shit.' I sat up properly. 'Do we have an ID?'

'Not officially. Twenty-something IC1 male, brown hair, cause of death suicide. That's all I know.'

'Brown hair . . . did you say twenty-something male?' Fear slammed into me with physical force. *Not Luke, please, not Luke . . . not when he's only just found him . . .* I managed a grotesque impression of a casual enquiry. 'Anything in the wallet to give us a name?'

'Cards in the name of Roderick Asquith. Mean anything to you?'

It meant the world. I didn't say it. 'I interviewed him a couple of days ago in the Paige Hargreaves case.'

'There you are. That's how he had your card.' Pettifer sounded pleased. Mystery solved. Poor, sweet Roddy. In the absence of any concrete details I imagined him lying on a hillside or hanging from a tree, his worries at an end. *Was it something I said?*

'What happened?'

'Suicide is all I've got. They wanted to let you know in case it was relevant that your card was in his wallet.'

I frowned. 'Have they moved the body?'

'Not yet.'

'Tell them not to. I want to take a look.'

'They won't be pleased. They want to get the scene cleared up.'

'I'll get there as soon as I can.' I threw back the duvet and started to get out of bed, slowing down as stiffness and bruising and raw grazes set up a morning chorus of complaint. 'Actually, where *is* there?'

'Middle of nowhere. I'll let them know you're on your way and send you the postcode.'

163

I rubbed my face, trying to think of something useful to ask. 'When did it happen?'

'No idea. The local CID called me a couple of minutes ago. I bet they'll be thrilled if you're getting involved.'

The county forces were overstretched, bogged down with targets and time limits. It was getting harder to find resources to allocate to major crimes. Much better to get the Met's deep pockets and infinite manpower involved, which was fine except that I was the infinite manpower in question and I'd almost reached my limit. I yawned. 'Right. I'm on my way. Want to come?'

'Nah. I've got a stabbing. You're on your own.'

On my own. I was glad of it as I drove down the A3, and very glad that no one had been in the flat to see me wince and hobble through an abbreviated version of my morning routine. I'd taken a handful of painkillers to deal with the physical aftermath of my fall, and they'd kicked in at last, but the emotional side was going to take longer to stop hurting. I thought about Roddy instead, and why he might have taken his own life, and if I had done the right thing by him. The satnav knew where she was going, even if I didn't, and I turned the green fields into a blur as I sped away from the congestion of London.

The address Pettifer had sent me truly was in the middle of nowhere, through a tiny village I'd never heard of. The satnav directed me confidently down a lane as narrow as a footpath and I swore, hoping I wouldn't meet anyone coming the other way. The trees met overhead and branches swept the sides of the car.

'Your destination is on your left,' the satnav purred.

I slowed down, watching for the entrance. I almost missed the faded board with hand-painted letters: Bladewell Brickworks. A police car was parked near the entrance, almost blocking access. It was a good way of discouraging any curious passers-by from investigating what was going on there if you didn't have enough people to leave someone at the gate. I nosed past it and parked beside two unmarked cars. No one came to greet me, which was fine by me. I got out of the car and walked slowly towards the huge shed that took up most of the site, trying to get my bearings. The roof was pitted with holes and big double doors sagged open, revealing rusting machinery. Behind the shed, a square-sided chimney stretched fifty metres into the sky.

I looked in through the open doors but nothing moved inside the enormous shed except for a couple of birds that shot up towards the rafters, panicked. A narrow roadway skirted the outside of the building, the tarmac fractured and peeling. Weeds had seized control, spiralling up through it wherever they could find a fissure to exploit. The abandoned brickworks was giving me the creeps. It felt completely isolated, with no other properties in view and trees crowding close around the site. I heard voices in the distance and headed in that direction, following the road.

As I came around the side of the building I saw a small knot of men standing together in what must have been a loading yard at one time. It was big and bare, and the only thing that was out of place was a twin streak of tyre marks across the cracked concrete that led to a vehicle smashed against the base of the chimney. I stopped dead, staring at it. The front of it had folded as if it was tinfoil. All the glass had shattered and lay around the car like snow. The vehicle was half the length it should have been and barely recognisable. A slick of dark liquid pooled on the concrete beneath it.

'Can I help you?' A grim-looking man in a suit detached himself from the group and came to intercept me.

I introduced myself and explained why I was there, and he looked relieved.

'I'm DC Frank Steele. We've been waiting for you to turn

up. Once you're finished here we'll get a crew of firefighters to extract the body, get the vehicle recovered and have this place cleared up.'

Not so fast, I thought, but I smiled as he introduced me to the other detective, the response officers and the pathologist, a Dr Sunbury.

'What happened?' I asked.

Steele answered me, taking the lead as before. 'The deceased drove in here some time before four this morning. There's no working CCTV, no guard on site, so we're a bit stuck on the exact timings. He came around the side of the building and stopped on the other side of this yard. Then he floored it. There's a farmhouse a bit further down the road. They heard the impact and called it in.'

'We got here about ten past five,' one of the response officers chipped in. 'No one here, no sign of any other cars. He wasn't wearing his seatbelt and there was an empty bottle of whisky in the car. Looked like a suicide to us.'

'And me.' The pathologist was short and round. 'I've taken blood samples but there's a strong smell of alcohol in the car. He would have been killed instantly. Massive head injuries.'

'Are you sure of the ID?'

'He took most of the impact on his forehead and the top of his head. The lower part of his face is fairly intact and it matches his work ID which was in his wallet. We'll double-check, of course.'

The relatively undamaged rear end of the car had a round blue-and-white badge that I could see from where I stood. 'It's a BMW. The airbag didn't deploy?'

'On the passenger side only.'

'I thought you couldn't switch off the driver's one.'

'You can take the fuse out,' the second response officer volunteered. 'If you're fixing something on the dashboard of the car you can set them off by accident, so it's safer to disable it. Dead easy. You wouldn't need to be a car mechanic to do it.'

'Who's the registered keeper of the vehicle?'

'It's a hire car.'

I considered that briefly. 'Any note?'

'No, and his phone was smashed.' The other CID officer held up a bag with the remains of the phone in it.

'I'd better have a look at the body.'

'It's messy.' That was Steele.

'I'm used to it.'

'Yeah, of course. I didn't mean to suggest you weren't.'

I smiled. 'I should be OK, but that doesn't mean I'm looking forward to it.'

He looked relieved that I wasn't taking offence, and I walked away, knowing that they were all watching me. If only Steele knew that I was essentially immune to sexist remarks after working with Derwent for so long.

Derwent. I sighed and put him out of my mind so I could concentrate on what I was doing, stopping a few feet from the car so I could walk around it and take in the damage. The metalwork gleamed where it wasn't damaged: a new car, hired for the occasion, cleaned between uses. I came round to the driver's side and looked in, deliberately separating the body in the car from my memory of Roddy as he'd been, except to confirm that this was the man I had met and interviewed. The force of the impact had pushed the engine block back into the vehicle, wrapping the car around his body like a fist. Impossible to guess at what damage he might have sustained to his lower half. It would take the firefighters a while to disentangle him from the wreckage, I anticipated.

The door was buckled so badly it couldn't be opened. I did as everyone else had done and leaned through the window to get a close look at him. As Sudbury had said, the smell of alcohol was overpowering, and stronger as I got closer to him. Blood and brain tissue had cascaded down from a massive wound on the top of his head, streaking his face and soaking into his clothes. The front of his shirt was saturated. His hands were still on the steering wheel, the signet ring shining. I took out my torch and took a closer look at his mouth and jaw.

'Problem?' Sudbury was right behind me, with Steele behind him.

'I'd say so.' I straightened up. 'Not suicide.'

'What makes you say that?'

'Roddy was epileptic. He wasn't allowed to drive and he'd never learned. He didn't have a licence and he wouldn't have been able to hire the car on his own. Even if he'd got someone else to hire it, he'd never have been able to drive down the A3 without attracting attention from a traffic unit – that's a fast road and someone inexperienced would stand out a mile. And even if he managed *that*, he'd never have been able to cope with the narrow lane that leads here in the middle of the night. It would have been dark.'

'Desperate men can do extraordinary things,' the pathologist said.

'I looked up this place before I got here.' I'd done my homework and I didn't mind them knowing it. 'It's on a handful of urban exploring forums, precisely because there's no security and no CCTV and no close neighbours and the gate isn't working any more. The only people who come here since it closed down are kids who get a kick out of abandoned buildings and criminals looking for somewhere quiet to go about their business.'

Steele nodded. 'It's fairly well known locally.'

'And further afield. I tried searching for "abandoned factory rural location near London" and it came up on the first page of results.'

'Even so,' Steele began and I held up a hand.

'I met Roddy recently and his teeth were perfect. Look at them now.' I stood aside to let them see. The two front teeth were chipped, a neat half-moon taken out of them.

'That could have happened in the crash,' Steele objected.

Sudbury was shaking his head. 'No. There was no impact on the lower half of the face and there's no bruising on his mouth.'

'This mark – what does it look like to you?' I shone my torch on Roddy's jaw.

'A bruise. A finger mark, maybe.' Sudbury bristled. 'I'd have seen it at the PM.'

'I was looking for it,' I said, which was generous of me, because he should have thought of doing the same. 'I think someone held his face and made him drink. Look at the amount that must have spilled down his shirt. When he was injured, the blood spread, as if the material was wet already. No droplets, just saturation. He was set up. This was staged.'

'People aren't in their right minds when they kill themselves, as a rule. You might spill your drink, mightn't you?' Steele said. 'And he could have got that bruise somewhere else. He could have been in a fight before he came down here. None of this is making me think murder.'

'OK, well, look at the car. This window broke inside the driver's door when it buckled. The window was open before the crash. Someone had to take the handbrake off, which isn't a job I'd have liked myself because the accelerator was already pushed down as far as it would go. When they recover the car, they'll need to look for something in the driver's footwell – a block, something heavy like that. The way the car was damaged, whoever arranged this accident wouldn't have been able to retrieve it, assuming that was their plan. If you check, you'll find it.'

'Who would do that?' Steele asked.

'I don't know yet. Someone connected with the murder I'm investigating, I presume.' I looked down at Roddy soberly. 'He knew something about it, I could tell, but he wouldn't talk.'

He looked appalled. 'And someone killed him anyway? Even though he didn't cooperate?'

'They're absolutely ruthless.'

'They must have a lot to lose,' Steele said, and I shivered in spite of myself.

22

The only thing worse than being ignored by Derwent was being the focus of his attention. I was reminded of this as I stepped out of the office lift at the end of a long day. For the second time in twenty-four hours I found myself stumbling off balance, but this time it was because Derwent had grabbed hold of my arm to haul me into an empty meeting room.

'What are you doing?' I shook myself free, rattled. 'Don't do that.'

'It wasn't him?' Derwent's face was taut with tension. No need to ask who he meant.

'No.' I brushed myself down, tucking my shirt back into place. 'How did you hear about it?'

He took a moment before he answered, and when he did his voice was shaky with relief. 'I asked where you were. Belcott said he'd heard from Pettifer that you were down in Hampshire since early this morning, because a young man from one of your cases had killed himself. He didn't know the name, obviously, and I couldn't get hold of Pettifer to ask him about it because he was tied up with some stabbing.'

'Why didn't you call me?'

'I wasn't sure you'd pick up.'

'I would have,' I said, stung. *It's not me who's gone off in a huff, mate.*

'I thought – if it was him – you wouldn't want to tell me over the phone.' He swallowed, the agony of the preceding few hours carving shadows in his face. 'So I didn't want to call you.'

'If it had been him, I'd have told you myself. It would have been the first thing I did.'

He looked as if he wanted to argue the point but he settled for asking, 'Who was it?'

'One of Luke's housemates. A guy called Roddy Asquith.'

'And he killed himself?'

'No. Set up to look like suicide.' I filled in the details for Derwent as he leaned against the wall and listened, his arms folded, his expression stern.

'So no one else picked up on it being murder?'

'No one else was thinking it might be murder, but then they had no reason to suspect it. They were delighted when I turned up and told them they'd got it wrong and there'd have to be a proper murder inquiry.'

'I'm sure you were charming about it.'

'I was nice,' I protested. 'But it was so *slow*. They'd wasted a lot of time before I got there. It took a couple of hours to summon up the SOCOs and start processing the scene, and then a fire crew had to cut the car open to get the body out. The pathologist is going to do the post-mortem tomorrow morning, but really only because I nagged him about it.'

'No better woman.'

'Thanks,' I snapped.

'Calm down.' Derwent had to be feeling more like himself if he was being so infuriating. 'Tell me about the crash. How did they set it up?'

'A weight on the accelerator, they think, but it will be a while before they can retrieve it from the rest of the car. There was something rigged up so the parking brake could be released from outside the car – the SOCOs found a sticky residue on it, like tape. It was a BMW 3-series with a switch rather than a lever for the handbrake. Easier to take it off.'

'Presumably that explains why they picked that model of hire car.'

'That and the fact that it was heavy for a relatively compact car. The run-up from one side of the yard to the other was short but the impact was massive.'

'And he didn't manage to turn the wheel to avoid it?'

'I think Roddy was comatose or close to it when the car crashed. He reeked of alcohol. He probably didn't even know what was happening. All the damage was on the top of his head. I think he'd slumped forward in the driver's seat so he headbutted the steering wheel when the car hit the wall. The airbag was switched off. Fatal, instantly.'

'Not a one-person murder.'

'What makes you say that?'

'The location was remote. They'd have needed a second car to get away after they fucked the first one against a wall. Two drivers, if your victim didn't drive there himself.'

He was right. 'I'll tell them to look for tyre marks.'

'Probably too late if you and a hundred other people have been driving on to the site. You'd park a fair way from the scene anyway, wouldn't you? Near the gate, out of sight of the road.'

'No harm in telling them to look there.'

'None at all. So why would someone want to kill him?'

'To stop him from talking, I presume.' I sighed. 'He'd given me a no-comment interview but he was a nice kid. I was planning to pay him another visit and ask him some more questions about the incident Paige was investigating. I think I'd have got somewhere if I'd had the chance to persuade him to talk.'

'Who else knew you were going to question him again?'

I bit my lip. I'd been hoping he wouldn't ask me, because

I could only think of one person. When I didn't answer straight away, Derwent frowned. 'Oh. I see. Luke.'

'Yeah.' I'd worked out in the car on the way back that Luke was the only person who had known what I intended to do next, and what questions I would be asking, and to what end. 'But that might be a coincidence. Or he might have said something to the wrong person by accident and tipped them off without realising it.'

'Or not,' Derwent said grimly. 'He might be in it up to his neck.'

I really wanted to say something reassuring, but I couldn't, and anyway Derwent wouldn't have fallen for it. He looked at me warily.

'Don't say anything to Burt about that yet.'

'Why not?'

'I managed to persuade her to let me work on this case, as long as Luke's not involved. At the moment he's not on her radar. You were happy with the answers he gave you in interview and he's not a suspect.'

'Not officially,' I said, troubled. 'But I'm not sure this is the ideal way to get to know him if that's what you want.'

Derwent made a dismissive gesture, as if that hadn't even occurred to him. 'I don't want to be stuck on the outside of this one. It's a big case. Burt wanted an inspector involved and I persuaded her it should be me. So don't give her any ideas about changing her mind.' He straightened up and checked the time. 'I'd best head off. Melissa will be sending out search parties.'

'Sorry for being so late.'

He nodded. 'Keep me in the loop, though. I need to know what's going on.'

'I will.' Another question popped into my mind. 'Hey, how did you know I hadn't been in the office today?'

'You'll see.' He hesitated, already halfway out the door. 'Is everything OK?'

'Everything's fine,' I lied.

He nodded. 'That's what I thought.'

'What does that mean?' I was too late; he was gone. I went thoughtfully through to the main office and stopped at the sight of my desk.

'Happy birthday!' One of the support staff smiled at me. 'We've been admiring them all day. And the scent! Amazing roses.'

'They are.' I tried to smile. 'Not my birthday, though.'

'Must be a *very* special occasion then.' I didn't answer, and she looked disappointed. 'Well, goodnight!' She took herself and her curiosity out to the lifts and I walked down to my desk, where half the contents of a rose garden had been crammed into billowing cellophane. The smell of the flowers hung on the air, a distinct improvement over the printer-ink-and-failing-deodorant ambience the office usually enjoyed. I looked for the card, ripping it out of the still-sealed envelope with shaking hands.

I'm sorry. Can I make it up to you?

I picked the bouquet up with some effort and carried it into the kitchen, where I rammed it into the bin. I tore up the card and shoved it down the side of the bin, my face hot with embarrassment and anger. It wasn't the apology I minded, particularly – it was nice of him to take the blame for a row that had been at least 50 per cent my fault. All that he had to apologise for was losing his temper when I had goaded him into it, and for leaving me on the street on my own. I'd fallen over all by myself. I hated that the flowers had sat there all day, a source of interest to the entire office. I despised the whole public production of getting a bouquet at work anyway, not to mention lugging it home on the underground, shoving it in a vase and watching the flowers wither and stink. I saw enough of death not to want it to happen in my home.

175

The one good thing about coming in so late was that most people had already left for the day, and anyone who was left in the office had more sense than to ask me about the flowers. I strode to my desk, glowering, and logged on to my computer to catch up with the day I'd missed. Of course Derwent would have known it wasn't my birthday or an anniversary. He would have spotted the flowers for what they were. *Is everything OK? That's what I thought* . . . I focused on my inbox, powering through messages with ruthless efficiency. An unexpected name appeared halfway down the page and I clicked on the message.

Hi there,

Sorry for emailing but I thought you'd want to know someone contacted me on Twitter to say she'd been talking to Paige about a story. Can you call me?

Bianca Drummond

It was getting late. Worth a try, I thought, and called her. The phone rang again and again, and I was resigning myself to leave a voicemail when she picked up.

'Bianca, it's Maeve Kerrigan. Thank you for the email.'

'I thought you'd like to know.' She sounded sullen, as if she was slightly regretting contacting me. 'You did ask me to tell you if anything happened.'

'I did, and I'm grateful. Who is this person who contacted you and what do you know about her?'

'Her name is Antoinette. She read a piece I wrote about Paige in an online magazine – a tribute to her. It did quite well and I got a big response from readers. One tweet was from this woman asking me to follow her so she could send me a direct message.'

'What did it say?'

'Not much. She'd been helping Paige with a story about

something that happened to her at Chiron House and she wanted to know if anyone was going to write that story now.'

'What did you say?'

'I said I was looking into it.'

'Bianca . . .'

'Well, I am now. She wants to talk to *someone* about this story – it might as well be me.'

'I don't think it's safe. We still don't know who killed Paige, or why.'

'Would you stop doing your job because it was dangerous?' She waited and I was silent. 'Didn't think so.'

'It's a bit different for me.' Time to take the gloves off. 'I don't want to end up picking bits of you out of the Thames, Bianca.'

'You won't.'

'With all due respect, you can't know that.'

'Look, you wouldn't even know Antoinette existed if I hadn't told you.'

'True, but—'

'I'm going to meet her tomorrow.' She hesitated. 'I was thinking – if she doesn't mind – you could come with me. Not to interview her, but you can sit in on our conversation. If you want.'

'She'd have to know who I was,' I said. 'I don't want her to be misled about anything. She's potentially an important witness.'

'Fine. I'm sure she'll say yes. She just wants to talk.'

I frowned. 'Don't get me wrong, I'm glad you got in touch, but why do you want me to come along?'

Bianca hesitated. 'I want to do my job but . . . I'm scared. And I don't know much about her.'

'You thought it might be a trap.'

'I don't know.' Her frustration and fear came through her voice. 'I don't know what to think. But I don't want to take any stupid chances.'

177

'Where are you meeting her?'

'The Barbican. We're meeting in the café on the ground floor at eleven.'

It was a good location, I thought, busy and big and close to public transport. Antoinette could hang back and see if Bianca was alone, or if she'd been followed, and no one could overhear them easily.

'Can you ask her if she'll let me join you?'

'I'd rather wait until I meet her. I don't want to scare her off. And you look nice,' she added, rather sweetly. 'You don't *look* frightening.'

I laughed. 'Appearances are deceiving.'

'If I say a police officer wants to come along, she'll get nervous. If I point you out to her and she sees you, she'll probably be fine with it.'

I made up my mind. 'OK. As long as you're clear with her about what I'm doing there.'

'I'll tell her everything,' Bianca promised.

23

It was a beautiful morning and the massive, pitted concrete
fortress of the Barbican was looking as attractive as it ever
could as I crossed the courtyard towards the arts centre. The
terrace outside the café was packed with people sitting in the
sunshine, but no one I knew. I threaded my way through
the crowds into the cool, faintly unsettling foyer with its squat
pillars and odd angles, then headed into the half-empty café,
scanning the tables for Bianca Drummond. She was by the
window, looking serious in glasses and a high ponytail as she
tapped at her laptop. There was an empty coffee cup in front
of her, the inside veiled in dirty brown foam. As she saw me
approach she slammed the laptop shut.

'You're early.'

'So are you,' I pointed out. 'And you've been here a while.'

'I don't want to miss her.' Bianca looked past me and bit
her lip. 'She's not here yet. She sent me a message to say she
was running a few minutes late. Could you . . . go away? I
don't want her to get scared.'

'How far away would you like me to go?'

Bianca either didn't hear or chose to ignore the sarcasm.
'Over there.' She pointed to the other side of the café. 'When
she comes, I'll explain who you are.'

I did as she suggested, detouring to get a bottle of water, then sat with my chin propped on my hand, scanning the crowds for anyone who looked burdened with terrible dangerous secrets. I had more or less given up hope by the time a young woman stalked into the café and passed the food without so much as looking at it. She had a haughty expression thanks to high cheekbones, narrow eyes and a small, discontented mouth. She went straight over to Bianca and said something to her. Very tight jeans and a plain T-shirt and wedge-heeled sandals: not English, I thought, and prepared to suffer for her looks. She cast a glance over her shoulder, tossing long straight chestnut-brown hair out of the way.

Bianca was shaking her head. She touched the woman's arm but she shook her off. She snapped something and began to stride away.

I was out of my seat before I'd thought about it. I reached her side in a few paces, as she stepped out onto the terrace and slid on vast designer sunglasses.

'Antoinette?'

'Who are you?' Unfeigned terror turned her face into a mask behind the glasses.

'I'm a police officer. A detective,' I said in a conversational tone, and showed her my ID as if I was showing her something on my phone, in case someone was watching. 'I'm investigating Paige Hargreaves' murder. I gather you might have some information for us.'

'I told her to come alone.' She scowled at Bianca, who had come to join us. Antoinette's accent was pronounced, an Eastern European inflection that thickened her consonants. 'I knew she wouldn't.'

'I thought you were going to tell her who I was,' I said to Bianca.

'She asked me if I was on my own and as soon as I said no she stormed off,' Bianca said. 'She didn't even give me a chance to explain.'

180

'Bianca knew I would need to talk to you,' I said. 'She was Paige's friend. She's been helping with the investigation.'

'I was her friend too.' The tip of Antoinette's nose reddened and she darted a manicured finger behind her sunglasses to swipe away tears. 'She was kind.'

'Please come and talk to us.' I tried to look as harmless and pleasant as possible. 'You contacted Bianca because you want to talk to someone about what happened to you at Chiron House. You talked to Paige already. If you tell me what you told her, maybe I can do something about it.'

She gave a cracked, bitter laugh. 'No one can do anything. It's too late.'

'What do you mean?'

'There's no evidence. It's my word against theirs. And who would listen to me? I am nobody. They are big important men.'

'I'll listen. And so will Bianca.'

Slowly, reluctantly, she turned and stepped through the doors into the café. Bianca pulled out a chair for Antoinette. 'Can I get you a drink? A coffee?'

'No, nothing.' Antoinette collapsed into the chair and winced; they were not designed for slumping. She folded her sunglasses and wrapped them in a cloth before stowing them in their Prada-branded case. 'I just want to talk and go.'

Bianca put her phone on the table, close to Antoinette. 'I'm recording this interview, is that OK?'

'Why not.' She looked listlessly from Bianca to me. 'What do you want to know?'

'Why don't you start by telling us the story you told Paige?' I suggested. 'Exactly the way you told her about it.'

She sighed and leaned forward, speaking in a low voice that was directed towards the phone. Aside from her accent, her English was extremely fluent and colloquial. 'OK. So, I moved to London three years ago. I worked many jobs – cleaner, barista, clothes shop. I came to learn English so I could work

in an office. In my country, I am an accountant, you understand? But here I have to study to be an accountant and it
costs a lot. Also, I need good English.'

'Where are you from?' Bianca interjected.

'Latvia.'

'And how old are you now?'

'Twenty-eight.' She could have been five years older or
younger, I reflected. 'Anyway, I worked hard. I saved. It's
difficult because of rent and the cost of living here, so I worked
as much as I could. I had a job in a shoe shop and it was my
lunch hour. I was sitting in the break room, registering with
temp agencies – you know, office work? I was so tired of that
job. People so rude and smelly, and children that didn't listen.'
She pulled a face. 'The assistant manager saw what I was
doing. I thought I would get in trouble for looking for another
job but she told me if I could waitress, there was an agency
that needed girls for evening and weekend work. Weddings,
that kind of thing. Of course I said I was interested.'

'What was the name of the agency?' I asked.

'Delahayes.' She spelled it for me. 'I phoned the number
she gave me and they said, yes, come round, let's talk. The
office was in Victoria, near the train station. When I arrived,
there were many girls there – ten, twelve. They looked at all
of us and said to five of us, yes, you come through here. The
others, they told to go.'

'How did they decide who to keep?'

'Some of the girls they told to go were fat. Some were not
good-looking or had no style. No grooming. One was too
old. One had gum, you know?' She mimed chewing. 'And bad
teeth. A couple of them had tattoos.'

'And the ones who stayed?' I prompted.

'We were all pretty, thin, nice. Some tall, some small. All
young. One very young. She said she was eighteen, but . . .'
Antoinette shrugged. 'Of course, I was not an idiot. I was
already thinking it was something for sex – a brothel, a club.

I was ready to leave. But the girls who worked there came in and told us it was waitress work and their clients were very wealthy so they wanted girls who looked respectable and nice and could behave themselves properly. And then she told us what the pay was. Three times what I could earn in the shop.'

'And was it waitressing work that they wanted you to do?' Bianca asked.

Rather to my surprise, Antoinette nodded. 'Waitressing, yes. They trained us in silver service. I did two . . . three weddings? And then special corporate events in the City. Lots of very rich people. It was places that didn't have usual staff – special venues. We were brought in for the evening. It was OK, you know? They had rules about your hair – no coloured dye – and your nails. My God, they would inspect you before you started work every time and it was like the army. They didn't allow anything.' She cackled. 'We called one manager the general because she was so strict. We had to walk the same, talk the same, wear our hair the same, no jewellery, no perfume. Lots of rules. But good money, and it was fun.' Her face changed. 'Until the Chiron Club almost two years ago. The twenty-second of July.'

'What happened?' I asked, my ears pricking up at the date she mentioned. That was the day before Luke's car had been spotted in Standen Fitzallen.

'It was a special event. Only the best girls picked.' She looked away for the first time. 'I was pleased to be chosen. There was a bonus, too. Two hundred pounds per girl, plus tips. We weren't supposed to accept tips – it wasn't usual to get anything over what we were paid, but we were paid well. The general told us the club members were generous and liked to reward the girls they liked by giving them cash at the end of the night. We were supposed to remember to smile and be nice and talk if they wanted to talk. Some of us were waitresses. Others were to sit at the tables in case the men wanted to talk.'

'Like escorts?' Bianca asked.

'No, this is another word for prostitute, yes? Not escorts. More like decorations. Like the flowers on the table. They were the most beautiful girls who were chosen for this.' She shrugged. 'I was a waitress. I thought that was OK. I didn't want to sit and listen to them talking all night. Men like that are boring. Always boasting. No one cares about your money, Gerald.'

I found myself laughing along with Bianca and Antoinette's mournful expression lifted for a second, a sparkle appearing in her eyes.

'We laughed at them, you see. That was why I liked the job.' The light went out of her face as she went on. 'That night, they gave us dresses to wear for waitressing – short but smart. They told us we had to wear very fine tights or stockings, and three-inch heels at least. Not fun for waitressing, but OK, I am used to heels, for me it was no problem. And then we were ready. The evening started at seven with a champagne reception.'

'How many men were there? What was the occasion?'

She shook her head. 'Two hundred? I think it was a special summer party or a celebration. I don't know. There was a big cake, I remember. Huge. Everyone was drinking a lot, shouting, cheering. The men, they started out polite, but they were watching us, and talking about us. We could all tell. You always know.'

I nodded. 'So you were uneasy.'

'A little. But a big group of men, they talk about sex. Always. So.' She looked uncomfortable. 'They were young, some of them. Handsome. Very rich. We were flirting, you understand? Playing games with them? It wasn't difficult. We were all thinking of the tips at the end of the night. Some of them pinched bums or groped us because it was crowded where the reception was. We warned each other who to avoid. I was black and blue, but I kept smiling, smiling, like I was having fun.'

'Of course,' Bianca said warmly. 'That's what you do.'

184

'I couldn't lose the job, you see. I wanted to work more. I thought I had to do it.' She shivered. 'One of them said he would give me a hundred pounds if I kissed him on the cheek. I wasn't sure but I said OK, and when I went to kiss him he grabbed me and put his tongue in my mouth.'

'Did you complain?' Bianca asked.

She laughed. 'Who to? The general didn't care. Anyway, I had said yes. He gave me the money afterwards and I felt horrible. Like a whore.'

'He tricked you,' I said. 'That wasn't what you agreed to.'

'No, but I was stupid to say yes.' Her face crumpled. 'I behaved like I was OK with it. They thought – well, maybe they didn't care. But I felt it was my fault, what happened later.'

'What happened later?' I asked gently.

'It was after the main course. We had served. One of them had put his hand in between my legs and I couldn't stop myself – I spoke to him sharply. He said he was sorry.' She shuddered. 'He looked so angry with me. But one of the other men, an older man, he told me I was right. Some of them were kind. I was so upset I needed a minute to myself. I ran out to find the bathroom. There were two young men in the hall, and I asked them if they knew where it was. I was confused. I hadn't been there before, and I didn't know how to get to the staff area.'

I waited, but Antoinette didn't go on. She was sitting very still, her eyes fixed on the table, and she was trembling. At last she said, 'I should have asked one of the other waitresses. My fault. I remember one of them laughing. The other said, "Yes, I know where it is. Come this way. I'll show you." He brought me to a door and said, "Here it is." I said, "Are you sure?" and he opened the door. The other one was behind me and he shoved me inside. It was full of coats, and dark. They put a coat over my head and wrapped it around, tight. Then they pushed me against other coats and I screamed as loud as I could, but no one heard. They took turns with me. I couldn't fight – they were behind me and I think one held me down while the other one did what he wanted. I was so scared. I thought I would die. There was no air. I went limp, as if I'd fainted – I thought that might make them stop, even if I couldn't fight.' She smiled bitterly. 'They didn't stop. Not until they were both finished.'

'I'm so sorry,' I said, appalled. 'I'm so, so sorry. But it wasn't your fault.'

'I should have known.'

'You couldn't have. You were there to work. You should have been safe.' I pushed my own anger down because it wasn't helpful, not then, but I knew it would resurface later. *These men and their entitlement.* 'Did they speak to you afterwards?'

She shook her head. 'They left me in the room, in the dark. I got dressed again – my tights were ripped, so I took them off. I tried to clean myself up. I came out and found the general but she wouldn't listen to me. She got one of the men who works at the club and he called a car for me. He told the driver I was ill, and to take me straight home. I was so shocked. I wanted to go to hospital, or the police, but the driver took me to my flat and made me go in. The man at the club said I should forget everything that had happened, that it would be best for me, too. I asked what he meant and he gave me an envelope full of money.' Her eyes filled with tears. 'It was so much money.'

'How much was it exactly?' I asked.

'Four thousand, eight hundred. I – I took it.'

'I'd probably have done the same. A rape trial is a nightmare for the victim,' Bianca said, with a wholly unwarranted glower in my direction.

'I knew they would say I'd agreed, if there was a trial.' Antoinette took out a tissue and dabbed at her nose. 'I knew they would say I'd kissed the other man. No one would have

186

seen anything suspicious. They would say I was an immigrant trying to make money off drunk men by lying about them. And I would lose the money. I would have nothing. It felt like the right thing to do to just . . .' she mimed wiping the air. 'It was gone. It never happened.'

'Did you ever make a complaint to the police?' I asked.

'I tried. About six months later, I was still thinking about it. I realised it hadn't gone away. I could still see their faces. They had probably forgotten everything, but I remembered.' She looked fierce for a moment, then sad. 'But I had got rid of all the evidence – thrown out the clothes, the envelope. Spent the money. I had some messages on my phone from that night, where I said I was raped, to friends. I could describe the men. Not enough.'

'It should have been enough,' Bianca said. 'Your word should be as good as theirs.'

'It's not that we wouldn't have believed the story. The Crown Prosecution Service won't take a rape case forward unless they think there's a good chance of getting a conviction,' I said apologetically. 'That usually means physical evidence or witnesses.'

'I asked some of the other girls if they'd seen anything. They said no.' Antoinette sighed. 'There was one girl who was always my friend. I tried calling her, texting her. Nothing. I never heard from her after that night. I don't know if something happened to her, but she was gone from my life.'

'What was her name?'

'Iliana Ivanova. She was Bulgarian. Very beautiful.' Antoinette welled up again. 'I went to her house and asked her housemates, but they said they didn't know who I was talking about. She'd disappeared, as if she had never been there.'

24

The girl behind the reception desk at Delahayes Opportunities gave me a long, assessing look when I walked in, her expression neither welcoming nor hostile. She was young, black and beautifully groomed from her braids to her manicured fingernails. Somehow, I passed the initial scrutiny because she slid a clipboard and pen across the desk to me and launched into an uninterruptable spiel delivered at high speed.

'Fill out this form with your name, age, nationality and legal status, what languages you speak, your current employment and what hours you would be able to work. Don't forget to reply to the questions on the other side about hair colour, eye colour, dress size and shoe size, height and weight. Don't lie because we will be double-checking all the information you provide us with.'

She turned back to her computer as I took the clipboard and wrote my name and POLICE OFFICER in the space for current occupation, then slid it across to her with my ID.

'You're finished already?' She looked at it. 'Oh. My God. I'm sorry. I thought – I mean, I *assumed*—'

'Don't worry,' I said kindly. 'Is the owner available for a chat?'

'I'll give her a call.' She picked up the phone and pressed

a couple of buttons, then changed her mind. 'I'll go through and see her. That phone – it's not working very well for some reason.'

'That's strange.'

'It happens from time to time.' She was starting to regain her composure. 'Take a seat.'

I watched her sashay through the door behind the desk, tossing her weight of braids nonchalantly as she went. Then the thunder of a pair of feet running upstairs at high speed echoed through the building, and I smiled to myself. Not as calm as she pretended to be, not by half.

Delahayes occupied three floors of a narrow, dingy office building on the corner of a busy street near Victoria Station, the kind of place you could walk past a hundred times without ever noticing it. The communal hallway outside was dirty and bleak, but the reception area had been recently redecorated and was a tasteful symphony of black and grey. The company's name was stuck on the wall in chrome letters, and a big vase full of white flowers looked impressive until you realised they were very good fakes. I thought of the roses Seth had sent me and suppressed a shudder. I had, in the end, sent him a text to say I'd got them, and he had phoned me, and we had talked for hours. He wasn't happy with how he'd behaved. He'd never meant to lose his temper. It had been the end of a bad day, he explained, but that was no excuse. It had been my fault as much as his, I had insisted. I had been difficult, moody, silent during dinner. High maintenance, he joked, but worth it, and I'd felt ashamed of myself.

'If I didn't care so much, Maeve, I wouldn't have lost my temper.'

'It upset me. I wasn't expecting that anger.'

'It's nothing more than another kind of passion.'

'Not the kind I like.'

'So what kind do you like?' There'd been a smile in his voice again, and a lazy kind of anticipation that turned my icy reserve to meltwater. And since then, a barrage of messages and jokes and an email confirming a reservation on the Eurostar and two nights at a hotel in Paris in July.

So I could forget all about it, I told myself, even as I caught myself easing my knee where it still ached.

'Miss Gould will see you now.' The receptionist tiptapped into the room, smiling nervously. 'You can go straight up. Top of the stairs, on your left.'

I hadn't formed much of an image of Miss Gould in my mind, but she was a surprise all the same: fiftyish, short fair hair, an engaging smile, an armoury of rings across her knuckles and enough chains slung around her neck to act as a fairly effective breastplate. She stood up as I entered and held out a hand.

'Edina Gould.' Her voice rang with money and good breeding. 'What can I do for you?'

'Detective Sergeant Maeve Kerrigan. I'm investigating a murder.'

The smile evaporated. 'What murder? What do you mean? If it was one of my girls—'

'I don't think she was one of your girls officially.' I sat down and took out my notebook, settling in, and after a moment's hesitation Edina Gould sat too. 'I'm here because of Paige Hargreaves.'

'Who?'

'Come on, Miss Gould. You can do better than that. Paige Hargreaves. She was a journalist. She came to see you a couple of months ago. She wanted to work for you because she had a story she was investigating, about young women being hurt for fun at the Chiron Club.'

Her face was mottled under the veneer of expensive foundation. 'I don't remember.'

'I think you do. I think Paige came and asked if you would take her on and you turned her down, so she explained who she was. She told you if you cooperated she wouldn't name this agency in her report. She wouldn't blame you for putting vulnerable young women in harm's way.'

'First of all, they're not vulnerable. That's why we have such a long and careful screening process. I only supply girls who have a reasonable amount of spirit and can keep their head in any circumstances. Secondly, I never put anyone in harm's way. I offer them an opportunity to work in a very high-end environment, among this country's leading business people and most powerful men. It's up to them how they take advantage of that opportunity. What you will find is that many of these girls embark on impressive careers having started out here. They make contacts, they listen, they learn. They're ambitious and they know their worth. No one is being victimised. Nothing illegal is taking place at the Chiron Club. If there was illegal activity, I would know about it.'

'You're supplying young women knowing that they'll be sexually harassed *at best* while they try to do their jobs.'

'Not at all. I'm not a madam. This isn't a brothel. I'm a professional recruitment consultant and I make it very clear to my clients that the girls are not there to be used. What private arrangements they make are up to them, of course, but I have nothing to do with that. It's the same as meeting someone in an office, except that they have very little chance of meeting men like this in any office where they might work. Haven't you ever started a relationship with someone you met through work?'

'Rape isn't a relationship,' I said thinly.

'I thought you were investigating a murder. Now you're talking about rape.' She flung herself back in her chair and rearranged the gold chains slung around her neck. 'Either way, I don't know anything about it.'

'Did Paige tell you the story she had been told? About a woman supplied by you as a waitress being gang-raped in a cloakroom?'

'Not at all. She told me that one of the girls had been paid off after having sex in a cloakroom with two of the club's members.' She smiled, not pleasantly. 'No names, of course. No further details. I had to tell her, I have no record of this happening at all. No one complained.'

'Your manager who was there that evening didn't mention it to you.'

'Of course not. And she would have told me immediately if there was anything to concern us.'

'My understanding is that the girl was raped.'

She gave a tinkly little laugh. 'I don't think you can call it rape when the girl is very keen to meet handsome, wealthy young men and . . . get to know them. Paige told me this girl approached them. Maybe things went further than she had expected. Maybe she was disappointed that it didn't lead to a closer relationship. Whatever her reason for complaining to Paige, she didn't go to the police.'

'Not immediately.'

A dent appeared between Edina Gould's immaculate brows. 'Has she reported it now? Formally?'

'I can't tell you that.'

Her mouth puckered as if her lips contained a drawstring. She unpursed them to say, 'She would be very unwise to make this a police matter.'

'It's already a police matter.' I leaned forward. 'Paige Hargreaves *died*, Miss Gould. Someone killed her, and cut her up, and dumped her in the Thames.'

'One would think that should be enough to make anyone think twice about causing trouble.'

'Do you know who killed Paige, Miss Gould?'

'Of course not. No one at the Chiron Club would bother with something like that. They'd get any negative stories killed before they were published. These people don't need to worry about bad publicity. Nothing ever makes the papers.'

'What about the internet? Anyone can publish anything these days.'

She shrugged. 'All deniable. And all open to litigation if you want to take that route. There aren't many journalists willing to take that kind of risk, personally, and there aren't many crusading websites with deep enough pockets to bear a long, expensive legal process.'

'You sound as if you approve of them silencing their critics.'

'It's how the world works. There's no point in trying to change that.' Edina sat up straight and rearranged her swag. 'Everyone backs down in the end.'

'Luckily for me, this is my job, and I'm not backing down,' I said quietly. 'Did you send Paige Hargreaves to the Chiron Club to work?'

'No. She asked me to, but I said no. I told her it would breach my contract with the club and I wasn't prepared to do it for any reason.'

'Did she find another way in?'

'I haven't the faintest idea. You'll have to ask them.'

'I will.' An idea had been percolating ever since the receptionist had mistaken me for a job applicant. 'Do the Chiron Club have any functions coming up that require extra staff?'

'Yes, there's a dinner next week that I—' She stopped and her eyes went wide. 'You wouldn't.'

'I most certainly would. I'd like to be sitting at a table, with the guests.'

'You don't look right.'

'I scrub up well,' I said. 'And I have a colleague who would make a brilliant waitress.'

'It's impossible.'

'It's really not. I want to get a closer look at how the Chiron Club operates and I want to do it without them noticing I'm there. You can make that happen. We are very discreet and very good at our jobs and if it works out as I anticipate, they won't even know we were there.'

'What if you arrest someone?'

'For what?' I blinked, bland as milk. 'You said you were

sure there was nothing illegal going on there. How could I arrest anyone if they're not breaking the law?'

'I'm not comfortable with this.'

'These girls – these intelligent, beautiful, ambitious girls you provide. They seem like the kind of girls who might think of suing an employer who knowingly exposed them to a hostile and dangerous working environment. It's only a matter of time before one of them thinks of it. What do you think would happen if a civil court heard that not only did you fail to take steps to protect your staff, but you refused to help with a police investigation aimed at rooting out the people who were causing them to be raped, or to disappear?'

'Disappear?' Edina Gould's voice was sharp. 'You mean Paige?'

'I mean Iliana Ivanova. Remember her?'

The name unsettled her, that was clear. 'These girls come and go. They go home. They get other jobs. They may drop out of sight but that doesn't mean I need to be concerned.'

'She was never seen again after the party on the twenty-second of July the year before last. She didn't leave the country by any official routes as far as we've been able to tell, and no one seems to remember she existed.' I leaned forward. 'But I do. And I'm going to find out where she went.'

Now

It was done, it was over; he could stop worrying about it. He only wished he could stop *thinking* about it. He pulled his chin above the bar, the muscles in his arms and shoulders and chest and stomach screaming, then lowered himself down again.

They hadn't been pleased.

'That's what we're here for.'

'You weren't handling it,' he'd snapped into the phone, cupping his hand over his mouth so no one in the park could hear what he was saying, or read his lips.

'With respect, you have no idea what we were doing or not doing.'

'You were letting them get too close.'

'We were letting them look. They won't find anything.' The same level voice that had spoken to him when he called the number on the back of the photographs, two years before, his whole body shaking. A woman. He'd never seen her. Voice like velvet, heart like a stone. 'There's nothing to find.'

'There are pictures.'

'Not where they can find them.'

'You need to destroy them.'

A note of amusement in her voice. 'If we destroyed every-thing every time someone was interested in us, we wouldn't have much left to work with.'

'Maybe that would be a good thing.'

'Really? Am I to understand you don't want our help any more?'

He hesitated. How he wanted to say no. He really didn't want them involved in his life. But if he said that, he had an awful feeling they'd hang the whole thing on him. And he wasn't guilty. Or at least, not as guilty as *some* people.

Anyone who'd got hurt had deserved it. And it had sent a message that anyone who tried to get in his way would get hurt. You had to take control of these situations. You had to make it clear you weren't going to let them take advantage of you. You weren't going to let anyone betray you.

(*What are you doing?* Roddy's face, white in the moonlight, and the other man holding the bottle, uncertain, staring at him like he was a stranger.

This is what happens to people who talk.

But I didn't say anything? His voice making it a question, shaking with fear.

Even then, Roddy hadn't realised it wasn't him he was talking to. It had been a warning for the man with the bottle, and given the way he'd looked afterwards – *white knuckles on the steering wheel, shock making fathomless holes of his eyes* – it had sunk in.)

Whatever he'd done, he told himself, levering up again, grimacing with effort, he'd done the best he could in a bad situation. And no one could blame him for that.

25

'Do you want some champagne?' The red-faced man – Roddy Asquith as he would have been if he'd lived another twenty years – grabbed the waitress's arm and towed her back to face me.

'I shouldn't, but I will,' I said, and giggled, and made eye contact with the stony-faced, sulky waitress for the briefest moment as I lifted a glass off her tray. If Georgia didn't watch out, she was going to get a proper telling-off from the Delahayes manager, the general herself, who had put us through a quick and brutal training programme so we would pass muster. It was thanks to the manager that my hair was currently wider than my shoulders, and my dress was as abbreviated as it could be while still counting as clothes. I'd worried beforehand that someone would recognise me but I'd walked right past Sir Marcus Gley as I came in and his eyes had been riveted on my legs and chest rather than my face. Orlando Hawkes wouldn't be there, with his housemate lying in a Hampshire morgue. I wasn't completely at my ease but with the hair and make-up I thought I could pass for a Delahayes girl. Georgia had been told to smile, and pay attention to what the men were saying to her, and to be polite. Currently she was looking as if she was ten seconds away from ramming her tray in someone's neck and making a break for the exits. I didn't blame her completely; it was difficult to carry a single champagne flute through the throng, let alone a whole tray of them. She forced a more pleasant expression on to her face as she offered her tray to someone else.

'Down in one,' Roddy's lookalike urged me, and I giggled again.

'I couldn't! I'd be on the floor.'

'I'd look after you,' he said gallantly, and squeezed me around the waist, which rucked my dress up. I managed to get a hand to the hem in time to tug it down and preserve my modesty, although we were all so thoroughly packed together there was no question of anyone seeing anything. In fact, the champagne reception was proving to be a bit of a challenge. It was so crowded that I couldn't move, let alone circulate, and I hadn't seen anyone I recognised so far. The noise level was extraordinary – a string quartet in the corner were scraping away but I couldn't hear a note. I could only imagine what the cacophony sounded like for the occupants of the unmarked van that was parked a short distance from the Chiron Club's front door. They were listening through the button microphone I had clipped to the centre of my bra (despite Pettifer's kind offer to help me to fit it). It was a tiny device, and even if the neckline of my dress slipped down, no one would ever spot it. The police hadn't really moved on from the old days in terminology – a wire was still a wire, even if it relied on digital transmission now – but I was glad we were past the days of actual recording units. My tiny, strappy, sparkly little black dress didn't offer many places where you could hide an old-fashioned wire.

'Hope you're getting all of this,' I said behind my champagne glass and Derwent's sigh gusted through my earpiece.

'That was some of the least competent flirting I've ever heard, Kerrigan. You need lessons.'

'Maybe she doesn't want to encourage them, *Josh*,' Liv snapped.

'She'll have them all lining up to take her in to dinner anyway, looking like that.'

'Shut up, Chris,' Derwent and Liv said in unison, which was precisely what I would have said to Pettifer if I'd been able to reply.

'What about a canapé? Are you hungry?' My companion was mainly ignoring me in favour of talking to his friends, but every now and then he remembered his manners.

'I'm fine, thank you.' I smiled at him, and then at the waitress who was offering me a platter of tiny vol-au-vents. Her eyes went wide and I recognised her with a start. Bianca Drummond, kitted out in the black dress and polished make-up of the Delahayes girl. It shouldn't have surprised me that she'd followed the same trail to the office in Victoria, but it did. I could cheerfully have strangled her, and then moved on to Edina Gould, who hadn't thought to mention that Bianca would be joining us too.

'Actually, no. I will take one.' I covered for both of us, in case anyone had noticed anything strange, but my companion had already returned to his conversation.

'What are you doing here?' she demanded under cover of the noise around us.

'I could ask you the same thing,' The canapé was a horrible, squelching thing and now that I was holding it I really didn't want to eat it.

The dimples flashed in Bianca's cheeks. 'They're disgusting. Here, put it back.'

I dropped it on her platter. 'How did you talk Edina into letting you do this?'

'Promised I wouldn't mention her in my story. You?'

'Threatened her, basically.'

She laughed, and moved away from me before I could ask her what she was planning and the crowd instantly closed around her. I looked past her, trying to spot Georgia so I could alert her, but there was no sign of her. *Typical.*

'Did someone recognise you?' Derwent sounded tense.

'Hold on.' I detached myself from the man beside me. 'I need to pop to the ladies.'

'Don't be too long – we'll be sitting down in a tick.'

'I'll be quick,' I promised, and slid away from him.

'Where are you going?' Derwent demanded. 'Don't wander around. I don't want you disappearing too.'

I reached the edge of the room, feeling like a swimmer clambering out of a crowded pool. Bianca had disappeared. I stepped out into the hall, pretending to look through my bag.

'Are you all right, madam? Have you lost something?' It was the tall, granite-faced man I'd seen when I interviewed Sir Marcus Gley – Carl Hooper, the head of security. I felt a thud of alarm as he crossed the black-and-white tiled floor and took my elbow, but there was no recognition on his stern face. 'What are you looking for?'

'My lipstick – it'll be in here somewhere – and the ladies room, please.' I kept my head down, still fossicking in my bag. I didn't want anything to jog his memory and I thought my usual voice might remind him we'd met before, so I had switched to a gentle, rural Irish accent. I had worked hard at school to shed the influence of my parents' soft voices – the 'r' that most English accents didn't pronounce, the hushed consonants, the longer vowel sounds, the very rhythm of their speech – and it was nice to let it seep back. Edina had agreed, reluctantly, that sometimes they did have Irish girls and that they were quite popular with the members, so I could be Áine O'Driscoll for the night.

'I'll take you to the ladies.'

'Oh, there's no need. Directions will do me fine.'

'I love it when you talk Irish,' Pettifer said reverently in my ear, and I cheered silently as he gave a yelp of pain. 'No need for that, Josh.'

Two men came out of the room behind us, their voices raised, drunkenness turning to the faintest hint of aggression. Hooper's head snapped up and I saw the watchfulness that was habitual to people whose job involved stopping trouble before it started. He let go of my elbow, which ached as if it might bruise.

'Up the stairs, second door on your left. Don't be too long. Dinner starts on time and you mustn't be late.' He walked away, his attention still absorbed by the men he'd noticed. As I ran up the stairs I heard his clipped, slightly metallic voice. 'Gentlemen, are you enjoying your evening?'

I was in the Chiron Club for two reasons: to see what they got up to behind closed doors, and to look for anything that might connect the place to Paige Hargreaves. It did occur to me that I might take the opportunity to have a quick look around – hadn't Sir Marcus said there were offices upstairs? – but as I turned the corner of the stairs, I saw a man sitting on a chair on the landing. He was wearing a grey suit, like Hooper, and he had the muscle and general demeanour of a prize bull as he got to his feet.

'What, miss?'

'Ladies room.'

He was blocking the entire hallway behind him. One massive hand gestured to his left. 'Please. This way.'

Meekly, I went where he had pointed. It was a tiny bathroom with a single cubicle and a basin the size of a teaspoon. Luckily for me, it was deserted.

'Right, can you let Georgia know that Bianca Drummond is here?' I said, keeping my voice low in case the man outside was listening. I couldn't talk to Georgia via my mic; they would have to relay the message. 'She's one of the other waitresses. Georgia knows her, so she might have recognised her already.'

'Got it,' Pettifer said. 'What's she doing there?'

'Same as us, presumably,' Liv said.

201

'I'd say so, but I don't want her to get in our way. Or get hurt, if it comes to that. I can't really talk to her in public again so Georgia will have to do it.'

'How's it going?' Derwent asked. 'Any sign of Ash?'

'No.' I said it reluctantly. In a team meeting before we'd left, it was Derwent who had pointed out, almost as if he wanted to prove he was able to be objective, that Luke Gibson was the only person who had mentioned Ash to us – that sending us on a wild goose chase looking for him might suit Luke very well indeed. I really didn't want to find out that Luke had lied to us. 'No sign of Ash or anything suspicious so far. The security staff are everywhere. Anyone in a grey suit is staff, and most of them seem to be muscle. Can you run a guy called Carl Hooper through the box? He's their head guy – he's the one I was talking to in the hall. Something about him feels off.'

'Consider it done,' Liv said. 'You'd better hurry up. They're starting to sit down.'

I reapplied my lipstick and sighed. 'I wish I'd brought my pepper spray.'

'If they get too handsy, stab them with a fork,' Derwent said.

I'd assumed the gathering would become more sedate when we sat down for dinner, but I was mistaken. I had found my way to a table of younger members, thinking that they were more likely to be able to tell me about Ash. They were already drunk, shouting in each other's ears, eyeing the women in the room with predatory intent. There were four women at the table and eight men, and I spent the first course trying to get the men on either side of me to stop groping me under the tablecloth. The one on my left was so drunk he could barely sit upright, but the man on the other side, Harry, was alert enough. I set out to charm him, and by the time the waitresses had delivered our main course plates, he was staring into my eyes.

'So,' I purred eventually, 'I have a friend who told me his friend was a member of this club. Ash, I think he said his name was?'

'Ash? I don't know him.' Because he had been brought up to be polite and helpful, Harry turned and nudged the guy next to him. 'Do you know a bloke called Ash?'

The question went around the table until it reached a slight, fair-haired man on the other side of the table from me. 'Yah,' he called. 'I know him. He's here tonight.'

'But I was looking for his name on the seating plan and I didn't see it,' I said, blinking as if I was completely befuddled.

'It's a nickname. His real name is Peter Ashington. Nice guy. We worked together for a while.'

'Peter Ashington,' I repeated for the benefit of the listeners in the van. *So he exists.* 'And where's he sitting?'

'Why are you talking about him? Talk to me,' Harry whispered wetly into my ear, and I giggled.

'In a second.'

'Now.' He leaned over and kissed my neck an inch under my ear, open-mouthed. It tickled at first; then I felt a sharp pain as his teeth nipped my skin. I cried out.

'What happened? Are you OK?' Derwent's voice was urgent, and I tried to laugh.

'You can't lean over and bite me! Not without buying me dinner first.'

'Fucking hell.' Derwent sounded as if he was on the verge of abandoning the surveillance van to deal with Harry.

'She's fine,' Liv said.

'Sorry, sorry.' Harry winked at me as he sloshed some more wine into my glass. 'Couldn't resist it.'

A glance around the room told me that the mood had changed as the waitresses cleared away the main course. Girls were sitting on the men's laps, or kissing them openly at the table. One man had his hand inside the top of a very young, very scared-looking brunette on the other side of the room.

Another was walking out dragging a blonde girl who was stumbling, barely able to put one foot in front of the other. Here and there men had simply passed out, sleeping peacefully amid the debauchery. Sir Marcus Gley presided at an all-male table of older members who should have been better behaved, I thought, but even as I watched one of them hauled a girl into his lap and made her straddle him. Gley said something and a shout of laughter went up from them. A waitress leaned over so someone at our table could slide a twenty-pound note between her breasts. She laughed when he groped them as she straightened up. I wanted to ask the fair-haired man where Peter Ashington was, but as I looked over at him he was straightening up, glassy-eyed, rubbing his nose, and I thought I might wait for the cocaine buzz to fade. The man beside him called to Harry.

'Oi, Hazza. We should take her with us to the house.' He meant me.

'What house?' I asked, leaning my chin on my hand and blinking as if I was too drunk to concentrate.

'A very big house in the countryside. You'd like it. Brilliant place for parties.' Harry put his hand on my thigh and slid it upwards and I edged out of reach. 'There'll be more wine and we'll have some fun.'

'Will Peter be there?'

'Who?'

'Ash. Peter Ashington.'

The man on the other side of the table frowned at me. 'Wait a second. Where are you from?'

'Roscommon.'

'Where's that?'

'Southern Ireland,' Harry drawled.

'We generally just call it Ireland. Or the Republic of Ireland if you want to be formal about it,' I said, forgetting for a moment that I was supposed to be looking pretty and saying nothing, and Derwent laughed in my ear.

'You tell him. Why don't you throw in a quick chorus of "A Nation Once Again" while you're at it?'

Harry raised his eyebrows and looked across the table at the other man, who was shaking his head.

'I don't think so, mate. Too much trouble.' He looked up as a wiry twenty-something with dark curly hair passed by. 'Hey, Ash. This girl's asking about you.'

'Yeah?' He checked himself and turned, looking puzzled as he saw me and didn't recognise me. 'What is it?'

'Are you Peter Ashington?'

'That's me.'

I jumped out of my seat and hurried over to him, weaving as if I was drunkenly enthusiastic rather than closing in on my prey.

'We've got a friend in common. Roddy Asquith.'

His face went white and his eyes flared with panic. He backed away from me, turned, and ran for the door as if the hounds of hell were after him, instead of one very irritated police officer in a skirt that was far too short and heels that were really too high for a pursuit.

26

The evening had degenerated into the kind of chaos that meant a man racing out of the dining room into the Chiron Club's hall didn't attract all that much attention. It also meant, however, that Peter Ashington didn't have a clear run to the outside world. He smacked straight into a vast, enormously drunk man who bearhugged him while laughing uproariously. As he fought to get free, I caught up with him and managed to grab hold of a flailing arm.

'Wait. I need to talk to you.'

Fear lent him the strength he needed to swing the huge man around so he cannoned into me. I lost my grip on Ashington, knocked off balance. For a moment I thought I was going to fall, my heels finding no purchase on the highly polished marble floor as the big man roared, outraged. Ashington wriggled free like a salmon thrashing upstream, and slid towards the door.

Like the answer to a prayer, Georgia appeared on the other side of the hall and, for once, took in the situation at a glance. She dropped her tray and ran forward to intercept him.

'Stop!'

Ashington shoved her, sending her flying as he made for the door through a throng of smokers returning from the steps outside. She fell against the wall with a thud that made me wince. The smokers stared at her with bland curiosity, none of them making a move to help her. That was someone else's job, presumably.

'Get ready, he's running,' I said for the benefit of the surveillance team.

Liv's voice was calm and assured. 'We'd worked that out. We can see him on the steps. I think he's trying to decide which way to go. Josh and Chris are already in pursuit and all the local uniformed teams are coming to help. Oh – there he goes.'

'Which way?'

'He's heading towards Blackfriars Bridge.' She caught her breath. 'That was close. Nearly got hit by a taxi. He's fast.'

'Too fast for us. And too strong. And too drunk to know what's dangerous.' I was crossing the hall to check on Georgia, aware that two grey-suited men were converging on her from the stairs and the main door and worried that she might give herself – and me – away as undercover police officers before I was ready for that. She was still crumpled in a heap where she had fallen. Genuine concern sharpened my voice. 'Hey, Georgia? Are you all right?'

She stared at me with an unfocused gaze. 'M'fine.'

'I don't think you are.' I helped her to her feet and steadied her as she wobbled against me. 'I think she might have hit her head when she fell.'

I said it for Liv's benefit, but as if I was talking to the taller of the two grey-suited men.

'Hurts.' Georgia put a hand up to explore the back of her head and winced. 'There's a bump.'

'She'll be all right,' the first grey suit said coldly. 'Won't you, love.'

'I get Mr Hooper,' the second said.

'Get an ambulance,' I said. 'She needs an ambulance.'

'Stand by,' Liv said, and went silent.

207

I was glad she was calling an ambulance for Georgia, because the grey suits made no move to help and I really thought she needed to be checked over. She was swaying like a sapling in a high wind. I steered her to a chair and sat her down. She had gone very pale and her lips were blue-tinged.

'Are you feeling OK?'

'Going to be sick,' she mumbled.

I grabbed an ice bucket from a nearby table and she put her face in it, groaning. I looked around for someone else to help her and came up with precisely no one I would trust. The two grey suits were standing in front of us, blocking us from the view of the members but otherwise not making any effort to help. Everyone else in the hall was drunk, or high, or both, and there was no sign of anyone from Delahayes. The members seemed to be very good at ignoring anything that didn't look as if it might lead to a good time. It wasn't that they weren't interested in what was happening to Georgia – they simply couldn't bring themselves to see it.

In the absence of anyone else, I knew I should stay with her, but I was desperate to find out if they'd caught up with Ashington yet. Only a minute or two had passed since he ran through the doors. If he disappeared – that had been our one chance to take him unawares . . . I couldn't stand not knowing. Besides, I wasn't achieving anything by standing beside her. 'Look, stay there, will you?'

'Mmmph,' came from the depths of the bucket, and I hurried outside to see how the chase was going. It wasn't yet dark, the sky a luminous blue that was still streaked with red and gold from what had been a glorious sunset at the end of a sunny day. The light was good enough and my vantage point was high enough for me to be able to see Peter Ashington racing across the bridge, almost at the other side, a trail of pursuers behind him. I shaded my eyes, confirming that the person behind Ashington was Derwent, who was running as if he had something to prove. Pettifer had dropped out of the race already but there were two uniformed officers flying after Derwent, losing ground with every stride. They would have been hampered by heavy equipment belts and thick-soled boots, whereas he was in trainers and jeans. His stab vest wouldn't be helping, I thought with a twinge of anxiety: they were so tight they constricted your breathing when you were exerting yourself, and they were heavy, and hot, and generally the last thing you wanted to be wearing in a foot pursuit on a warm evening. He was gaining on Ashington, though, and even as I watched he made a grab for him. Ashington evaded him with a dodge that had to have been pure instinct. From my vantage point I could see that two other uniformed officers had set off from the other side of Blackfriars Bridge and were heading towards them, so someone was going to catch him eventually. Ashington noticed them a split second after I did, and it unsettled him enough to slow him as he tried to work out his options, none of which were good: jumping into the river over the low parapet, hurdling the cycle lane and the anti-terror concrete barriers to cross the fast-moving traffic that was speeding across the bridge, or letting himself be caught by the police who were closing in on him. Ruthlessly, sensing weakness, Derwent put in an extra effort, and this time when he pounced Ashington went down.

'He got him,' I said, excitement and relief fizzing through my blood, and Liv cheered.

'Ambulance is two minutes out. Is Georgia OK?'

'She wasn't the last time I saw her. I think she was being sick.'

'And you left her?' There was a quizzical note in Liv's voice and I winced, knowing that it wasn't really acceptable to abandon a colleague – even one you didn't like particularly – just because you wanted to see what was going on.

'I'll go and check on her now.'

'I think you should.' Definite disapproval. The adrenalin of the chase ebbed away and I trudged inside, thoroughly ashamed of myself, to find Carl Hooper bending over Georgia, and Bianca Drummond crouching by her side.

'It's fine.' Georgia tipped her head back and looked up at me sleepily. 'Maeve. Tell'm.'

'She hit her head.' I said.

'She probably just needs to lie down for a while,' Hooper said dismissively.

'I've called an ambulance for her.'

Hooper rounded on me, irritated. 'Was that really necessary?'

'I think so.'

He turned to another grey suit who was standing behind him. 'Get rid of the ambulance.'

'She needs to be checked over,' I protested. 'She's been throwing up and she's confused. She has concussion at the very least.'

'We'll get a taxi to take her to the nearest A&E.' He glanced at me. 'You can go with her if you're so concerned.'

'Absolutely not. She shouldn't be moved until she's been assessed.'

He gave me a look full of cold loathing, which I returned with enough force that he actually gave in. 'Then tell the ambulance crew to go to the rear of the building. We can't have an emergency vehicle parked outside. The members won't like it.'

'You can't make her walk through the building,' Bianca protested. 'She's hurt.'

'We can arrange for someone to help her.' He looked around for another grey suit as if he could summon one up by sheer force of will.

'You won't be moving her anywhere,' I snapped. 'She's going to wait here to be assessed by paramedics and they will decide when and where she goes. And if you don't like emergency vehicles being parked outside, I have some bad news for you.

I'm Detective Sergeant Maeve Kerrigan, Georgia here is an undercover officer, and we are very far from finished with the club this evening. Based on what I've seen, we have enough concerns about illegal activity on the premises to get a warrant to search the club.'

Hooper stared at me for a moment, recognising me at last. He mumbled something, stepping backwards like a cat that had stepped in something unfortunate.

'Carl, what's going on? What's all this about?' Sir Marcus came trotting across the hall, his face red with fury. 'This isn't acceptable at all. Can't you clear this away?'

'Sir Marcus . . .' Carl croaked.

'What's wrong with her?' He eyed Georgia coldly. 'Get her out of here.'

'Not now, Sir Marcus. The police are here. And an ambulance.' Hooper gestured weakly as two green-uniformed paramedics bowled in through the front door and Gley caught his breath.

'Hello, how are you, darling? What's your name, my love?' One of the paramedics bent over Georgia, while the other one turned to me.

'What happened?'

'She banged her head on the wall a couple of minutes ago. She's been sick and she seems a bit confused.'

She nodded, then turned to help her colleague. I might have had reservations about Georgia's professionalism and indeed her personality, but it was a relief to see her being cared for properly. I hadn't realised how worried I was for her until they started to assess her.

While I was distracted with the paramedics, Sir Marcus had melted away like snow. I nudged Bianca. 'I want to check what's happening outside. Could you stay here until I come back?'

'Of course.'

I paused before I left, looking at Hooper. I had no reason

to arrest him, and I sensed that he would know that. I settled for warning him, 'Don't go anywhere. We'll need to talk to you.'

'Of course.' He made a stiff little bow. 'I wouldn't dream of leaving.'

Outside, I saw a small procession had made it back to our side of the bridge, moving far more slowly on the return journey. They all looked exhausted. Derwent was holding on to a handcuffed Peter Ashington, whose head was hanging down so low it was bouncing on his chest. His dinner jacket had come off one shoulder and his trousers were sliding down his hips. I came down the steps and walked over to the surveillance van, where Liv was standing with Pettifer. She was holding a bottle of water that was fogged with condensation.

'The van is on its way.' She meant the transport van that would take Ashington to custody. 'And indeed here it is. What a beautiful sight.'

It was barrelling towards us, siren wailing. Liv waved to flag it down. I glanced over my shoulder at the windows of the Chiron Club, where some members were staring out with undisguised horror at the scene that was unfolding on the Embankment. More faces began to appear behind them, intoxication evaporating into confusion and wariness. Police meant publicity, which meant public scrutiny, which could only be a bad thing when you thrived on secrecy.

The van pulled in right in front of us, and the uniformed officers escorting Derwent stepped out to stop the traffic so he could cross with Ashington. His arrest, his prisoner. Scowling, Derwent shoved Ashington off the pavement and manhandled him across the road. Then, at last, he gave him over to the two largest response officers who bundled him into the van with brisk efficiency. We wouldn't be able to interview him until he had sobered up – and doubtless lawyered up if he took the same approach as the other Chiron Club members I'd interviewed.

'Well done.' Liv threw Derwent the bottle of water which he caught with a nod of thanks.

I eyed him, noting the way his chest was heaving under his stab vest and the sweat that glistened on his skin and darkened his hair. 'You look as if you need to take off some clothes.'

He paused in the act of taking the cap off the bottle and looked me up and down, slowly, insolently, taking in every last detail. 'Yeah. Yours.'

There was a silence that seemed to last far too long while I realised what he'd said, before the shout of laughter went up from Pettifer and the officers who were standing around. I'd offered him the opportunity on a plate, and of course he'd taken it. I knew I was blushing, and couldn't do anything about that, so I settled for shaking my head at him as he drank his water.

'I literally never learn.'

He gave a huff of amusement that sent bubbles rushing through the bottle. When he stopped for a breather, he said, 'It's what keeps me going.'

'Happy to help.'

He grinned at me, the lines lengthening around his eyes, up to his old tricks and unrepentant about it. I turned away to find Liv had moved off to the rear of our van. I caught up with her, concerned in case the stress was getting to her.

'Are you feeling OK?'

'I mean, are *you*?' She checked she was out of sight, then fanned herself theatrically. 'I don't know if it's the hormones or what, but that almost turned me heterosexual for a moment.'

I laughed. 'Steady.'

'Don't worry, it's worn off now.' Her face was alight with amusement and curiosity. 'He's quite something when he turns it on, isn't he?'

'I'm used to it. Anyway, it was just a joke.'

'Uh-huh.' Liv put as much doubt into those two syllables as a QC might fit into a whole defence speech.

'Oh, come on. He wasn't flirting with me. That was designed to put me in my place.'

'It sounded a lot like flirting to me.'

'You can't take it seriously.'

'I wouldn't,' Liv said, 'but maybe you should.'

'What's that supposed to mean?'

She raised her eyebrows at me, and gathered her belongings from the van. 'We've got work to do.'

'That's exactly what I was about to say.' I pulled a sweatshirt on over my ridiculous dress, and then followed her up the steps into the club.

27

The paramedics were gathering up their equipment as we came into the hall. I looked down at Georgia. She still seemed utterly dazed.

'How's she doing?' I asked.

'We're going to take her to Casualty and get her checked out properly,' one of the paramedics said and I nodded, relieved.

'There's no need.' Georgia waved a hand. 'Don't need to go anywhere.'

'You got a hell of a knock. Better safe than sorry.' I looked around. 'Where's Bianca? She was here a few minutes ago.'

'I – I don't know. I didn't see her go.' Georgia winced as she turned her head. 'I thought she was standing right there. I'm sure she was.'

'What's up?' Derwent had arrived behind me.

'Bianca Drummond has disappeared.' I was looking around, hoping to spot her. 'She was here a minute ago. She was standing beside—' I broke off. 'Damn it.'

'What's wrong?' Liv asked.

'Where's Carl Hooper?' I stalked over to the enormous grey-suited man who had been stationed at the top of the stairs. He was coming down slowly, looking wary. 'Where's your boss?'

'No idea.' He shrugged, his shoulders almost swallowing his head. 'I called him on the radio and he didn't answer.'

Shit. 'He said something about a door at the rear of the building?'

'Yes. Downstairs. Past the kitchen.'

Derwent was already moving in the direction he'd indicated. 'Leave that to me. Liv, get the warrant sorted out. And someone grab the officers from outside. We're going to need them to search the place properly.'

Liv was leaning forward so she could see into the dining room. Whatever she saw made her eyes widen. 'We'll need to clear this place out too.'

I turned to the squat grey-suited man. 'Did you hear that? You can tell your colleagues the party's over.'

Once we had our warrant, we were allowed to roam the entire building. It didn't take long to confirm my worst fears: Bianca Drummond had disappeared and so had Carl Hooper. I took the details of all the staff who were still in the building: chefs, waitresses, foreign kitchen hands who were palpably terrified to come in contact with officialdom, the grey-suited security staff and the porters. None of them had seen Bianca leave, they assured me, not meeting my eyes. None of them had seen *anything*.

Derwent found me in the staff changing room.

'What have you got there?'

'Bianca's jacket and bag.' I showed him what was inside the bag. 'House keys, phone, money, cards. She wouldn't have left this by choice.'

'You think something happened to her.'

'I do.' I shoved the jacket and bag into an evidence bag and wrote a label for it, my writing an edgy scrawl. 'I should never have left her. Carl Hooper must have realised who she was. Or maybe she saw something she shouldn't have. I should have arrested Hooper the minute I identified myself.'

216

'For what? He hadn't done anything wrong then.' He was watching me closely, his arms folded.

'If it comes to that, we don't even know he's done anything wrong now. But I have a bad feeling about him.'

'I've just been talking to Pettifer,' Derwent said slowly, reluctantly, as if he didn't want to be the one to break the news. 'He's got the background information on Hooper. Multiple convictions for violent behaviour.'

I swallowed hard. 'So a little light kidnapping would fit in very nicely.'

'You're overreacting.'

I glowered at him. 'You don't know that. I hope I am. But it wouldn't be the first time a woman connected with the Chiron Club disappeared into thin air, and nothing good happened to the others.'

Derwent would never admit I was right, but he did abandon the argument. 'There's nothing else here. Come on.'

I followed him into the deserted kitchen. Trays of glossy petits fours lay where the staff had abandoned them, unserved because we had brought the evening to an end early. Derwent pulled a clean linen napkin off a stack in the corner, unfolded it with a brisk shake, then opened a massive freezer and disappeared inside it.

'What are you doing?'

He emerged with a handful of ice on the napkin which he bundled up and pressed against my neck. 'Hold it there. It'll help with the bruising.'

I put my hand up cautiously to keep the ice in place. 'Does it look bad?'

'It's a proper bite.' He shook his head. 'It's not really your style. Keep that on there for a few minutes.'

I knew I should be grateful to him for thinking of it, but I didn't care about my neck at that moment. What was shredding my nerves was the thought of Bianca being scared. Worse was the thought of her being silenced permanently. Why would

Hooper take her away unless it was to make sure she couldn't tell me what she knew?

'Where's Liv?'

'Collecting the drugs she found under the tables in the dining room.' Derwent grinned. 'Half of London's coke supply is all over the carpet upstairs. It looks like a blizzard hit. The members did not want to be caught in possession of illegal substances.'

'What a shame for them.'

'I've got a list of all the members who attended this evening. We can interview them when they've sobered up and find out if anyone saw Bianca leave.'

'They won't have seen anything.'

'Pettifer is reviewing the club's CCTV.'

'That might be more helpful,' I allowed.

'If she was wearing a recording device it might have been transmitting to her phone. Let's fast-track it and see if the tech guys can download anything useful for us.'

'That's a good idea.'

'It's not your fault. She came here because she wanted to play investigative journalist. You tried to warn her.'

'I'm well aware of that.'

Derwent raised his eyebrows. 'OK. I'm only pointing it out.'

'I'd better get a move on.' I tipped the ice into the nearest sink with a clatter, and carried my evidence bag out to hand it over to someone who could make Bianca's phone talk to us.

The last place we searched was the Chiron Club's administrative offices, housed in three poky rooms right at the top of the building. I sat on the floor, my torture-device heels next to me, and worked through the contents of a filing cabinet while Derwent and Pettifer ransacked the desks and drawers and Liv yawned through correspondence. It was punishingly late, but I didn't want to leave until we had gleaned every last detail from the files. The only advantage we had was surprise. I hoped that meant we would find something useful, but so far we had found nothing that helped with any part of the investigation. Even the CCTV had been useless, the camera covering the back door unaccountably failing to record for the period where Bianca had disappeared. We would try to get something from cameras on the streets around the club, but for the time being we were groping in the dark.

'Anyone got anything good?' Derwent asked at last.

'Not me. Nothing but complaints about the food and the fixtures and the conversation at the members' table during weekday lunches.' Liv waved a handwritten letter at us. 'This one is about the paper in the lavatories. It goes on for *pages*. I would honestly go mad if I had to deal with these people all the time. The administrators are saints.'

'What about you?' I asked.

'I found the accounts.' Derwent tipped open a giant ledger that looked as if it had been used for decades, the used pages puckered and yellowed. 'The membership fees seem to vary a lot.'

'Everyone pays according to what they can afford. That's what Sir Marcus told me.'

'Most people can afford a lot.'

'Have you found expenses? Petty cash?'

'Yeah, there's another ledger for that.' Pettifer brandished it.

'Can you look up the twenty-second of July two years ago?'

He started flipping through the pages. 'What am I looking for?'

'A payment in cash. Several thousand pounds.'

He ran his finger down the page. 'Four thousand, eight hundred quid?'

'That's the money they gave Antoinette as a pay-off to stop her from reporting her rape.'

'It's got "repaid in full x 2" written beside it.'

'Then I guess they passed the cost on to the guys who did

219

it. That proves they knew all about the rape and they knew who to ask for the money.'

'Only if a court is prepared to believe Antoinette's story,' Derwent pointed out. 'They can say that money was paying another debt. Gambling or something. A bar bill, even. There's nothing to say it was a rape pay-off.'

'Yeah, I can't imagine why they didn't write it down.' I got up, tugging my skirt down. 'Let me have a look for a second.'

Pettifer turned the ledger around and I read the next few entries, frowning.

'Problem?' Derwent asked.

'What do you think PPCS is?'

'No idea. Why?'

'It's listed here as a payee the weekend after that party when Antoinette said she was raped and Iliana Ivanova disappeared. Two payments of cash, but it doesn't say how much – there's just a symbol. And the money was never repaid. This bill was covered by the Club, not an individual member.'

Derwent considered it. 'What do you think it was?'

'I don't know but the admin staff are meticulous about noting how much cash they spend. It's weird that they won't even write down the amount for this. Who gets paid secret money in cash? Apart from contract killers and drug dealers?'

'There's a safe in the other room,' Liv said from the doorway. 'I can't open it but they could have quite a bit of cash on the premises.'

'We'll have to get one of the administrators to open it for us in the morning.' I checked my watch. 'In about four hours.'

'PPCS,' Derwent said, more or less to himself, and pulled out a drawer in the desk. He pawed through the pen tray and found a white biro with blue writing. He turned it to show us. 'PPCS. Contract killers don't usually bother with promotional stationery.'

'Can I have a look?' Beside the initials was a complicated

line-drawing logo of a cat, dog and horse. I stared at it, trying to remember if I'd seen it before.

'Could it be veterinary supplies? They could be sourcing their drugs through a crooked rep. Horse tranquilliser is a lot of fun.' We all turned to look at Liv, who shrugged. 'So I've heard, anyway.'

I did a quick internet search on my phone and scrolled through the results. 'That is a surprisingly popular acronym.'

'Search PPCS and animals,' Liv suggested.

'Postoperative pulmonary complications in dogs.' I put my phone down with a sigh. 'Not much help.'

'We can look them up properly.' Pettifer yawned massively. 'Tomorrow, maybe.'

'Bored?' I asked with an edge in my voice.

'Tired.' He pointed at Liv. 'And so is she. We're all tired.'

'Then maybe you should all go home.'

'What about you?' Derwent was throwing the white pen up in the air and catching it, apparently absorbed.

'I've got to finish going through the filing cabinet.'

'You're not going to find Bianca Drummond in there.'

I *was* tired, I thought, or I wouldn't want to cry. I rubbed my eyes with the heels of my hands. They came away black and I stared at them in horror. 'Oh God. Have I given myself panda eyes?'

Derwent got up and shook out an evidence bag.

'Come on. We're not the only people who are looking for Bianca and Carl Hooper. A briefing has gone out to all the Met response teams. His car will ping any ANPR cameras it passes. If Bianca is out there, someone will find her.'

I nodded, knowing he was right.

'Let's take as much of this paperwork as we can carry.' Derwent held out the bag for Pettifer to drop his ledger into it. 'I'll get an officer to stay here until we come back so they can't clear the place out. We can have a bit of a rest while we're waiting for analysis of the phone and the CCTV images we've requested. The most important thing is finding Bianca, but we've gone as far as we can here. Time for a break.'

'Maybe we could get something to eat,' Liv suggested.

'Good idea.' He picked up my shoes and handed them to me. 'And if you're very good, Kerrigan, we can stop on the way to the office and get you some bamboo.'

28

At the office I let the others get started on the food. I went to the locker room instead and had a shower, rinsing away the sticky residue the Chiron Club seemed to have left on my skin. Scrubbing off the last of the eye make-up was satisfying, but not as much of a relief as it was to pull on jeans and a thin grey jumper instead of the tiny dress. All the bones in my feet were complaining from being forced into high heels and my neck throbbed where Harry had bitten it. There was something dead in my eyes, something missing that I didn't want to think about or name. I put on trainers, tidied my hair and smudged on enough make-up to look presentable, clamped a composed expression to my face like a mask and went back to the others.

'Now you look more like yourself,' Liv said through a mouthful of burger as I walked in.

I waved the dress I was carrying at her. 'You didn't like this either?'

She smiled, cheek bulging, and managed a muffled, 'I think everyone liked it.'

'We did,' Pettifer said earnestly. 'We liked it a lot.'

Liv finally swallowed her food. 'You should take it home. Try it on for Seth.'

I dropped it into a bag along with the heels and shoved the lot under my desk. 'Ugh. No. He would not be pleased.'

'Why not? Is he blind?'

'He doesn't like me to dress like that.' I went over to inspect what was left from the take-away we'd picked up: a bag of chips, still just about warm, crusted with salt and soggy with vinegar, absolutely what I wanted to eat. I sat on the edge of my desk and took out a chip. 'He would definitely have wanted me to be the waitress instead of Georgia. And I think Georgia might have preferred that too, given what happened to her.'

'What did happen?' Pettifer asked. 'I still don't know how she managed to get herself hurt.'

'She was trying to stop Peter Ashington from getting away and he knocked her over.' I shrugged. 'It was bad luck. Not her fault.'

'I called the hospital.' At the sound of Derwent's voice I jumped; I hadn't realised he was there. 'She's fine. They're keeping her in for another few hours to make sure she doesn't have any issues, but they don't think there's anything to worry about.'

'That's good.'

'Do you want the bad news?'

My stomach clenched. I put the bag of chips down.

'The tech guys say Bianca's phone was set to record but it didn't work. They haven't been able to recover anything usable. They think she was out of range of the phone so it couldn't pick up whatever she transmitted.'

'She may not have realised she was going to have to leave it downstairs by the kitchen.' I chewed my lip. 'That's disappointing. Anything on the CCTV from the local area?'

'On its way,' Liv covered her mouth as she yawned. 'As soon as it comes in, I'll get started on it.'

'Where does that leave us? What else can we do?'

'There's still Ashington to interview,' Pettifer pointed out.

'They breathalysed him when he was arrested and he blew

over a hundred. We're not going to be able to interview him for a few hours,' Derwent said, and I felt my shoulders drop with disappointment and frustration.

'Can we get a search warrant for his house?'

'I've already done the paperwork.' He held it up. 'Let's go and wake up a magistrate.'

Peter Ashington lived alone, in a luxury new-build flat marooned in the hinterland of King's Cross Station. It was a little too far away from the Granary Square development that had brought restaurants and shops to what had been one of the grittier parts of London, but it wasn't quite in Islington. Vast banners hung on the sides of the building proclaiming that the complex was 70 per cent sold, though one-bedroom flats were still available from the low, low price of £670,000.

The developers had aimed for a high-end look but the white finish of the building was already dingy, while the landscaped grounds were too newly planted to look attractive. The security guard was a languid man from West Africa, who nodded at our search warrant as if that kind of thing happened all the time. He found a master key for us and directed us to the fifth floor. The lift was tiny and mirror-lined. I caught a glimpse of my reflection and pulled my hair forward to hide the bruise on my neck. The space was so small, Derwent's shoulder brushed mine.

'Are you all right?'

'Why do you ask?'

He shrugged. 'Just checking. You look tired. You could have stayed at the office and had a nap.'

'I couldn't. Not with Bianca missing. I'd rather be out doing something.'

'I know that feeling.'

The lift doors slid open on a narrow, grey-carpeted hallway.

'He's in flat 53.' I pointed. 'That one.'

Derwent knocked before unlocking the door. He went in

first, wary in case anyone was waiting for us. It didn't take long to search the place, which was surprisingly poky. Floor-to-ceiling windows at the end of the living room gave him an incredible view towards the City, and that had to have been the main selling-point for the flat. An L-shaped sofa took up most of the living room. The kitchen was black and white and seemed almost unused: no dishes in the sink, no crumbs on the worktop. I checked the fridge.

'Champagne, beer, vodka in the freezer. Otherwise nothing.'

'Not a cook, then.' Derwent was sorting through a pile of post that had been left on the small dining table.

'Maybe he eats out a lot.'

'Or he has a girlfriend and she feeds him.' He pulled out a letter from a bank and whistled. 'Unauthorised overdraft. Naughty Peter.'

'How can he afford membership fees at the Chiron Club if he's in the red?'

'Good question.'

I opened a large cupboard in the hall. 'Suitcases, skis, about a hundred pairs of trainers.'

'For running or fashion?'

'Running.' A handful of medals hung by their ribbons from a hook inside the door and I jangled them. 'Marathons.'

Derwent loomed behind me. 'Has he done London?'

'Twice. Berlin, Vienna, Chicago, Sydney . . .' I craned my neck to see. 'What's this one?'

'Marathon des Sables.' Derwent shook his head in grudging admiration. 'Even I'm not mad enough for that. Six days in the desert, fifty-degree heat, two hundred and fifty-one kilometres. It costs a fortune to enter as well. He must be a proper runner.'

'But you still caught him.'

'I was just thinking that.' He stood up a little straighter, pleased with himself, and I wondered why I'd thought his ego needed any stroking.

'So as far as we can see he spends his time not eating, and running, and probably going to the gym. He doesn't have any photographs up of his family or friends or even himself. No books, no DVDs. Do you see a computer?'

'No.' Derwent moved to the kitchen and started opening drawers. 'He's got an iPad. It's locked. We can take it with us.'

I was taking down boxes from the top of the cupboard and opening them to find winter clothes, more running gear and ski stuff.

'There's nothing illegal here. I was expecting drugs at the very least. Why do you think he ran?'

'You scared him.'

'I did not!' I looked over my shoulder to see he was grinning. 'I mean, obviously I did, but I wasn't trying to frighten him. As soon as I mentioned Roddy Asquith he took off.'

'Maybe we're not the only ones who know Roddy was murdered.'

'And he thought I was threatening him?'

'It's possible. Or he was involved in setting up the fake accident. If you'd killed one of your friends, you'd be twitchy too.'

'Why would he kill Roddy?'

'If Roddy knew something that implicated him, Peter could have decided to shut him up.'

'Roddy gave a no-comment interview. He didn't even risk making a statement.'

'He started off doing what he was told. That probably wouldn't have lasted long once DS Kerrigan started working on him.'

'What's that supposed to mean?'

'You're persuasive. People tell you things they meant to keep secret.'

Derwent disappeared into the bedroom and I followed him, wondering if he was talking about Claire and how I'd found out about their son. But that had been luck, I thought, uneasily, not my investigative skill. The bedroom was tiny, just big enough for the bed, two bedside tables and a wall of fitted cupboards. He was already looking through the suits that were hanging up in one cupboard so I took the other, a mixture of open shelves and sliding wooden drawers that still smelled of cedar. Cashmere jumpers, pristine shirts, folded silk ties, serried ranks of socks.

'Maybe it's so characterless because he hasn't been here for long.'

'Or he spends all his time at work.'

'Or with the mythical girlfriend.' I pulled out the top drawer. 'Maybe not so mythical.'

'Oh?' Derwent peered around the door, instantly curious.

I held up a condom. 'A couple of these.'

'Only two? Amateur hour.'

'Luke had two boxes of them, which tells you something about his love life. At least he's careful.'

I'd said it without thinking, and by the time I'd finished talking I was all the way in the middle of the minefield, with no way back. Derwent's eyebrows twitched together, but all he said was, 'He has more sense than I did.'

'I don't want to think about it,' I said truthfully.

'You brought it up.'

'Well, I didn't mean to.' I looked at him, trying to judge his mood. It was too good an opportunity to pass up; we were hardly ever alone and I needed to know if he had forgiven me. 'Are you still angry with me?'

'Let's not talk about it.'

'That means yes.'

'What do you expect?' There was no answer to that. He disappeared again and I heard the sound of hangers scraping the rail as he slid them to one side, working through them.

I wavered. *Say something or say nothing.* Well, he was angry with me anyway. I had nothing to lose.

'I can't begin to imagine how you must feel, finding out you have a son you didn't know about.'

'I'm sure you can't.' I couldn't detect any encouragement to keep talking in his tone.

'What does Melissa think about it?'

He appeared around the door again. 'Stop, now.'

'What?'

'I'm not telling you how she feels. It's none of your business. It never was your business.'

I quailed. 'Sorry.' Common sense suggested I should stop talking about it. I was short on common sense at the best of times. 'Look, I worry about you. This is a big thing. You're a father.'

'I don't think it's going to change anything.'

'You don't?'

'I doubt he'll want to get to know me. Not after all this time.' A bleak look crossed his face. 'Melissa told me the best thing I could do is forget about him.'

'Oh.' I tried to keep my feelings out of my voice.

'He doesn't need anything from me and I have no right to ask anything from him.'

'Maybe he does need you.'

He shook his head; for someone who thought highly of himself he was being surprisingly negative.

'You can't just let him go. You have to try.'

'That would be selfish.'

'Why?'

'Because getting to know him would really be for my sake, not his.' His voice dropped. 'I always wanted a son. I never imagined it would happen like this.'

I couldn't find words to respond to him. His mouth tightened, as if he regretted saying so much, and he walked out. I heard noises from the bathroom: the lid of the cistern clanking and cupboard doors clattering.

I finished searching the wardrobe, my throat tight with

suppressed emotion. *Concentrate, Maeve.* Definitely *do not cry*. I couldn't even work out why I felt so upset on Derwent's behalf, or on my own. Everything had changed, and no matter what Melissa said, none of us could forget that.

The bedside table was empty too, aside from a charger for a phone – not a reader, I thought. I pulled the table away from the wall, almost as an afterthought, and stared blankly at the A4 envelope that was taped to the back of it.

Derwent appeared in the doorway as if I'd called him, all business. 'Nothing in the bathroom. What have you got?'

'Not sure yet.' I took some pictures, then detached the envelope from the bedside table. The envelope had been opened but someone had sealed it up again, wrapping the ragged ends of the envelope in so many layers of tape that it was stiff.

Derwent had opened out an evidence bag and laid it on the floor. I knelt beside it.

'Over here. Open the other end.' He handed me his penknife and I slit the closed end of the envelope carefully. I shook it and the contents slid out with a sigh, fanning themselves out as if I'd arranged them that way: five photographs printed on glossy paper. Derwent moved them around delicately with his gloved fingertips, putting them in order, and we looked at them in silence for a while.

'I think I can see why he ran,' I said at last.

Derwent straightened up. 'Look at it this way. At least we know what to talk to him about now.'

29

Jeremy Fallon had changed his tie and his suit but not his manner; his eyes still had all the warmth of the blue heart of an iceberg.

'Mr Fallon, so nice to see you again.'

'The pleasure is mine.' He squeezed my hand in both of his. I remained uncharmed. I had changed into a suit, worn with a shirt that had a high collar to hide the bruise on my neck, and it felt like armour. I introduced Derwent, who had been briefed by me outside the interview room about Fallon and his techniques. He shook hands with Fallon, then looked down at Peter Ashington, who was huddled in his chair, a slight figure in a paper boiler suit. One foot tapped constantly and he swallowed every couple of seconds, as if his mouth kept filling with saliva.

'All right, mate? You gave me a run for my money.'

Ashington glanced up at him and then returned to staring at the floor but his foot-tapping intensified.

'I do hope we can bring this to a satisfactory and speedy conclusion.' Fallon eased himself into his seat.

'That depends on how helpful your client is inclined to be,' I said. 'He's charged with a couple of very serious offences already.'

'I think we both know that assault is a very *variable* offence, Sergeant Kerrigan.'

'He gave a police officer concussion.'

Ashington roused himself. 'She didn't say she was a police officer. I didn't know.'

Georgia hadn't identified herself, I remembered. She had only told him to stop. 'It's still a serious assault. She spent the night in hospital.'

Fallon seemed taken aback. Ashington looked up at me, his eyes tortured under thick dark brows. 'It was an accident.'

'I saw what happened,' I said quietly, and left it at that while I started the tape running and began the interview formally.

We started by going through the events that had led to Georgia's injury, and Ashington stuck to his accident line stubbornly.

I leaned across the table. 'Even if it was an accident, why were you running away?'

'I don't know. I'd had a lot to drink.'

'When I mentioned Roddy Asquith, you ran. Why was that?'

'Don't know. I can't remember.'

Fallon flicked a look at him and I thought I read approval in it. *Don't tell them anything. Stall them. They can't do anything if you're vague.*

'You know Roddy's dead, don't you.' Derwent was deceptively relaxed beside me, like a tiger lying in the long grass before it starts the hunt in earnest.

'He crashed his car.'

'Not *his* car. He couldn't drive.'

'I didn't know that.'

'Well, you did.' I smiled at him, and Fallon, who was looking wary now. 'You used to drive Roddy around, didn't you?'

'I don't have a car.'

'No, and that's why you were insured on Luke Gibson's

car. You used to borrow it whenever Roddy needed to be driven somewhere.'

'Who told you that?'

'Luke did.'

Ashington widened his brown eyes, belatedly coming to the realisation that we knew more than he had anticipated. 'Uh, yeah. I mean, it was a while ago. I'd forgotten about it.'

'Something else you'd forgotten about,' Derwent said.

'Let's talk about the twenty-third of July two years ago.' I watched for a reaction from Ashington, and was disappointed. Fallon wrote himself a note and circled it with a savage slash of his biro.

'I – I don't know what happened on the twenty-third of July two years ago.' Ashington sounded baffled.

'It was one of those occasions when you borrowed Luke's car,' Derwent said. 'He was away on holidays, so you probably didn't even need to ask permission. This time you drove it into the countryside. To a place called Standen Fitzallen.'

If I'd thought Peter Ashington was pale before, I had a new standard for that. His face was entirely bloodless, his lips white. 'How – how do you know about that?'

'What were you doing there, Peter?'

'P-picking someone up.'

'Who?'

He shook his head, but it lacked conviction. 'No one I knew.'

'You drove to Standen Fitzallen for a stranger.'

'No. Roddy asked me to.'

'Was it Roddy Asquith you picked up?' I asked.

'No, he was with me—' Ashington stopped himself and took a deep breath. 'I drove there because Roddy asked me to. We picked someone up. I didn't know him. He slept on the back seat while I drove to London. I took him to Roddy's place, parked the car and left.'

'It was a Sunday, wasn't it?'

233

'Sunday afternoon.'

'Were you all right to drive?' Derwent asked.

'I was fine.'

'I suppose it was late enough by then. You must have had a hell of a hangover though.'

Alarm came off Ashington in waves. 'What do you mean?'

'You'd been out the night before at the Chiron Club. Big night, wasn't it? A special celebration?'

I clicked my fingers. 'A celebration of Sir Marcus Gley's presidency, wasn't it? They published a special little book about him to mark the occasion.'

'Yeah.' He shrugged. 'So what?'

'So you were there,' Derwent said. 'You and some friends.'

'Are you building up to charging my client with drink driving based on the notion that he might have had too much to drink two years ago?' Fallon chuckled. 'This really is a remarkable turn of events.'

I had the sense that he was playing for time on Ashington's behalf, giving him some breathing space to prepare for what was coming next. What I couldn't decide was whether Fallon knew what was in the envelope we had found in Ashington's bedroom. He was clearly employed by the Chiron Club. I wondered if he was a member himself. I would have to get Liv to check the members' register which we had removed from the club.

'Peter, you were in the club that night. Did you see anything illegal taking place?'

He blinked at me. 'Not really. I mean, a few people might have been using drugs. Not me. Some people. That does happen from time to time.'

You could see the hope dawning that what interested us might be the drugs after all. I ruined it for him with my next question.

'What about the women who were there? Did you see anything happen to any of them?'

He considered it, then shook his head, his face a polite blank. 'There were girls. Waitresses and so forth. But I didn't see anything happen.'

'That's strange.' Derwent opened the folder in front of him and pushed a photograph across the table. 'That's you, isn't it?'

The picture was of two young men standing in the hall of the Chiron Club. They wore black tie, their hands were in their pockets and they were deep in conversation. One faced the camera; the other had his back to it. The one facing the camera was clearly recognisable as a younger version of the man in front of me, his face rounded and childish.

Ashington reached out a trembling hand and drew the picture towards him.

'Where did you get this?'

'Same place we got the rest.' Derwent drew a second picture out and slid it across the table. 'That's you talking to Antoinette Breve.'

'Who?'

'She was working as a waitress that night,' I said. 'In this picture, she was asking you if you knew where the ladies' bathroom was.'

'In this one, you're pretending to show her.' Derwent produced the third image: the slight figure between two dark-suited men who were guiding her towards a door.

'That's not the ladies' bathroom, is it?' I said. 'That's a glorified coat cupboard. Why did you take her in there?'

'No. It wasn't me.' He shook his head.

'Is this you coming out?' Derwent showed him the fourth image. The other man's face was obscured with a black square, but Peter Ashington was clearly visible. He was laughing, and zipping up his fly.

'That's me, but that doesn't mean anything. I was getting something out of my coat and – and – those trousers were really annoying, and the zip kept sliding down all the time.'

'Here's Antoinette coming out. She doesn't look so happy, does she?' Her face was contorted, her mouth a rectangle as she sobbed. I pretended to be dispassionate as I looked from the photograph to Ashington but anger smouldered in the pit of my stomach. 'Her clothes are all over the place.'

'Antoinette says you and your buddy raped her.' Derwent leaned across the table. 'She's told us the whole story.'

'No. She was into it. She wanted us to do it like that.'

'She wanted you, two strangers who didn't even know her name, to hold her down and cover her head with a coat so she could barely breathe, and to rip her underwear off and rape her while she was working as a waitress, trying to save some money for her education.'

'I don't know about any of that. It wasn't *bad*.' Peter shook his head. 'The girls – that's what they're there for. They know what they're getting into. They're there to make more money and this is the kind of thing they do. You have a bit of fun, you pay them, everyone's happy.'

'She was paid,' Fallon said. 'Did she tell you?'

So the lawyer knew exactly who she was, and what had happened to her. I felt the heat in my face, but I held on to my composure. 'She told me the whole story, even down to the amount of money she was given as a bribe to stay silent.'

'Let me guess. It didn't go as far as she thought it would and she's looking for a further payment.' Fallon flicked his fingers. 'This is a waste of our time. And yours. I know you're required to take these complaints seriously but this would never stand up in court. A jury would never believe her.'

'Who sent you these pictures?' Derwent asked Ashington. 'You left them in the same envelope they came in, which was useful for us. They were addressed to you at your old address. We found them hidden carefully in your current flat so we know you saw them.'

'I – I don't know who sent them.'

'The postmark tells us they were sent the Friday after these events took place.'

He shrugged. 'So?'

'So we had a good look at them,' I said. 'Before we talked to you about them, we wanted to know as much as we could about the pictures and who took them and who sent them to you and why.'

'These are copies,' Derwent said. 'We've kept the originals. But this is a photograph of the reverse of one of them. See this mobile telephone number? It's faint. Written in pencil.'

'So?'

'We rang the number,' I said. 'Someone answered.'

'How very thrilling for you,' Fallon snapped.

'It was quite exciting, yes. Especially when we realised it was the police constable who was on duty in the members' offices at the Chiron Club, answering a mobile telephone that was in one of the file drawers.'

It was Fallon's turn to look deeply uncomfortable. Beside him, Ashington had dropped his head to his chest. When he raised it, I saw he was laughing silently.

'Is this funny?'

'Yes. Yes, it is.' He shot his solicitor a look of pure dislike. 'You're screwed now. You've been holding this over me for long enough. I still don't think I did anything wrong – I mean, I was told to behave that way. I was *promised* it was all right. They said she'd put up a fight for show but she was in on it all along.' He looked from me to Derwent. 'If I didn't know, it doesn't count, right?'

'It counts.' Derwent's face was grim.

'She took the money.'

'You still raped her.'

'Debatable. She was acting, whatever she says now. It's my word against hers and she has to explain the money she took.'

He was right, and we all knew it. The chances of getting him prosecuted for rape were tiny. I knew there was no chance

237

a jury would believe Antoinette, with her accent and her ambition, when Ashington had nice manners and good looks and wouldn't have *needed* to rape anyone. His lawyers would destroy the case – and Antoinette – and think they'd done a good job.

'If you weren't worried about being prosecuted, why did you keep the photos?' I asked.

Ashington glanced at Fallon. 'Shall I tell them everything, Jez?'

Fallon's head seemed to have inflated. 'I don't think I can represent you any more. I advise you to say nothing else until you have arranged other representation.'

'What do they have on you, Mr Fallon?' Ashington laughed. 'It must be good.'

Fallon stood up, mumbled something and made for the door.

Ashington looked at us. 'This is what they do. They create a situation where you have to be grateful to them, and then you owe them. They buy your loyalty with your own blood. You have no choice about it.'

'There's always a choice,' I said.

'OK, yes. They loaded the gun, I pointed it at my own head.' He mimed shooting himself with his finger. 'I didn't know what I was doing. I didn't know what it would mean.'

'Why would they do this?' Derwent asked. 'What do they want? Money?'

'I really advise you to say nothing,' Fallon said again from the door. He was breathing heavily, his face glossy with sweat.

'It's not just money. For me it was access to my dad. Do you know who my dad is?'

I shook my head.

'Vince Ashington. He runs one of the top venture capital businesses in the UK. He's richer than you can imagine. He barely gives me any money. I mean, you've seen where I live. He would only buy me a shitty little one-bed flat. It's embarrassing. He wants me to make my own way in the world.'

'You're old enough to stand on your own two feet,' Derwent said.

Ashington laughed. 'Oh my God, you sound just like him.'

A commotion at the door was Fallon leaving the room. I explained his departure to the tape and asked if Ashington was happy to carry on without him.

'Might as well.'

'Does your father pay your membership fees at the Chiron Club?' I asked.

He nodded. 'But he's not a member. They tried to get him to join when he was at university himself but he said no. He's much, much cleverer than me.' Another laugh. 'I'm what happens when you marry a trophy wife who's as thick as two short planks and she gives her brains to your kids.'

'But he pays for you.'

'I can't afford the fees myself,' Ashington said. 'And I have to keep paying them.'

'After this?' I gestured at the pictures.

'That and . . . some other things.'

'Like what?'

'I think I've said enough.' He laughed again, his eyes bright: he was almost high on the reckless excitement of letting it all out. 'But put it this way – they've got me for life. And through me, they've got my dad. He can't face the idea of me being publicly humiliated. It would reflect badly on him. So he pays for my membership fees, and when they need a bit of invest-ment for a member's project, they get on the phone to him. He's put up millions for them. Tens of millions. And some of it worked out OK.'

'But some of it didn't,' I said.

'Yeah. Well, that's business. Sometimes everyone makes money, sometimes no one does.'

'Is this something they tried with you, or do they do it to everyone?' Derwent asked.

'Everyone, to some extent, for some reason or other. All of

us are in the same boat. They tricked us all.' Ashington ran his hands through his hair. 'The things they've done. The people they own. You wouldn't believe me if I told you. Politicians, judges, media bosses, billionaires. They've got them all.'

'What happened to Paige Hargreaves?'

'Who?' His face was blank.

'This woman.' Derwent produced her picture and Ashington stared at it.

'Nope. Never seen her before.'

'What about Iliana Ivanova?'

'Never heard that name before either.' He looked at me earnestly. 'You should ask Carl Hooper. He's the only one who knows what's really going on. He's the guy in charge of all of this shit.'

'We're looking for Mr Hooper at the moment.'

'You've lost him.' Ashington threw his head back and laughed. 'That's hysterical. You got me and let him go. You really need to find him. He's the big bad wolf. I'm nothing but a cub.'

'Do you have any idea where he might be?'

'No. No idea at all.' Ashington blinked, serious again. 'I mean, I assume you checked the house already.'

'The house?'

'There's a house in Highgate. The Bishops Avenue.' He shuddered theatrically. 'That's where the real shit goes down. Or so I've heard.'

'What kind of thing?'

'It's where you go if you don't cooperate, or if you fuck up too publicly. That's where they sort problems out.' He nodded to himself. 'That's where you don't want to go.'

30

I'd known immediately that gaining entry to the Bishops Avenue house was not going to be a matter of knocking on the door, but I hadn't anticipated the sheer number of armed officers who were going to be needed to cover the numerous exits from the property. As the third carrier emptied out, I moved aside so I wasn't in their way. The armed officers weren't there as back-up: they would be going in first and we would be some of the last people who entered the property. There was every possibility that the inhabitants of the house were armed, and that they might panic when we walked in. The armed officers were experts at avoiding confrontations before they started, and even better at ending them. It tended to be a fairly dramatic and final way of solving the problem, though.

I checked the time: eleven o'clock at night. The operation had been arranged at great speed, driven by my conviction that Bianca Drummond was somewhere inside the house, alive or dead. Some house: the properties on the Bishops Avenue belonged to the wealthiest people in the world. It was a long road that ran between Highgate and Hampstead, a mixture of extremely luxurious apartment buildings and vast houses. The most modest detached house on that road currently cost somewhere in the region of twelve million pounds. The house that belonged to the Chiron Club was a red-brick mansion with a white Palladian porch; it looked more suited to oil magnates in Dallas than the top end of London society. Crucially, it had high security gates and stood some distance from its neighbours on either side, so it was private. Access was difficult for us, and getting out would be impossible if you were a prisoner there.

Fortunately, the house next door was unoccupied. Like several of the other properties on the road, it was a bricks-and-mortar bank account for its super-rich owner, a status symbol rather than somewhere to live. I could see why the road appealed to the Chiron Club. There were hardly any nosy neighbours to avoid if you wanted to carry out any activities you might not want to publicise. On the other hand, it was a gift to us, since we could gather in the garden next door and avoid approaching from the front.

The commander who was running the operation finished her final briefing and sought Una Burt out from the crowd. Una nodded agreement and the teams of armed officers formed up, then jogged swiftly into the darkness. The commander's voice issued orders over the radio as the teams soundlessly found their way into the grounds of the house and fanned out, surrounding the property. Five exits: front door, side door, garage, French windows from the dining room on to a terrace, basement door. All covered. It wasn't the sort of visit where you knocked; a shouted warning was followed up with a small explosion as the doors went in simultaneously. I winced and held my radio away from my ear as the air filled with shouting: *police, police, you,* you, *hands, lie on the ground, show me your* hands, *fucking hands* now *where I can see them, how many other people are here, is anyone armed, don't look at me, did I ask you to look at me, don't fucking look at me . . .*

'I've always said one of the major skills you need to be on an ARV crew is the ability to shout convincingly,' Derwent said, strolling over to me.

'They haven't found her.'

'Not yet.' He was frowning and I thought he was doing the same thing as me: imagining them moving through the rooms we'd seen on the floorplan the council had provided. Four floors and it would take time to search it from the basement gym to the final dressing room on the top floor. A lot of rooms, a lot of cupboards. A lot of places to hide.

'The front gate is open,' Una Burt informed us, and the small team of detectives hurried from our holding point down the road. A figure in the petrol-blue uniform of the armed response crews held the gate open and closed it behind us. I looked up at the façade of the house, at the lights blazing in every room.

'Any sign of her?'

'I don't know, sorry.'

The front hall was empty apart from a massive chandelier and I stopped to look at the wrought iron and marble staircase that swept down the centre of the house. The sound of boots on bare floors echoed, as if most of the rooms were empty. Voices came from the room to my left: a study, on the plans. I went to investigate and found Carl Hooper sitting in a swivel chair at an expensive golden oak desk that matched the flooring. There was nothing else in the room apart from three armed officers. Hooper's face was reddened along one cheek, as if he'd hit the ground hard.

'Mr Hooper. You left without saying goodbye.'

'What?' He looked at me blankly, then with sudden and hostile recognition. 'You're the copper who was in the club.'

'Yes, and I thought I told you to stay put.'

'I like you better when you've got your tits out.'

'Language,' Derwent said from behind me, coldly, and I held up a hand to let him know I was fine, I didn't need rescuing.

'I'm not here to be liked. I'm here to find Bianca Drummond.'

'Who?'

243

'You left the club with her. She hasn't been seen since. Don't pretend you don't know who I mean. What have you done with her?'

'I don't know what you're talking about. I've only just got here.'

'He drove in about ten minutes ago,' one gravel-voiced officer said. 'That's his Merc outside.'

'See? I haven't been here.' Hooper looked smug, but he was holding on to the arms of his chair with a grip that had turned his fingers into claws.

'Who else is in the house?'

'No idea.'

'Keep him here,' I said to the gravel-voiced officer, who nodded. I walked rapidly through the ground floor, the rooms from the floorplan leaping to life around me, as bare as they had been in the line drawing. Whatever it had cost the club to buy the house, they'd saved a fortune by not furnishing it. The drawing room led to the dining room, then to a butler's pantry, plant room, a vast kitchen . . . four more armed officers stood here, cradling their guns, standing over two men who were sitting at the table. I recognised one from the club but the other one was new to me. Both were the same type as Hooper: muscled, tough, the kind of men who found jobs on both sides of the law because they were physically capable. This pair sat with their heads hanging down.

'I'm looking for a woman called Bianca Drummond. Five foot five, brown hair, medium build, mid-twenties. Ring any bells?'

They looked at me warily and shook their heads. The one I didn't recognise looked past me for a second before he returned to staring at the table, and I frowned.

'No one upstairs.' The commander came in with Una Burt. 'No sign of your lady.'

'She was never here,' Burt said. 'It was a good guess, but wrong.'

'Did someone check the pool house?' Derwent asked and the commander nodded.

'We've been over every inch of the property.'

'What about the basement?' I asked.

'We've checked everything.'

I looked around the kitchen, frustrated. It was a huge room with a wall of windows overlooking the dark garden. Apart from the table and twelve chairs, it was empty. A multi-coloured rug lay crumpled on the floor between the cooker and the island that housed the sink and dishwasher; it was the only rug I'd seen in the whole house. I glanced at the man I hadn't recognised and saw he was watching me, his expression intent. Was it the rug that had caught his attention before? Was that where he had been looking?

I went over and flipped the rug against the cupboards, revealing that the smooth wood of the floor had a rectangular shape cut into it, with a brass ring inlaid halfway along one side.

'That's a door,' Una Burt observed brilliantly.

'What's down here?' I asked the man.

'Nothing. A wine cellar. It's empty.' He had a French accent. Blue eyes, very short dark hair, muscles, a deep tan. I was willing to bet he did well on Tinder.

'Let's have a look,' the commander said, and nodded to two of her men, who got into position immediately. One hauled the door up while the other covered the widening gap. A staircase disappeared into the darkness. The one who'd opened the door shone his torch down the stairs, sweeping it around. From where I stood I could see empty shelves and racks, as the Frenchman had promised. The man with the torch leaned forward, then made an exclamation before rattling down the stairs at high speed. His colleague followed, only pausing to punch the light switch so the cellar was properly lit. I went after them and got hauled back by Derwent, who had a good grip on my stab vest.

'Don't go down there. You don't know it's safe yet.'

'They've found something.'

'We need paramedics,' the second armed officer called. 'There's a woman here matching the description you gave us.'

This time, Derwent let me go. I flew down the steps and swung around behind them where the two officers were crouching over a small figure. One of them peeled tape off her mouth and she cried out.

'It's all right. We're the police,' the officer said. 'We're here to help you.'

Her eyes were screwed up against the light. I leaned forward. 'Bianca? It's Maeve Kerrigan. Are you hurt?'

'I – I don't think so.'

She looked cold, though, her lips blue. The air in the cellar was fresh enough but the room wasn't heated and the floor was bare cement. The space was small – there was barely enough room for the three of us to stand while she was sitting down. I looked around for food or water.

'Have you been here the whole time?'

'Upstairs.' She held her hands so the police officer could cut through the tape that was wound around her wrists. 'They only put me down here a couple of hours ago. I was in a bedroom.'

'Why did they put you down here?'

'They said . . .' she started to shiver uncontrollably. 'They said they were going to kill me, like they killed the others. When you came down the stairs, I thought it was time.'

'Who said this to you?'

'Hooper. His men. And his boss.'

'His boss?'

'The president of the club.' Her shivering had intensified. 'Sir Marcus Gley.'

I took a moment to respond, stunned. I'd thought Gley was an odd little man, but this was on another level. 'Why did they want to kill you?'

'The security staff saw me talking to a kitchen porter, so they were suspicious of me. Then when Georgia was hurt, they thought I was a police officer too. I told them I was a journalist, like Paige. They were afraid I'd found out what happened to her, I think, but I hadn't.' She squinted at me. 'They were terrifying.'

'Paramedics are here,' Derwent said, leaning into the stairwell. 'You'd better make some room.'

I climbed out of the tiny, chilly cellar with a feeling of indescribable relief, and the paramedics clambered down cheerfully. They were two young women and seemed completely unshockable.

'You found her.' Una Burt sounded far less excited than I felt she might have been. 'Well done.'

'We'd have found the wine cellar on the plans,' the commander said. 'We wouldn't have missed her.'

'Of course you wouldn't,' I said politely, but they had missed her and they'd been thinking about giving up.

'Can I have a look at the plans?' Derwent asked, and the commander handed them over. He spread them out on the kitchen island and stared at them intently.

'What are you looking for?'

'A safe. There's bound to be one in a place like this.'

I looked up at the men who were sitting at the table. 'What about it, guys? Do either of you want to cooperate with us? We've got you for kidnapping and false imprisonment so far, and those are not minor charges.'

'Fuck off,' one of them said under his breath. The other, the French one, flicked a glance at his colleague and then made eye contact with me meaningfully.

Not in front of him . . .

'Have we got a transport van sorted out?' I asked.

'It's outside now,' the commander said.

'Then let's get these two out of here. Him first.' I pointed at the uncooperative one and in a very short time he had been lifted out of his chair and dragged down the hallway, swearing all the way.

As soon as he was out of earshot, the Frenchman turned his blue eyes to me. 'I have not worked here for very long. I don't know everything or I would tell you.'

I believed him; he had a skin to save, after all.

'The safe is under the main staircase. I know the code. I can open it for you.'

'Show me,' I said.

31

'This is a bit of fun, isn't it?' Kev Cox put down the crate of equipment he was carrying and looked around the enormous hallway. 'I don't think I've ever searched a private house this size before.'

'Fun is not what I would call it.' I took the lid off another box from the safe that had spilled its contents all around me. The safe was enormous, a walk-in structure lined with shelves that were loaded with boxes, and going through the contents was proving to be a nightmare.

'This place is like a hotel.' Kev was revolving on the spot, enchanted. 'Imagine living here.'

'Imagine having about six chairs, a desk, a table and no spare loo roll to go in your nine bathrooms and seven bedrooms.'

'Nine? Seriously? Brilliant.'

I couldn't help laughing. 'Are you going to be this happy in twelve hours' time when you're not even halfway through?'

'Probably.' He beamed at me. 'Have you found anything in there?'

'A lot of cash in various currencies and a few portable hard drives that have gone off to be examined. And a lot of paper.'

'What am I looking for?'

'Anything dodgy.' I got up from where I'd been kneeling and stretched. 'One of the staff has been more forthcoming than the rest. He says he hasn't worked here for very long but he was warned by the other guys that things happened here from time to time that weren't very nice.'

'What kind of things?'

'He went vague on us but he admitted he'd heard things about torture and intimidation and disposing of bodies. This is where they deal with people who step out of line, as I understand it. Including, I hope, my dead journalist from the Thames.'

'Ah, you think this is where she was killed.'

'Or where she was cut up. It's a big house and the neighbours are far away. Half the houses on the street seem to be being rebuilt. They could have used power tools on her and no one would have heard anything.'

Kev nodded happily. 'I'll see what we can find.'

Derwent emerged from the study and nodded to Kev, who was marshalling his troops, then scowled at me. 'Find anything?'

'I'm working on it. I take it Carl Hooper isn't being very helpful.'

'How can you tell?'

'Your sunny demeanour.'

'He's a twat. He's denying everything.'

'I'm shocked.'

'He says he left the club because he was worried he'd get arrested, given his record. Bianca left at the same time, but not with him. He says she turned up here on her own and broke in. The lads who were minding the house didn't know what to do with her and couldn't get hold of him, so they stuck her in a bedroom. When Sir Marcus Gley finally made contact with Hooper, he'd found out about Bianca and panicked. They decided they should scare her into giving up the idea of writing about the club. That's what Hooper's paid for, he says. His job is to protect the club and its members, and that's all he did. They threatened her and put her in the wine cellar for a couple of hours but they were planning to let her go. They knew about Paige because of what you told them, so they pretended they'd been involved in her murder to scare Bianca.'

'She didn't say they brought her here, now that I think about it,' I said slowly. 'Maybe he's telling the truth about that part. We can get Liv to ask Bianca about it at the hospital.'

'Sounds to me as if she was trying to make it all sound more important than it was.' Derwent saw me raise my eyebrows. 'What makes a better story? "I was kidnapped by thugs and tortured" or "I went round to a house that belongs to some rich people and annoyed their security guards". I know which one I'd want to read. She wants to write something that'll sell. Of course she's talking it up.'

'You just don't like journalists.'

'I don't hate *all* of them. Most of them, maybe.'

I knelt down again and pushed an unopened box towards him. 'Have a look through that. All I've found so far are membership records and archives. I'm sure it's fascinating if you're a fan of the Chiron Club but it's leaving me cold.'

He took the lid off and tilted his head sideways as he flicked through the contents. 'Did you look in here already?'

'No. Don't tell me I accidentally gave you something interesting.'

'Hanging files. Alphabetised.' He was working through them. 'Here's Peter Ashington's file. Ah, there's a surprise.'

'What's in it?'

'The pictures they sent him. Same images, different prints. The face of the other guy is still blacked out in these. No chance of identifying him from this.' He took out a small plastic bag filled with something soft and black and turned it over. 'What's this?'

'Oh, don't open that – it could be Antoinette's tights. She said she left them in the cupboard.'

'Kept for the DNA, presumably.' He put it back where he'd found it. 'That'll be useful if we get to prosecute. What's this – Roderick Asquith. That's your victim, isn't it?'

'Don't tell me they had something on him.' I shuffled over to see the sheaf of pictures Derwent had taken out of the file, and wished I hadn't. 'Oh God. She looks young.'

'Very young.' A muscle tightened in Derwent's jaw as he whipped through the pictures of Roddy lying back in an armchair, his bow tie crooked, while a slim, pale girl performed a lap dance for him. She was completely naked and boyish, her hips narrow, her chest flat. In several of the pictures she was touching him. In the last, his hand was between her legs. 'And . . . what a surprise. A copy of her birth certificate and an affidavit to say she was fourteen when she did this.'

'He probably had no idea.'

'Doesn't matter, does it? But I think he did know.' Derwent looked at me. 'You knew she was underage the second you saw her. He wasn't stupid, presumably, or blind. He saw what he wanted to see and he did what he wanted to do.'

'I liked him,' I said sadly.

'He probably wouldn't have done it if they hadn't supplied the girl and told him to go along with it. But he did it all the same.' Derwent shook his head. 'Even nice guys will do horrible things if they think no one's going to find out.'

The file was mainly photographs – twenty or thirty sets featuring all manner of perverse and illegal behaviour. Humiliation was a popular angle – mortification in a hundred different ways. I thought I would do anything to prevent pictures like that from getting out, if I featured in them.

'What's the issue with this one? That's just sex, isn't it? They're both into it.' Derwent showed me a couple of pictures from the last set: two men photographed in explicit detail. 'I suppose if you're homophobic – or your dad is – that would make you do what you were told.'

I glanced at the pictures. 'Suppose so. Or one of them is married, maybe. I imagine it's hard to explain that kind of encounter to a wife.'

He dropped the pictures into the file. 'Persuasive stuff. Did you notice they're all around the same age? This file is the twenty-something members. There must be files for the older ones too.'

'I got that from the shelves near the back. Go and see if there's anything more there.'

He disappeared into the safe and I returned to my very boring pile of papers, leafing through it. There was at least nothing sexual about a stack of invoices. I'd seen enough already. I turned over a page and stopped dead.

'Guv?'

'Yeah?'

'Remember PPCS?'

'The people with the animal logo?'

'The very same. I know who they are now, and what they do.'

'Go on.'

'Parnassus Pet Cremation Services. They're in Berkshire. And the Chiron Club are good customers.'

He came out of the safe. 'Show me?'

I handed him the invoice and he read it, then whistled. 'Ten grand for a pet cremation? That's steep, isn't it?'

'Check the date.'

'Twenty-fourth of July two years ago. That's the day after Ashington drove down to Standen Fitzallen. This is the invoice that goes with the records we found in the club where they were paid in cash.'

'It sure is. And remember, that's two days after Iliana Ivanova disappeared.' I handed him the next invoice. 'That's another ten thousand the same day. They were disposing of something else. Or someone else.'

'Guys, are you busy?' Kev rustled down the stairs and came into view. 'Only there's something you should see.'

I knocked on the study door and put my head into the room. 'Ma'am, sorry to interrupt. Inspector Derwent and I have found a few interesting things.'

'Come in and tell us about it.' Burt had taken Hooper's place at the desk. He had been relegated to an upright chair from the kitchen. It stood in the middle of the immaculate wooden floor. He lolled on it, looking unimpressed as Derwent and I walked in.

'Parnassus Pet Cremation Services.' I laid the invoice on the desk. 'What do you know about them, Mr Hooper?'

He was as still as if he'd been turned to stone, his expression now nothing short of stark horror. 'Where did you find that?'

'In the safe. We found the register of expenses in the club's offices too.' I leaned forward and pointed. 'The dates match, look. So we know you used these pet cremation people for some reason that weekend. I've looked them up and the most they charge is eight hundred pounds, and that's for a horse.'

'Did you have a lot of horses to dispose of?' Derwent asked. 'Over that weekend? You could have got rid of the whole field for the Grand National at that price.'

'I don't know what that was for,' Hooper managed.

'If we go and ask them what the two payments of ten thousand pounds were – and we will – what do you think they're going to say? Do you think your name might come up?' Derwent asked softly.

Hooper swallowed, his expression grim.

'If I was in your shoes, I'd want to get my story in first. Especially given what we found upstairs,' I said.

'What did you find upstairs?' Una Burt was looking highly entertained.

'Well, Kev found it really. Did you know there are nine bathrooms in this house?'

'Nine? My goodness.'

'I don't think they use all of them. This one was locked.'

'Why was that?'

'Someone had made an awful mess of the bath,' Derwent said flatly. 'The surface was badly damaged. Cut marks, Kev said. As if someone was using heavy tools to cut through something dense and difficult, like a body.'

'You don't know when that happened,' Hooper ground out. 'Or how.'

'Do you know the answer to either of those questions? Would you like to tell us?' I asked. 'It could have been two years ago when Iliana went missing. Or it could have been more recent than that. It could have been when Paige Hargreaves started asking questions.'

'Kev sprayed it with luminol. Do you know what luminol is, Mr Hooper?' Derwent asked. 'It's a chemical that detects blood. Lights it up like a Christmas tree. The bath upstairs, those scratches, they glowed for us. The only thing we need to know is whose blood it is.'

'You've got the wrong idea,' Hooper muttered.

'What idea would that be?'

'The cremations, the cuts on the bath – that all happened around the same time. There were two bodies.' He shook his head. 'Look, in the moment it seemed like the right thing to do.'

'What did you do?'

'Disposed of the bodies ourselves. It was an accident that they died. That's the first thing. That's what you have to understand.' He chopped his hand down, emphasising his words. 'No one wanted anyone to die.'

'Who died?'

'The girl – Iliana. But she was the second one.'

'Who was the first?'

'A young man who told us his name was Jonas Powell, but it was a pseudonym. I was never able to trace his family and he was never reported missing. No one seemed to miss him. I did try to find out who he was.'

Derwent frowned. 'Why would he lie about who he was?'

'Because of what he was doing for a living. He was a rent boy. A drug addict, too, though I wouldn't have hired him if I'd known. He said he was clean. He had a whole panel of tests at a sexual health clinic – AIDS, the works. He was healthy. So we hired him for a party.'

'What kind of party?'

'An after-party,' Hooper said tiredly. 'Following on from the big celebration of Sir Marcus's presidency. We took some of the young members down to a house near Swindon and turned them loose. We do that from time to time, in various venues, and take pictures of what they get up to. It's part of the club's ethos. It's how it survives – we ensure total commitment from the members. No one was forced to do anything, and no one was supposed to get hurt.'

'But two people died,' I said. 'That's not an accident.'

'It was two accidents, one after the other.'

'Rubbish,' Derwent snapped and anger flared in Hooper's eyes.

'I'm telling the truth and if you give me the chance, I can prove it.'

32

'Carl Hooper is the sort of man who likes to have an insurance policy in his back pocket, in case things don't work out quite the way he planned.' I looked around the conference room, seeing total concentration on all of their faces: Una Burt, Derwent, Liv, Pettifer, Pete Belcott who was still snuffling with his cold, a pale-faced Georgia and Colin Vale, our resident technical expert. 'He was fully committed to doing exactly what was required of him by his bosses at the Chiron Club, but he was also concerned that if it ever came to light, he wasn't going to take the fall. They didn't pay him enough for that, apparently.'

'I bet he got paid more than we do,' Belcott said.

'Oh, undoubtedly. But he worked hard for his money. He was in charge of creating situations where illegal behaviour could occur, and making sure it was recorded when it did. He taped a lot of it himself on his mobile phone and with a secret body-worn camera in his lapel, and he copied footage from other sources. According to him he didn't *personally* blackmail anyone with the information he recorded but it would not shock me if he had a side hustle that he won't admit, especially having watched what you're about to see.

'Now, he's no Spielberg, but this is a rough cut of the

events that took place at the Chiron Club two years ago, and at the after-party. The first part of the tape is footage from the club.'

I pressed play and Derwent hit the lights as the big TV on the wall flashed into life. The footage was amateurishly shaky but organised, starting with a long shot of the big, brass-mounted calendar in the hall showing it was the twenty-second of July. The recording cut out, to be replaced by a shot of three men huddled together, snorting coke off the back of their hands. The camera panned over their faces and then swung away to face the floor.

'Do we know who they are?' Burt asked.

'I don't recognise them,' I said, 'but I'm sure Hooper knows exactly who he was filming.'

The next few minutes consisted of jumpy, poorly filmed incidents – a fist fight, a man groping a waitress, another forcing his dining companion's head down towards his crotch while she fought to free herself and the other men at the table roared. He had filmed Antoinette's conversation with Peter Ashington and his companion through a doorway. They walked out of view, Peter turning to grin knowingly at the other man whose face was still hidden. I felt sick as I watched her disappear to her fate, knowing what awaited her.

'That's the girl who was raped in the cloakroom,' I explained for the benefit of the others. 'Here's footage of Hooper getting the funds to pay her off. That's one of the administrative staff at the club. We don't know if she knew what the money was for, but as you can see, she doesn't seem surprised to be asked for it.'

The angle was off, the woman appearing diagonally as she counted out the money, licking her finger to speed up the process. She looked bored, as if this was routine. Hooper filmed the stack of money disappearing into the envelope. Then a jump to Antoinette, her mascara smudged under her eyes, sobbing as a grey suit helped her into a car.

258

'This all corroborates Antoinette's story,' I said. 'If we want to charge Peter Ashington with rape, this is going to be useful.'

'Why wouldn't we charge him?' Colin Vale asked.

'I need Antoinette's cooperation to take it further, and the CPS may not approve a charge if they feel there's no chance of getting a conviction. He says she knew what was going to happen and pretended to put up a fight so they had the thrill of forcing her. She took the money afterwards, which helps his case. And he's plausible. I actually think he believes that story even though I know Antoinette was telling me the truth. But who's going to get the benefit of the doubt?' I pulled a face. 'I don't know if I'd give evidence in her shoes. It wouldn't be fun.'

'It's not meant to be fun. It might stop him from doing it to someone else,' Derwent snapped. 'Don't you think she has a duty to other women to try and have him locked up?'

I looked at him in the half-light from the TV, surprised at his tone. 'I think it's up to her to decide what's best for her recovery.'

'What happens next?' Una Burt asked.

'Then we get some footage of Sir Marcus making his acceptance speech. Hooper filmed this properly, with his camera the right way up. Presumably no one minded him filming it.'

The screen filled with Sir Marcus bowing and laughing as he prepared to cut an enormous cake with a long sword. Two of the men grabbed one of the girls and bent her over so he could pretend to cut off her head. Then he drew up her skirt and smacked her bottom with the flat of the sword. A roar of approving laughter went up from the throng. When the men released her, she stumbled away, clearly upset.

'Those bastards,' Georgia said clearly. 'I want to arrest all of them.'

'This is the part where they were playing nice,' I said. 'It gets a lot worse later on.'

She shuddered and wrapped her arms around herself, as if she was cold, though the conference room was stifling.

'Right, the next part is in a car, on the way to the house in the country for the after-party. According to Hooper, the premises will have changed a lot since this was filmed. He said the house belonged to an elderly club member who had died. His family were planning to sell the place but they hadn't done anything with it apart from emptying it out, so it was basically derelict. Since this party it's been sold and completely refurbished to turn it into a luxury spa hotel, so everything you see here is gone and you can forget being able to recover anything forensically.'

I pressed play and we watched two young men in dinner jackets groping drunk, slack-jawed girls while they were squashed together in the back seat of a car. The pair on the right progressed to full sex, unnoticed by the other couple who were drinking and pawing one another. Hooper had filmed from the driver's seat. As he put the phone down it caught the passenger for a split second. He was asleep with his head turned away from the camera. Light-brown hair, a neat ear, a square jaw: I thought it looked like Luke, and from the way Derwent shifted uneasily, he'd thought the same thing. No one else in the room appeared to have noticed, I thought, and was glad of it. He had been in Peru, I reminded myself.

He had *said* he was in Peru, and I'd accepted it based on some Facebook posts. I didn't want to find out I'd been wrong. But he wasn't a member of the Chiron Club; they'd never have let him go to their private parties. It was just a coincidence.

'This is inside the house, is it?' Burt asked and I forced myself to focus on answering her.

'Yes. Hooper explained this to us. Basically, these are the people he recruited as the entertainment for the evening. This is backstage.'

Two model-like girls looked up and waved as one passed a joint to the other. They looked dazed. The taller of the two wore a dress that had slid off her shoulder so one small breast was exposed, though she seemed oblivious. A beautiful dark-skinned man practised capoeira moves as a breeze moved the curtains of the open window behind him. A young man wearing ripped jeans and nothing else threw the camera a grin then dropped to perform a few push-ups, clapping his hands between each one. The tattoo on his arm flexed as he moved. I paused the video for an instant.

'This is the man who said he was Jonah Powell.'

The camera panned away from him, to a girl in a black dress who was winging her eyeliner with a steady hand. I paused it again.

'And this is Iliana Ivanova, the girl who disappeared.'

'Is that it?'

'There were a few others who came down in the cars. Hooper told us this was an exclusive little event. They only had ten members here, and half of them left early to go somewhere else. The club were targeting one or two of the men who hadn't blotted their copybooks yet. The kids they hired in for the night were told they would double their money if they managed to provoke any bad behaviour. That was a lot of money for them. It was a competition, fuelled by drugs that Hooper supplied.'

'What kind of drugs?' Belcott asked.

'Ecstasy, for starters, and then GHB and mephedrine. It was designed to lower their inhibitions, along with the alcohol.'

'Did it work?'

'All too well,' Derwent said. 'This is Iliana dancing.'

She spun around and around on a terrace, her dress flying up as she laughed. One of the men, now without his dinner jacket, got up and caught her, then carried her away into the darkness.

'Who was that?' Burt said sharply.

'Don't know, but it doesn't matter. Whatever happened to her in the garden didn't kill her. You'll see her again in a bit,' I said. 'This is Jonah again, in the pool.'

A naked man with dark curly hair and a beard ran into view, moving away from the camera. He was unrecognisable, no matter how much we'd played with slowing the images and trying to sharpen them. He leapt into the water. Jonah whooped, exultant, and gathered him into his arms, and the two of them kissed, hard. Jonah tangled his hands in the other man's hair. They sank under the water, their bodies twisting, play-fighting like otters.

'How much more of this is there?' Colin asked.

'Not much.'

'I'm sorry, it's just not my cup of tea,' he said plaintively, and the room dissolved into laughter. I waited for everyone to calm down again.

'I get the impression that Hooper left them to it for a while. Maybe he felt he was getting in the way. The next thing he filmed is inside the house.' I let the video play: a rumpled bed, filmed from the doorway of an otherwise empty room. Jonah was getting up, clambering past the man who was asleep face-down. He paused to drop a kiss on one of the man's buttocks, grinning at the camera again afterwards. He was naked but totally unselfconscious about it, a performer enjoying the attention.

'Did you have fun?' Hooper's voice was quiet as if he didn't want to risk waking the sleeping man.

'Always. I'll be feeling it tomorrow though. He was tougher than he looked. He was mean to me, Carl.' Jonah stuck out his bottom lip, then picked up his jeans and took something out of the pocket. The tattoo on his arm moved as he did, the dragon swelling with breath as his bicep bulged.

'What's that?' Hooper demanded.

'A little something to help me come down.' Jonah flashed his trademark wide smile and swallowed the pill he'd palmed. He turned away and his hand went up to his throat as if the pill hadn't gone down properly.

'Are you OK? Jonah?'

One minute he was standing there, his back to the camera, his muscles moving under his skin. The next he had fallen heavily to the floor where he clawed at his face, his mouth frothing.

'He's having a fit,' a male voice said from behind Hooper. 'Help him.'

'That's not a fit. That's an overdose.'

On the floor, Jonah had started to jerk spasmodically. His eyes were fixed on the ceiling, staring. The froth slid out of his mouth and down his cheek.

'Do something.'

'I can't. He's *fucked*.' Hooper sounded genuinely upset, and furious. I paused the film.

'Right, I asked him about this. He said he had supplied the best quality drugs and he knew exactly what everyone had taken. He said Jonah arrived with this, without Hooper's knowledge. He doesn't know what it was but he thinks it was something that was cut with rat poison or something else toxic and that's why Jonah reacted this way. We never got to test his body so we don't know. It could have been the cumulative effects of all the other drugs he took reacting with whatever this was.'

'This next bit is a proper horror show.' Derwent turned away from the screen and I didn't blame him. We had watched it twice together, which was twice too often.

On the screen, Jonah continued to spasm. He vomited foamy purple slime. Dark, reddish-brown liquid seeped out from between his legs.

'What is that?' Belcott demanded.

'That would be the contents of his bowels.'

'He's dying,' Georgia said.

'And Hooper is still filming,' I pointed out. 'Which is good, in a way, because then we get this.'

A woman's scream tore through the room and Hooper swung the camera around. A small grey-haired man stood

263

swaying behind him in trousers and an undone white shirt: Sir Marcus Gley, barely recognisable as the suave gentleman who had tried to charm me. Beside him was Iliana, who wore black suede heels and lace knickers and nothing else. Her make-up was smudged under her eyes now. She screamed again.

'Help him! You can't just watch. You animals, you animals, you killed him. You *killed* him.'

Sir Marcus snarled, 'Shut up, you stupid bitch. *Will* you shut up?'

She ignored him. 'You killed him. You're murderers. *Murderers*.'

'Then I'll make you shut up.' He grabbed her by the neck, squeezing her throat. Her face went red, her eyes popping. She clawed at his hands but his grip tightened.

Hooper turned away to check on Jonah. He bent over him, swearing softly. The young man's eyes were rolled back in his head and his chest was still. Hooper pressed his fingers into Jonah's neck, searching for a pulse, then gave up.

'He's dead.' He turned as Sir Marcus took his hands away from Iliana's throat. She slid to the floor, lying at his feet in a clumsy tangle of limbs. The strings had snapped; the puppet was broken. Only the dead could manage to look so totally abandoned.

Silence hissed on the recording for a few seconds. Sir Marcus was rubbing his hand over his mouth again and again, staring down. Hooper spoke again.

'You killed her.'

'No, I didn't.' Sir Marcus looked up. 'It was an accident. You saw.'

'I . . . did.' He sounded uncertain.

'Oh, come off it, Hooper. Don't pretend you care. She wasn't worth much alive and she's worth less dead. Make it go away.'

'What?'

'All of this.' He waved at the room. 'The boy. The girl.

264

Make them disappear. You'll get some kind of bonus for it, obviously.'

'Thank you, sir.'

'Get my car.' He started to button his shirt, his hands trembling. 'This was supposed to be fun.'

'I'm sorry, sir.'

'Hell of a way to end an evening.' He walked away, accidentally kicking one of Iliana's shoes down the hall in front of him. I felt he would have liked to kick her too.

The screen went black and Derwent put the lights on again. I turned to face the others.

'That's the end of the film Hooper made. According to him, they staged the scene to make it look as if Jonah had drowned in the swimming pool because they wanted to guarantee that the man who slept with him would stay silent. Hooper thought that a dead body would shut him up more effectively than anything else, and it did seem to work. They'd already decided to dispose of both of the bodies in the crematorium though. They fished Jonah out of the pool once the guy had left, transported both corpses to the house in London, cut them up and took them to their friendly body disposal facility in Berkshire.'

'Why didn't they do that with Paige Hargreaves?' Derwent asked.

I shrugged. 'Maybe they couldn't use the crematorium for some reason. The river is right in front of the club – it wouldn't require a massive leap of imagination to dump her there.'

'So we need to arrest Sir Marcus Gley,' Una Burt said. 'Wonderful.'

'Not yet,' Derwent said. 'He's well known and he doesn't know we have this footage. He might run between now and when we're ready to arrest him, but we can alert the border agencies in case he tries to hop on a plane. Before we bring him in I think we need to trace the other people who were at the party, ideally including the man who was in the swimming pool with Jonah and the kids who were paid to be there. Hooper couldn't or wouldn't ID the swimmer for us but we'll get a name from one of the other members if we ask around. We need to talk to the crematorium and get their version of events, and then we need to make some arrests there too, for assisting an offender and unlawful disposal of a corpse. Anything we can think of, basically, to put pressure on them to talk. The bodies were cut up in the house on the Bishops Avenue so the crematorium staff could pretend they didn't know they were burning human corpses, but the club paid ten grand each for the cremations. The staff at the crematorium must have known they were being paid to look the other way.'

'We've tangled with the lawyers from the Chiron Club before,' I said. 'They're not fun. We want to have all the facts before we arrest him. And we still need to process the Bishops Avenue house forensically, and talk to Bianca about what actually happened to her there before we found her.'

'And go through the rest of the paperwork from the club and the safe at the house,' Liv said. 'That'll take a week, minimum.'

'Right,' Burt said. 'Well, now that Bianca has been found, this investigation no longer requires a fast-time response. Some of you have been working silly hours and you look half dead. It's Saturday, and it's a bank holiday weekend, in case you hadn't noticed. Take some time off and come back on Tuesday with as much energy as you can all muster. Let's aim to arrest Sir Marcus towards the end of next week. That should give us time to get organised.'

'Thanks, boss,' Derwent said, looking surprised and gratified.

'You deserve it.'

I was startled at the wave of relief I felt at the thought of time off. It was so long since I'd slept properly, or eaten an actual meal. I could rest for two whole days. It was as good as a holiday.

'But when you come back, I want you at your best. I want to lock that man up for a very long time,' Una Burt said, waving a finger at the screen. 'I want him ruined for what he did to that girl. And the rest of them. He needs to be dealt with and we're going to do it properly.'

33

The mistake I made, looking back on it, was telling Seth that I had the rest of the weekend off.

'So can I come over?' he said immediately.

'Tomorrow?' I suggested. 'I really need to get some sleep. I'm shattered.'

'You can sleep when I'm there.'

'I usually can't,' I said, teasing him. 'You take up a lot of the bed and you know how you toss and turn.' Besides, he wouldn't want to sleep, if I knew him, and I didn't want to do anything else. I was afraid that he wouldn't understand, that he would take it personally. The truth was that watching the video of the women being mauled at the Chiron Club and the after-party had made me feel nauseated. I flashed back to it when I closed my eyes. I didn't want him to touch me until I'd shaken it off. 'Look, come over tomorrow. The weather forecast is really good. We can go out for a picnic or something.'

'Or stay in.'

'Or stay in,' I agreed, knowing that he meant in bed. Somehow I managed to keep the reluctance out of my voice. It wasn't his fault; he had no idea of how I'd spent that day or what I'd seen. The job seeped into your personal life, even if you tried to keep the two things separate. You had to deal with it yourself so your partner didn't have to.

I was in bed by nine, and drifting off to sleep when my phone chimed. I would have needed to be dead or approaching it to ignore a message, so I checked it. Liv.

Did Josh ever apologise for what he said to you outside the club?

I rolled my eyes and texted her back to the effect that she should know better than to ask; Derwent didn't do apologies, and especially not when I'd provided him with such a beautiful opportunity for a good line, which was all it had been.

I think he always wants to take your clothes off.

I laughed at that, and shook my head as I typed my reply.

Stop troublemaking. Your hormones are out of control.

Then I switched my phone to silent and sank gratefully into the depths of sleep, thinking no more about it.

The forecast hadn't been wrong: it was a glorious morning. I sang as I tidied the flat and changed my bedsheets and put a load of laundry on, feeling like a normal human being. I found a cotton sundress with a flared skirt in the back of my wardrobe and even put on sandals because I needed a decent antidote to weeks of sensible trouser suits. The local deli was crowded but I managed to elbow my way through the throng to get French bread, olives, three different kinds of cheese and some roasted peppers. At the supermarket I bought juicy little cherry tomatoes and frosty grapes, pâté and fat strawberries that smelled as sweet as jam. The day stretched ahead of me, full of potential and sunshine. I would coax Seth into going somewhere green and leafy, where we could spend a leisurely couple of hours over our picnic. I added a bottle of prosecco to my basket, because why not? I wasn't on call and the weekend had two more days in it and the case was coming together so I needn't worry about it, or anything else.

The streets were quiet, as if London had emptied out for the bank holiday that always felt like the official start of summer. I noticed all the neighbours who lived downstairs and beside the flat were away, their cars gone from the street outside and curtains closed against the sun. My spirits lifted at the thought of the months that were to come: barbecues and riverside walks and white-clad cricket on all the green spaces across London and the sun on my skin; lazy games of tennis in the parks, followed by dripping ice cream and cold wine in big glasses in noisy beer gardens and a trip to an outdoor cinema and those hot, short nights when the air felt heavy . . .

Seth turned up at eleven on the dot and I ran downstairs to let him in. He was looking particularly handsome in a polo shirt and navy shorts, and I felt a little hum of pleasure at the thought of spending the day with him.

'You look beautiful,' he said, and I laughed.

'I'd be flattered but you sound far too surprised.'

'It's a good look on you. I like this.' He tweaked the skirt of the dress, then stepped close to me, sliding his thigh in between my legs as his mouth found mine again. He pushed me against the wall, grinding against me. I kissed him with moderate enthusiasm, trying to imply that yes, I thought he was extremely attractive but no, I did not want to abandon my plans so we could go to bed immediately. As if he'd heard what I was thinking he let go of me.

'I've got everything ready upstairs,' I said brightly. 'I just need to finish packing the basket.'

He followed me up the stairs without saying anything and I wondered if I was reading too much into his silence.

'Are you OK? Was it something I said?'

'No, of course not.' He held up his phone. 'This has died on me. The battery isn't charging properly. Can I use your phone for a second?'

'Sure.' I unlocked it for him and went into the kitchen to get the picnic things out of the fridge. He would cheer up once we were lying on a rug under a tree with the sun gilding patches of grass through the leaves. I hummed to myself as I packed the basket, pleased with myself for the planning and execution.

'Maeve?' he called from the living room. 'Could you come in here, please?'

I don't know what I thought he wanted. I know I wasn't worried as I walked through the hall towards him, that I didn't even think about finding a way out. I didn't so much as glance down the stairs to the front door.

'What's up?'

He was standing in the middle of the room, holding my phone. 'What the fuck is this?'

'What are you talking about?' I was confused, not scared. I should have been scared.

'I think he always wants to take your clothes off,' he read, and showed me the screen: Liv's message to me from the night before.

'That was a joke.' I blinked at him. 'Did you take my phone so you could read my messages?'

'I wondered what was going on when you wouldn't see me last night.' He reached out and caught me by the jaw, his fingers digging in as he twisted my head so he could look at my neck. I knew what he was glaring at: the love bite that had faded to a purple-green-yellow smudge but still looked exactly like what it was. 'You must have thought the marks would be gone by today, or that I wouldn't notice they were there. You must think I'm stupid or something.'

'No, of course not.' I knocked his hand away and stepped out of range. 'I got this when I was doing an undercover job a couple of days ago. Some dickhead bit me. He was drunk and showing off to his mates. It wasn't a big deal so please don't overreact.'

'Why didn't you tell me about it?'

'Because it was a non-event. I forgot all about it.'

'You forgot.'

'I've been busy,' I pointed out. 'I had better things to worry about.'

He changed tack. 'What did Josh Derwent need to apologise for?'

'He made a stupid joke.' I held out my hand. 'Can I have my phone?'

'What was the joke?'

I shook my head. I'd been too surprised to be outraged before, but I was starting to feel anger singeing the edges of my composure. 'That doesn't matter.'

'It matters to me.'

'Why? It was a stupid joke. I've told you, it didn't mean anything. Why can't you take my word for it?'

'Because I think you're lying to me.'

'I'm not.' I could see my beautiful day evaporating into ugliness and recrimination. It wasn't what I'd wanted and all of a sudden I'd had enough of it – of trying to be perfect, and always failing. 'Seth, I can't do this. You don't trust me even though I've never given you a reason to doubt me.'

He laughed, a harsh sound. 'Oh, you haven't?'

'No, I haven't.' I stood my ground. 'Look, it is what it is. You've tried so hard with me and I've tried too but I keep coming up short. I can't relax around you.'

'Because you're aware you're not good enough for me.'

I sighed. 'If that's how you want to put it, fine. I might as well take the blame. You haven't done anything wrong.

You've been the perfect boyfriend. I don't know how you could have done more. But it's not making me happy.'

'It's not making you happy,' he repeated. 'You aren't happy. How do you think I feel?'

I threw up my hands, frustrated. 'Well, if I'm making you miserable too, let's just stop this now. It's over.'

He tilted his head to one side, quizzical now. 'I make you miserable?'

'I didn't say that—'

'It's funny if you think this is me making you miserable. I haven't even started.'

The words I was going to say died in my mouth; I stared at him, wary now.

'You should be trying to please me.' He leaned forward, getting into my face. 'You should be on your knees begging me not to dump you. What gives you the right to tell me it's over?'

'I think it's for the best.'

'Fuck you.' The air in the room was vibrating with his rage. I'd seen his temper long before I'd ever agreed to go out with him but I hadn't realised how angry he could be until now. 'You don't get to dump me. You piece of shit. I tried to help you. I tried to look after you. What did I get for my trouble? Fuck all.'

'Then cut your losses,' I said, striving to remain calm. 'Look, if you need to be the one who does the breaking up, God knows I've given you enough reasons to end it. Say whatever you want and go.' I turned to walk away, and he threw the phone at my head. It missed me, and I watched it slam into the wall instead and spin into several pieces, and I still didn't expect to find his fist coming towards me when I looked back at him. I wasn't even aware of it making contact. The pain lit up the inside of my head with the blinding whiteness of a nuclear explosion. I saw it more than felt it, but I tasted blood and knew I was hurt, that I was falling, that I'd taken him for someone he was not, and I would pay a price for being wrong.

At least, I thought, once I was on the floor it would stop; he would stop.

I was wrong about that too.

34

I had no idea where I was or what had happened to me when awareness came back to me, peeling away the darkness that was like a lead blanket weighing me down. I was alone and I was lying face down on a hard surface, but I couldn't make sense of what I was able to see out of the one eye that was working. This was not my bedroom, nor any bedroom I had ever slept in before. I stared at the corner of the room, which stubbornly refused to turn into something I might have expected to see. Perhaps I was still dreaming, I thought, and made to sit up. Even before the pain shrilled through me, catching me in a hundred places with hooks as sharp as talons, I knew it was a mistake.

Maybe I would stay where I was for a while.

The second time I tried to move, I was more cautious. Slowly, I began to raise my head. That wasn't going to be possible, I registered after trying for a few seconds, and not because my muscles were complaining: I was physically stuck. I slid one hand towards my head, ignoring the fact that my fingers felt heavy and swollen and didn't seem to want to bend. After a few minutes of delicate exploration, I worked out that my hair was glued to the floor and that I needed to free myself before I could sit upright. I picked at it, freeing it one strand at a time, my eyes closed against the dim light that filled the room. I was lying on the living room floor, I finally concluded, and I was hurt. That was as far as I got. The rest of the facts were standing outside a door I slammed in my mind because I wasn't ready to know them.

Eventually I'd unpicked enough hair to be able to lever myself up. Unthinking, I tried to put some weight on my left elbow to support myself and lost the breath from my body at the pain. Worse than the discomfort was the horrifying sensation that something was adrift further up, something integral. Wary exploration produced a flare of agony as I probed my collarbone: broken, I guessed, and therefore not doing the job of holding my shoulder in place or letting my arm be of any use. My ribs sang their own song of pain, and everywhere there were bruises. I sat staring stupidly at the dried blood that had soaked into the carpet, at the bruising under the skin all the way down the outside of my right thigh, at the red and swollen fingers that had possibly been stamped on . . . and I hadn't even seen my face yet, to find out where the blood had come from, but it felt taut, the skin stretched. Some injury or other had swollen to seal one eye closed completely. I sniffed, trying to clear my nose. No joy.

Well, I could breathe through my mouth. And eventually, when I was able, I would get to my feet, and begin the process of calling for help. I would need to go to hospital, I thought, to get checked out.

I would have to tell them what had happened to me.

I closed my one working eye and allowed myself to feel utterly dreadful for a little while.

Prosaically, what got me off the floor was that I needed the loo and I wanted to cling on to whatever dignity I still possessed, so I had to get to the bathroom. I puzzled over what that simple need meant as a distraction while I gathered myself for the titanic effort to get to my feet: I must have been unconscious for a few hours. I wasn't wearing a watch and the blinds were all down in the living room, but it was still light outside. I was quite glad of the dimness as I levered myself up and found a friendly wall to lean against while the room stopped spinning. Hobbling the short distance to the bathroom was an awkward, gruelling struggle, and I got through it by saying as many rude words as I could remember, and by propping myself up on the wall. Later I'd realise I had left a long dragging smear of tacky blood behind me as I moved, but at the time I was oblivious.

I waited until after I'd used the loo to look at myself in the mirror, and when I did I wished I hadn't. My hair was matted from a deep, jagged cut on my hairline that had bled spectacularly, coating the side of my face and my ear. I had a black eye, as I'd anticipated, but the cheekbone below it was wildly blown out, the skin shiny. My nose was swollen and the nostrils were black with dried blood. Fuzzily, I tried to wipe the worst of it away, then gave up. The sundress had had it: blood stained the front of it and one shoulder strap had been ripped away. I undid the buttons down the front and let it fall at my feet. I would never wear that dress again, I thought, and felt utterly bereft because I was not the person I had been before, when I put it on, when I sang for the fun of summer and being happy.

Small triumphs: I had done laundry that morning so there were clean yoga trousers to step into and a loose T-shirt that I managed to get on, supporting my left elbow to make up for the jangling discomfort from my collarbone. Getting my arm through the sleeve required another round of swearing, but I felt marginally better once I was dressed. I was operating a long way below my normal cognitive level, but I could manage a phone call to the ambulance service, I thought, and to remember my address, and there was every chance I could make it down to the front door to open it for the paramedics so no one would have to put the door in.

My first problem: the last time I'd seen my mobile it had

been in five or six pieces. My second problem: when I went looking for them in the living room, they were gone.

So was the landline, and the router for the WIFI.

So was my work phone.

And so was my radio, along with all of the personal protective equipment I carried on duty.

I spent far too long creeping around the flat, searching, losing track of what I was even looking for. I was forgetting what I'd done with them, I convinced myself, and then, as the truth seeped into my mind, I refused to think about what it might mean. It was the third or fourth time I hunted through the flat that I made myself face up to the fact that he had taken all of my means of communicating with the outside world.

I would have to leave, I thought, and started searching for my keys, and then for the spare keys, and then, with rising panic, for a key to the back door. I had to be mistaken, I told myself, and took a long, shuffling, unsteady trip down the steep stairs to the hall, where I turned the latch and absolutely failed to open the door.

It was locked, from the outside.

I couldn't get out.

I could only wait until he came back.

I'd like to say that sobbing in the dimly lit, poky hall behind a door I couldn't open was the worst I felt on that endless day, but it wouldn't be true. When I eventually dragged myself back up the stairs I forced myself to return to the living room, to pull up the blinds. I was in the middle of London, not walled up in a prison cell. I was resourceful and determined and OK, yes, everything was taking a long time and I couldn't seem to coordinate my movements properly and I was swinging between exhaustion and terror, but I could still call for help the old-fashioned way.

Except that when I went to open the blinds, I found he had

nailed them down, driving small tacks through the material to hold them in place, and no matter what I did I couldn't manage to open the window. I wasn't strong or coordinated enough to drag the blinds down off the wall, or rip them free. With the blinds secured as they were, I couldn't even break the window glass.

It's a mark of how utterly destroyed I was that at this point I simply gave up. Helplessness gutted me in a way that pain could not. I had been out-thought, out-manoeuvred, out-done. I hadn't been able to fight him when he hit me, despite all of my training, because he had caught me off guard. I had simply submitted to the punches and kicks, hoping it would end, preferably before I died. Now, when he wasn't even there, I was still in his power. I wasn't able to leave, or call for help. I was cut off from anyone who might be able to help me. By chance he had all the advantages, from the fact that the neighbours were away to the two clear days off Una Burt had allowed me. No one would be looking for me until Tuesday morning at the very earliest. It was Sunday now, drifting towards evening I guessed, given the warmth and angle of the light that glowed through the blinds. That left me a whole day and two nights to survive.

That gave him a whole day and two nights to come back.

I couldn't begin to guess what he had been planning to do when he locked me in, but I had every reason to think he intended to finish what he'd started.

35

I had expected it – I had planned for it – but when I heard a key scraping in the lock downstairs my immediate reaction was blind panic. I drew myself together, making myself as small as I could in my hiding place. It wasn't a good hiding place, but it was the best I could achieve. If he thought I had somehow managed to leave, he might go too, and this time he *might* forget to lock the door. That was it: that was the plan I'd worked out over the previous hour or so, as the sun slipped lower in the sky and the world carried on, oblivious to me and my terror. Sirens split the air but not near the flat; they were speeding to the rescue for other people. I was on my own, and I'd accepted that I couldn't fight Seth off, even to save my life. I only had one working arm, my balance was off, my depth perception was shot since one eye was still sealed shut and my reaction times were pitiful.

So, I hid.

The flat wasn't overburdened with places to hide, admittedly, and I wasn't at my most inventive. The bed was too low to the ground for me to be able to slide under it, but the bedroom had a chimney breast with a recess on either side. One contained a wardrobe and the other, by the window, was filled with a chest of drawers that was narrower than the space it filled. I had shifted it to one side and forward, then eased myself in beside the chest of drawers and fluffed the curtains out to disguise the gap as best I could.

It felt very much as if I'd made the wrong decision as he came up the stairs with a measured, wary tread, not hurrying. He stopped at the top of the stairs and I pressed my hand against my mouth so I wouldn't make a sound. I imagined him listening, stilling himself so he could hear the tiniest noise. At last, he moved, his pace slow and deliberate, as if he was placing his feet carefully. A floorboard creaked and I knew he was standing in the doorway of the living room, looking at the place where I had been when he last saw me. Bloodied carpet, a room in disarray, walls marked with scrapes from the phone and smudges I'd left behind: a classic crime scene that had once been my home.

He didn't go into the living room. Instead, he came to the bedroom door and looked into the room for what felt like forever. I listened to his breathing and tried to muffle mine. I was shaking and couldn't stop; the trembling came from deep within me.

Another creak and I shut my eyes: I couldn't tell if he was coming towards me or moving away. Then a drawer in the kitchen rumbled open, which reassured me very slightly – at least he wasn't in the bedroom any more. I didn't know what he was looking for. I'd discovered all the knives were gone from the knife block and the cutlery drawer. He'd taken everything bladed, even scissors. He had thought of everything.

In my mind I moved with him to the bathroom. I tried to imagine what he was seeing there: my dress, of course, abandoned where I'd stepped out of it, crumpled like a flower that was past its best. I had recovered, I willed him to think. I had cleaned myself up, got changed, and somehow found a way out of the flat. I must have hidden spare keys somewhere, and he'd missed them. There was nothing here for him. I was long gone.

Wishful thinking.

The footsteps moved through the hall again, and did not pause at the kitchen or the top of the stairs. They came closer, to the threshold of the bedroom, and then inside it. He crossed the room without hesitating, as if I had called out to him. I dropped my head on to my knees, bit the inside of my bottom lip and prayed, though what I was asking for I didn't really know. A miracle, perhaps.

He tore the blind away from the window sill with a muttered curse and my head came up slowly. I could see a narrow strip of the room, and his hand as he pulled the blind cord, drawing it up. Late evening sun turned the room red, and I'd got my miracle after all.

'Josh.'

I will give Derwent this: he didn't so much as flinch. I would have jumped out of my skin, but he just pulled the curtain out of the way, so he could see me in my hiding place. He gave me a searching, assessing look that was three parts detective to one part ragged relief.

'There you are.'

'Yeah,' I said, my voice rusty from not using it.

'Can you come out?'

'I'm not sure,' I said, clearing my throat and trying to match his matter-of-fact tone. 'If you move the chest of drawers, probably.'

It took very little effort for him to move it, or so it seemed to me. He left it standing sideways in the space, and squatted so we were on the same level.

'What about now?'

I uncurled a few inches, then stopped because I had stiffened up while I was hiding and everything suddenly hurt twice as much. The pain must have been written all over my face because Derwent touched my knee gently to stop me.

'Stay put.' He straightened up and took out his phone to make a terse, competent phone call to the emergency control room requesting an ambulance as soon as possible. I shut my eyes while he talked to them, drifting a bit now from sheer relief and exhaustion and the pain. He seemed to be having a very calm argument with someone about how long it would take and how urgent it was. I missed him leaving the room and when I returned to what currently passed for full alertness he was holding a glass of water.

'Drink?'

'Yes, please.' I was proud of holding the glass myself as I sipped, my teeth chattering against the rim.

'The ambulance is going to be about ninety minutes. They're getting slammed, according to the control room. I did my best, but—'

'It's fine.' I put the glass down on the floor beside me. 'I can wait.'

'You're in pain. It's not fine.'

'It's fine if I don't move, I mean.'

'That's all right, then,' he snapped.

'Don't be cross with me.' The words seemed to have more significance than I'd intended, once I'd said them. *Don't be cross with me for not realising the danger I was in. Don't be cross with me for letting you down when you deserved to know about your son. Don't be cross with me for making the best of this horrible situation.*

His expression softened. 'I'm not cross with you.'

'Come and sit down. Stop looming over me.'

He lowered himself to the floor and slid over so he was beside me, on the opposite side from the broken collarbone. He leaned against the wall, a solid figure, sane and steadfast, not touching me. I let myself rest against him and shut my eyes.

'Wake up.'

'I'm not asleep.'

'Has he done this to you before?'

'No.' I shifted, trying to find a comfortable position and failing. 'Not exactly.'

'He did something or he wouldn't have sent you the roses.'

'You don't miss much, do you?'

'It's my job,' Derwent said simply.

'What happened before was nothing like this. It was an argument that got a bit out of hand.' I looked down at myself. 'I should have known, though.'

'But you didn't. That's all there is to it.' In other words, I shouldn't blame myself. 'What happened?'

A policeman's question; he'd waited long enough to ask it and I gathered myself to answer it.

'I annoyed him. It was stupid. He thought I was cheating on him and he wouldn't believe me when I said I wasn't.'

'Why didn't you call me?'

'No phones. No radio. He took them with him.'

'Did he indeed?' Derwent said softly.

'That wasn't all.' I listed all the things that he had taken out of the flat, and Derwent listened to me intently. From where I sat I could only see the side of his face and the corner of his mouth. I knew his expression was grim.

We sat in silence for a while after I'd finished. I was fading again, struggling to keep my eyes open. Then a sound made me snap to attention, trembling again. 'What was that?'

'What?'

'I heard something from downstairs. A noise.'

'I didn't hear anything.' He dropped a hand onto my knee and held on to it, and I felt very slightly reassured. 'It's all right.'

'I don't want him to come back,' I said, as I let my head fall onto his shoulder again.

'Me neither.'

I was caught up in my own fears and couldn't quite follow what he meant. 'But you're not scared of him. Are you?'

I felt rather than heard him laugh. 'No. I'm not scared.'

'Then why?'

'He needs to be prosecuted for this, so he needs to be

arrested and cautioned and interviewed properly. There's no margin for error. It needs to be by the book.'

'And if he turned up now, it wouldn't be?'

'I don't think so, no.'

'Because you would hit him.'

'I might.' He made a fist of his other hand and looked at it absent-mindedly. 'I might kill him.'

'You must be furious with him.' I yawned. The urge to close my eyes was overwhelming. 'He's wrecked your flat. All the blinds . . . and there's the carpet in the living room—'

'I don't care about that. Not at all.'

We stayed there, sitting on the floor side by side, until the paramedics rapped on the door downstairs.

36

There were dizzying numbers of uniformed police officers in the A&E department of the nearest hospital, but not for me. It was a busy night, as the ambulance service had warned, and the cops were there to deal with drunken bad behaviour, fights and domestics, and patients in the throes of mental illness threatening violence to themselves or others. I was used to being on the other side of the chaos, watching it spill through the streets, mopping up afterwards instead of being caught in the tide.

On the other hand, as I reminded myself, being in the hospital was nicer than being trapped in the flat. It was a relief to have access to some decent painkillers and the loving care of the nurses. They were charming to me, and side-eyed Derwent, stiff-legged with suppressed hostility, until I explained that he was not responsible for the three broken ribs, fractured collar bone, broken nose and broken cheek-bone, not to mention the multiple soft-tissue injuries that didn't appear on the X-rays. At that point he got a chair and a cup of tea.

'He saved my life,' I told the nurse who was preparing to stitch up the long laceration on my head that had bled so comprehensively, the one that had effectively glued me to the carpet. 'If he hadn't come to find me, I don't know what would have happened.'

She was young and from Galway, and had been in London for eight months. She had told me already she was thoroughly enjoying her life in the big city, though I noticed she hadn't lost her wide-eyed stare. 'So did you call him? Is that how he knew you were hurt?'

'No, I didn't have a phone.' I tried to look at Derwent without moving my head, but it was impossible: he was sitting too close to the head of the bed. All I could see was a dark blur in the corner of my vision. 'Actually, how did you know I needed to be rescued?'

'Liv called me. She said you hadn't picked up the last message she sent you, so she called every number she had for you and you didn't pick up. She knew I had keys to the flat and she knew I was worried about you so I'd go round straight away.'

'You were worried about me?' I really wished I could see his face.

'Ah, that's lovely.' The nurse waved a mouthpiece at me. 'Now this is going to sting, and it's going to take a while. You should have some gas and air.'

'I'm fine.' I was already on about eight different kinds of pain relief and I felt as if parts of me were floating off the bed, tethered to invisible balloons.

'The local anaesthetic really stings going in, and then it's a horrible sensation being stitched. Especially with a head injury.' She held it out to me again and looked stern, and I took it meekly. When I inhaled, I instantly felt a hundred times better than I could remember ever feeling before, chemical happiness bubbling through my bloodstream.

'That is really good.'

'Enjoy it!' The nurse looked over at Derwent and beamed, I presumed at my expense. I didn't care. It was a proper second-glass-of-champagne buzz and it made me feel as if the pain in my head (which was considerable, once she started digging around) didn't matter in the slightest.

'So, the two of ye are friends, are ye?'

'We work together,' Derwent said. I reached out my free hand to him and he took it. 'We're friends too.'

I rolled my eyes. Here we were again, trying to define the indefinable. He wasn't even getting close to the truth. *If you want something done, do it yourself.* I took the mouthpiece out. 'Honestly, we're much more than friends.'

'Is that right?' the nurse said.

'Yes. I love him.'

'Whoa there.' Derwent shifted his chair along the side of the bed so I could see him. He was grinning. 'This is a bit sudden.'

'Shut up.' The gas and air was starting to wear off; I was sobering up far too fast. 'It's not like *love* love.'

'You're doing well. Keep talking.' He held up a hand. 'In fact, no, have some more gas and air, then keep talking.'

'Stop it, you're terrible.' The nurse was laughing so hard I could feel the bed shaking.

'You know exactly what I mean,' I said coolly, with total dignity as far as I was concerned. 'It's not the gas and air, either. Ow.'

'You need it. Have a bit more,' the nurse said, and held the mouthpiece up for me again. I floated away on it again, but I still had something to say so after a few deep breaths I took it out and addressed the nurse.

'The thing is, it's that feeling. When you think about them and the feeling you get is too big to fit inside your chest. And you worry about them if you don't see them, and just seeing them makes everything better, even if they're annoying or you don't see eye to eye. That's love, isn't it?' I looked at Derwent. 'Isn't it?'

'Yeah, it is.' He squeezed my hand, and I felt as if I'd

actually managed to say what I meant for once, so that he understood me.

I was on a lot of drugs at the time.

From the moment he found me in the flat, Derwent didn't leave my side, until the officers came to take a statement from me about what had happened. He made it through the DASH form that all victims of domestic and sexual violence had to fill out, which I answered as honestly as I could. When I looked at the questions coolly and unemotionally, it was plain there was a pattern to Seth's behaviour that I had failed to see, despite everything I knew about violence in relationships. He had behaved like a perfect boyfriend but his goal had been to control me, and isolate me, and I had let him do it. My voice got quieter and quieter as the officer worked through the form, the shame of it all sinking into my bones. The officer was small, mid-forties, with kind eyes and very good make-up. After answering the final question on the form I asked about her manicure and the advantages of shellac nail varnish while I regained my composure. We both knew I was avoiding the next part, and her manner was gentle when she brought me back to their reason for being there.

'And now can we talk about what happened specifically in this incident today?'

I'd been dreading it, but it had to be done. Maybe I would feel empowered, I thought, once I'd actually said it. Derwent was standing with his arms folded, looking at the floor rather than at me, his head bowed.

'Um. He had wanted to come over last night.' I looked around. 'Wait, what day is it now?'

'Technically Monday.'

'Well, he wanted to come over on Saturday night and I put him off. I was too tired.' I heard the shake in my voice and clamped down on the emotion that was threatening to break through. 'When he came over on Sunday – yesterday morning – he saw a bruise on my neck that I got at work. He was suspicious that . . . that I had received it from a colleague.'

Derwent's eyebrows snapped together. So he *was* listening.

Of course he was listening; I would have been listening if it had been someone else telling this story. I looked away from him and focused on the policewoman. She didn't have a hair out of place and she had to be well into her shift. I needed to know how she managed that. Industrial strength hairspray, maybe.

'And then what happened?'

'He got hold of my phone and saw a message from another colleague. She had made a joke about something that someone had said to me. It was a throwaway remark. Nothing. I mean, it wasn't important in the least.'

Derwent hadn't moved. He was so still, you might have thought he was asleep.

'And he didn't like the joke.'

'No, I wouldn't tell Seth what the joke was. I thought he would overreact, and it was none of his business anyway.' I managed something like a laugh. 'Maybe I should have told him what she was talking about.'

'It was what I said, wasn't it?'

The police officer looked around at Derwent. 'What was it?'

'Do you know what? It doesn't matter. It could have been anything anyone said. He was looking for an excuse.' I understood that now, as I hadn't before, and I wanted to be sure Derwent understood it too. There was no reason for him to feel guilty. 'He would have invented a reason if he'd had to.'

He nodded, and a couple of minutes later I noticed he had left. I assumed he was going to make a phone call or something, and I didn't think any more about it until the police officers had taken photographs of my injuries and departed, leaving the curtain open. I could see him sitting on a chair at the nurses' station with his head in his hands. A nurse was standing between me and him, her hand on his shoulder as if she was comforting him, and my throat tightened. Was it worse to be hurt or to feel responsible for someone else's pain? I knew the answer to that one. I only caught a glimpse before an orthopaedic consultant came in to discuss treatment options and fracture clinics and keeping me in overnight, which was, in fact, what happened because they were concerned about potential complications. And then Derwent seemed completely normal when he came to tell me I was being transferred to a ward and he'd have to go, so I decided not to say anything about what I'd seen.

'I'll tell your parents where they can find you.'

'Why would you do that to me?'

'Because I'm more scared of them than I am of you.' He looked at me seriously. 'They would want to know.'

'They never liked him.'

A gratified expression flitted across his face. 'You should listen to them more often.'

'I'm not sure that would be wise.' I yawned. 'What time is it?'

'Ten past three.'

'I'm so sorry. You must be exhausted.'

He shrugged. 'I'm used to this.'

'Yes, but this weekend is supposed to be your time off too. You should be at home with Melissa and Thomas.'

'I wouldn't have wanted to be anywhere else. I'll talk to you tomorrow, OK? Get some rest.'

I nodded and he stood at the end of the bed for a beat, as if he was weighing something up. Then he picked up his jacket and left.

37

They didn't let me out of hospital on Monday after all. Some of it was the languor of the wards during a bank holiday when the staffing levels were low. Some of it was genuine concern about how I was, and whether my collarbone was likely to heal without an operation. If it had been up to my mother they would have kept me in for at least a week, if not two, because I couldn't get into trouble in hospital. In much the same way that I appreciated the care I was getting in hospital but couldn't wait to go, I was fretting under her attention even though I was glad of it. She arrived as soon as visiting hours began on Monday, armed with Lucozade and chocolate biscuits and books, and commandeered two extra chairs for beside my bed, one for my father and the other for her belongings.

'Look at the state of you. Your lovely face, Maeve.'

'It'll heal.' That was the wrong thing to say.

'Yes, well one of these days you're not going to heal. You need to take care of yourself. Did you chip your teeth?'

'*I* didn't chip anything. I didn't do this to myself, Mum.' I relented. 'My teeth are fine.'

'So it's just everything else.' She looked me over with the proprietary air of a farmer inspecting her favourite cow, and I returned the look, admiring her fine-boned good looks that were lasting well despite her official status as a grandmother, and her general air of elegance that she had somehow managed not to pass on to me. 'You haven't been eating properly either. I can tell.'

'I've been busy.' I wanted to smile but it hurt too much. 'I'm not in here because I haven't been getting enough protein.'

'No, you're here because of that – that – *shit*.'

It was so unlike her to swear that my mouth popped open in pure shock. My father moved from his stolen chair to sit on the end of the bed where he held on to my ankle through the bedclothes.

'Maeve, are you all right in yourself?'

'I will be.' I was in the state of mind where I was perpetually on the verge of tears and kindness seemed to tip me over the edge every time. 'I'll be OK.'

He nodded. 'Good girl.'

They stayed for the whole day, my mother taking the opportunity to tell me long and detailed stories about their neighbours and the extended family and even neighbours of the extended family until I was desperate for some peace and quiet. The ward was hot and my whole body ached viciously. But when they gathered their things to leave, I found myself asking what they were doing the next day – would they call me?

'We'll see you tomorrow of course.' Mum looked at me as if I was insane. 'We couldn't have you here on your own. Besides, we want to know what the doctors have to say and we know there's no point in waiting for you to pass it on. You never tell us anything.'

You were never so low that you couldn't be taken down a peg or two by your mother, I mused after they had gone. I missed them though, and I missed my phone, and I missed being able to move without catching my breath. I was acutely conscious that Derwent hadn't come as he'd said he would. It was the bank holiday, I reminded myself. He would have had other places to be. I still half-expected him, late into the evening, since visiting hours were the kind of rule that he regarded as an irrelevance. I stayed awake longer than anyone else in the ward, jumping in case every movement from the hall meant he was about to saunter in. And then, when I settled down to try to sleep I found myself tormented with worry about why he hadn't come, if he blamed me for what had happened or if he blamed himself – if things would never be the same.

I managed to get some sleep at last but the hospital machinery began to grind early, breakfast arriving long before I was ready for it. My mood deteriorated after an agonising session with a bright and cheerful physiotherapist who left me with a handful of leaflets, a sheet of exercises and strict instructions to limit myself to light desk duties for two or three months.

'You're going to have to go easy on yourself,' my mother said, nodding in support. 'You have to listen to them, Maeve.'

I did listen, and I listened to the doctors who came and offered various opinions about my injuries, and I asked very politely if I could be discharged sooner rather than later, and then I asked less politely, and then I offered to discharge myself if they wouldn't agree to do it, and then I told them I was going to walk out. At that point I got official permission to leave, plus a goody bag from the hospital pharmacy.

'You don't even have any clean clothes,' Mum fretted. 'Those clothes you came in are filthy.'

'They'll do. I'm only going home,' I pointed out, by which I meant my parents' house because I was not remotely ready to be on my own again.

'These might help.' A bag landed on the end of the bed and my parents leapt up to embrace Derwent, who they adored. I was hugely relieved to see him and covered it by going through the bag to see what he'd brought me from the flat: jeans, a loose short-sleeved shirt, underwear, trainers.

'Not bad. I'm not sure how I feel about you pawing through my knicker drawer, though.'

'I didn't look at anything. I did it by touch alone.'

'Oh God, why is that worse?'

He grinned. 'You're looking nice, by the way.'

'You should have seen me yesterday. It wasn't as colourful then.' I had seen myself in a number of mirrors by now and my appearance was getting worse as I healed.

'Her poor face, Josh.' My mother's face crumpled. It was only then I realised that she'd been holding herself together for two days, hiding her feelings by talking compulsively and sniping at me for my many shortcomings.

Derwent took her hand and patted it. 'She's tough. She'll be fine.'

'She's not as tough as she thinks she is,' my mother snapped.

I rolled my eyes and Dad, the soul of tact, put his arm around her and guided her away. 'We'll get a cup of tea in the café down the hall while you're talking.'

Derwent waited for them to move out of earshot, then turned to me. 'How are you, really?'

'I'm really OK. Ready to get out of here.'

'I believe you.' He sat down in one of the chairs and stretched out his legs. 'Are you pressing charges?'

Wrong-footed, I started re-folding the clothes he'd brought. 'I haven't decided.'

'They can prosecute him without you, but it'll be better if you're involved.'

'I know that.'

He watched me, saying nothing, and I wondered why I had wanted to see him.

'Look, it's difficult.'

'Thought you might say that.'

'Don't make me feel bad about it.'

'If you're wondering why I didn't come to see you yesterday, I spent some of it at the flat with the coppers who are investigating the case. When we got there, what do you think we found?'

'I can't begin to guess,' I said shortly.

'The phone, and it was working perfectly. Your police radio and your ASP and your PAVA spray were all there. The router was plugged in. The cutlery was in the drawers and the knives were in the block. The blinds were all up – they had little holes in them, but you might not make much of that if you didn't know how they'd been before. And your keys were on your bedside table along with your mobile phone.'

I had started to tremble again. 'There was blood everywhere.'

'Yeah, there was. And you're injured. But there's no sign he intended to do anything more.'

'He trapped me there. You know I'm telling the truth.'

'I do. But you need to convince a jury of that.'

'You saw it.'

'And I'm happy to give evidence to that effect. But it will only work if you're prepared to step up and say what he did. Your injuries are one thing – the way he left you is another. And you need to give that evidence in court.'

'I know I should.'

'When I saw he'd put everything back—' he shook his head. 'This wasn't a moment of madness. He didn't lose his temper and punch you, and he doesn't regret anything except that he missed his chance to go to the flat while you were there. He planned this, over time. I know you have feelings for him, but he's dangerous, Kerrigan. He needs locking up.'

'I don't have *feelings* for him. That's not why I don't want to take it further.'

'Why then?'

I'm ashamed. I couldn't say it. I looked down instead, folding the sheet in concertina pleats.

'The other thing I did yesterday was talk to a girl called Rae. Did he ever mention her to you?'

I shook my head.

'He went out with her last year for about six months. It ended when he beat her so badly she had double vision for

296

weeks afterwards. She still gets headaches. She didn't report him because she thought no one would take her side against his – he *told* her they wouldn't believe her. She's terrified of him. He locked her in her home and told her he would kill her if she ever told anyone. She promised him she'd keep her mouth shut and until I talked to her, she did.' He leaned forward. 'It's not you, Maeve. You didn't make him do this. You aren't the first person he's treated this way and you won't be the last, unless he's stopped. You don't want to go to a house and find a dead girl because you didn't do anything in time, believe me.'

'How did you find her in a day?'

His face went completely blank; by chance I had asked the one question he didn't want to answer. 'I didn't. I found her last week. I looked Taylor up online. There was a picture of them together at a legal party last year. She's another solicitor and the caption mentioned her by name. I tracked her down through her LinkedIn profile.'

'You did this last week?'

'After he gave you the flowers.' Derwent winced. 'I knew something was wrong. I thought he was up to something. I should have said as much to you. But you'd told me to stay out of your private life—'

'And you were angry with me about Luke.'

He looked shocked. 'I would never have left you in harm's way because of that. I was trying to work out how to talk to you about it. I thought I had time.'

'So when you came to the flat on Sunday . . .' I said slowly.

'I thought I was too late. I thought he'd killed you.' He managed a particularly grim smile. 'You might understand now why I don't want you to have that experience.'

I moved over to sit on the edge of the bed, close to him. 'If you hadn't come to find me, I don't know what would have happened. You've told me not to blame myself, but you shouldn't feel guilty either. If you'd warned me about him, I probably wouldn't have listened.'

'You were in love with him.' Derwent was taking a keen interest in the floor so he didn't have to look at me.

'No, I wasn't. But I wanted to be.' It was hard to admit it, but I had to be honest. 'He seemed as if he was completely right for me. He could be really charming and persuasive, and he pretended to be in love with me. He made me think I was lucky to have him. I wanted to believe it was all true. I thought I was the problem. I should have realised that he really was too good to be true.'

'You haven't had much luck with men lately.'

'You can say that again.'

He glanced up at me with a quick grin, but before he could reply his phone began to ring and he took it out, frowning at the screen. He killed the call, but his expression had faded to a tired kind of resignation.

'It's Melissa.'

'You should go.'

'Yeah.' He made no move to get up though.

'You spent so much time on me over the last couple of days.' I felt ashamed for having expected him to come and see me the previous day, and I was glad I hadn't complained about it. 'I hope you got to do something with Thomas and Melissa yesterday.'

His mouth tightened. 'That wasn't the most relaxing part of the weekend.'

'Did you have a fight?' Not the sort of question I would have dared to ask usually, and not the sort of question he would answer, but he had seen me at my most vulnerable two days earlier and maybe it made him feel he could talk openly.

'She's not happy about Luke. She's jealous.'

'What happened with Claire happened a long time before you met her.'

'Yeah, obviously.'

'And you don't want to be with Claire. You never did, as I understand it.'

He shook his head. 'She thinks I won't stay with her now. That I won't need Thomas any more because I have a son of my own.'

'That's ridiculous. You'd never lose interest in Thomas. You love him. And there's more to your relationship with Melissa than him, isn't there?'

He looked at me for a beat, his eyes shadowy and unreadable. Then he stood up. 'Look, I'd better head off.'

'Of course.'

'I'll swing by the café and tell your folks you're getting changed.'

'Thanks,' I said, meaning it. He nodded and turned to go, and I couldn't let him leave without saying the last thing that was on my mind, in case I didn't get another chance.

'Josh, I'm really sorry for not telling you about Luke.'

He looked back at me. 'I know you are. I'll get over it.'

'Will you?' I sounded dubious, because I was.

'Yeah. Probably.' His phone started to ring again and he walked out, his shoulders bowed as if he was supporting the weight of the world on them.

38

I was on the point of leaving hospital when a trim, perfectly made-up woman appeared by my bed and smiled. 'You probably don't remember me, Maeve.'

'I do! You're the officer who took my first account the other night.' I'd have known her manicure anywhere.

She smiled. 'Got it in one. Alice Schneider is my name.'

'It's nice to meet you when I'm not bombed out of my brain on painkillers.'

'You were absolutely fine the other night. Very lucid, very helpful.'

While my parents introduced themselves and shook hands with her, I thought about what was important enough to bring her to the hospital. I'd been trying not to think about Seth, and what might be happening to him, but I'd have to face up to it sometime.

'Do you want us to leave while you're having a chat?' Dad asked.

'Stay. I'd like you to hear what's going on. Otherwise I'll have to explain it to you after Alice goes.' I turned to her. 'How helpful was I on Sunday, exactly? Did you make any progress?'

She sat down on the edge of the bed. 'Well, we arrested

him. We picked him up yesterday morning, at his address, and took him in for interview.'

'And?'

'No comment all the way through. No surprise there, given what he does for a living. I'm sure he advises his clients to do the same.'

'How did he seem?'

She thought for a second. 'I've never met him before, but he seemed quite normal. Calm, but not too calm. A bit rattled to have us knocking on his door so early in the morning. He listened to everything I told him you'd said, and made notes on all of it.'

'Of course he did.'

'It's tricky interviewing them when they know what you're asking and why.' She grimaced. 'I did my best, but I couldn't get him to say anything that implied guilt.'

'That doesn't surprise me at all. He's very bright and he's good at what he does.' I swallowed. 'My colleague was here earlier. He told me the flat wasn't how we left it when you went to look at it yesterday.'

'No, it wasn't.' She smiled. 'I do wish you could have heard him when he saw it. I learned a lot, let me tell you.'

'I can imagine. He doesn't hold back.'

'No, he does not. Did he talk to you about giving us a proper statement?'

I nodded.

'And have you made any decision about that?'

'I have to, don't I?' My voice was husky and I cleared my throat. 'I mean I should.'

'You have to do what's best for you.' She looked sympathetic. 'Don't feel you've got to do this because you're a copper – that'll drive you mad. Forget it for now. But you should think about how you might feel if he's never charged. Would that make you feel worse than giving evidence against him?'

'I've seen what they do to victims in court.'

'Me too. And I've seen victims after their attackers walk out of court, even if they've done their best to give evidence against them.' She tilted her head to one side, assessing me. 'It's not an easy thing to do at all.'

'What do you want her to do?' Dad asked.

'We really need Maeve to give us a proper statement,' she explained. 'We only have her first account at the moment and it's not detailed enough on its own for us to be able to charge him with a realistic expectation of getting a conviction.'

'If I give a statement, I'm basically agreeing to give evidence against him at trial,' I said.

'And if you have her statement, what happens then? Will he be locked up?' Mum asked. She was trembling.

'He'll be rearrested and charged immediately,' Alice said. 'He'll appear at the magistrate's court tomorrow, and they'll refer it to the Crown Court because we'll be going for Section 18 – you probably know it as GBH or grievous bodily harm – given that Maeve has serious injuries such as fractures. They will grant him bail at that stage, but he won't be able to approach Maeve or you or anyone else connected with her between now and the trial. We'd pick him up for witness intimidation straight away, and then he would be remanded in custody to await trial.'

'When would the trial be?' Dad asked.

'In a few months. The first hearing at the Crown Court would be in about four weeks but the actual trial date won't be set until then.'

'Can he work if he's awaiting trial?' I asked. 'I should probably know this already.'

Alice smiled. 'I had to ask the CPS lawyer about that. He'll have to inform the SRA that he's been charged with an offence but it's not dishonesty or fraud so he should be allowed to work. If he's convicted, they may take a view on letting him remain a solicitor. There'd be a disciplinary committee hearing.

But as I said, he wouldn't be allowed near you before the trial. You won't be running into him at court.'

I could feel the three of them watching me as I thought about it, and Derwent's face when he talked about thinking I was dead, and how I would feel if the same thing happened to someone else, or worse, because I hadn't felt like being some barrister's target practice for a couple of hours.

'I'd say he's hoping you won't make a statement,' Dad said delicately. 'I'd say that's his dearest wish.'

'So you think I should?' I turned to look at him, surprised. He wasn't a vindictive man, as a rule. I thought of him as a peacemaker, and forgiving to a fault. Now he smiled at me, his eyes soft.

'I think you should do everything in your power to ruin his life, my dear, since he did his very best to wreck yours.'

I turned to Alice Schneider. 'I'm ready to make a statement, whenever you like.'

Going to my parents' house to recuperate involved a trade-off between security and self-determination, but I'd known it would be like that before I got out of the car. When I was under their roof, they owned me, and I had no say in the matter. For the first couple of days I spent most of my time in my room, sleeping and trying to get comfortable and thinking. Mealtimes came round with impossible frequency as Mum did her best to fit a year's worth of feeding-up into a single week.

I was standing in the kitchen on Friday, staring with minimal enthusiasm at a buttered scone, when I heard a knock and then voices at the front door. A small boy ran into the kitchen at top speed, and stopped when he saw me. He was taller and thinner than he had been the last time I saw him.

'Thomas?'

'What happened to your arm?'

I glanced down at the sling that was supporting it. 'I hurt it. What are you doing here?'

'He comes here a fair bit.' My dad followed him in and guided him to the table. 'We were going to have a go at chess again, weren't we? Can you remember the rules?'

'Yes. Some of them,' he added with a smile that made a dimple flash in one cheek and melted my heart. He sat down next to my dad and reached across him to start setting out the pieces on the board, greeting each of them like an old friend. 'Hello bishop. Hello queen.'

'Hey.' Derwent was in the doorway. 'How are you?'

'Surviving.' I nodded at Thomas. 'I almost didn't recognise him. He's grown.'

'They do that.'

'He looks at home here.'

'Your parents look after him now and then. When Melissa is busy and I'm working.' He stuck his hands in the pockets of his jeans, suddenly awkward. 'They didn't tell you?'

'Keeping secrets goes both ways in this family,' I said tartly, knowing that my dad was listening. He was smiling to himself when I looked across at him. It made sense to me, in a way; Derwent had moved to a house near them, and he and his girlfriend had no parents nearby to help out with Thomas. For reasons that escaped me, my parents loved Derwent. They must have been only too happy to involve themselves in his life. My brother Declan had two girls and they had been vocally disappointed that they didn't have a grandson. It was up to me to provide one, Dec had informed me, because he was finished. I had done precisely nothing about that.

So, of course, my parents had taken matters into their own hands and found a substitute. I didn't know why I was surprised.

'Thomas, are you hungry?'

He nodded, his eyes round and hopeful.

'Would you like a scone?'

'Yes please.'

With some relief I put the plate down beside him and watched the scone disappear.

'Better than a Labrador,' Derwent said. 'Can I have a word?'

'Sure.'

He jerked his head towards the hall and I followed him out of the kitchen.

'Are you bored yet?'

'Out of my mind,' I confessed.

'Thought you might be. I brought you something.' He handed me a folder and I flipped it open one-handed.

'Kev's report on the Bishops Avenue house. It's exactly what I wanted. How did you know?' I sat down on the bottom step of the stairs, already reading.

'I had a feeling you'd want to see it.' He leaned against the wall, watching me. I flipped through the report quickly, skimming for the gist, then closed the folder and looked up at him.

'Very interesting.'

'Understand any of it?'

'Some parts,' I said carefully.

He grinned and took out his phone. 'He told me to call him so he can talk you through it.'

I put Kev on speakerphone so Derwent could hear both sides of the conversation. Kev sounded as if the only thing he had ever wanted to do, his whole life, was explain his report to me. 'It was an interesting one! Big house, lots of visitors. It's going to take a long time to identify all of the people who left their DNA in and around the place.'

'What about the bathroom with the damaged bath?'

'The whole room had been thoroughly cleaned many times, but I lifted the rubber sealant from around the bath and guess what? Blood. It gets everywhere, luckily for us.'

'Do we know whose?'

'We identified one sample as being likely to belong to Iliana Ivanova. She was reported as a missing person at home in

Bulgaria and they had familial DNA on file in case a body turned up.'

'Why didn't we know Iliana was a missing person?'

Derwent answered. 'Her family had no idea what had happened to her. One July day two years ago she didn't answer her phone when they called. They never heard from her again. They did try to get the Met to take an interest in looking for her, but the case wasn't progressed. As far as I can tell, a PC went round to her last known address, they said she'd moved on without leaving a forwarding address and the file was closed.'

It was all too easy to disappear, I thought, especially when you weren't from the country where you went missing and no one there much cared you were gone.

'What else did you find, Kev?'

'Blood from three other sources, but I haven't been able to identify any of them so far.'

'Three? We only know of one other person they cut up – the man in the pool.'

'I'm afraid so. Two of them are very small samples – hard to work with. We're doing our best to get usable DNA.'

'They were a bit too relaxed in that video when Iliana died. They'd used that method of disposing of bodies before.'

'Could be they've used it since,' Derwent said. 'Too good a way of disposing of bodies not to take advantage of it.'

'What about Paige Hargreaves? Did you find any trace of her?'

'I didn't find any evidence that she was there, but I didn't find anything to say she wasn't.'

'Cagey,' Derwent commented.

'I'm not going to tell you anything I can't prove, you know that,' Kev said happily. 'But I'm still looking. We're removing all the fittings from that bathroom so we can make absolutely sure we haven't missed anything. We'll take everything into the lab and go through it millimetre by millimetre.'

'And in the meantime, we have Carl Hooper being very forthcoming about what he did and did not do on Sir Marcus Gley's instructions.' Derwent laughed. 'You'd think he'd been waiting for a chance to drop his boss in it.'

'So basically, we know how Iliana died and we know how her body was disposed of,' I said. 'We know how the guy with the tattoo died, and we've been told his body was disposed of the same way, but we still don't know who he was and no one has reported him missing. We have two other sources of blood which may or may not be from dead bodies and no missing persons to match up with them.'

'Correct.'

'But Paige Hargreaves is still a mystery.'

'Bang on,' Kev said happily. 'You must be feeling better.'

'Getting there.'

'When are you coming back to work?'

When I'm able to face everyone, I thought, and couldn't say it. 'I'm not sure yet.'

'I hope it'll be soon. We miss you.'

'Thanks, Kev.' Derwent took the phone from me and ended the call while I blinked furiously, trying to hide the tears that had welled up.

'Well, that's helpful.'

'Even though it doesn't get you any further with Paige Hargreaves.'

'When is Gley being arrested?'

Derwent's eyes gleamed. 'I wondered if you'd ask that.'

'It was supposed to be around now, wasn't it?'

'We're working towards Monday.'

'Monday,' I said thoughtfully.

'Want to come?'

'Yes.' I looked up at him. 'But do you think that's a good idea?'

'Definitely not.' He grinned. 'I'll pick you up.'

39

It was still dark when Derwent's car pulled up outside my parents' house. I hurried out, closing the front door as quietly as I could so I didn't wake them up.

'Morning.' He looked at the tin I had balanced on my knees as I put on my seatbelt. 'What's that?'

'Cake. Mum made it for the team.'

'Brilliant.' He sounded genuinely delighted. 'I knew it was worth picking you up.'

'I wasn't sure you'd come.'

'Why not?'

I shrugged. 'I thought you'd change your mind. I am supposed to be on sick leave.'

'I don't see why some miserable little shit's emotional problems should deprive you of being at Gley's arrest. If you hadn't nosed out the Chiron Club story, we wouldn't know anything about Gley or Iliana. This is all down to you.'

'Thanks.'

He nodded, concentrating on the road. 'You deserve this. And Burt agreed with me.'

'You got permission?'

'Everything by the book.'

I waited until we had stopped at a red light to pop the lid

of the cake tin. The smell of chocolate filled the car. Derwent leaned over and inhaled deeply.

'That is beautiful.'

'She said it was your favourite. Why does my mother know your favourite kind of cake?'

'She's that sort of person.'

'And I'm not?'

'No, and please promise me you'll never bake me a cake.'

'You'd be lucky.'

'Yeah, lucky to survive. I've seen your cooking. I wouldn't risk it.'

'I won't bother then,' I snapped.

He gave me a sidelong smile that was sweet and surprising enough to defuse my anger. 'Just promise me you'll keep it away from Liv until I've had some. She's like a python at the moment. She'd down it in one.'

The quiet road in St John's Wood where Sir Marcus Gley lived had never seen anything so shocking as the dawn raid on his house, complete with three police cars, one van and two unmarked vehicles. We weren't expecting trouble, but it was best to go prepared for it. In addition to a lot of uniformed officers and Derwent, the team consisted of Chris Pettifer, Pete Belcott and Colin Vale, who had left the office for the first time in months. No Liv, who was limited to desk duties. I wasn't officially there either, but I was glad to be included, and Derwent made sure I wasn't pushed out of the way as we trooped up the narrow path to the front door. The houses weren't huge but they were late Georgian, complete with fanlights over the doors and high windows, and only very wealthy Londoners could have aspired to own one. The brass knocker on the door gleamed in the morning light with the sheen of proper elbow grease. I heard a chorus of soft chirps around me as the uniformed officers switched on their body-worn cameras to record whatever happened next.

Sir Marcus himself came to the door when we knocked, before the officers had to use the battering ram known familiarly as the big red key. He was plum-faced and rumpled, lashing himself into a brightly coloured dressing gown.

'What on earth is going on?'

'Sir Marcus Gley?' Derwent asked.

'Yes.' He smoothed his hair, suddenly self-conscious. 'What can I do for you gentlemen?'

Gentlemen. I was standing right in front of him.

'We're here to arrest you,' Derwent said.

There was nothing jolly about his face now: I recognised the terrifying temper he had unleashed on Iliana Ivanova in the video of her death. 'On what charge?'

'Murder.' Derwent recited the caution smoothly as Sir Marcus took a step back, shaking his head.

'What? There's been some mistake. This is insanity.' His eye fell on me at last. 'You. I recognise you. You came to the club. You asked about a journalist. Is this about her?'

'Indirectly,' I said.

'Ridiculous. I told you I never saw her. I don't know anything about what happened to her.' He peered past me, looking across the road to where a small knot of neighbours had gathered to watch what was going on, even at that early hour. The spinning blue lights on the emergency vehicles would have given the game away. 'This is harassment! I'm going to sue the police for this. You're damaging my reputation for no reason. My lawyers are going to make you pay for this.'

'We need to search the premises.' Chris Pettifer handed him a warrant. 'Is there anyone else here?'

'My wife. You can't disturb her. She's still in bed.' He was calling after Derwent, who was halfway up the stairs already, two uniformed officers in tow.

'I'll be nice,' Derwent promised, which was even less reassuring if you knew him.

The rest of the detectives and officers fanned out through

310

the house. I stayed in the hall with a PC who was guarding the door, and Sir Marcus, who looked at me blankly.

'You're making a terrible mistake, you know. I didn't kill that journalist.'

I wrote it down. He'd been cautioned properly; he should have known not to talk. *Anything you do say may be given in evidence.* 'I'm not here to arrest you for that.'

'For what, then?'

He really didn't remember, I realised. There was nothing feigned about his bemusement. Iliana had mattered so little to him, alive *and* dead, that he had forgotten all about killing her. If it hadn't been on video, there would have been no evidence at all that he'd done it, assuming Hooper had never decided to talk. Gley and his money had wiped every trace of her off the face of the earth, and his arrogance had removed even the memory of her death from his mind.

Our plan was to take Sir Marcus to the office once he'd got dressed and we'd conducted a preliminary search of the house. We intended to leave a PoLSA team at the house to go through it with more care, in case there was something useful buried in a cupboard or a drawer. Somewhere he would have the clothes he had worn the night he killed Iliana; it was a long shot but there might be trace evidence there, if we were lucky and the dry cleaners hadn't obliterated it. He struck me as a man who owned more than one evening suit. I hoped it might have been hung up and forgotten.

What I hadn't appreciated was that Gley had lived in the house for forty years or more, and every inch of it was densely cluttered with heavy antique furniture filled with junk and paperwork. We were slower than I would have liked to get moving. At last, we were ready to take him to the van. Pettifer had no sooner cuffed his hands in front of him than Belcott popped his head in.

'Boss, just to let you know, someone's tipped off the media.'

Derwent swore. 'Who's done that?'

'You probably did it yourself,' Sir Marcus said bitterly and Derwent shook his head.

'Not me. More likely one of your neighbours.'

'What sort of media does he mean? Are there cameras? I can't be on camera like this.' He looked around wildly. 'You have to help me.'

I was wearing my jacket over my shoulders to accommodate my sling. I slipped it off and dropped it over his wrists to hide the cuffs.

'People will know I've been arrested anyway,' Gley complained.

'Yes, that seems likely.' Derwent's face was poker straight.

'But they'll jump to all sorts of conclusions.'

'They might think you're a criminal.'

'Exactly.' He gave Derwent a look of pure loathing. 'You think this is funny.'

'On the contrary. I want to get you into the police van with as little trouble as possible.' He gathered a few of the biggest officers and surrounded Sir Marcus with them. 'Don't get separated, don't get distracted, and let's do this as quickly as we can.'

I moved to the side of the hall, out of the way. Derwent looked for me and nodded, relieved.

'Stay out of trouble.'

That had been the idea, I thought but didn't say, confining myself to a glower that made the corners of his mouth turn up.

It wasn't Derwent's fault that the transfer to the van was the opposite of smooth. As soon as the front door opened, a photographer snapped a picture of Sir Marcus. The flash of the photograph startled him and he stepped back, encountered a large policeman behind him and stepped forward again, but lost his balance on the step. He pitched forward, and the photographer got a second shot which would appear in several of the next day's newspapers. In it, his mouth was open and his eyes were wide with horror. His hair floated away from his head like cobwebs. Someone caught him and set him on his feet before he actually fell, but the momentum was gone. Reporters and cameramen jostled for the right angle, and the whole ungainly mob pushed into the hall before the police took control and moved through the scrum, Gley all but invisible in the middle of them. I peeled myself off the wall where I'd been stepped on, squashed and dragged, easing my arm where it ached.

'Are you OK?' Colin asked, his eyes wide.

'Never better,' I said, and to my total shame toppled forward in a dead faint, as Derwent stepped forward smartly to catch me.

40

'I didn't know you were coming in! Are you back?' Liv perched on the edge of my desk and looked at me dubiously. '*Should* you be back?'

'I'm not officially here. I'm still on sick leave but I wanted to see Gley's face when we knocked on his door.'

'Was it worth it? Doesn't look as if it was to me.' She was scanning my face, which I knew was deathly pale.

'I got in the way during the arrest. I'm fine.'

'You always say you're fine.'

'Leave it,' I said through gritted teeth, and because she knew me well, she did.

In a low-key way I had been dreading the return to work. I knew my colleagues would have discussed what had happened to me; there was nothing worse than a room full of detectives for sheer gossip. But in the end, it had been easy to slip in behind Derwent and make my way to my desk, and by the time Liv noticed I was there I was already working. That meant I was legitimately able to brush off a big welcome, had one been on offer.

'I would have come to see you but Josh said you weren't in the mood for visitors.'

'Did he? He's not completely wrong.'

'Why?'

'I still feel stupid,' I muttered, and Liv leaned in so she could whisper.

'That's ridiculous. You couldn't have known what Seth was going to do.'

'So you say, but you never liked him.'

'No, but he's not my type.'

'Josh didn't like him either.'

'Firstly, he doesn't like *anyone*. And secondly, he doesn't like anyone you go out with.'

'That's a grand total of two men in the time I've known him.'

'So maybe it will be third time lucky.'

I shook my head. 'Never again. I'm celibate from now on.'

'Shame. Cup of tea?' Liv asked, straightening up again.

'I would really love one,' I said, and went back to reading through my inbox. I had to catch up on what I'd missed, but the words were dancing in front of my eyes.

'If it's not something that'll help me question Gley, forget it.' Derwent leaned over my shoulder to look at my screen, then reached around me to start closing windows.

'There are things I want to see. Reports,' I protested. 'People are waiting for answers.'

'Unless they need them today, they're not getting anything. You have to go home.'

'Not yet.' I turned to look up at him. 'One, I have work to do—'

'Which I've already addressed.'

'—and two, I don't feel up to dealing with public transport.'

'I'll drive you.'

'You can't. You have to be here to question Gley.'

'He's locked up with his lawyer.' Derwent checked the time. 'We've got two or three hours before we'll get anything more from the PoLSA team and I want to keep him waiting a while anyway. I don't have to charge him until tomorrow morning and unless he decides to plead guilty to manslaughter when he sees the video, I doubt I'm going to get a confession out of him. So I'll drive you.'

'Someone else could do it.' I looked at the screen where the contents of my inbox were scrolling past. 'Hold on a second. That's from the officer in Roddy Asquith's murder. It might be important.'

'You've got five minutes. Then we're leaving. I'm going to see if there's any cake left.' He straightened up and walked off, sidestepping Liv who had returned with the tea.

'He's so bossy. You must hate it,' she said, as if she thought the opposite. 'But this time I think he's right.'

'So do I.' The email from Frank Steele was brief and had a report attached: pages of forensic detail from the car crash, complete with pictures. I gave up on reading it, secretly glad I had a reason not to plough through it immediately, and forwarded it to Liv, who had taken over the case in my absence. My head was aching and I felt exhausted. Maybe there was a point to sick leave after all.

'This isn't the way to my parents' house.' We were heading east, not south.

'Yeah, I said I was taking you home. Your home.'

A metallic taste filled my mouth along with a rush of saliva that I swallowed. *Please God, don't let me be sick in the car.* Derwent would never forgive me, even if he deserved it.

'I'm not ready. It's only been a week.'

'Eight days. And you need to go back or you never will.'

'I don't want to.'

No answer. He kept driving, his attention fixed on the road.

The anger that poured through me pushed the nausea and weakness out of its way. 'Are you listening? I don't want to go there, and you can't make me.'

'No, I can't.' His jaw had tightened but his voice was calm and level. 'If it helps, I do know how you feel.'

316

'I really doubt that.'

'You never want to see the flat or anything in it again. You find yourself thinking about it when you least expect or want to. You remember every detail of how it looked when you left it. How it smelled. The food you'd bought that day. The blood on the walls. Every morning when you wake up there's a second where you think you might be there on the floor, with no way out.'

'You *shit*,' I said softly.

He glanced across at me, his eyes very bright. They saw too much, I thought. 'Too accurate?'

'No. Not at all accurate, in fact.' I stared out of the windscreen, refusing to look at him again. He didn't seem to care, driving on in silence. The oldest trick in the book: not saying anything so the other person felt compelled to talk. There weren't that many people who could bear the sound of silence. It was Derwent's bad luck that I was one of them, I thought, clamping my mouth shut on the words I wanted to say. He couldn't force me to talk. And he could take me to the flat but he couldn't make me go inside.

For once the traffic was light and we made good time. Much sooner than I had expected or wanted, we were pulling into the street. The flat was at the end of the terrace. Of course there was a free parking space right outside, when usually I would have to circle for ages, waiting for someone to leave. I often had to park on the next street over and lug my shopping or work back. I corrected myself: I *had* often had to do that. Not any more.

'I'm not going in,' I said, after he turned the engine off.

'No.'

'You don't know everything.'

'No.'

I swallowed the knot in my throat. 'How did you know about what happens when I wake up? I haven't – I haven't told anyone about that.'

'It's part of recovering from a difficult experience. I've had a few of those.'

'So you've felt this way.'

He shrugged instead of answering.

'And got over it.'

A sidelong look this time.

'Sort of got over it,' I amended.

'Sort of.'

'I don't want to go in.'

'I know.' He dug in his pocket and took out a set of keys, which he placed carefully on the dashboard in front of me.

More silence: a few seconds of it this time, before I snatched the keys and got out of the car. Better to get it over with and go than sit there full of fear, I told myself, and hated it, and did it anyway.

My damn-it mood got me up the path and through the front door but I stopped once I was in the hall.

'Problem?' He was behind me, not too close.

'It smells different.'

'Paint.'

I turned to look at him. 'Paint?'

'Go on.' He nodded at the stairs. I made myself walk up them, my feet silent on the carpet, and found myself thinking of Paige making her way into her flat up those narrow, echoing wooden treads. That distracted me all the way to the top, where I stopped again.

'You painted the hall.' It was grey now instead of cream. It felt bigger, the ceiling higher.

'Yep.'

'The blood wouldn't come off?'

He shrugged. 'It needed doing.'

In the living room, a new carpet covered the spot where I'd bled all over the floor. He'd moved the furniture around, changing the feel of the room, and new pale grey-green curtains hung at the windows. The walls were the same shade.

'It feels like a different flat.'

'I always meant to redecorate.'

I nodded. 'I like it.'

'Good.' He leaned against the wall and blew out a lungful of air. I realised with a rush of affection that he'd been nervous about what I'd think.

'Anything else you need to tell me about?'

'There's a new bed.'

'There was nothing wrong with the bed.' I was genuinely puzzled.

'I thought you could do with a fresh start.'

A new bed so I hadn't slept with Seth in it. I hadn't even thought of returning to a bed I'd shared with him and how that might make me feel. Derwent had been so kind it made me want to cry. To cover it, I gave him a hard stare. 'I suppose all of this is being added on to my rent.'

'Every penny,' he said gravely. 'Plus I'm charging you danger money.'

'Why?'

'I cleaned out the fridge.' He shook his head. 'The things I've seen.'

'You didn't touch the bottom shelf, did you?'

'Not without gloves.'

'That could have been a new antibiotic.'

'It could have killed us all. What was it originally?'

'Leftover curry.' I pulled a face, apologetic. 'The container leaked.'

'You should have cleaned it up straight away.'

'I didn't notice for a couple of days. By the time I realised what had happened, it had settled in.'

'Yeah, it's hard to kill something with a personality.'

Only Derwent could have made me laugh standing in the room where I'd been so badly hurt. I looked around again. 'You didn't have to do this.'

'I know.'

'But I'm glad you did.'

'Take a few minutes. I'll wait outside. When you're ready to move back in, let me know.'

'It might be a while.' I followed him into the hall.

'You can't stay at your parents' house forever. They'll drive you up the wall.'

'I thought you liked them.'

'I do.' He was halfway down the stairs already. 'They're not my parents though, and they don't comment on everything I do.'

'Not in front of you, maybe.'

'Oh, is that how it is?' He looked up from the bottom of the stairs and grinned. 'I thought I got off lightly.'

'Compared to some people you do.'

'Good.' Two strides took him to the front door and he slammed it behind him. I heard his footsteps receding down the path, and the soft thud of the car door closing.

On my own again, in the flat. It felt strange.

It felt *right*.

I walked into every room, noticing what had changed and what had stayed the same, and I felt as if I was at home.

41

The following morning, my mobile rang at one minute past six. I fumbled it off the bedside table and under the covers.

'H'llo?'

'Don't tell me you were asleep.' Derwent sounded offensively pleased with himself.

'I was, actually.'

'Guess who I just charged with murder.'

'Gley?'

'None other.'

I pushed the duvet off and eased myself upright, leaning against the stack of pillows that was supposed to make my shoulder more comfortable in bed. I thought it couldn't be *less* comfortable, but I wanted to get back to work quickly so I would do as I was told. For now.

'Did he confess?'

'Nope.'

'What did he say to the video?'

'Nothing whatsoever. But you should have seen his face. His lawyer too. I think we need to start handing out sick bags before we play stuff like that.'

'And he didn't cop to it even though he saw the video?'

'Oh, he offered a plea to manslaughter at four o'clock this morning. Or his lawyer did. Gley cried.'

'You made him cry!'

'I said what I imagined you would say if you were there and it was surprisingly effective.'

'Thanks.'

'You're welcome. Anyway, the CPS said no to manslaughter. He strangles her for almost a minute and shows no remorse afterwards and it's all on video from start to finish. It's murder. I reckon we'll get a guilty plea at some stage but he wants to hurry up and do it before it gets to trial because he'll lose out on credit for a guilty plea.'

'I'm sure you're very worried about the amount of time he serves.'

'I don't care if he dies in prison,' Derwent said cheerfully, 'but there's much less work to do if he goes straight to a plea.'

'Well, that all sounds good.'

'It is.'

There was a note in his voice I recognised though, a note that I associated with nothing good. *Trouble coming.* 'What else has happened?'

'Nothing. But you might want to have a look at the *Times*.'

'Why?'

'Bianca Drummond has written a piece about the Chiron Club.'

'Saying what?'

'Nothing prejudicial. The lawyers must have been all over it. She basically explains the club is a den of iniquity behind closed doors. They use young women as toys and consume illegal drugs openly and get up to all kinds of bad behaviour. She does say there are credible accounts of sexual assault at the club and even rumours of murder. She also says she went undercover and observed a lot of this behaviour herself and that there's an ongoing police investigation that she's helping.'

'Is she helping? I hadn't noticed.'

322

'She's an important witness, you know.'

'Does she mention Paige?'

'Nope.'

'What about Gley or Hooper?'

'In passing. She stops short of saying that Gley is a killer but she mentions he's been arrested. One of the pictures is of him from yesterday morning. Not a flattering shot.' I heard the newspaper rustling. 'Not like the main picture they've used for the article. That's very striking.'

'What is it?' I snapped.

He read the caption. '"Fighting the good fight: an undercover police officer dealing with a member's unwanted attention." In fairness, you can't see your face. Only someone who knows you very well would recognise you.'

'I suppose you identified me immediately.'

'I'd know that bottom anywhere,' he said solemnly.

'Oh *God*.'

'Nice clear image. I wonder what equipment she was using? The technical side of covert surveillance has really come on a lot.'

'What's he doing?'

'He's got his arm around your waist. You're all standing up drinking champagne.' More rustling. 'I mean, you might as well not be wearing a skirt.'

I put one hand over my eyes. 'How bad is it?'

'At least an inch of cheek. But on the bright side the world can see you were wearing underwear.'

'He grabbed me. There was nothing I could do. I thought it was too crowded for anyone to see anything,' I wailed.

'It's a lucky shot through the crowd. They must have moved apart at precisely the right moment.' No one ever sounded smugger than Derwent did then.

'Is that everything?'

'I think it's probably only the start,' he said, and hung up before I could reply.

*

323

I did look at the article online after breakfast, because I wanted to read it rather than because I was keen to see the picture, although I saw that too. I was, thankfully, unrecognisable, as Derwent had promised, but he hadn't exaggerated at all about how much of me was displayed in a national newspaper and internationally on the website. I focused on the words instead, frowning as I read it. Bianca had started by explaining a bit about the history and public reputation of the Chiron Club, and who the typical members were, establishing it as a haven of male privilege. Then she tore into it. The article was expertly written to suggest a lot that was, as yet, unsaid, but an intelligent person could read between the lines. I read it twice, then sat and thought for a while, then read it again. There was what it said, and what it didn't say.

I was on sick leave. I needed to recover. The previous day had shown me I was far from back to full working order.

It still bothered me that I hadn't found out who killed Paige Hargreaves, and it bothered me that her name wasn't mentioned in Bianca's article. She was disappearing from view, lost forever like Iliana, except that Paige didn't have a family to grieve for her. There was no one to hound us to get a result – no one to mourn. Without that there was every chance she would slip down the pile, an unsolved case, a file on a shelf and a small collection of body parts waiting for disposal.

Well, not if I had anything to do with it. I set about collecting what I needed and made a couple of phone calls. The following day I put on jeans and a clean shirt, tied up my hair and headed for Greenwich with a spring in my step. It was good to be doing something useful. I felt that way for the first half of my journey, before the hot, sticky, crowded underground began to drain the energy from me. Someone jostled my elbow as I emerged from the station and the resulting wave of pain left me sick to my stomach. I trudged slowly around to Paige's street and when I reached her house

I leaned against the railings for a moment. I shut my eyes. Maybe I shouldn't have come on my own.

'Are you all right?' A woman's voice, close to me: Paige's neighbour, Mila. I stood up straight and blinked myself awake.

'I'm fine. Having a break.'

'What happened?' She was looking at the sling, and the fading bruises on my face that were still visible in the right light.

'An accident. Not work-related.'

She looked different, I thought. There was something softer about her appearance: pale pink lipstick instead of red, but also a gentler look to her face. She was wearing a white linen dress and a huge straw hat. 'Thanks for agreeing to meet with me at such short notice, Mila.'

'You were lucky. It happened to fit in with my plans.' She was the sort of person who gave offence casually, without being aware of it, and considered it a point in her favour that she was a straight talker. She clearly wouldn't have changed her plans one iota if it hadn't suited her to meet me. 'Do you want to come in?'

I couldn't face the steps up to the front door, I discovered. 'No, thanks. I don't want to keep you for long. I wanted to ask if you could look at a few photographs for me.'

'An ID parade?'

'Sort of. Unofficially, for now.' I handed her the sheaf of images I'd printed off at home on my parents' dodgy printer that had to be hand-fed every page. 'Have a look at those and tell me if you see the man who came round to look at Paige's flat before we did.'

She shuffled through the printouts, shaking her head as she went. The familiar faces slipped past: Roddy, Luke, Orlando, Peter Ashington, Carl Hooper and a few others I'd thrown in like Pete Belcott and Chris Pettifer to round out the collection. She got to the end and sighed.

'No. None of them.'

325

'Have another look. Take your time. He would probably have looked very different in a suit. These images aren't great quality.'

'They look as if you found them on Facebook.'

And a few other places, I thought. 'Once more. Please.'

She looked again, more thoroughly this time, sliding her sunglasses up on to the top of her head. I almost had a heart attack when she hesitated over Luke's picture but at last she moved on to the next one, and the next. She went through all of them and then pulled out one which she handed me.

'That could be him.'

'OK,' I said. 'That's a help.'

'He looked older. His hair was different. Slicked down, not sticking up. And he was wearing a suit, as I said before, not casual clothes. But I think it was him.'

'Leave it with me.'

'All right.' She looked up at the house. 'Do you know when you're going to be finished with Paige's place?'

'Soon, I hope.'

'The landlord has agreed I can tackle the mould upstairs before he rents it out again. Paige simply wouldn't consider it. She didn't want the upheaval. But he says he's going to let me have the whole place refurbished – all the damp addressed, everything. It's wonderful.' Her cheeks had flushed with excitement.

'Are you paying for it?'

'Contributing. I view it as an investment in my own property. And if he ever decides to sell, I've got first refusal on it. I could turn the building back into one house.'

'That sounds like a worthwhile project.'

She nodded, looking up. 'I want to get on with it now.'

'I understand. We're still trying to find out what happened to her though, so . . .'

'Oh, of course.' She slipped her sunglasses into place as if she was lowering a mask over her face. 'I should have asked if you had any leads.'

'Some. We're making progress,' I said cautiously, thinking of the absolute lack of any forensic evidence to link Paige to the Chiron Club currently, and how frustrating that was.

'That's good.' She was frowning though. 'Are you sure you're all right? You do look pale.'

'I'm fine.' I thanked her, and said goodbye, and waited until she had gone inside before I took out my phone to make one more call, even though it could only cause me trouble.

42

As the car drew up on double-yellow lines outside the café the hazard lights started to blink, the universal acknowledgement that the driver is doing something unacceptable and knows it, but is going to do it anyway. Derwent opened his door into the path of a scooter that tooted indignantly as it swerved. As he got out, his jaw was tight with irritation. I slid down a few inches in my seat as he slammed the door. *Temper, temper.* He shouldered his way into the café, yanked his sunglasses off and glared around, visibly unimpressed with the charms of Carlo's. I lifted a hand and waved to attract his attention. The sight of me did nothing to improve his mood.

'What do you think you're doing?'

'Having a break?' I slid a coffee across the table. 'I got you this.'

'I don't want it.' He slid it back. 'I want to know why you're in Greenwich conducting enquiries instead of at home with your feet up.'

'I got bored. I wanted to work.'

'I thought you'd had enough of that on Monday. I only let you come to arrest Gley because I knew I'd be there to keep an eye on you. When you come back to work officially

328

– which should be when you're fully recovered, and not before – you're supposed to be on restricted duties. That means paperwork. That means being in the office, not wandering around using your own initiative to get yourself into trouble.'

'I know,' I said quickly, 'and I'm absolutely going to take things easy from now on. But I had an idea.'

He frowned. 'What kind of idea?'

'How to find out who impersonated a police officer at Paige's address and removed her computer and notes. But I need you to help me.'

'Go on.'

I passed him my set of photographs and explained how I'd shown it to Mila Walsh. I tapped the top one. 'This is the guy she picked out, which is exactly what I thought would happen. I want to go and see him. I think if we confront him, he'll admit it.'

He picked the page up, then held it to one side as the picture below caught his attention. 'Is that . . .'

'That's Luke.'

He stared at the picture intently, almost hungrily, as if he hadn't had the chance to look at him properly before.

'Did you look like that when you were twenty-five?' I asked eventually.

'I was better looking. Obviously. Like now.'

'All right, handsome.' I nodded at the window. 'Let's see if your looks can work some magic on the traffic warden that's about to give you a ticket.'

Ticketless, because Derwent was jammy like that, we drove across the river while I explained who we were going to see and why I thought he had taken Paige's notes. When I got to the end, Derwent nodded.

'Makes sense. Were you planning to do this by yourself before you had a funny turn, as a matter of interest?'

'No, I was going to ask for help even before that.' I looked at him sideways. 'I'm not reckless. Besides, this is right up your street. You're far more intimidating than I am.'

'You have your moments.'

'I would have to say now is not one of them.' I leaned against the headrest and shut my eyes. 'I've felt perkier.'

'Are you sure you want to do this now?'

'Yes. I don't think we're going to find out what happened to Paige otherwise.'

'And that's more important than how you feel.'

'Of course.' I looked at him, surprised. 'You'd be the same.'

Derwent shook his head, but said nothing more to try and put me off.

When we arrived in Whitechapel, he looked up and down the street. His lip curled. 'I don't know how any coppers patrol around here. You wouldn't get five feet before you had to nick someone. How would you even pick which criminal to arrest first?'

'Don't arrest anyone yet.' The intercom crackled beside me. 'Bianca? Maeve Kerrigan.'

'Come on up.' She sounded cheerful and Derwent raised his eyebrows as he followed me into the hallway.

'What did you tell her?'

'Not much. She thinks I'm here to update her on the inves-tigation.'

'Which is true, in a way.'

'I would never lie.' I blinked innocently at Derwent, who grinned back. There were lies and lies, as we both knew.

She was waiting for us with the door open when we reached her floor. She looked at me with open curiosity. 'I heard you were off sick – what happened?'

'An accident. I'm on the mend now.' I moved past her into the small, cluttered sitting room and nodded to her boyfriend. 'Hi, Sam.'

'Hi.' He jumped up, wiping his hands on his jeans nervously. 'Do you want to talk to Bianca on her own? I can go somewhere else.'

'Actually, I want to talk to both of you.'

'That doesn't sound good.' He tried to laugh.

'What's this about?' Bianca looked from Derwent to me, her eyes wary.

'It's about someone going to Paige's flat after she disappeared and removing her computer and her notes for the story she was working on. The story that was going to transform her career. The one that made her so excited, she couldn't stop talking about it, even though she wouldn't tell you what it was about.' I smiled. 'She didn't trust you, did she? And she was right. Because the first chance you got, you went to her flat and took everything you could find that might be of any use to you, so you could write Paige's story yourself.'

'That's not fair. I didn't want all her hard work to be for nothing.'

'Not when you could benefit from it yourself, no. Even if it slowed our investigation into Paige's death – even if it distracted me from finding her killer – your career and the story was more important. That's how you knew about Antoinette. She didn't contact you, you contacted her. I called her and checked this morning and she confirmed the story you told me was a lie.'

'I made sure you knew about Antoinette. If I hadn't let you know I was meeting her, you still wouldn't know she existed.'

'That was only because you were worried about your own safety. It suited you very well to have police back-up while you were investigating the Chiron Club. You knew about the Bishops Avenue house because Paige had found out about it and you were following her lead.'

'They took me there.'

'They did not. We've found CCTV from the area near the club that shows you following Carl Hooper when he left the club but he drove off without you.' One of my phone calls the previous day had been to Colin Vale, who was happy to describe the little scene he'd cut together from various cameras, and how very annoyed Bianca had looked to be left behind. 'You made your own way to the house, knowing that we would probably turn up sooner rather than later and come to the rescue if you needed us. They found you poking around and shut you away while they tried to work out what you wanted, but you didn't even know what you were looking for. The only reason you were there in the first place was because of Paige. But of course you couldn't give that away to anyone without revealing that you were the person who stole the files from her flat.'

'I didn't. I wasn't even there!' Bianca said.

'No. You sent Sam instead.'

He had been following the conversation with his mouth hanging open, alarm written all over his face. 'What?'

'We have a witness who saw you. She spoke to you. I showed her your photograph and she identified you, even though you had changed your appearance by slicking your hair back and wearing a suit.'

'The woman downstairs. She scared the shit out of me, asking if we knew who'd killed Paige.' He looked wildly at Bianca. 'You said they would never find out. You promised me I wasn't doing anything wrong.'

'Shut up, Sam,' she hissed. 'Don't say anything else.'

'I didn't know I was going to get in trouble.' He turned to me. 'We had a key. Paige had given us a spare set because she kept losing hers and locking herself out. So it wasn't burglary, was it?'

'Maybe it was murder.' Derwent had his arms folded; he looked very big and very stern. 'Did you kill Paige Hargreaves?'

'No!' Sam stared at Bianca. 'Tell him! Tell him I didn't!'

'What do you do for a living, Sam?' I asked, knowing the answer already.

'I'm a tree surgeon. Why?'

'Tree surgeons have access to all kinds of tools. From the body parts we recovered, we know Paige was dismembered by someone who knew how to use tools.'

'Not me.' He shook his head. 'Not me. Please, Bianca. Tell them.'

It was crystal clear that Sam was not the sharpest tool in his own van, and that Bianca made all their decisions. I looked at Bianca.

'Well?'

'She was already missing when he went to her flat. That's why we knew it was safe for him to let himself in and look around. I persuaded him to dress up as a detective in case someone saw him, as a cover story. He thought it was funny. It was all my idea.' Bianca's voice was harsh. 'I told him what to look for. He took her computer and her notebooks and a load of other stuff, in case I needed it.'

'I didn't touch anything else,' Sam said, slightly desperately.

'Where is the computer now?'

'In a storage unit down the road. I didn't want to keep it here in case someone found it.'

'We're going to need it.'

'You can have it. And the notes. I've read it all now.'

'Oh, well, that's all right then, isn't it?' Derwent glowered at her and she quailed.

'You've found out what she knew, I swear it. She was trying to find out what had happened to Iliana. She'd got hold of someone who used to work for the club who saw them bringing in bodies and cutting them up at the Bishops Avenue house. He would only talk to her off the record so I don't know who he is – she used a code name for him and I never tracked him down. But it's all there in her files. She was really close to getting to the truth when they killed her. When you said she was cut up, I knew what had happened. I knew they'd got her too.' Bianca's eyes were brimming with tears. 'I shared as much as I could with you. I did what I could to help, honestly I did.'

'No, you obstructed the investigation by stealing key evidence that could have helped us find her killer.' I didn't bother to keep the contempt out of my voice. 'And you just admitted you already knew she was missing when you went to her flat. You deliberately delayed reporting that to us until you'd retrieved the information you wanted. Our investigation – and Paige's safety – mattered less than your career. Unless you knew she was already dead and there was no point in looking for her.'

'I had no idea what had happened to her, I swear. All I knew was that I had one chance to find out what she was investigating before we reported her missing. If I hadn't taken it, she'd have died for nothing. The story would have gone nowhere. I was making sure her work counted for something.'

'Very noble,' Derwent said.

'I don't expect you to understand, but it wasn't self-interest. I really believed she had found out something important. People need to know how the world works. The self-interest. The lying and cheating. There's one rule for the rich kids and another for the rest of us.' Bianca's eyes had filled with tears. 'It's not fair, and it's my job to reveal that. Paige would have wanted me to have her notes. She would have wanted me to carry on where she left off.'

'That's what you told yourself,' I said.

'It's true.'

'Are you going to arrest us?' Sam's eyes were huge.

'We haven't decided,' Derwent snapped. 'We'll need you to make a statement about what you did. Every detail.'

'Why should we help you?' Bianca was starting to recover, which meant she needed squashing again.

'If there's something on that computer that could have got us a conviction and we lose it because you nicked it and disrupted the chain of evidence, that's going to come back to you. Your best bet is to cooperate or you'll be even more screwed than you are already,' I said.

'This is so unfair.'

'No. It's the law. And though you might not want to believe me, it applies to everyone.'

43

Liv shook her head as I walked into the office. 'I knew you'd never stay away. What's the excuse this time?'

'Not an excuse. Some business that couldn't wait.' I explained that Derwent and I had been interviewing Bianca and her boyfriend, and why.

'What a bitch.'

'She's ambitious.'

'At her friend's expense.' Liv bristled. 'I'd arrest her for perverting the course of justice.'

'That option is still on the table, but the pair of them are being very cooperative.'

'Now that they've been found out.'

I laughed. 'OK. No sympathy for Bianca. But we've got Paige's notes and her computer and phone, so we can find out exactly what she knew and who she was dealing with when she died. I actually think we might be able to solve her murder.'

'Well that's good news. That only leaves a few hundred to work on.'

'Said like someone who is going on maternity leave in a few weeks and won't have to care about it for a year.'

'Pretty much,' Liv said happily. 'Hey, did you get a chance to read that email about Roddy Asquith?'

'Not yet. That was on my list of tasks before I leave again.'

'I couldn't see anything useful in it,' she confessed. 'It's highly technical. All about how the car was rigged to run into the wall but nothing that points a finger at anyone in particular.'

'What about Carl Hooper? Did he admit to knowing anything about Roddy's murder?'

'No. He denied all knowledge. He said that as far as he knew the only actual murder in the club's history was Iliana's. He doesn't know anything about Paige or Roddy.'

'Or he's heavily implicated in both and doesn't want to give himself away. He's already in serious trouble for assisting in disposing of the bodies. He's looking at prison time.'

Liv looked dubious. 'Hmm, he's being very forthcoming about what he did and did not do on Sir Marcus Gley's instructions, but when we ask about Roddy and Paige, he's at a loss.'

'Maybe he was out of the loop.'

'He clearly knew too much already.'

I sighed. 'Is there anything new I haven't seen yet?'

'We've got CCTV footage from the rental agency where the BMW was hired but we haven't been able to identify the man yet. The quality is terrible and he's wearing a cap. You don't get a clear look at his face. Also, he used a fake licence as ID.'

'Send the CCTV to me,' I wheedled.

'Absolutely not. You're supposed to be on sick leave. You're not supposed to be working.'

'Watching a few minutes of video is hardly work.'

'It's more than you're supposed to be doing.'

'I might recognise him. I spent more time in the club than anyone.'

Liv rolled her eyes. 'If you insist. But you shouldn't be here. I don't want Josh to shout at me for encouraging you.'

'I'll zip through my inbox, and then I'm gone,' I promised.

I meant it, too, and it might even have worked out if the fifth email I opened hadn't been the one from Frank Steele in Hampshire. This time I read through the report in more detail, and got to the final appendix of pictures from the forensic examination of the car's wreckage. They had finally located and identified the object that had weighed down the BMW's accelerator. I looked at it, then looked again with closer attention and a creeping sense of dread: a circular five-kilo weight with a hole in the middle, the kind you add to a set of dumbbells.

The kind Luke Gibson had under his bed when I searched his room before Roddy died.

I wasn't going anywhere.

'I'm getting pretty tired of coming in here.' Luke was sprawling in his chair, affecting to be relaxed, but he was fidgeting in a way I hadn't seen before. Blue shadows under his eyes hinted at too many sleepless nights in the previous couple of weeks. There were innocent explanations for that, of course; it could have been grief. It could have been that he was worried about being in the building where his biological father worked. Equally, it could have been his guilty conscience, I reminded myself sternly. He had agreed to come with me when I'd asked him to be interviewed again. He had allowed himself to be measured and opened his mouth obediently for the DNA-sampling swab of his cheek, cooperating without questioning why we wanted this information. At the same time I had the sense that he was desperately worried and on his guard. The good humour was a very thin veneer today.

He raised his eyebrows. 'I'm beginning to think you're coming up with excuses to bring me in because you want to see me.'

I didn't smile at him; I was a long way past jokes. 'As I explained earlier, I've asked you to come in today because we've found something that we'd like you to explain. The

338

weight that was used to bring about Roderick Asquith's murder matches the weights you own. When I visited your house this afternoon, I located your weights and discovered that you were missing one that matches the one recovered from the crime scene. You were unable to account for its absence.'

'I'd noticed it was gone, but to be honest I assumed you'd taken it on one of your searches. There seemed to be quite a wide and random selection of things that disappeared from the house. I found it hard to keep track.'

'When did you notice the weight was missing?'

'I don't know. A few days ago.'

'Can you identify the weight in this picture?' I slid it across the table and he glanced at it.

'It's the same make as mine. It's the same size as the one that's missing. It could be mine. I can't say without any doubt. I don't remember that it had any marks on it or anything that would make it stand out as mine, and it's a well-known brand.'

'Did you kill Roderick Asquith?'

'No.' A muscle flickered in his jaw and I did my best not to think about Derwent, who was watching a video link from the interview room. He had been silent since I told him what I'd found, and had withdrawn from the investigation at Una Burt's request, but nothing on earth would have kept him from watching his son while I questioned him. No one had tried to stop him.

'Do you know who killed Roddy?'

'No.'

'Who had access to your room?'

'Anyone who came to the house, I suppose. I don't lock the door to my room.'

'Who would have known you had weights under your bed?'

'I don't know. They weren't hidden.' He shifted in his chair, uneasy.

'They weren't easy to see either, were they?'

'No.' His mouth tightened. 'I suppose not.'

'Someone would need to know where they were if they wanted to take one. They wouldn't come across them accidentally.'

He shrugged, helpless. 'I can't say if that's true. I didn't keep them in a particularly prominent place but they weren't a secret.'

'Do you know if Roddy had any enemies?'

'No. No way. He was a good guy.' He sounded definite.

'Did you ever fall out with him?'

'No.' The answer came instantly. 'He was the kind of person who didn't like arguments. He'd go out of his way to avoid upsetting anyone.'

'Did he talk a lot?'

'Yeah, all the time. You couldn't shut him up.'

I thought of the no-comment interview he had given me, of how he had hardly dared to open his mouth. 'Was he good at keeping secrets?'

Luke actually laughed. 'No. Orlando used to call him Roddy FM because he broadcast everything he heard at school. If you wanted to spread a rumour, he was your guy.'

'Is that why he talked to Paige Hargreaves about the Chiron Club?'

The smile faded from his face. 'I don't know.'

'Did he ever talk to you about the Chiron Club?'

'Not in any detail.'

'Did he mention any concerns or worries he had about the club or its members?'

'No.'

'Did he ever talk to you about the time he borrowed your car without asking and had a friend drive it to Standen Fitzallen?'

'No. I was away for a while and then I suppose he didn't think of it. I didn't get the chance to ask him about it after you told me they'd taken my car.' Luke jammed the heels of his hands into his eye sockets for a moment, emotion catching him unawares. He got control of himself. 'I was hoping to ask him about it. You questioned me about it . . . and then, afterwards, I went home for a couple of days because my mum was upset.'

We both knew what had upset her; there was no need to record it on tape.

'By the time I went back to my house, I'd already heard that Roddy was dead. So no, we never talked about it. But I wish we had.'

Orlando Hawkes had lost weight since the first time I met him. He was verging on gaunt, his cheeks hollow, his eyes sunk in his head. I wondered if he had been ill. The cocky arrogance was gone, and so was the Chiron Club's fancy lawyer. This time he had a quiet young woman who looked about twelve, if she was small for her age – the opposite of intimidating, though I knew better than to assume she'd be easy to handle.

When I came into the room, Orlando looked up at me.

'How's Luke?'

'He seems fine.'

'Have you let him go?'

'Not yet.' I settled down at the table, Chris Pettifer beside me, and we began the formal interview process. He had been cautioned already and had gone through the same measuring and DNA-sampling process as his housemate, but Orlando hadn't been able to pretend he was relaxed about it. He had shaken like an overbred pedigree puppy throughout.

'Do you know why you're here, Mr Hawkes?'

'Because you found a weight in the wreckage of the car Roddy was driving when he killed himself and you think it's significant.'

I tilted my head fractionally. 'Why do you say he killed himself?'

'That's what happened.'

'We're investigating it as murder.'

He shrugged. 'I don't know if you've got a quota to hit or something but it wasn't murder. Roddy was under intolerable pressure because you were harassing him. He wasn't the kind of person who could cope with that sort of stress. He topped himself. No great mystery there.'

'But plenty of forensic evidence that someone else was involved.'

Orlando gave a nervous laugh. 'What kind of evidence?'

'All sorts,' Pettifer said. 'Like CCTV from the rental place where someone hired the car that killed Roddy.'

'Would you like to see it?'

Orlando swallowed convulsively and said nothing, and Pettifer made a big deal out of turning his laptop around and making sure the screen was angled so Hawkes and his solicitor could both see clearly. They watched the footage closely. I'd seen it many times that day and didn't look at the screen; I knew it was miserable quality. When it came to an end Orlando sat back and smiled, a little too relieved for my liking.

'That could be anyone.'

'You're right,' I said. 'We don't have a good shot of the guy's face, and he's wearing nondescript clothes – nothing identifiable. But we were able to use the images to calculate his height. It's not Luke. He's too tall. And it wasn't Roddy, because he was much broader than this man. But this person is in or around the same height as you.'

'Totally circumstantial,' the lawyer said. I ignored her.

'So we have someone who could be you renting the car for Roddy, and we have a weight taken from your house as a means of wedging the accelerator down to drive the car at the base of the chimney. It must have been a bad moment when you realised you couldn't retrieve it because the engine was on top of it.'

'I—' He shook his head.

'You knew Luke had weights under his bed. Luke was away.

Roddy trusted you. There was nothing to stop you from setting this up.'

'Roddy was my best friend. Why would I want to kill him?'

'We actually know the answer to that one. You were worried he'd give away your secret, and you wanted to make sure Peter Ashington understood he'd get the same treatment if he told us what he knew about you.'

'Ash . . .' Orlando's face was bloodless.

'I spoke to him just now, after I talked to Luke.' I smiled. 'It was very interesting. According to him, you wanted to make sure he didn't say anything about your little adventure in Standen Fitzallen. Two people knew about it and one of them was Roddy, who was your best friend since school. You knew he couldn't be trusted. You didn't know about Ash. So you used him to help set up Roddy's death, to give yourself something to hold over him and to show him you meant what you said. If he talked, you'd kill him too.'

'I did wonder,' Pettifer said heavily, 'why he was so keen to talk about the rape he carried out the night before he picked you up. It turns out he knew he could probably get acquitted if the rape case made it to court. He wasn't at all sure he could get away from you if you decided he had to die.'

'Was Roddy already drunk when you put him in the car?' I asked. 'When did he realise you were going to kill him?'

Orlando squeezed his eyes closed and I guessed he was remembering what he had done, and how Roddy had been.

'Was he scared?' I asked quietly, and Orlando winced.

'He . . . I don't . . .'

I waited, but this time instead of breaking down he rallied.

'I didn't hurt him. I wouldn't. He was my friend.' He blinked at us, focused again. 'I wouldn't.'

'But you did. And we know why.' I slid them across the table, one by one: images we had found in the safe at the Bishops Avenue address. A slender, raffish young man with a beard and curling hair and languid dark eyes, lounging in evening wear on a terrace, the smoke from his cigarette looping through the night air. The same man swimming naked in a pool with another man whose tattoo was a dark shadow in the water. The two of them kissing. Teeth sinking into a shoulder. One pinned against a wall by the other. Both of them on a bed, tangled together. The bearded man dragging the other man's head back as the strain made the tendons stand out of his neck like guitar strings, and his face contorted. The room was completely silent.

'In the last couple of years, you've lost the beard, cut your hair, put on a bit of muscle and kept your nose clean. But in July, two years ago, you were this guy here. And this one' – I tapped the tattooed man's face – 'he didn't make it home that night. He died.'

Orlando lifted his hands to his face, his whole body trembling. 'Oh fuck. Oh fuck. Oh *fuck*.'

'What was his name?' I asked.

'You don't have to answer that,' the solicitor said, but Orlando ignored her.

'I n-never knew it. I – I don't even know what happened. You have to believe me. I was out of it – drink, drugs, fuck knows what I'd taken. When I woke up, he was floating in the fucking *pool*. There was nothing I could do. He was dead by the time I found him. I mean, I don't think I did anything to make that happen. I didn't hurt him. Apart from – you know.'

'We know how this guy died,' Pettifer said. 'There's a video of it. You weren't involved.'

'What?' The emotion leached out of his face, leaving utter blankness that was somehow worse. 'You know how he died?'

'He OD'd. You were asleep. Nothing to do with you,' Pettifer said gruffly.

I tapped the photographs. 'This was a scandal that you could have lived down.'

'If it was only the sex, then I wouldn't have cared. I mean, shit, it's embarrassing to see myself like that, but fuck it.' He gave a strained little laugh. 'We're all somewhere on that spectrum, aren't we? Not a big deal to cross the line. Lots of guys do it.'

'But you thought you'd killed him,' I said. 'And the Chiron Club let you go on thinking that so you'd be a good little member and get your father to use his considerable wealth and influence to have land rezoned for housing in commuter towns around London.'

'They set you up,' Pettifer said helpfully. 'You made it easy for them.'

'And the only person you told was Roddy, because you needed his help to get home to London, but Roddy needed to involve Ash because he couldn't drive. Then when we started investigating Paige's murder, you were so scared that you were going to be found out you decided Roddy knew too much to be trusted and it would teach Ash a lesson too.' I leaned across the table, dropping my voice so he had to concentrate on what I was saying. 'You killed him, and you set up Luke to take the fall for you.'

'I never wanted that to happen.'

'Come off it, Orlando. You could have used a few bricks to wedge the accelerator down. You took something of Luke's because when it came down to it, he was as expendable as Roddy. You put yourself first, over and over again.'

'No. I wanted to get the weight back. I didn't realise what would happen to the car.' His solicitor winced but there was nothing she could do; she couldn't stop him from talking if he wanted to, and the truth was spilling out of him. Privilege was a double-edged sword, after all. Orlando simply didn't believe he was going to get in trouble for what he'd done. He looked from Chris to me. 'It was nothing to do with Luke, I swear it. He's never been involved at all.'

'The best thing you can do for him is to start at the beginning and tell me exactly what you did.' I relaxed, giving him some space. It was all falling into place, the pieces arranging themselves without needing much help from me. 'Tell me about Paige. When did you decide you had to kill her?'

'Paige? I barely knew her.' He shook his head. 'I never hurt her.'

I stared at him. 'But if you thought Roddy had told her what you did—'

'I never thought that. Roddy fancied the arse off her so he told her as much as he could about the club, but a lot of it was rumours and gossip that he came up with as a way to impress her. He was trying to get her into bed but I wasn't worried he'd give me away to her. I'd warned him. He knew the score.'

I was puzzled. 'But you also warned him not to talk to me, didn't you? And he didn't.'

'I could have convinced Paige he was talking shit if she'd asked me about it. She wasn't the police. She was really full of herself and everything she was going to achieve but she wasn't all that bright. She'd get obsessed with something she was writing about and bore on about it, like everyone else should care too. Totally self-absorbed.' He blinked at me. 'You'd know, though. He'd have told you everything and I'd never have been able to fool you into thinking he was lying. You're much too clever for that. I had to shut him up . . . because of you.'

It was the kind of compliment I could really have done without.

44

Derwent was waiting for me in the corridor when I came out of the interview room where I'd been with Orlando Hawkes, lounging against the wall with his hands in his pockets.

'Good interview.'

'It was a good result,' I said. 'I didn't really have to do much. He was very forthcoming once he got started. I think he was so relieved he hadn't killed Jonah Powell he almost forgot it was worse to admit he'd staged Roddy's death.'

'You had him on CCTV, though, at the rental place.'

'Have you seen the footage? He's halfway off the screen for most of it and the quality of the recording is dismal. You never get a proper look at him. No one would ever ID him off it.'

'What about the height?'

'We pushed the analysts to give us something to work with but they told us not to rely on it because it was such a rough estimate.'

Derwent whistled. 'And I thought you always played fair.'

'Well, I was right to say the heights matched, because it *was* him in the CCTV, so it would have been the same.' I stretched, trying to ease the ache in my shoulder. 'Roddy Asquith wasn't perfect but he didn't deserve to be rammed into a wall at sixty miles an hour. I wasn't going to let Orlando Hawkes get away with it.'

'I heard him blaming you. Don't let that get to you.'

'Of course not,' I lied.

'Where does that leave Luke?'

'He wasn't involved. He was either at work or staying with his mum during this whole period. We've got his Oyster card and his mobile phone records and we can see his movements. Unless he has the power of bilocation he was nowhere near the house in Fulham or the brickworks.'

'He's a clever kid. He might have worked out how to provide himself with an alibi.'

I shook my head. 'You don't have to worry about him any more. There's nothing to link him to the murder. I even double-checked his alibi for the night Iliana died and he was thousands of miles away, like he said. Besides, there's no question in my mind that Orlando was acting alone. He wouldn't have wanted to involve anyone else – that was the whole point. If he'd been able to work out a way back to London without telling Roddy what had happened at the house party, he would have done that. Unfortunately for Roddy, he couldn't. Roddy was the only person he told, and he regretted it. He wasn't going to make that mistake again.'

'But he dragged Ashington along when he killed Asquith.'

'As a warning. I don't think Peter Ashington had any idea what was going to happen to Roddy. And I suspect Orlando would have ended up killing Peter Ashington too, because he would have wanted to tie up the last loose end. He couldn't afford to take any chances. I think we'd have found Ashington at the bottom of a cliff somewhere, apparently overwhelmed with guilt about raping the waitress at the club.'

'Which would have given it away, since he doesn't give a shit about her.'

'But a coroner might have believed it was suicide. And then Orlando would be free.'

'So are you going to talk to Luke now?'

'I was going to.' I raised my eyebrows. 'Do you want to do it?'

'No, you can give him the good news.' Derwent was still standing there, though, as if he was waiting for me to say something.

'Do you want to come with me?'

'I wasn't sure if that was a good idea.' He looked at me helplessly. 'I don't know what to do here.'

'Well, it's uncharted territory for both of you.' I sighed. 'Oh, Josh, I don't know what to say. It might go really badly but I think you should try to talk to him. You'll regret it if you don't.'

'What if he doesn't want to talk to me?'

'I think you have to prepare yourself for that. He wasn't looking for you – you've dropped into his life without warning. And it's not as if he's been having a nice time over the last few weeks. His whole life has fallen apart, he's probably going to have to find somewhere to live and he's lost two of his best friends because one killed the other. It's horrible timing.'

Derwent shook his head ruefully. 'Typical, isn't it, that I only find out I've got a son because he's a suspect in a murder.'

'This isn't how it's supposed to be but it's the situation you've got to deal with. And it might not be so bad.'

'Claire won't have told him anything nice about me.'

'She was really fond of you – I think she still is, if it comes to that. But Luke belongs to her. Of course she's going to be protective of him, and she has every right to be.'

'Yeah, she did all the hard work.'

'Look, you weren't there when he was growing up. I think you'd have been a great dad if you'd had the chance, for what it's worth, but it didn't happen. That doesn't mean you can't get to know him now. But it only works if he wants to get to know you. You have to leave it up to him to decide. He is a grown-up.'

'Isn't he, though.' Derwent managed a lopsided grin. 'Makes me feel old.'

'Well . . .'

'Oh, come off it, Kerrigan.'

'You deserved that after the dress comment.'

'I'm sure I apologised for that already.'

'And I'm sure you didn't.' I tapped on the door of the other interview room and went in before he could reply.

Luke glanced up, his open, hopeful expression changing as Derwent came into the room after me and shut the door behind him.

'Do you want the good news or the bad news?' I adopted a bright and breezy tone in the hope it would cut through the atmosphere that was building in the room, crackling with electricity like the air before a thunderstorm. Luke was staring at Derwent with an expression that was as close to hostility as anything I had seen from him before.

'The bad news first, please.'

'Orlando has confessed to the murder of Roddy Asquith.'

Luke shut his eyes for a moment and winced. 'Did he do it?'

'Yes, he did.'

'Why, though?' Luke looked infinitely sad. 'They were best friends. Roddy loved him. He'd have done anything for him.'

'That was really the problem. Orlando decided he knew too much about something he'd done in the past. That time he borrowed your car, when you were trekking in Peru, he was helping Orlando out. Orlando mistakenly thought he'd killed someone at a party. He was afraid Roddy would tell us what he knew.'

'But Roddy wouldn't have wanted to get him in trouble. Ever.'

'You said yourself Roddy was indiscreet. He talked to Paige Hargreaves about the club, which was supposed to be a secret. Orlando was afraid he'd give the game away.'

'That club. What a stupid, pointless, selfish—' Luke's voice was rising before he cut himself off. 'What a mess.'

'Orlando was very keen to make it clear that you weren't involved, even though he used your weight to set up the accident.'

'Nice of him.'

'The least he could do,' Derwent said from behind me, his voice as dry as the Sahara. Luke looked at him again, his eyes wary. It wasn't hostility, I thought with a rush of understanding and sympathy. It was fear. They were both terrified the other one would do the wrong thing.

And I was standing in the middle.

'So you're free to go whenever you like,' I said. 'You're off the hook.'

Luke's mouth curved up at the corners, irresistibly. 'I've heard that before.'

'As far as I know it's true this time. But I always say that, so . . .' I shrugged.

'What about Paige Hargreaves? Did he kill her?'

'I don't know yet.'

'But you'll find out.'

'I hope so.'

He stood up, pushed the chair into its place at the table, politely, then stopped. I glanced at Derwent and saw they had both adopted the same stance unconsciously, feet apart, hands jammed in their pockets, heads lowered. The look in Derwent's eyes made my throat tighten.

'I'll just . . .' I headed for the door but Derwent reached out to catch my arm as I passed and swung me back. 'Don't go.'

'I'm in the way,' I protested.

'No, you aren't.' It was Luke who said it. 'Please, don't go. There's something I want to say to both of you.'

Be kind. Say something kind and then you can go. Don't break his heart . . .

'I talked to my mum. About both of you,' Luke added, and grinned. 'We had quite a bit to discuss. I heard all about *you*.'

Derwent, the you in question, cleared his throat. 'We were very young. And your mum was brilliant, even then, but I was a dickhead.'

'That's not exactly what she said. She really liked you.'

'But not as a father to her baby.'

'She wanted to do it by herself.'

Derwent nodded, his face remote. There was no suggestion he thought she had been wrong about that. He would never criticise her, I thought, even if Luke did.

'There were times when it would have been really good to have a dad around, I'm not going to pretend there weren't. But mostly, I had a good childhood. We were a close family. My grandparents were there for me when Mum couldn't be. We were happy.'

'And you did well on it, so she was right,' Derwent said.

'I did OK.'

'Better than OK.'

'Some things worked out. Others didn't, so much.' Luke looked at me. 'I wanted to say in front of . . . um, *him*, I know it wasn't your fault. Mum told me she made you promise not to tell him. I know what she's like – she would have gone mental if he'd turned up on the doorstep. She'd never have let me see him. So, you not breaking your promise is probably a good thing.' He looked at Derwent. 'You really need to forgive her for that.'

'I already have,' Derwent said, with the smooth confidence of someone who had neither said it nor planned to in the future.

Luke took a deep breath. 'If you'd asked me two or three years ago if I missed having a dad, I'd have said no. If you'd come to see me when I was at university, I'd probably have told you to fuck off. I didn't have a dad and I didn't need

352

one. I was proud of growing up on my own and I wouldn't have wanted to change a thing.'

'And now?' His tone was carefully matter-of-fact. There would be no emotional appeal; he would accept whatever Luke wanted, even if it broke his heart, and Luke would never know.

'I don't know.' Luke shrugged. 'It's a bit late to start playing football together.'

'I could buy you a pint.'

The silence seemed endless before Luke nodded. 'I'd like that. And to be honest, I need a drink after today.'

'Have a lovely time,' I said, beaming at the pair of them.

'Oh, you're coming too.' Luke looked at his father. 'Isn't she?'

'If she wants.' Derwent raised his eyebrows at me. 'How about it?'

'I'd get in the way.'

'No, you wouldn't.' They said it in unison, and then grinned at one another, and I suddenly saw how it would make everything easier if there was someone else to talk to, someone who wasn't in the grip of any emotion stronger than joy to see someone I cared about feeling happy for what might have been the first time since I'd known him.

'Well, maybe for one.'

It was a beautiful evening, warm and clear, and the pub's customers had overflowed across the pavement. The rumble of conversation rose like the smoke from cigarettes, evaporating into the blue air. Laughter spilled out from the group next to us and I found myself smiling at it instead of minding the noise.

'Are you all right to stay out here?' Derwent asked me. 'Or do you want to find somewhere to sit down inside?'

'Out here is fine. I'm not feeling as bad as I was. I must be on the mend.' I found a place where I could lean against the wall while Derwent disappeared into the pub, a tall dark figure cutting through the crowd without difficulty. There was something about him that made people give him space. Luke watched him go.

'Is he always like that?'

'Like what?'

'Effective,' Luke said at last.

'Pretty much. He'll get served straight away.'

Luke looked thoughtful, watching the door like a dog that wasn't sure its owner was coming back. There was a sweetness to his face that I'd never seen on Derwent's – a lack of cynicism that was touching. Maybe Derwent would have been like that if his life had been less difficult. Maybe he would have gone to Cambridge and got a well-paid job and laid waste to the pretty girls of London if he hadn't been struggling to make his way in the world on his own.

'This must be strange for you,' I said gently. 'But remember it's strange for him too.'

That got his attention. 'How does he feel about it? About . . . well, about me?'

I hesitated. If I said too much, it might make Luke feel overburdened with Derwent's need to build a relationship. Too little, and he might think it didn't matter.

'I don't want to speak for him, but he wouldn't be here if he didn't want to be.'

'You know him well, don't you?'

'He's not easy to know. You have to get past a lot of defences before you find the real him,' I said carefully. 'But I can tell you that he has the biggest heart of anyone I know, and for as long as I've known him, he's been looking for something to do with it.'

Luke nodded. 'I know that feeling. Like there's something you've never had but you miss it all the time.'

'Exactly.' I looked around, checking to see he wasn't in earshot. 'The main thing is that you can trust him. He's never let me down.'

He smiled down at me. 'You look out for him, don't you?'

'I don't want either of you to get hurt.'

'No. And speaking of being hurt, what happened to you?'

I didn't have to answer straight away because Derwent returned with two pints of bitter and a gin for me. He had heard the question and I was aware of him watching me to see how I would respond. And in the end, it was easy to tell the truth. I felt safe with the two of them, and I wasn't afraid of being judged.

'My ex-boyfriend beat me up.'

'Shit.' Luke looked horrified. 'Are you OK?'

'I will be.'

'Are you going to get him locked up?'

'If I can. Someone told me I should, and he was right. I don't want him to do it to anyone else.' I sipped my drink. Derwent was smiling to himself.

'So he's now your ex-boyfriend,' Luke said slowly.

'Very much so.'

'And that means you're single.'

Derwent snorted. 'Forget it, pal. She's well out of your league.'

'It's worth a try.' Luke was staring into my eyes. 'Isn't it, Maeve?'

'No, it isn't.' Derwent snapped. He looked at me. 'Why are you laughing?'

'Because there's no need for a DNA test,' I said. 'This is definitely your son.'

45

Two weeks later I was back in Greenwich on a hot, sunny day, on my own again, with the keys to Paige Hargreaves' flat in my hand. The front door was propped open when I arrived, though, with a crumpled dust sheet on the floor and plastic sheeting taped all the way up the stairs. A radio burbled in the distance and there was the rhythmic sound of industrious sanding from the living room.

'Hello?'

'Who's that?' A middle-aged man in white painter's overalls backed into view, peering down the stairwell. 'All right, love?'

'Can I come up? I'm a police officer.' I pulled out my ID.

'Am I in trouble?' He slapped his forehead. 'Did I park on a double yellow?'

'I don't care if you did. I'm not a parking warden.' I'd reached the top of the stairs. 'Wow, this place looks bigger without all the stuff in it.'

'They got a clearance firm to come in and take the lot.' The painter looked around. 'It'll be all right when it's done up but it was a proper shithole, if you don't mind my saying so.'

'I don't think the previous occupant cared about that kind of thing.'

'What happened to her? Someone told me she died.'

He had a kind, ruddy face and I felt he wasn't asking because he wanted a cheap thrill.

'Someone murdered her.'

'Here?'

'I don't know. Possibly.'

'Oh my days.' He shook his head. 'What a thing to happen. Was she a young lady?'

'She was twenty-eight.'

'Same age as my Nina.' He shook his head again. 'Have you worked out who did it?'

'Not yet.'

'That'll be why you're here, I suppose.'

I nodded, though actually I wasn't sure why I was there. The flat had been returned to the landlord, the forensic work having been completed. We had taken a few things and let the rest go. You couldn't keep every piece of clothing and every dish in case you'd missed something – a skin cell, a speck of DNA – but it bothered me that the answer to who had killed her might have been right there in the flat and we hadn't found it.

'I'd better get on with it.'

'Course. Let me know if I'm in the way, love, and I'll go and get a coffee.' He checked the time. 'Almost eleven. I do need a break.'

'I don't mind,' I said. 'There's a good café around the corner though, if you're looking for somewhere to eat. It doesn't look like much but the food is lovely. Carlo's.' I gave him directions and described the outside.

'Thanks. I'll give it a try.' He headed off to wash the paint dust off his hands, whistling as he went.

I was glad he'd decided to go; I wanted to be on my own. Not knowing what had happened to Paige was eating away at me. Her links to the Chiron Club had seemed so promising but I felt as if they had dissolved into dust in the cold light of day. Once I'd been given her files I'd read every word of her notes, every draft she had begun to write, and I had no sense that she'd come close to anything that might have put her in danger. Carl Hooper said he knew nothing about her death. None of the other grey suits seemed to recognise her.

I walked around the main room, where the entire kitchen had been ripped out already, exposing the walls. A large patch of new plaster covered the spot where the black mould had grown. Where the cabinets had been, old layers of wallpaper and tiles peered through rips in newer layers. The people who had chosen them were long forgotten, as Paige would be. Someone would put in a neat new kitchen – probably IKEA's cheapest model – and a new resident would make their home in the renovated flat that smelled of nothing worse than paint, unaware that anything had happened. I wondered if the mould had really been dealt with or if it would return, seeping through the new plaster, hinting at what lay underneath . . .

'I'll leave you to it,' the painter said, popping his head in. 'If you don't mind waiting until I get back.'

'No problem. Are you redecorating the whole place?'

'Everything except the stairs. The woman downstairs said not to bother with it because it wasn't done that long ago, but—' he grimaced. 'Not a proper job at all. Someone slaps some magnolia paint on a wall and thinks it's painted but they don't understand what they're doing. Look at this.'

I went obediently and stood at the top of the stairs, half listening as he pointed out the marks that had been missed, the splashes on the ceiling where someone had gone too fast and not taken care, the overall shoddy job that he hoped no one had paid for because it was amateur work and careless too. The sunlight from outside was so bright the hallway was lit up as if there was a spotlight shining up it and I could see what he meant. There were drips in places, and great arcs where someone had dragged the roller quickly across the wall. I wondered what he would make of the job Derwent had done on the flat. Josh was obsessively neat and believed in attention to detail; I had a feeling his work would pass muster. He had covered up every trace of what Seth had done to me. You would never even guess something terrible had happened in my home, unless Kev went at it with the luminol, I thought idly.

'I could go on about this all day,' the painter said at last with a rueful grin. 'You probably go on about murders when you're down the pub.'

'I try not to,' I said, grinning.

He saluted and headed off, whistling again.

Paige's bedroom also seemed much bigger without all the clothes rails and the clutter on the floor. I knelt where the bed had been, under the open skylight, imagining her there. She had lain in bed, drinking champagne (because she had found out something that would make her article devastating, or because she had it in the fridge and why not?). Someone had come to see her. Someone had ended her life. Someone had disposed of her body. Her friends had worried, but they'd seen an opportunity too. They waited to report her missing until they had been to the flat and retrieved the computer, so Bianca could take advantage of her missing friend's research. They had known she was dead.

They had known she was dead because they had killed her and then cut her up, using Sam's tree surgeon tools.

No.

We had looked at Sam's (filthy) tools. There was no trace of blood on them. Bianca and Sam were both adamant that they hadn't harmed her. And Bianca had pointed out that she'd known nothing about the cut-up bodies until she got her hands on the computer because Paige hadn't trusted her enough to tell her about it.

I'd looked again at the Chiron Club. With better tech at my disposal, I'd found out that the inside source Paige had found was a grey suit who had worked at the Bishops Avenue house before being fired. His replacement was the charming Frenchman who had tipped me off about where Bianca was hidden. A bitter ex-employee repeating rumours as fact wouldn't have been enough to scare the club into killing a freelance journalist, I thought. Not when they had covered their tracks so well. And the very fact that the bathroom had been left in such a poor condition proved to me that they thought they had got away with it. Their first act to cover it up should have been to strip out any evidence of the dismemberment and dispose of it. Arrogance, laziness and (I suspected) the thought that they might do it again had kept them from replacing the bath, to our benefit. But we still hadn't identified the three unknown sources of blood we'd found. They'd got away with more than I'd have liked.

Orlando still denied having anything to do with Paige's death. Could Roddy have killed her? I puzzled through possible motives: if she rejected him sexually, after all the time he'd spent wooing her, if she found out about his lap dance from a young teenage girl, if he lashed out in frustration or fear.

People killed for money, or because they were humiliated, or because they were frustrated. And people killed to protect themselves or those they loved.

Maybe it had been the father of a Chiron Club member who feared their son's evil doings being exposed. A contract killing, efficient and controlled. No personal connection between the victim and killer.

Untraceable.

I had no evidence to suggest it was a contract killing but I believed they were capable of it. To the kind of men who frequented the Chiron Club she would be insignificant – an obstacle that had to be removed.

Standing in her home, I thought I'd never known a murder victim as entirely alone in the world as Paige. No parents, no friends she could trust. Unlike me, she had nowhere to go when life had kicked her in the teeth, except to her small, grim flat. No wonder she had thrown up walls around herself. No wonder she had celebrated and grieved and lived behind closed doors. And now, when she was gone, every trace of her passage through this world was being eradicated under a coat of fresh paint. Her belongings had been cleared out and scattered like the parts of her body, absorbed into an uncaring world.

I walked through the flat, my heels echoing on the bare floorboards, remembering how Mila had objected to the officers pounding up and down the stairs. This would be worse. I hoped she was away, because it would take the painter a while to work through the whole flat on his own. At a guess, it had been a long time since the flat was redecorated.

So why would anyone redecorate the stairs – the tiny, narrow passage up to the flat – instead of tackling the serious refurbishment the rest of the flat needed? The stairwell was the sort of place that never got painted. It shouldn't have been anyone's first priority.

I stood at the top of the stairs, looking down, and thought about motives and deceit and covering up, and how we had followed a trail that had been created for us to follow from the very start. Clues, hints, suspects, helpful remarks, all pointing us in the wrong direction, and I had gone willingly down that path, pleased to find it was so easy.

Who killed Paige, and why?

The answer had been right in front of me all the time.

46

The low, windblown bungalow crouched alone in flat grassland, where the roads petered out towards the distant edge of Sheppey. It faced the Swale, a channel of the Thames estuary that cut the island off from the Kent mainland. There was nothing to protect the house from the salt-laden sea breeze that tugged at our clothes and blew my hair into confusion – no trees, no shrubs, no other houses in sight. There was nothing around us but the vastness of the sky filled with the whirling flight of the plovers and harriers that thrived in the wetlands.

It took Mila Walsh a few seconds to make sense of what she saw when she answered the door. I suppose it was hard for her to place me when I was so out of context. She was wearing ancient jeans and an oversized white shirt and flat sandals: her off-duty look, I guessed.

'Sergeant Kerrigan. What are you doing here?'

'Following up on a few things. Can we come in?' I didn't wait for her to answer but pushed the door wide open and trooped into the hall followed by Liv, Derwent, Pettifer, Georgia, Pete Belcott and Kev Cox carrying a toolbox full of forensic kit. Behind us, outside the house, two other forensic investigators were pulling on protective shoe covers. We were there in force and it was designed to intimidate her.

'You can't just come in here. You have to take off your shoes.' Her hands fluttered helplessly. 'You can't be in here, all of you.'

'I'm afraid we have to be.'

'Mila? What's going on?' A man emerged from the back of the house. He had huge, rough hands that were coated in something white and dusty, and his arms were muscled and scarred. He had a deep tan, as if he spent a lot of time out of doors. His hair and beard were longer than they had been in the picture I'd seen of him in a magazine, but still a gleaming silver-grey.

'Harry Parr?' I checked.

'Yes?' He turned round blue eyes on me.

'We're Metropolitan Police detectives.' I showed them the paperwork as most of the others fanned out through the house, beginning to work room by room. 'We've got a warrant to search this address.'

'Why? What are you looking for?' His voice was a low rumble.

'Tools,' Derwent said. 'Cutting tools.'

'Plenty of them out in the studio,' Harry said with an attempt at a laugh.

'Stop it, Harry,' Mila snapped. 'Don't say anything. Don't say *anything*.'

I sat with them in the small living room, the two of them perched on a mid-century daybed covered in white leather, holding hands in silence. The murmur of conversation made Mila flinch from time to time, and I watched her eyes darting around the room as she licked her lips nervously, chewing off her lipstick, fidgeting with her hair. Harry sat still with his eyes closed and a half-smile on his face, meditating. I used the time to admire a huge abstract painting over the fireplace and a giant bit of driftwood that filled the hearth. Otherwise the room was bare, like Mila's London home. I was sitting in a plywood chair that curved around me and was surprisingly comfortable. It looked like a classic Danish design, in keeping with the spare artist's aesthetic the couple favoured. One big window faced on to flat fields and the infinite sky. Somewhere beyond the horizon, invisible, was the sea.

Footsteps rustled through the hall and I looked up to see Derwent and Kev, who waved an evidence bag at me, triumphant.

'I've swabbed a few of the saws and cutting tools out in the studio and then did a quick Kastle-Meyer test. I got a positive reaction for blood from three of them so far. We'll take the lot.'

Harry opened his eyes and blinked as Mila began to cry.

'I do cut myself sometimes,' he said mildly. 'When I'm working.'

Kev gave him a little bow. 'We'll test for DNA. There's very little that's visible to the naked eye but it's enough for our purposes.'

I cleared my throat. 'Mila Walsh and Harry Parr, you are both under arrest for the murder of Paige Hargreaves. You do not have to say anything, but it may harm your defence if you do not mention when questioned something which you later rely on in court. Anything you do say may be given in evidence.'

'Harry,' Mila said, dissolving into tears. 'Harry.'

'It's all right, my darling.' He leaned his head against hers, his eyes closed again. Then he made a quick, furtive movement, palming something from his pocket, and I was too far away to reach him, and too slow.

'Watch him!'

Before the words were properly out of my mouth Derwent had caught hold of his wrist, using all his force to turn the sculptor's hand away from his body as the tendons stood out under Parr's skin and his muscles bulged with effort. A tool clattered onto the bare wooden floor: a chisel, small and lethally sharp. For a moment we were all still, staring at it.

Mila's mouth was open and her eyes were wide with horror. I wondered if it had been intended for her, after all, but then Harry settled the question.

'I can't go to prison. I'd rather *die* than go to prison.' His anger made me shiver. Mila hung around his neck like a garland, limp, getting in the way as we attempted to handcuff him for his own safety, and ours.

'I don't understand,' Mila said dully. It was the first thing she'd said since we got to London, to the office and the small, windowless interview room where Derwent and I were preparing to take her apart.

'Neither did I, until I thought about the dates,' I said.

'What dates?'

'The first time I met you, you told me about the detective who searched Paige Hargreaves' flat. He told you his name was John Spencer, but he was actually a guy called Sam Williams.'

A flash of the old Mila: 'I've never heard that name before.'

'That's all right. I assumed you didn't know him. I tracked him down, though, and he told us that while he was there, you asked him if anyone knew who killed Paige.'

'That's right. He was very convincing, I told you. I believed he was a police officer.'

'Yes, you did. But that doesn't explain how you knew Paige was dead.'

'What?' Mila was frowning, still lost.

'She hadn't even been reported missing, officially. You *could* have been aware of not seeing her for a few days. You *could* have been concerned that she was missing, even though you told me that Paige came and went and kept odd hours and you weren't really aware of her too much, so even realising she was missing would have been a stretch. But to know she was dead before we'd found so much as a scrap of her body in the river – that means you had to have been involved.'

'I must have misspoken.' She had a hand to her throat, her elbow braced in the fingers of her other hand. 'Or he's misremembered it.'

'He remembers it very well. You frightened him.'

'Ridiculous.' Mila's voice was flat. 'How would I know she was dead?'

'Because you killed her.'

'No. Absolutely not.' She gave a strained laugh. 'Why would I do that?'

'There are parts we have to guess,' Derwent said. 'I'll admit we don't know exactly what happened.'

I took over. 'We know she had been drinking – lying in bed, swigging champagne from the bottle, celebrating the fact that she'd found a brilliant source for the story she was working on. She thought it was going to make her career. I suspect she told you about it when you knocked on her door. She was a little self-obsessed. Life had taught her to be selfish, to be her own hero. She wasn't remotely interested in talking about what *you* wanted to talk about.'

'And what was that?'

'Mould.' I had expected her to bluster, to laugh, to sneer at the very suggestion, but she didn't. The colour was gone from her face and I didn't think she could speak, even if she had anything to say. 'I looked your partner up after we spoke the first time. Harry Parr. I found an interesting article about him. A profile of the celebrated sculptor, who had come through a period of life-threatening poor health. The piece was about how he had fled London to live in Kent, because the bungalow was new and clean.'

'What of it?'

'He left London because he was sick. He started having scary symptoms – aches, pains, dizziness, loss of appetite, depression and anxiety. His immune system was overreacting to everything. He said it felt as if he was allergic to the modern world. You couldn't get a diagnosis for him, no matter how many doctors saw him. Then he realised he felt better at the bungalow. He found an expert in environmental allergies who confirmed your worst fears – he had developed an auto-immune disease as a reaction to the mould he had been exposed to. The house in London was toxic. He couldn't live there with you.'

'So what?' Mila still sounded truculent but it was a half-hearted effort.

'So you completely stripped your whole place and had it redecorated. You'd taken it back to the bricks and lifted the floorboards to be absolutely sure you'd eradicated every trace of mould.' I sounded sympathetic because I was, a little; they had fought hard for Harry's health. 'You couldn't do anything about Paige's flat though. You went in to her flat at least once, by your own account, to check whether she'd left a tap running – water leaks are the worst source of mould, so it must have been a real concern for you. You saw the black mould that was all over her kitchen wall, right above the bedroom you and Harry had shared. No wonder he got sick. I got hold of the landlord, by the way, and he confirmed he was prepared to allow you to go ahead with renovating the flat as long as you paid for it, but Paige refused. The mould didn't bother her and when you begged her to reconsider she said no. She didn't care. She wanted to be left alone to work and she didn't want the disruption of the building work you wanted to do.'

Mila swallowed, and said nothing. Her eyes were fixed on mine.

'I've heard a lot about Paige, and formed my own opinion of her. She was single-minded to a fault. She was the cat that walked by herself – and as a result she'd taught herself that she didn't need anyone. When you spoke to her she was drunk enough to be chatty, but she only wanted to talk about her work, her exciting project that was occupying all of her time and energy. She flatly refused to pay any attention to you. And so you killed her.'

'That's ridiculous,' Mila spat.

'There was no sign of a struggle in the flat, which confused me. It wasn't until I went there again on a sunny day and the front door was propped open that I noticed the paint on the walls in the stairwell. A quick job, poorly done according to an expert I consulted.' The decorator *was* an expert, I thought. And he'd been right about the shoddiness of it. 'The flat hadn't been redecorated in years. Why would someone want to paint the stairs in a hurry?'

'We found a few specks of blood spatter on the ceiling in the stairwell,' Derwent said. 'Tiny, but they were there, when we looked.'

'You did a good job of cleaning it up but not good enough. We are sure Paige died there, on the stairs. Did you shove her, or stab her, or hit her over the head?' I waited, but Mila said nothing.

'You could say it was an accident,' Derwent prompted. 'Most people go for that option. But then you'd have to explain why you didn't help her.'

'People kill for lots of reasons.' I looked at her with some sympathy. 'Wanting to protect the person you love most is a big one. Harry must have been so touched that you were prepared to kill for him.'

Her face was unreadable, remote.

'What we think you did after she died was to call your boyfriend,' Derwent went on. 'Between the two of you, you came up with a plan. Paige had told you enough about her story that you knew she was investigating the murder of a girl whose body was cut up. You decided to make use of that so we would assume it was connected with her work instead of paying attention to the downstairs neighbour who had keys to Paige's home and a motive growing all over the walls of Paige's flat. Your boyfriend is good at anatomy. He knows how bodies fit together. That means he knows how to take them apart. He also has a large collection of tools.'

'There's that picture of him in his studio. Loads of hand tools, ideal for cutting up the wood and bone he uses in his pieces.' I smiled. 'All you had to do was cut her up, leave the pieces somewhere we'd find them and wait for us to jump to the wrong conclusion. Unfortunately, Sam took Paige's computer and everything that related to the story, so it took us a while to find out about the other dismembered girl. In the meantime, we were looking far too closely at the flat for your liking. But first time round we missed the blood in the stairwell. It was only when we went looking for it with luminol that we found traces of it.'

'You only missed a couple of places,' Derwent said encouragingly. 'Really, you had done a good job. But the places you missed lit up like the night sky.'

'It was you who took the carpet away,' I said. 'I did wonder how you could bear to have Paige running up and down uncarpeted stairs because it was so noisy when we were there and that obviously bothered you, but of course you didn't have to bear it before she died.'

'You went and bought plastic sheeting and tape from your local DIY store, and quite a lot of bleach, and some magnolia paint, and a roller set. We've got CCTV of that.' Derwent played the short film clip on his laptop. Mila watched herself as she moved quickly around the DIY shop. On the screen she looked harried. In real life her face was stony. 'That was nine days before Paige's disappearance was reported to us,' Derwent said, and clicked it off.

'Harry cut up Paige's body on the hall floor, where we spoke the first time I met you. You had covered the whole place with plastic sheeting but afterwards you cleaned it with bleach, in case you'd missed any blood, and lit a candle to hide any remaining smell. I noticed the candle when I was there, but nothing else. By the time we came to look around, the new paint smell was gone. Anyway, the flat upstairs stank.'

'You did a much better job in your own flat. When we

went and looked at it yesterday, we didn't find blood there, but we did find tape residue on the walls.' Derwent shrugged. 'And then you slid her body piece by piece into the Thames, some of it near the Chiron Club, some of it in other places. Maybe you dumped some at sea while you were in Kent. The advantage of cutting her up was that she was easy to carry around. Worth the effort, as far as you were concerned.'

'This is all a fantasy.'

'Harry will admit his part in it. You know he will. He's terrified of going to prison for a long time. He'll talk if there's a reduced sentence on the table. But all the evidence we have points towards you as the killer.' I stared at her. 'We know what you did, Mila.'

Her face was white in the harsh overhead light. She leaned forward, and through clenched teeth she snarled three short words. 'Then prove it.'

47

Prove it.

The words echoed in my mind as I stood in the witness box and recited the oath, as I had countless times before. But this time was different. This time, I was not there in a professional capacity.

This time, I was the victim.

'I swear by almighty God that the evidence I shall give shall be the truth, the whole truth and nothing but the truth.'

The prosecution barrister was a young woman, Emma Khan. I had seen her animated, out of court, her hair tumbling around her shoulders, throwing her head back to laugh at another barrister's joke. Facing her in Court 3 in the palatial Victorian grandeur of Snaresbrook Crown Court was like being in front of another person altogether. Here she was composed and dignified, her face a serene light-brown oval under her wig. She had a trick of pulling her gown into place before she introduced a new line of questioning, and a calm manner that slowed my racing pulse to a manageable trot.

'And what do you do for a living, Miss Kerrigan?'

'I'm a detective sergeant with the Metropolitan Police.'

There was a ripple of reaction from the jury box. I tried

not to look across at them, aware of them only as a blurry entity in the corner of my vision.

'What sort of crimes do you investigate?'

'Murders.' No way to say it without sounding dramatic. 'I've worked on a murder investigation team handling complex cases since I became a detective constable.'

'Is that a challenging job?'

'At times.'

'Do you enjoy it?'

'At times,' I said again, this time with a smile. I felt rather than heard the amusement in the courtroom.

The first part of my evidence was all about establishing who and what I was, and how I had met Seth. He was sitting in the dock, beside a dock officer who looked bored. I knew he was on bail and I had seen him earlier in the park that surrounded the court building. The shock of it had been like touching an exposed wire, but I was glad I'd been able to look at him before I saw him in Court 3. He was wearing an impeccable suit – not too fashionable, but very well cut – and his tie was sombre. He had had his hair cut. He looked like what he pretended to be, a handsome and confident solicitor, and he did not look at all like a man who could coldly and deliberately beat me unconscious, even though that was exactly what he was.

'How did you meet?'

'He was professionally involved in a murder investigation. His client was on trial.'

'So you were on the other side.'

'Yes.'

'And even so, you fell for each other.'

'He was injured and had to take time off work. I visited him. We started seeing one another more seriously about ten months ago now. Before Christmas.'

'And were you happy?'

'Yes. Very,' I said, simply. 'He was very attentive. He made

372

a point of telling me how much he loved me. He gave me presents, often, until I told him to stop because I was embarrassed at his generosity. He took me out for dinner a lot. He encouraged me to be more aware of my health, taking more exercise and improving my diet.'

'The ideal boyfriend.'

'So it seemed.'

'Did anything worry you?'

'He disliked most of my friends and colleagues, and they had reservations about him which they expressed to me on a number of occasions. I felt as if I had to choose between him and my colleagues. I felt isolated, at times. I felt as if I had to get his permission to have any kind of social life.'

'Did anything else upset you?'

'He was highly critical of me. He kept warning me I wasn't reaching the standard he expected in my conversation or behaviour.' I swallowed, hard. 'It was upsetting and unsettling. I felt as soon as I managed to do something properly, he would change the rules, until it was impossible for me to be good enough.'

'He was violent towards you?'

'Not at first. He liked to be in charge. He made all the decisions and plans. I went along with it because it seemed to be easier to live that way. Over time, I became worried about making any decisions without checking them with him.'

She led me through an account of the incident where we had argued in the street and I'd fallen and had to make my own way home, then moved on to the main event.

'Tell us in your own words what happened that day.' Her voice was heavy with sympathy.

I did my best to go through it calmly, setting the scene, explaining that we hadn't seen each other for some days, describing the bruise on my neck and how he had jumped to the wrong conclusion about it. When it came to telling them how he had beaten me, I faltered.

'Please speak up, Miss Kerrigan,' the judge said sharply. He was a small, lipless man with cold eyes, and as I spoke I worried that he had taken Seth's side, that he hadn't believed me and nor had anyone else. The jury probably hated me, a voice said in my head. A police officer who had let herself be abused. A stupid woman telling lies about her handsome lover who had dumped her.

'I remember him hitting my face with his open hand and then a fist. I remember my nose cracking. I remember him holding on to me so I didn't fall because it was easier for him to hit me if we were standing up. I remember him kicking me on the floor. I don't know how long it went on for – it felt like hours but that's probably not the case. And then I blacked out. The next thing I remember is waking up on the floor, on my own.'

I described the flat, the lack of phones, the locked doors, the utter helplessness I'd felt. I described hiding, and my landlord – *yes, he is a colleague* – coming to see if I was all right because he had been concerned for my welfare. I described my injuries. The jury looked at their jury bundles, where the photographs from the hospital were reproduced in lurid colour. I was barely recognisable in them, my eyes glazed with shock and pain.

'Do you suffer from any lasting side-effects from this incident?'

'Not physically.' I had healed well, my bones restoring themselves, the bruises fading. 'I still feel devastated that it happened. I find it hard to trust people. I am more nervous than I was, especially when I'm on my own.' *I sleep with the house keys under my pillow and a spare set hidden on top of the bathroom cabinet, just in case.*

'Do you find it harder to do your job?'

'I try not to think about it at work. We don't tend to deal with domestic murders but when we do, I find it harder than I used to.' And that was true. Every woman who was strangled by an ex-partner, every girlfriend who was beaten to death – I could have been any of them, or all of them. I had trusted the wrong person and paid the price, but they had lost everything. Those cases still kept me awake at night. *Give me a nice straightforward gangland shooting any day.*

The defence barrister had thirty years and eleven inches on Emma Khan, and the swagger to go with it. He gave me a small, patronising smile as he stood up to begin his cross-examination and I breathed out slowly.

Do not let him make you angry.

'Is it professional, Sergeant Kerrigan, to find your boyfriends during murder investigations?'

'People often meet partners through work,' I said evenly. 'My focus at work is not on my personal life.'

'It's not your first time to meet someone through work, though, is it?'

'I had one other boyfriend who was a colleague before we became close.'

'And was that a serious relationship?'

'Yes, it lasted several years.'

'When did it end?'

'Two years ago.'

'And since then, have you had many relationships? Of any length?' he added.

'No. Your client was the first.' *So you can't try to pretend I'm always on the hunt for male attention.*

'Would you say you were quite keen to make this relationship work?'

'I tried.'

'Mr Taylor is a cut above most of the people you meet through work, isn't he? He's well off, ambitious, some would say handsome . . .' he paused for a laugh that came on cue. 'He was interested in you. He was "very attentive". He told you how much he loved you. He sounds rather perfect.'

'He did seem that way.' I was trying to guess where this line of questioning was going.

'But things weren't working between you, were they? You

had argued. He sent you roses to apologise. What did you do with them?'

How did he know? 'I put them in the bin at work. I didn't want them.'

'Were you disappointed to receive a large bunch of flowers from him?'

'I didn't like being the subject of gossip at work. I like to keep my private life separate.'

'Wasn't it the case that you wanted him to propose to you? That other people at work assumed the roses were a sign that this had happened, and you were cruelly disappointed?'

I smiled at that, my composure intact. 'No. People at work may have assumed they were a romantic gesture but I knew they were an apology and I took them as such. I would have preferred a less ostentatious approach.'

'But you did want to marry my client.'

'It was the last thing on my mind. We weren't living together. We saw each other once or twice a week. I was certainly not waiting for him to propose.'

'An eligible, attractive, successful man held no appeal for you, even at an age when many women would be keen to settle down.'

I shook my head. 'It wasn't something I'd considered.'

'Isn't it the case that he was unhappy in your relationship? He broke up with you on that day in May when these events took place, didn't he? And you were furious.'

'No, I told *him* we should go our separate ways.'

'You attacked him, in a rage.'

'Absolutely not.'

'You are trained in combat, aren't you?'

'Yes.'

'Before the incident in May, when was the last time you had done a course in self-defence and restraint?'

'April,' I said.

'What sort of thing do they teach you on these courses?'

'Safe restraint when someone is taken into custody. Situational awareness. Techniques for ensuring compliance. Self-defence.'

'What techniques ensure compliance?'

'Generally putting people into stress positions, where they are uncomfortable, so they lose interest in fighting back. The techniques are designed to avoid causing harm to the individual.'

'If I can translate this for the jury, you know how to hurt someone.'

'Yes.'

'And you know how to defend yourself from being hurt.'

'I'm trained for that, but—'

'And you are quite tall, aren't you?' the barrister said loudly, cutting me off.

'Five foot ten.'

'An inch or so shorter than my client.'

'He weighs a lot more than I do,' I said calmly.

'Still, you were more evenly matched than many. You were trained in self-defence. You knew how to cause pain. You were arguing and you lashed out, intent on hurting him. My client was concerned to defend himself against your attack. By your account, you then did nothing to protect yourself. You were helpless.'

'I was in my own home, with my boyfriend. I wasn't expecting to be the victim of a physical assault.'

'You couldn't defend yourself.'

'I tried to protect myself.' I swallowed. 'I wanted him to stop. I thought he would calm down if I didn't fight back.'

'With all your training.'

'Yes.'

'And all your experience of violent crime.'

'Yes.'

'Did he hit you?'

'Yes.'

'Kick you?'

'Yes.'

'Punch you?'

'Yes.'

'And you did nothing. You allowed yourself to be his punch bag.'

'I – I tried,' I said lamely.

'Isn't it the case that you knew very well that being accused of this crime would have a devastating effect on my client's reputation? That if he was convicted, he would lose his job?'

'I was aware of that.'

'Sergeant Kerrigan, we have heard your account of this relationship, this regrettable incident and the lasting effect it has had on you. You were angry that your relationship was ending. You decided to take revenge on him by provoking him into an unwise physical assault. You suffered significant injury around this time, you allege through my client's actions although he disputes that. You created a narrative to suggest he imprisoned you in your flat, cut off from the world so you couldn't ask for help, though investigating officers found that all of the things you alleged to be missing, such as the phone and your keys, were all inside the flat where they should be. You set out to trap him, to make his life a misery and take his career away from him. You knew the consequences of accusing him of this, and you did it anyway, so you could punish him by bringing him to court and destroying his reputation once and for all.'

'I would have given anything not to come here and give evidence.' I was trembling and hoped it didn't show. 'I'm here because I do my job so I can keep people safe. I don't want this to happen to anyone else. You keep saying I knew the consequences of accusing Seth of attacking me, but he knew the consequences too, and he still did it. I promise you, I don't want anything like revenge. I just want justice.'

48

Once I had given evidence, I was technically allowed to go into the public gallery and listen to the rest of the trial but for two reasons I decided against it. Firstly, juries were popularly supposed to dislike seeing the complainant in court, as it looked vindictive. I didn't want to lend any accidental credibility to Seth's barrister's suggestion that I was going through this as an act of revenge. Secondly, I didn't want to spend another minute in that courtroom after I'd endured my time in the witness box. It had gone quickly because I was concentrating, but afterwards my knees felt exceedingly unreliable as I followed the usher out of court. I was tired and worried that I'd said too much, or not enough. I had been likable, I hoped, but serious enough to show the jury that this mattered to me.

And it did matter. I didn't want Seth to walk away unscathed. I had been brutally honest about what had happened between us, and it had cost me something. All I wanted was for the jury to recognise my honesty and respect my account of events. If they refused to convict him – and juries could go either way; they were as unpredictable as an English summer – I would feel as if I had been found guilty and I wasn't sure how I would deal with that.

I sat on the bench outside the courtroom, because I had nowhere else to be, and couldn't stop shivering even though the building was overheated. The last prosecution witness was giving evidence. Then the defence case would begin, with Seth's own account of events. I dreaded the thought of it. He was good at arguing, and plausible. Five men, seven women: those odds were in his favour, it seemed to me.

A rattle at the door made me jump. It opened and the prosecution witness stepped out, smoothing his tie, scanning the hallway for anything amiss out of pure habit. I watched him walk across to me, checking off the details: dark suit, navy tie, new white shirt, recent haircut, general air of confidence, a touch of swagger at all times. He looked notably unruffled by whatever the defence had asked him.

'All right?'

'Yes.' I didn't sound sure of it, though. I cleared my throat. 'How did that go?'

'Usual stuff.' Derwent smoothed his tie again. 'Nothing that should worry you.'

Because he was a witness too, he hadn't seen my evidence. 'Did he suggest to you that I'd made it up because I resented being dumped?'

'He did. That was fine. I told him getting married was not on your radar and it was hard to get you to commit to lunch, never mind an engagement.'

'What did the jury think of that?'

'They laughed.' He stretched. 'Juries love me. You know that.'

'I couldn't look at them. I don't know what they made of me.'

'You make a decent impression.' He hauled me to my feet. 'Come on. You look done in. Let's go to the canteen and I'll buy you a cup of tea.'

'It'll be terrible tea and it'll cost a fortune.'

'Don't be ungrateful.'

'I'm not,' I protested. 'In fact I should buy the tea to thank you for doing this.'

'I wouldn't have missed it for anything. The look on his face when I walked into court.' Derwent shook his head. 'If nothing else, I got to see him in the dock.'

'I didn't really look at him.'

'Probably for the best. It might have put you off. It inspired me, I'm glad to say.'

'Oh God.'

'I was *phenomenal*.' He put his arm around me and guided me down the corridor, holding forth about his own brilliance all the way.

The canteen was to the left of the front door, a few tables and chairs becalmed outside Court 1. I found a table near the window and looked out at the brilliant October day and the trees fiery with leaves they hadn't yet shed. Snaresbrook had been built as a massive Victorian orphanage; Crown Court was merely the latest of its incarnations. It was the only court I could think of with a duck pond.

'Here you go. Looks good to me.' A cup and saucer clattered on to the table in front of me and I gave a soft wail of distress.

'It's pale grey. Since when was tea grey?'

'Nothing wrong with it.' Derwent drew it back to his side of the table and gave me the other one.

'That looks more like it.' I sniffed it, suspicious. 'How did you manage that?'

'Natural charm. I asked for two teabags in yours.'

'Thanks.'

'Drink it while it's hot. You do look as if you need it.'

'I'm OK.'

'Really?'

When I looked up, he was watching me with that unnerving focus I had come to fear. 'Yes. It's just weird, that's all.'

'What is?'

'Being the victim.'

He leaned across the table and covered one of my hands with his. 'Whatever happens with this trial, you're no one's victim. He didn't take anything from you. You're still you. And you're the bravest person I know.'

I shifted in my seat, embarrassed. 'I don't feel brave.'

'Coming to court and giving evidence was brave.'

'You didn't give me the impression that I had any choice,' I pointed out.

'You always have a choice.' He sat back. 'For instance, you could have chosen to do the wrong thing.'

'But you would never have forgiven me.'

'Probably not.'

'And you'd have made my life a misery.' I corrected myself. '*More* of a misery.'

He grinned, his eyes bright with amusement. 'I'd have been very understanding.'

'Oh sure. You always are.'

The two of us sat there, drinking our tea, talking about anything and everything but the trial that was going on elsewhere in the building, where a man's fate hung in the balance with mine.

The jury went out at the start of the third day after a summing-up of the evidence from the judge. I thought of his spare, haughty face and worried that he would guide the jury away from believing me. His would be the last voice they heard before the usher took them away to consider their verdict.

'If they come back quickly, it's usually a good sign for the defence. Easier to acquit than convict.' Emma Khan chewed her lip, looking nervous, because the outcome turned on how well she had done her job. It was always like that, the police and the CPS and the victim expecting a conviction and the prosecutor having to explain why it hadn't worked out. I told her I thought she'd done well, which was true, and we agreed that juries were unpredictable, and then the two of us fell silent as the minutes passed.

Somewhere, Seth would be pacing up and down, like I was. The stakes were higher for him. All I had to lose was my faith in the legal system, imperfect and underfunded though it was. He could lose his freedom and his job. The not-knowing would be a kind of punishment in itself, I thought, and tried to comfort myself with that. Whatever happened, I had made him come to court and explain himself. Whatever happened, I had spoken up for myself, and for all the women he had harmed. The officer in the case had tracked down two of them but neither had wanted to give evidence against him. I was on my own.

But I was on my own with a fair number of people to help and support, from Alice Schneider, the officer in the case, to Emma herself. And even as I thought that, a familiar figure came into view at the end of the corridor and sauntered towards me, his hands in his pockets.

'Any news?' Derwent asked as soon as he reached me.

'They've been out for an hour.' I smiled at him. 'I didn't know you were coming today.'

'I didn't want to miss this. It's the best bit.'

'All parties in the case of Taylor to Court Three,' a voice intoned over the tannoy. Emma set off for the door at a half-run, dropping her wig on her head as she ducked through the double doors. I grabbed on to Derwent's arm.

'This is it.'

'Or the jury want to ask a question. Come on.'

As we came into court, Emma was leaning over to talk to the court clerk. She looked around at us and mouthed, 'Verdict.'

I sat in the public gallery with a humming in my ears and my eyes fixed on the floor, faintly aware of the other seats filling up with Seth's family and friends and the reporters who had followed the trial. Derwent sat beside me, his knee pressed against mine for support, or because manspreading was what

383

he did. He glowered at anyone who tried to sit near us. The rumble of conversation in the corner caught my attention: Seth, waiting to be let into the dock by the officer who was coming up from the cells. He was practically dancing with impatience to get this over with. He saw me look and flashed me a dazzlingly white smile: I might want to think he'd suffered during the trial but he was determined to give me the impression that he'd had no concerns at all.

We stood as the judge arrived, summoned by the flat-footed and weary usher. The judge glanced around the court as he sat down and I imagined his eyes lingered on me.

'We have a verdict,' he announced to the court. Then he eyed the usher. 'Jury, please.'

Slowly, the twelve of them shuffled in, self-conscious now that the entire court was waiting for them to play their part in this strange theatrical ritual. I waited to see if they looked at Seth once they had found their places. When juries didn't look, it meant they had decided the defendant was guilty. I would know for sure in a moment, but I couldn't help agonising over what they had decided.

The clerk stood up, holding a copy of the indictment. 'Will the defendant please stand?'

In the dock, Seth got to his feet. He looked completely self-possessed but his hands were clasped so tightly the top one left a mark on the lower one.

'Would the foreman please stand?' the clerk droned. It was routine for him, of course.

The foreman was, in fact, a round, middle-aged woman. She clutched a piece of paper with white knuckles, as if it was her shopping list on Christmas Eve an hour before the supermarket shut.

'Will you please answer my first question yes or no,' the clerk said, drawing out the final word. He pushed his glasses up his nose and squinted at the jury. 'Has the jury reached a verdict upon which you are all agreed?'

'Yes.' Her voice was clear and loud enough that we could all hear her. I wondered briefly if she was a teacher – she had that air – then made myself focus again on what was happening.

'Do you find the defendant guilty or not guilty of causing grievous bodily harm with intent?'

She answered immediately, but her voice seemed to come from a long way off. I watched her lips move before I heard the word so that I understood it.

'Guilty.'

A sigh swept through the public gallery. In the dock, Seth seemed to stumble, swaying on his feet. The dock officer reached out and steadied him.

'Thank you. You may sit down.' The clerk did the same and started writing something inscrutable on the papers in front of him.

Emma got to her feet. 'The defendant has no previous convictions.'

'Yes, thank you,' drawled the judge.

As she sat down the defence barrister rose. 'It's my application for reports, your honour.'

The judge's face tightened. 'Mr Colebridge, we all know what sentence I must pass in this case. I'm not wasting the probation service's time.'

Mr Colebridge sat down again, his head bent. Not a good day for Mr Colebridge, or his client.

The judge turned to the jury. 'Ladies and gentlemen, your role in these proceedings is finished. I will now sentence Mr Taylor. If you wish to stay, you are welcome to. If you don't wish to stay, please indicate that and the usher will take you to the assembly area.'

None of them made a move. They were all looking across at Seth, their expressions revealing that they had no doubts about their verdict at all. I looked for pity on their faces and saw only distaste.

'Yes, Mr Colebridge.' The judge nodded to him, and the barrister got up to start his mitigation. I stopped listening, aware that it was designed to make Seth sound as good as possible. As if it was being transmitted via a poorly tuned radio, the odd phrase broke through the humming in my ears. *Unblemished record . . . good character . . . maintains his innocence . . .*

Colebridge wound up with: 'The offence falls towards the bottom of the range and I would request you take that into account in your sentencing.'

The judge nodded, and turned to the dock. 'Stand up please, Mr Taylor.'

Seth dragged himself to his feet. He had never had any doubt that he would be acquitted and now reality was crushing him like a juggernaut.

'Mr Taylor, I must now sentence you for an offence of grievous bodily harm with intent.' Coldly, clinically, he recited the facts of the case for the final time. I almost forgot it was me he was talking about. His voice was like ice when he said: 'The jury has rejected your version of events, and in my judgement, rightly so. In my judgement, I am sure that you did lock her in the flat, which significantly aggravates the offence.'

He had believed me and not Seth. I stayed completely still, not smiling, but the relief I felt was as warming as if a light had been switched on inside me.

'I listened very carefully to the personal mitigation advanced on your behalf very ably by Mr Colebridge. I do not punish you for having a trial, but the effect of that is that I can give you no credit for your plea.' He began to talk about sentencing guidelines and I looked around to see a handsome woman, Seth's mother, weeping silently. I had never met her while we were dating. Now was not the time, I thought, to make her acquaintance, but I handed Derwent a tissue, and nodded in her direction, and he passed it along to her.

'This case,' the judge intoned, 'is so serious that an immediate custodial sentence is necessary. The least sentence I can impose is one of four years' imprisonment. You will serve half of that sentence in custody and the remaining half on licence. Mr Colebridge will explain to you exactly what that means.'

Lucky Mr Colebridge. At least his client knew what it meant. Seth was grey now, visibly shaking, his good looks lost to despair.

'Is there anything else I need to deal with?' the judge asked and Emma shook her head. He looked across at Seth and flicked his fingers. 'Take him down.'

The judge went one way, the jury another. Mr Colebridge headed off glumly to the cells and his devastated client. Emma Khan skipped away to the robing room to pack up her belongings, clearly delighted with the result. Derwent gripped me by the elbow and steered me competently past the reporters and Seth's supporters, moving too quickly for anyone to intercept us. We walked down the corridor, passing the main exit without a second glance at the bright sunshine outside. The press would be there, waiting, and that was the last thing I needed. The full scandal of the Chiron Club had broken during the summer, with week after week of lurid revelations, much of it written by Bianca Drummond. The wave of public interest had splashed over me too – *Undercover Stunner Was Club's Downfall*, one headline screamed, much to my irritation. I'd avoided the press as much as I could, concentrating on preparing for the many trials that arose out of the investigation. Orlando Hawkes had already pleaded guilty to murdering Roddy Asquith, and despite giving evidence Peter Ashington had found himself with a long custodial sentence too for the part he'd played in it. It almost didn't matter that Antoinette had backed away from giving evidence against him. Almost. It nagged at me that he'd got away with it, and that we'd never identified the second man who attacked her. Like the mould in Paige's flat, they poisoned the very air around them, but they were an invisible evil. They hid in plain sight, behind handsome faces and the swagger of wealth.

The most important trials, Sir Marcus Gley and Mila Walsh, would be taking place in December and January respectively. Gley was still trying to suggest Iliana's death had been a simple accident, even though he was the star of the snuff movie we had found. The CPS were still having none of it. Mila had refused to talk, unlike Harry, who had told us everything he could. But I still didn't know exactly how Paige died, and I thought I probably never would.

It would be nice to be professionally rather than personally involved in a trial for a change, I thought. The stakes were so much lower, whether you won or lost. Seth had lost, but it didn't feel like much of a victory to me. I shivered.

'All right?'

'He looked distraught.' Somewhere behind us Seth was locked in a tiny cell, confronting his disgrace and his bleak future. He had two years of incarceration to look forward to, and almost certainly no job when he came out. I wondered how much he hated me now.

'I'm glad I didn't get my hands on him,' Derwent said thoughtfully. 'It would have been fun, but watching him go to prison was far more satisfying.'

'He'll be out in two years.'

'You're right. I can do it then.'

'You'll have forgotten all about it.'

Derwent shook his head. 'Unlikely. But I can wait. I'm good at that.'

We slipped out through the side door, unobserved by anyone, and walked away across the leaf-strewn grass together.

Acknowledgements

I'm so grateful to the whole team at HarperCollins including my amazing editor, Julia Wisdom, her brilliant team including Kathryn Cheshire, Finn Cotton and Phoebe Morgan, Charlie Redmayne, the lovely Kate Elton, Hannah O'Brien, Fliss Denham, Katy Blott and everyone else who has contributed so much hard work on my behalf. I'd also like to thank the wonderful team in the HarperCollins Dublin office, especially Tony Purdue, Ciara Swift, Patricia McVeigh and Jacq Murphy. Anne O'Brien provided astute insights, as usual, when copy-editing the book, and Charlotte Webb proofread the book with great care and attention to detail.

A special thank you to my exceptional agent, Ariella Feiner, her superb assistant Molly Jamieson, wonder-agent Sarah Ballard and the whole team at United Agents for looking after me so well.

I get tremendous support from booksellers and librarians in the UK and Ireland. Bookshops and libraries seem to me to be the essence of a civilised society and they are worth cherishing: use them whenever you can.

In researching *The Cutting Place*, I spent a morning on the Thames foreshore, mudlarking under the supervision of the Thames Explorer Trust. The Shard is the highest point you can currently observe London from; the foreshore is the lowest. It gave me a new perspective on the city and on my book. (Many of Maeve's stupider questions in the first chapter were based on the questions I asked our infinitely patient guide. Any mistakes are, of course, mine.)

I am so lucky to be part of the close-knit and kind crime-writing community, including the Killer Women and other friends who are genuinely too numerous to list. For their great support and friendship I must mention Liz Nugent, Sinéad Crowley, Catherine Ryan Howard, Andrea/Andy Carter, Patricia Gibney, Hazel Gaynor, Carmel Harrington, Vanessa Fox O'Loughlin, Bert Wright, Maire Logue, Bob and Marta from the Gutter Bookshop, Pat Kenny, and Rick O'Shea for running a wonderful book club among his many other duties. Susie Steiner, Sarah Hilary, Erin Kelly, Colette McBeth, Tammy Cohen, Amanda Jennings and Ruth Ware are frequently my shoulders of choice to cry on: wise and brilliant authors all. Also a massive thank you is due to the Lord Peter Wimsey Casting Club (Harriet Evans, Sarah Hughes, Anna Carey, Aoife Murphy and Sarra Manning) for many hours of amusement. (You are all wrong.)

Huge thanks also to my two book clubs for reminding me how much I love reading and talking about books that I haven't written, and to Alison Gleeson, Jo Anderson and Sarah Law for making me laugh every Friday morning.

I couldn't write anything at all without James, or Edward and Patrick who mudlarked with so much enthusiasm and found so many revolting (but not human) bones, or Fred (who actually doesn't help at all but I adore). Thanks also to my inspiring parents Frank and Alison, to Philippa, Kerry, Mary, Michael and Bridget and the rest of my family.

Finally, my special thanks to Claire Graham, who is a wonderful person and a great friend. This book is dedicated to her; she truly deserves it and so much more.